THE FABRIC OF THE REALM

S.B. RYAZAKHOV

EDITED BY
SERENA SMITH

ILLUSTRATED BY
AMAIMANIS

First published by Rendered Realms Publishing LLC 2025

Copyright © 2025 by S.B. Ryazakhov

First edition

ISBN 979-8-218-58282-1

CONTENTS

To the people whose names I hold dear: T, P, & B.

And

To those of you who have lost the music within your own soul—those of you who find solace in Sleep Token lyrics and fantasy worlds—may you hear your own beautiful notes again.

"Where the wave of moonlight glosses
      The dim grey sands with light,
      Far off by furthest Rosses
      We foot it all the night,
      Weaving olden dances
      Mingling hands and mingling glances
      Till the moon has taken flight;
      To and fro we leap
      And chase the frothy bubbles,
      While the world is full of troubles
      And anxious in its sleep.
      Come away, O human child!
      To the waters and the wild
      With a faery, hand in hand,
      For the world's more full of weeping

"The Stolen Child" by W.B. Yeats

NOTE TO THE READER

Readers should be aware that this book contains themes of maternal mortality, arranged marriage, fighting, kidnapping, violence, murder, blood, and mental health topics such as anxiety and trauma. There is a scene intended to be a magical interpretation of EMDR (Eye Movement Desensitization and Reprocessing), which aims to show that even fantasy characters need help processing. It is my hope that this book does these topics justice and reverence.

If you have experienced trauma or any other mental health concerns, you are not alone. There is help waiting for you. In the US, you can reach out to the 988 Lifeline or the Crisis Text Line at 741741. Wherever you are in the world, you can contact your local mental healthcare providers or emergency department.

THE CORRUPTED REALM

SILVINE'S PLAYLIST

This is a sample of my very eclectic playlist for Silvine's story. If you enjoy the music, I encourage you to listen. If it's not your thing, it won't impact your experience of *The Fabric of the Realm* at all. You can find the full playlist by searching Silvine's Playlist on Spotify.

1. "Escape (feat Hayla)"- Kx5, Deadmau5, Kaskade, HAYLA
2. "I Found" - Amber Run
3. "Dreams" - Fleetwood Mac
4. "Wicked Game" - Daisy Gray
5. "Silver Springs" - Fleetwood Mac
6. "Here Comes the Rain Again" - Eurythmics, Annie Lennox, Dave Stewart
7. "Jaws" - Sleep Token
8. "I Found" - Amber Run
9. "Possession" -Sarah McLachlan
10. "Paradise (feat Dermot Kennedy)" - MEDUZA, Dermot Kennedy
11. "Dreams" -The Cranberries

PRONUNCIATION GUIDE AND INFORMATION

It is important to give credit to the cultural inspiration behind my novel and the languages that have inspired my story as well. Although I have done extensive research, I take full credit for any and all errors that may appear with regard to these languages. I encourage you, the reader, to learn more about Gàidhlig, Gaeilge, Cymraeg, and Latin, as well as their cultures of origin.

Silvine- Sil-veen. *French name meaning "forest," derived from the Latin "silva."*

Gilla- Jill-uh.

Morair- Mor-air. *Gàidhlig for "lord, nobleman."*

Cardoc- Care-dock. *From the Welsh name "Caradoc," meaning beloved.*

Quaestor- Kwy-stor. *From Latin, a Roman government position. In Ainmean, the Quaestor is responsible for overseeing the treasury, including fines.*

Fluellen- Floo-eh-luhn. *A Welsh surname, derived from "Llywelyn." Also the name of a character in Shakespeare's Henry V.*

Macha- Mah-kuh. *Gaeilge name for one of the three goddesses of the Morrigan.*

Bav- From Badhb (Bah-v). *Gaeilge name for one of the three goddesses of the Morrigan, goddess of war.*

Cian- Kee-an. *From Gaeilge, meaning "enduring one."*

Guval- Goo-vahl. *Inspired by the Welsh name "Gwawl" (G-wow-l), a name of a figure in The Mabinogion.*

Ainmean- An-yuh-min. *Gàidhlig for "names."*

Regina- Reh-gee-NAH. *Latin for "queen."*

Donadas - Do-nah-dus. *Gàidhlig for "badness, evil." **

Dùn Falaich- Doon Fal-ach. *Gàidhlig for "hideout."*

Talamh Fuar- Tal-ahv Foo-air. *Gàidhlig for "cold earth."*

Rafflesia- Ruh-flee-zia. *A parasitic flower.*

Phos- F-oh-s. *From the Greek root for "light, bringer of light."*

Ollam- Oh-lav. *From Gaeilge "ollamh," meaning "master, expert."*

Donadais is the genitive form of Donadas, used in terms like "King of Donadais."

PROLOGUE

The Avartagh, In the Beginning

Thirst was The Avartagh's first companion. He was born into the barren, empty sensation of unmet needs.

As a babe, thirst was the first thing he knew. His mother had been slaughtered moments after giving birth. His father remarried within two days, nuptials taking precedence over finding a wet nurse. When they finally placed him in her care, he was no more than a waif. All his crying had ceased, the babe accepting that it was useless to mewl and scream if no one was coming.

His life began in his father's sunless, dwarvish kingdom. The dwarves of The Avartagh's land, unlike the others, were unusually tall, hardy, and cruel. Their bodies were designed to labor with minimal food and sunlight, like plants thriving in a sunless desert. Destined to use his strength to excavate the earth's riches and serve a merciless tyrant, he craved a more fulfilling life than the one he knew.

The Avartagh's powers were unlike anything that had been seen in centuries. He could kill with the lightest touch. While he watched the tyrant who sired him push his subjects to the brink time and time

again, he felt their thirst: their unmet needs, their lust, their yearning for a better world.

His life changed when a mage was born, and she whispered to him of the world she saw across the sea. Together, they dreamed of the salt of the sea and the wonders of the lands beyond.

One fateful night, he crept into his father's command chamber. The Avartagh's mage, his brother, and their most trusted comrades crept in behind him.

His father was meeting with his advisors, discussing the output of his mines. "Production is lower than I want. How many whippings have we—?"

The Avartagh gritted his teeth. The answer to his father's question was "too many." Too many had suffered to fill his father's coffers. Resentment tightening every muscle in his body, he drew his blade. "There will be no further whippings," he promised, swiftly slitting his father's throat.

Screams and protests echoed in the chamber as The Avartagh and his companions made quick work of the king's most trusted advisors. These were the very people who had let him suffer for decades. He would be the one to deliver retribution.

He saved the queen, the mother of his half-brother, for last. She stood in the corner. The jewels, which adorned every inch of her, clanged as she shook in terror, and The Avartagh looked down at them, crinkling his nose. Every jewel had been added to her collection while The Avartagh and his brother went hungry, while their people died in the mines.

"I hope those jewels were worth the bloodshed," The Avartagh whispered.

The queen shook her head and pushed herself against the wall, but The Avartagh was unmoved by her show of emotion. Instead, he took his time, slicing each gem from her wrists and neck before placing his palms at her temple.

Tears slid down the queen's cheeks as black smoke wafted from The Avartagh's hands, and he drained the Life from her.

The Avartagh and his companions then carried torches through the depths of the earth, offering freedom to every miner who bent the knee. They promised to reward them in the days to come. Staunch supporters of the king, or those reluctant to swear fealty, were granted the mercy of a swift death.

His mage set fire to the mines, the flames consuming the underground castle and the rest of Rafflesia with it.

With their new followers in tow, The Avartagh and his men fled by sea, ash from the burning mountains falling like snowflakes onto the decks of their ships.

Arriving in a lush, green world where the sun shone brightly and the Fae sang and reveled endlessly, they realized that power was theirs for the taking. Water, sunlight, and resources were plentiful. Yet, The Avartagh's thirst was not quenched upon arrival in The Realm. Instead, his throat was dry and his tongue heavy with the need for Life he'd never known before.

The Realm was full of strange traditions and fantastic creatures: walking trees, river nymphs, and Fae who could shift into animal forms. The birds did not chirp; they sang entire songs, complete with verses and choruses. Wildlife lived in harmony with the Fae. There was no central ruler, but many rulers over different domains. There were two high rulers, however, who oversaw all the others: The Modrona, Ruler of Life and Nature, and The Euron, Bringer of Nature's Wrath.

The Modrona was the loveliest creature The Avartagh had ever seen. She epitomized all the Life and beauty in The Realm. She was the gold of his father's mines, shimmering in the sunlight he'd never known. When she spoke, her voice as melodious as bells, everyone listened. He was captivated by her, finding every excuse he could to see her. While The Realm had countless other powerful creatures, he wanted only her. His thirst became unending desire.

He wanted to drink deeply from the love and Life that poured out of her. Refusing to heed the warnings from his mage, he knew in the depths of his soul that the only thing he needed was The Modrona. She was the panacea for the insatiable longing he'd felt all of his miserable existence.

Together, he and The Modrona would have limitless might. His thirst would be quenched.

What he couldn't comprehend was the one-sided nature of his obsession. He interrupted her council in the forest. She went silent until her raven chased him away. He came to her palace uninvited, and her guards escorted him out. He appeared to her while she was bathing in a crystal-clear, alpine lake, and she screeched at him to leave.

The Great Silver Bear, the Fae who held dominion over Nature and its Wrath, kept The Modrona from him. Each time she rejected The Avartagh's advances, The Great Silver Bear made his displeasure known with an earthquake, a dust storm, or a torrential downpour.

The appreciation The Modrona gave The Euron made The Avartagh's jaw clench until it ached, and the Death power in his fingertips demanded to be released. She showed appreciation for The Euron with every Wrathful act he delivered. The Avartagh offered her promises of love and luxury, but she barely looked his way.

As long as The Euron lived, The Avartagh could not have The Modrona. Ridding The Realm of him became The Avartagh's obsession.

The most important law that ruled The Realm was hospitality, but the dwarves of Rafflesia had never known such rules. Their only rule had been to strive endlessly. Hosting a feast provided the perfect opportunity to take advantage of the Fae. The fools took his invitation at face value. To them, hospitality was akin to morality.

They were eager to see the newly-constructed fortress of this migrant power, so new to their lands. The fortress was a wonder, constructed of marble, fluorite, serpentine, jade, and feldspar mined below the depths of the earth.

Preparing for a toast, cup filled to the brim with wine from the coastal vineyards, The Great Silver Bear never saw the end coming. Not even the oracle, Macha, foresaw The Avartagh's betrayal.

Owain, nicknamed The Hunter, had been seated beside Euron. The Hunter was a Fae of The Realm who came to align himself with the values of the dwarves. While his hunting prowess was praised throughout the land, he had never been offered more power than mere lip service. His talent and knowledge made him a vital asset to The Avartagh.

Rubbing a knee he said bothered him from his forest-dwelling days, Owain didn't rise when The Avartagh called them all to clank their cups together. Instead, The Hunter took the poison-tipped, iron blade offered to him by his brother, Finnegan, and stabbed The Great Silver Bear in the neck.

Blood spattered on the table. The Euron fell forward, gagging on his own blood. His mouth opened and closed, silently cursing his murderers. Gasps and shrieks replaced the sound of clanking glasses. The Avartagh forced his eyes to widen, clamping a hand over his mouth.

Owain and Finnegan fled. They followed The Avartagh's orders, absconding to the seat of Ainmean. They soon claimed The Euron's province for themselves. Owain and Finnegan married human women, gave themselves mortal last names, and spun tales of how they'd saved the province from the evil Great Silver Bear. The humans of Ainmean came to see Owain's act as the most important part of their heritage. Eventually, no accurate memories of their former ruler remained.

The Avartagh's chest swelled with satisfaction, knowing the centuries where he had yearned were coming to an end. He sauntered over to The Modrona, ready to offer her his protection. This would be the moment when she came to see him as her hero, as the one she needed.

Blue eyes, the color of the clearest, purest waters, studied him cautiously. Her fists clenched at her sides.

"Fear not, I will protect you," The Avartagh promised, offering her his hand. "The betrayal we just witnessed will not be forgotten, and I will ensure your safety."

Her hands, surprisingly strong and calloused, shoved him away. His illusion of the gentle Modrona began to crack, but he found her strength even more appealing than her meekness. That kind of strength would be an asset in his mission to build a vibrant kingdom.

"You protected no one. You violated our Realm's laws of hospitality, the very fabric of our existence, the one inviolable rule set forth by The Creator. Don't pretend you didn't orchestrate this atrocity. You do not order your servants to slaughter a king and call yourself a protector. This is an act of war," The Modrona spat. "Do not delude yourself for a moment. We will do everything to protect The Realm from you."

Her words struck The Avartagh harder than any blow he had ever endured at the hands of his father. Why couldn't The Modrona see that he could be her everything?

Macha, whose powers The Avartagh did not yet fully understand, stepped in front of The Modrona. One of Macha's sisters, little and fierce, flanked The Modrona's side. "Our people will remember this day as The Great Betrayal. You are an enemy of The Realm. Do not take this further, or a curse will befall you and all your kind," she warned. Then she touched her palm to The Modrona's, and they vanished.

As the others fled his fortress, riding away on wings and powerful horses, The Avartagh sat at his blood-stained table, drinking wine until he was too numb to feel the longing that burned him from the inside out.

The Modrona had looked at him as though he was a monster. She'd spoken of The Great Silver Bear as her king and the laws of hospitality as the most important in The Realm. He yearned to make her see that he could be her everything. But how could he prove himself to her?

CHAPTER 1

BITTER WORDS AND HONEYED WINE

Silvine

Silvine clamped her hands over her ears, blocking out the hum of village life that overtook her senses. The cacophony of sounds made her head spin. Children pestered their mothers and playmates. Carts rolled down the cobblestones. Merchants called out to passersby, attempting to make midday sales. Similar routines and customs ruled all life in Ainmean.

To others, the sounds of daily life probably felt like a comforting reminder of the regimens they'd had for generations. To Silvine, it was another reminder of the way her father, Lord Morair, ruled the province with an iron fist. It was always, "The great Lord Morair says this," and "Our Premier likes it this way, and we must honor his leadership," but never a question of why the descendant of Owain Morair deserved to lead in the first place.

Silvine's best friend pulled her from her thoughts, throwing an arm around her shoulders. "Should we get a bottle of honey wine?" Ana asked. In her arm lay a wicker basket filled to the brim with cheese, vegetables, and fruits from the market stalls. Summer in Ainmean provided a rare opportunity to enjoy fresh produce.

"Make it two bottles," Silvine said.

The two strode over to the stall where mead was sold. In exchange for a few coins, they acquired two large bottles of their favorite honey wine. Since their picnic basket was overflowing, Silvine opted to carry the items.

From across the square, a tall, dark-haired woman laid eyes on them and began walking in their direction. It was Ophelia, Silvine's half-sister. Silvine cringed inwardly, dreading the encounter.

Ophelia darted in front of a cart, which was being towed by an aging buckskin mare and was loaded with turnips. The cart's driver jerked the reins backward. Turnips were sent flying across the cobblestones.

A loose turnip struck Ophelia's temple. She whirled around to glare at the cart driver. He leapt from the cart and began issuing profuse apologies. "Lady Ophelia, I did not see you. I am so sorry. Are you hurt?"

Rolling her eyes, Ophelia waved him away and stomped toward Silvine and Ana.

"Are you ready for the sparring match?" Ana whispered in Silvine's ear. Silvine winced. A lifetime, twenty-two years to be exact, hadn't been preparation enough for Ophelia's antics.

Ophelia studied the two bottles of mead in her sister's hands. "I see you continue to act *common*. Do you think it's necessary to buy drinks in the middle of the day?"

Silvine studied a loose cobblestone beneath her feet, avoiding eye contact.

Ana lifted her chin. "Is that the only thing you have to worry about today? You must be so bored."

Ophelia wrinkled her nose. "I worry about what my sister might do to our family's reputation every day. Your father looks over guilds and weapons. Our father is the Premier of an entire province. Silvine should do something to further herself and Ainmean."

Silvine's brows rose. Unable to hold her tongue, she bit out, "What are *you* doing to further yourself or Ainmean?"

Ophelia's face lit up as she gloated. "I joined our father in a meeting with the quaestor today. I learned so much. I learned a great deal about the unpaid fines in the village and crimes to be prosecuted. I even ran into *Cardoc* while I was there."

Her words struck a low blow, hitting their mark with precision. Nearly two years ago, Silvine had planned to run away and marry the village blacksmith, Cardoc. Instead, he'd left her waiting at their spot in a clearing in the woods.

Ana had delivered the message of Cardoc's departure, ending the romance and all of Silvine's hope for a future she could control. In his scrawling handwriting, Cardoc released her from his life forever in four sentences. *I shouldn't have played games with your feelings. I never actually loved you. I've been promised a good match and opportunity for advancement in the village. Move on with your life, and let your father find you a match as well. -Cardoc*

Cardoc had been married to the quaestor's niece for nearly two years. No longer obligated to work at his blacksmith shop, he enjoyed a position of status in the village and hired someone to run his business.

Though Silvine and Ophelia's father would deny it to his dying day, all evidence supported the conclusion that Lord Morair had gotten wind of Silvine and Cardoc's romance. He'd even attended the wedding between Cardoc and the quaestor's niece. Two years later, the wound of the betrayal still stung.

Ana looped her arm through Silvine's. "Ophelia, it's been a pleasure, as always, but Silvine and I have to hurry back to my house now. Try not to cause any more accidents." She glared at Ophelia before whisking Silvine away.

Neither of them looked back as they hurried toward the Fluellen estate. Gilla, Ana's mother, met them at the door, wiping her hands on her wrinkled apron. "No shenanigans planned for the day? I'm almost disappointed." A smile, genuine and maternal, lit up her face. As petite as each other, with the same chestnut hair and heart-shaped face, Gilla and Ana were mirror images.

"Who says we don't have shenanigans planned? We decided to come loot the wife of the Head of Guilds," Silvine joked. "I hear she has free time and plenty of things from the best forge in the province for us."

When they were small girls, Silvine and Ana had broken into the Fluellens's armory, playing soldier throughout the house, until they slashed through both of their dresses and an ancient family tapestry. Lord Morair had to send for a seamstress from far-off Phythia to repair the tapestry, much to his great irritation and expense.

Now, Ana's mother waggled her finger. "If I recall correctly, the last time two girls ransacked the house armory, they didn't even have the decency to use *arms*. They used my good forceps and scalpels to destroy the manor and themselves."

Gilla served as the village midwife and stored her spare medical tools in the armory. Her medical implements, perfect in size for eight-year-old warriors, were their weapons of choice.

They'd been no older than eight, quite naïve to the tools of womanhood *and* war, and in desperate need of adequate adult supervision. Nene, the Fluellen family's nurse of the past two generations, snored beside the parlor fire while they wreaked havoc.

"Is Nene available this afternoon, Mother?" Ana asked, lugging her basket down the hallway. Although they were fully grown women, society dictated that they still required supervision by their elders, especially when not in open, public places. Lord Morair insisted it was to protect their reputations. Silvine thought it was to control them.

"She's making a new batch of poultices. The miller's wife's pains have begun, so I'll be gone tonight. It's her first babe, so it may take a long while for it to enter the world." Gilla squeezed Silvine's hand, perhaps to reassure her that, if she had any say, the baby would enter the world safely. And the mother would make it, too.

The topic of midwifery led Silvine down darker mental roads. Her chest tightened as she thought about her own mother, Pulchra, and her demise. Pulchra had died giving birth to Silvine. Shaking her head, Silvine suppressed the hot tears that gathered in her eyes. The loss of her mother was a pain she carried everywhere.

The shadows of her thoughts must have crossed her face because Gilla squeezed her hand a little tighter. "Those tools are meant for good, you know, even if we can't always control what Fate has planned for us in child-bed." Gilla smiled. "It's an honor to know that, in my home, the Premier's daughter learned the difference between a scalpel and a dirk."

Silvine and Gilla looked at each other and began to giggle. It felt easy to simply *exist* at the Fluellen house. Though Master Fluellen managed all of the industries in the village, working closely alongside Silvine's mirthless father, he maintained a mirthful home.

Gilla leaned closer. "They say when The Old Ones lived among us, bringing children into the world was a beautiful, peaceful process. It wasn't so dangerous. Something shifted a thousand years ago, and now it comes with the risks you know all too well. I will always do my best for mothers and babies."

Nene peeked around the corner, shaking her head. The ancient nurse was notorious for her stories of evil, malevolent Old Ones. She gave anyone who said otherwise a scowl and a scolding. Gilla waved her away.

"Don't tell Ophelia this, but we are going to go meander through the gardens unattended," Ana called from a side room. She'd found a larger basket for their bounty and was filling it with supplies.

"Your secret's safe with me." Gilla patted Silvine's shoulder and lowered her voice. "The Earth loves its own. Someday, everything will make sense."

The two best friends lay lazily beside the pond, birds chirping in the background. This was their favorite spot, sheltered beneath ancient trees. The bygone Fluellens, though they lived inside the village itself, had sequestered and tamed several acres of the forest. Ana's forebears put up a stone wall around it then cleared the rest of the land that became the village.

The two girls luxuriated in the warmth of the late-afternoon sun, in one of the few places deemed safe enough for them to be, ignoring the walls that kept them in. They took turns sipping from the bottle of mead.

Silvine plucked the petals from a daisy one by one. "You know those paintings in my father's study?"

Ana sat up and looked back at Silvine. Earlier in the afternoon, they'd woven flower crowns for each other. Ana's flower crown consisted of white and red flowers, the perfect color scheme for her mahogany hair. Blue flowers adorned Silvine's golden locks.

"Yes, I recall seeing those a time or two... or twenty. I think they make up stories about lovely forest ladies being pampered by lovely forest creatures so we won't be as afraid of The Old Ones," Ana said, tossing the stem of a leftover flower into the pond.

The Fluellen's gated garden was one of the few forested areas considered safe. Silvine sat up, tossing the daisy's stem into the pond. "How come Ophelia and Father get so crazy about any talk of the forest?"

"That's Ophelia being her usual delightful self. Both of them can't come to terms with the fact that our Lady of Asturia was as arrogant as her daughter. Hunting on the sandy plains is far different than hunting here. No one has hunted these forests in hundreds of years, and for good reason."

The Asturian lands had been cleared of all traces of forest centuries before. No Old Ones or monsters lurked in their lands. It was true. Ainmeanian forests were far more dangerous than the cleared lands of Asturia. Although Lord Morair insisted Lord Creon, the Premier of a rival province, caused his first wife's death, his wariness of the forest seemed to contradict his claim.

Silvine swallowed. She feared she shared Ophelia's mother's arrogance. The forest called to her.

"What if it isn't as bad as they say?"

Ana sighed. "Nothing is as bad as your father says it is."

It wasn't until dusk that Silvine remembered she needed to return home. She hoped she would beat her father there. It would require all her skills to sneak into her bedroom and avoid conversations with prying, two-faced servants. Aethel was a notorious tattletale. As was the ever-troublesome Ophelia.

Her father's estate was past the village about a mile, surrounded by the orchards planted long ago. It abutted the forest to the north, with the same kind of gray, towering wall around it that the Fluellens had around their own home.

One market stall remained open, and Silvine quickened her pace, head down. It wouldn't do to be spotted by a well-meaning but nosy villager.

A crone of an old woman, one Silvine didn't recognize, was packing up for the day.

Odd, Silvine thought. She'd been certain she knew everyone who sold their wares at the market.

"Modrona, the Earth loves its own," the old woman croaked. Silvine halted, startled by the familiarity of her words.

The crone's skin was the texture of crepe paper, worn down and ashen, no hint of life in it. Her figure hunched forward painfully, and her voice was as haunting as the shriek of the wind. Frozen in place, Silvine felt her skin pebble like goose flesh.

The crone hobbled toward her, something silver glimmering in her hand. She thrust it toward Silvine.

In the woman's palm was the most unusual piece of jewelry Silvine had ever seen. It looked as though life and night were crafted into a single pendant. The stone was an oval-shaped obsidian, marked with flecks of silver and white. It reminded Silvine of the constellations in the sky. Criss-cross patterns of silver chains caged the stone in, as though a mere pendant could not contain a stone of such rarity and magnitude.

"Modrona, the Earth loves its own," the crone insisted, holding the necklace up. Silvine looked into the woman's eyes, barely able to tell where her pupils ended and her dark irises began. Age flecked her eyes with bits of white. The gaze was so intense that Silvine quickly broke from it.

It was an odd coincidence that the proverb from Gilla earlier came out of the mouth of this crone. The phrase sounded much more sinister coming from the lips of the ancient woman.

Maybe she's just desperate for an end of the day sale, Silvine thought, trying to settle her nerves.

Silvine drew back, trying to put space between her and the crone. "I didn't bring my purse with me."

"I could not sell The Modrona's own goods to her. This is yours," the crone's voice cracked. "I'm just the deliverer, returning the Earth's stone to its rightful owner."

Silvine shook her head. A sense of unease made her hands shake.

With shocking speed and dexterity for her hunched state, the elderly woman snuck behind Silvine and clasped the pendant around her neck.

The crone was in front of her as quickly as she'd gotten behind her. "It is yours, like it was your mother's, and hers before her. Protection, power, empathy. The cycle of death and new life in one. You must never take it off."

Alarm bells were ringing in Silvine's head. Everything about this interaction was shadowed by a sense of foreboding, for reasons she couldn't place. Against her better judgment, Silvine answered the irresistible urge to touch the stone. Its warmth in her palm surprised her. Something about it felt strangely *right.*

"You have accepted the gift. Do you accept the call?" the woman asked.

It became too much. Silvine's heart began to pound, a strange humming playing in the background of her mind. Images of things she could neither explain nor understand flashed through her mind in rapid fire.

She saw white-robed women with golden hair living, dying, loving, and passing on crowns of leaves to other golden-haired women. Flashes of white light, rapidly growing vines, walking trees, crumbling castles, bloodied bodies on a barren battlefield. There was a strange melody that hummed as her brain filed through each image rapidly.

Bile rose in her throat. Unable to stand another moment of their exchange, Silvine took off in a sprint. She ran like a thief in the night, faster than she'd ever run before.

"You can't run from it, Modrona," the crone shrieked after her.

She certainly *could* run, and she did.

Silvine ran the whole way home, desperately trying to shake the strange visions she'd seen. If the necklace hadn't bobbed against her throat with each step she took, she would have convinced herself she'd made it all up in her head.

The servant who met her at the door, long-suffering Aethel, looked her up and down as she took her sweat-drenched, muddy cloak. Wordlessly, Silvine tromped upstairs to take a hot bath and think of something, anything, besides what she'd just experienced. The necklace, however, remained where the crone had fastened it, a persistent reminder of the bizarre encounter.

CHAPTER 2

VOICE OF THE FOREST

Silvine

A feminine voice was calling her out of the orchard, the world around a blur of colors and giant trees. "Silvine! Silvine, my dear, come to me," it beckoned.

Silvine dropped the pear she'd been eating, its core left on the ground. A raven croaked in the distance, and she could hear the beating of wings overhead.

"Hurry, my girl, faster now," the voice called, its sound as delicate and lovely as a small bell. "Come to me, and the world will be right again." The voice was coming from the forest—the verdant, inviting forest. Birds were chirping, singing the most beautiful and other-worldly songs she'd ever heard.

If she could only reach the voice, she would find her belonging, leaving behind the confusion of Ainmean for a future that made sense to her. No matter how fast she ran, she could not seem to catch up.

Silvine looked down at her legs, willing them to move faster. They were the legs of a child, short and chubby.

In the distance, the voice continued. "All the world is yours, my

dear, if you only come and find me. You must be faster. Faster!" The voice grew more distant as Silvine ran toward it.

She reached the forest and made it to a meadow clearing bathed in golden sunlight, where flowers bloomed in abundance. She leaned down to pluck one and caught sight of her small, child's hands.

As her fingertips touched the blue flower, cold hands yanked her to the floor. She felt fire burn her like nothing she'd felt before. Silvine yelped in pain, reaching to touch her head. Her vision grew hazy. Time itself seemed to pause. The heat threatened to consume her, and the smell of burning flesh and thick smoke made her gag. She wriggled, kicking her feet against the floor, fighting to put an end to the overwhelming pain.

A cold voice said, "I will rid The Realm of this abnormality. No more of this wicked forest creature nonsense."

Silvine gasped, hoping fresh air would clear her senses. When the smoky air only thickened, she began to heave. She tried to clutch at her face, to save her ears, but strong arms kept them pinned at her sides. Unable to fight it, she threw up. Vomit soaked her neck and her dress, pooling around her body on the ground.

Steady hands pulled her away from the pain, and everything went black.

"Silvine!" a man's voice called.

Silvine opened her eyes, reaching her hands up to touch her scarred ears. Her father, Lord Morair, sat on the edge of her bed. He clutched his velvet robe tightly around himself with one hand while holding a candle in the other.

The pain was gone, but her scarred ears remained.

"Did it happen again?" Lord Morair asked.

"Obviously not, since I don't have fresh blistering on my ears," Silvine snapped. Her father's lips thinned, and she hugged herself tightly.

Lord Morair placed the candle on her bedside table. He reached out to squeeze her shoulder. "You know very well what I mean, Silvine. At some point, you must overcome this propensity for fixating on what happened to you when you were five. You are made of things much stronger than this... *feminine* weakness."

Silvine rolled her eyes and reached for the cup of water beside her bed. "Ah, yes. I must be strong enough to forget my mother in the grave, the tortures that left the tips of my ears disfigured, and yet, dainty enough to be a marriageable bargaining chip for you."

"Yes, that is what I expect," her father answered dryly. "There is a balance in all things, and you must come to know where you fit in that balance. You could easily overpower a husband if you aren't careful, and that would endanger us all."

Silvine interpreted that to mean that most men were too delicate to tolerate having an intelligent wife. More than the forest, more than money, more than the dangers of childbirth, Lord Morair feared that his daughter would someday outsmart the man to whom he would give her away.

The sound of her metal cup slamming back on the nightstand made the Premier wince. She blew a forceful breath and rolled away to face the wall.

After a long pause, Lord Morair left the room, taking the sole source of light with him. Alone in the darkness, Silvine allowed the tears to stream down her face. Her father was as evasive with answers about how her ears came to be disfigured as he was with the truth about his interference with Cardoc. He danced around the truth and deflected blame at every turn.

Whenever Silvine asked her father for answers, to explain what happened to her ears, he said, "Some people suffer from derangement and depravity. We are not sure how it happened or what happened.

You must move past it and be glad nothing worse has happened in your highly privileged life."

Silvine steadied her breath. After her nightmare and conversation with her father, she was unlikely to fall back asleep.

CHAPTER 3
VIOLET LIVERIES

Silvine

The next morning, Silvine sat at the dining table, half-asleep after her night terror robbed her of rest. Her chest was tight, as though heavy chain mail armor weighed down each breath. She braced herself for a morning of sparring with her family. In the Morair household, words were the weapon of choice.

Seated at opposite ends of the long oak table were her father and sister. Ophelia busied herself with petty demands for the maid. The biscuits didn't have enough marmalade. The piping hot tea was somehow too cold. An invisible chip on her plate meant she needed a new one.

Meanwhile, her father was buried in a pile of correspondence, likely dull reports about neighboring provinces and the status of his mines. Neither Lord Morair nor Ophelia seemed to notice that Silvine hadn't touched her food, and the maid was too busy dealing with the minutiae of serving Ophelia to mind.

Sitting in silence, Silvine absentmindedly toyed with the necklace from her strange encounter the evening before. When sleep evaded her after her nightmare, she'd snuck into her father's study to

find an ancient tome on lapidary. The author had been dedicated to his work, including detailed color drawings of every stone, gem, crystal, and rock he knew. She'd been able to identify the stone easily. The star-like crystal was galaxy obsidian, incredibly rare.

Myths abounded about the power of such a stone. The galaxy obsidian had flecks of quartz, said to have come from fallen stardust when The Creator stitched together the fabric of The Realm and spoke creation into being. The Old Ones believed such stones offered power and protection to its bearers.

Thoughts drifting back to family life, Silvine decided not to fight her demons alone today. The silence would consume her. "Father, I would like to spend my day at the Fluellen manor."

At her sister's words, Ophelia sneered, but before a word came out of her upturned mouth, her father waved his hand in Silvine's direction.

"You would find yourself there anyway, regardless of my consent."

Ophelia's face fell, and Silvine flashed a look of mock-demureness at her. Silvine had caught her sister in a compromising situation in an alleyway the week before and had been letting her fret about what she might say to their father.

Ophelia widened her eyes, perhaps remembering her own leverage, and her sneer returned. "Father, she bought mead like a commoner just yesterday, out in the open. You should get her under control. People are going to start to think *we're* common."

Their father put his papers down, raising his brows. "Indeed, I should. And *you'd* do best to stay out of alleyways with *common* men if you'd ever like to marry a man of quality outside of this village."

Silvine stared at her lap to hide her amusement.

Ophelia gawked, her face flushing as red as the apples in their orchards. She stood up from the table and yelled to the maid, "Aethel, go to the stables and tell them I'd like my horse ready immediately."

Aethel stepped into the room, bowed in acknowledgment, and turned on her heels to run to the stables.

Jaw clenched, Ophelia turned to her sister. "Careful, Silvine. The high and mighty have much, much farther to fall than the rest of us do." Before Silvine could return her jab, Ophelia fled the room.

"Someday, you will understand—" her father began.

Before he could finish, a messenger clad in violet flew into the room, Aethel at his heels. "Premier," Aethel panted, "he let himself in. You'll have to pardon me."

An icy glare spread across Lord Morair's face. "To what do I owe the pleasure of your visit? His majesty deigns to think of the humble province of Ainmean?"

Silvine froze. She knew her father's feigned ease all too well, but she could tell he was afraid. She faked her way through stressful situations in the same manner. At least, until everyone around the estate could hear her screaming in her sleep.

"Premier, you are to read this and act upon it immediately," the messenger said, a threatening edge in his tone. "I have orders to see that you depart your home. We can ride together if it pleases you." The messenger thrust a sealed piece of paper into Lord Morair's hands.

While her father read, Silvine's eyes traveled to the long, thin sword at their visitor's hip.

Lord Morair's sharp blue eyes darkened as he folded up the letter. "Very well," he said, pushing his chair back. "Silvine, meet me in my study in a quarter of an hour. You, sir, can wait for me at my stables. Do see if my groom can render your horse any services. I'm sure it's been a journey."

As everyone left the dining room, the butterflies of anxiety in Silvine's belly hardened into knots. She was glad she hadn't yet eaten food, or it certainly would have been trying to come back up now. Her father never rushed for anyone, and yet, here he was in a great hurry.

Silvine's leaden feet weighed her down, but she managed to get up and walk to the study. Although the estate was, by village standards, impressive, it was only its size that made it grand. Her father's ancestors were keen to assert their dominance over the people, ensuring that no one would get any democratic notions about the Premier position, so they constructed the tallest stone building they could manage. The secret was that their estate was sparsely furnished for generations, relying mostly upon locally hunted furs and exquisitely carved but cheap wood to give it an air of luxury. It was Ophelia's mother's lavish Asturian tastes that furnished it with decor from around the known world.

Silvine paused in front of the heavy oak door, breathing deeply to still her thudding heart. This could not be good. The king of The Realm hardly ever sent his messengers. The king never summoned his leaders to depart from anywhere with such haste. Could it be war? Their people had not gone to war in generations, but the stories of the wars of old were bloody and brutal. Provinces were laid to ash at the capricious whims of angry rulers. Ainmean, a small province of its namesake village and surrounding sprawling forest, was fortunately isolated and unappealing enough to stay out of the worst of such things.

As soon as Silvine crossed the threshold and closed the door behind her, she plopped down on the blue velvet chaise and smoothed out her pale gown.

Moments later, her father burst into the room. He'd changed into his signature blue riding tunic, blue velvet cloak, and leather breeches, which made his typically stern appearance more youthful. He ran his hands through his faded, salt-and-pepper hair and glanced at his daughter.

"Silvine, I wish I spent more time on your education," he announced, striding toward her.

"This seems like it's hardly the time to worry about how fluently I speak The Old Language, Father."

Silvine gave her father a playful smile, and he frowned. "This is also hardly the time for that winning 'humor' of yours."

This was something serious, indeed. Silvine slid her palms down her thighs over and over, focusing on her pale hands.

"I will be away for… a while," Lord Morair continued. "Several weeks. The king has summoned all the officials of The Realm, and his court is a five-day ride from Ainmean. We so rarely get to relish in one another's company that I anticipate we will take our sweet time before we say goodbye to one another again." Sarcasm and bitterness dripped from his voice. "I have been negotiating a potential match for Ophelia, so naturally, the timing is not ideal. The suitor's estate is en route to Court, so I will have to take her along and see how they all feel after she visits for a few weeks. She's clearly too… bored here."

This version of her father was new. He never deigned to share a hint of plans or concerns with his daughters.

"Yes, Father," she said, her throat dry.

"You have no idea why I'm sharing all these details with you, naturally. I suppose I should expect no less of *you*. What I mean to say is that you're the only Morair who will be left to represent the household. Do it well. Fluellen will stand in for daily governance, but I expect you to carry yourself with dignity. It will convey stability to the villagers."

Skies above and Earth below, I loathe him sometimes, Silvine thought. She hated every insult he lobbed at her. She hated that he was such a cold schemer.

Trying her best to ignore her father's words, Silvine looked up at the portrait of her mother, Lady Pulchra, on the wall between the paintings of naiads and dryads. It struck her that no images of *Ophelia's* mother remained. Perhaps Pulchra did hold a soft spot in the Premier's cold, hard heart.

In the portrait, Pulchra smiled, her flowing platinum hair wrapped around her tiny waist, indigo flowers in her hands the same color as her deep blue eyes. Her dress was flowy and white, with vines embroidered around the sleeves and skirt. She looked far from fashionable, yet undeniably ethereal, like a queen of the forest. She looked like she belonged among the creatures in the paintings beside her, not running day-to-day affairs at a Premier's estate.

As Silvine admired Pulchra's image, she could feel her father's gaze on the back of her neck. Undeniably, he was waiting for Silvine to agree to his proposition. She was to remain in Ainmean to represent her family.

She kept her tone bland as she asked, "Shall I lock myself away in the tower until a prince comes to rescue me?"

Lord Morair huffed impatiently. "I mean that your presence here secures our authority. Peasants have been known to revolt in other villages, but never ours. Others hear from mages and mercenaries of the wide world out there, and they get... ideas. Be girlishly happy with Ana Fluellen. Do it publicly. Sell them the idyll of village life. And if you see any strangers who look troublesome, report it immediately to Master Fluellen."

Silvine tilted her head. "By playing dumb and happy, I am meant to keep your people laboring away for you, never believing they can change things?"

"If you can follow my simple directions, maybe you shall prove I'm wrong about you. Maybe. You'll never be as beautiful as my Pulchra, but sometimes you are too keen about the practicalities of Premiership. I will be having enough merriment at His Majesty's palace that I do not wish to worry about any merriment here at home. He's never summoned me before, and I worry what it will do for the kingdom's stability. He is a largely uninterested ruler."

"Understood," Silvine replied, returning to an intent study of the blue vein that curled toward her index finger.

Lord Morair snapped his fingers, bringing Silvine's attention back to him. "Where did you get that necklace?" He reached for the chain, revealing the shimmering black and white stone pendant encased in a diamond pattern of silver chain. He pulled his fingers away rapidly, hissing.

Silvine's eyes widened. She felt as though she'd done something wrong, but she couldn't place what it was.

Lord Morair nearly snarled. "Now is not the time to gape at me. I will ask again. *Where did you get that necklace?*"

The sense of wrongdoing Silvine felt amplified. Her father never cared what she wore, so long as she looked presentable. "An elderly woman gave it to me at the market. I thought it impolite to refuse. It was so... unusual."

"I buried that necklace nearly twenty-four years ago with its owner," Lord Morair whispered, his voice harsh. "She wore it every day. Never took it off her beautiful neck. She said it was a relic of her people. It's primitive, nothing like the jewels found in my mines, but she loved it more than anything I ever gave her."

There is no way this was my mother's necklace, Silvine thought. A small voice in the back of her mind reminded her of the crone's words about returning the necklace to "its rightful owner" and saying it had been her mother's. How could it have left the grave to find its way to her, all these years later?

Silvine clutched at her necklace protectively. The galaxy obsidian was unlike any stone she'd ever seen, as magnificent as the constellations in the sky. The "primitive" pendant symbolized the entire Realm. Civilizations may have grown and fallen. Great men may have crumbled and died, but the celestial bodies above saw all. *The stars are eternal*, she thought.

She saw beneath her father's mask for the first time: he was a lost man, grieving for the one woman he'd ever loved. The compassion she'd never been able to find for him burned like an ember in her soul. He was just as lost in this world as she was.

Lord Morair pinched the bridge of his nose. "I never want to see or talk about the necklace again." He waved his hands as though he was waving away thoughts of Pulchra and the jewelry she'd been buried in. "Now, some rules. Under no circumstances are you to interact with Cardoc or go into the woods unattended."

Silvine cringed, fighting the urge to cover the tips of her ears.

"If you need anything outside of what the household provides, you may visit the quaestor. He will oversee household finances in my absence. I hope to see you in a few weeks' time."

Silvine would beg the Fluellens for a coin advance before she went to visit that old lout for money. Pushing the irritation away, she returned her father's gaze. "Farewell. I hope Ophelia's suitor and his family do not flee after hosting her."

Her comment was based on a justified fear that the match wouldn't work out. Ophelia's first suitor, sent by her Asturian aunt, witnessed one of her outbursts and immediately rescinded his offer. The damage control in the following weeks occupied a considerable amount of Morair's time.

With the tension of uncertainty hanging in the air, Morair and Silvine practically raced one another out of the study, Silvine rushing to her bedroom and her father heading to the stables.

When she reached her room and stared out her window at the stable below, Silvine watched Ophelia's tantrum begin. She threw her riding cap at the groom, the king's messenger waving his arms in outrage as it barely missed his head on its way to her target.

Lord Morair calmly pointed at the house, presumably insisting that Ophelia pack up her belongings. Silvine's sister stalked toward the front door, yelling about missing Festivale.

Skies above, Festivale is in four days, Silvine realized. She would have to preside over the activities, as the only available member of the Morair family. Festivale was dreadful enough to observe, let alone lead.

CHAPTER 4

BEARS AND BOARS

Silvine

On the day of Festivale, Silvine found herself bedecked in layers of nonsense. Every part of her look was carefully curated with the symbolism of the upcoming ceremony. Her heavy brocade skirt, tight bodice, Morair insignia necklace, and updo twisted in knots to resemble the Morair insignia, made it impossible to get into the family carriage without help. Ana, in contrast, slipped into the carriage with ease in her loose-fitting, green gown. Ana had covered her mouth when Aethel finished coating Silvine in layers of talcum powder and gold jewelry, concealing the amusement Silvine knew was threatening to bubble out of her.

The Morair carriage saw use once per year, as part of the Festivale ritual. In fading paint, there was an image on the side of the carriage of Owain Morair, founder of their family's dynasty and the political system of the village. Beside him was Finnegan Fluellen, the first Master of Guilds. In The Old Language, it said below the two men, "Fear not, Morair, for I am a Fluellen, and beside ye, I will remain."

Festivale served as a Thanksgiving of sorts, an annual expression

of gratitude for Owain's sacrifices, and a strengthening of the relationship between the villagers and their leaders. Silvine would be the Morair to seal that bond.

"A very picture of beauty," Master Fluellen said as he helped them into the carriage. Silvine wished at that moment that she could become a member of his brood. Her father, after all, would never have given her a compliment like that.

The groom, who was moonlighting as a footman, held the carriage open for her. Silvine always thought him a premature curmudgeon, eternally scowling and blustering, despite being in his mid-twenties. In this moment, though, the groom flashed Ana a rare smile. Her alabaster skin seemed to glow like the sun under his attention.

"I shall see you there," Fluellen said as he mounted his horse.

Ignoring Fluellen's comment, the groom winked at Ana as he closed the carriage door. "I shall take my sweet time escorting such precious cargo."

Ana batted her eyelashes in response.

As Silvine watched their exchange, a knot tightened in her stomach, she silently berated herself. She remembered so keenly what it had been like to receive such attention. She experienced a grand total of half a dozen kisses with Cardoc. Yet, more than mere kisses, the anticipation, the flirting, and the knowing looks had been what felt utterly intoxicating. Her heart longed to feel that way again. Love was a thrilling thing, filled with moments of rare and forbidden beauty.

Pulling Ana close, Silvine whispered, "Unless you plan to run away with my father's groom, I suggest you stop before you find him married off to someone you can't stand."

Ana's eyes widened in feigned innocence. "It's only flirting. I'm practicing is all." Silvine hoped Ana was right, for her own sake.

As the carriage began its slow amble toward the village, Ana erupted into guffaws, which Silvine surmised she'd been holding in until they were alone. "You look like a sacrificial bride from one of those old ballads."

Silvine shrugged. "I *feel* like a sacrificial bride from one of those old ballads. I'm so weighed down that I certainly couldn't run away from anyone with ill intentions."

Winking, Ana lifted the hem of her robe. Underneath, she had a long dagger strapped to her thigh. "I'll use my dirk on anyone who tries you. You are my fair lady, after all."

"I can't imagine anyone wanting to get too close to me. The aura of talcum I'm giving off and the clang of these bracelets is enough to put off even the most senile of men," Silvine joked, patting her thigh. "Besides, I've got my mother's dagger. I can jab someone myself."

"I'm sure you can. Regardless, sister of my heart, you'll never be too off-putting to me. I know this is going to be a lot for you, but I'll be here the whole time. I know you're being sarcastic because, Skies above, you hate these kinds of things. But you don't have to uphold the entire Morair dynasty alone. You've got a Fluellen at your side." Ana sprang to her feet, limber and quiet as a cat, and wrapped her arms around Silvine.

As they reached Festivale, the orchard's overseer announced their entrance. "In the Morair carriage, we have our Lady Silvine Morair and Miss Ana Fluellen. Forever shall we be under the protection of a Morair, with a Fluellen serving loyally by their side."

The crowd cried out, "Fear ye not, Morair!"

Silvine took a deep breath and plastered a look of serene calm on her face. Ana did the same, facing out the other side of the window. Both of them waved to the crowd.

Through her teeth, Ana said, "I brought a flask." She dug around in her robe's pocket, producing something small and silver.

"I'll sneak a few sips once we stop," Silvine said, feeling thankful for the offering of liquid courage.

"Don't sip. Chug."

The oblivious crowd clapped. *Such easily placated people*, Silvine thought. They had no idea of the scheming and control exercised over them by their leaders, nor did they seem to care. They blindly trusted, just as their forebears did. Ainmean remained safe from rebellion, for now.

Finally, the carriage stopped at the town stage. Located in the middle of the village, it served every purpose imaginable. Public executions, court hearings, village announcements, traveling troubadour shows, and everything else of importance was held there.

Silvine pulled down the crepe window shades of the carriage for a moment and chugged from the flask. She willed herself to swallow the burning liquid. Whatever Ana put in it was from her father's liquor cabinet, not Gilla's sweet vintage.

Ana snorted at the face Silvine made and finished off the flask. "Let's go," she said, grabbing her best friend's hand as the groom opened the carriage door.

The sun burned Silvine's skin as she walked. To her, the crowd's continued noises of support sounded more like a roar, and the smell of sweating bodies and cheap ale overpowered the flowers that were placed all around the stage. She focused on walking up the steps, trying to block out the bright light, loud noises, and body odor.

As Silvine reached the top of the stage and sat in the golden Morair chair, the crowd went silent. Ana took her place beside her father and mother.

The quaestor ambled over to Silvine and knelt at her feet. Her stomach lurched as he grabbed for her left hand and kissed it, leaving a trail of saliva behind. His knees cracked, and he gasped for air as he stood back up. "My good people of Ainmean, I present to you, the hope of our village. The blood of Owain Morair flows through her veins, and we shall forever be safe under Morair protection."

Everyone clapped.

"Thank you, our good people. Silence please," the quaestor continued. "The bloodletting ceremony is about to begin."

The bloodletting ceremony was performed with a wild boar, a substitute for the extinct bear. Bears had long been wiped out of the area. Even the most expert hunters could not find them in the woods. Ophelia's mother long ago sought a trophy bear, with no success.

The absurdity of pretending a hairy pig with tusks remotely resembled the greatest creature that ever roamed the woods was not lost on Silvine. The ceremonial nonsense, cultivated and glorified by her father, served as a reminder of Lord Morair's constant scheming.

Silvine held her breath as a golden-haired, tall figure, who radiated sunshine, appeared in front of her. Cardoc. He was carrying a bound wild boar, which he dropped at her feet. Though it was attempting to thrash, bobbing from side to side, the creature could hardly move with the way its feet and snout were bound.

As Silvine stared at the boar, her eyes widened, her heart pounded, and her breath quickened. She wasn't sure she could do it. This creature deserved to roam free and die a noble death, not in a public humiliation ceremony.

Silvine looked into Cardoc's warm eyes, finding nothing but calm. He unsheathed the dagger at his side and handed it to her. The tips of his sun-bronzed fingers brushed along her palm, and the jolt of electricity between them left her yearning.

"For you, my lady," Cardoc said, kneeling as he offered the knife, his eyes fixed on her.

Silvine knelt, too. Her hands shook as she whispered to the boar, "I'm sorry for this." In one swift motion, she sliced across its neck. Blood spilled onto her hands. The crowd stayed silent, watching. She couldn't bear the sight of it, so she held Cardoc's gaze until the quaestor stepped in front of them.

"The blood has been let. Long live the Family Morair," he called out.

The crowd began to whoop and clap, repeating the quaestor's words, "The blood has been let. Long live the Family Morair!"

Cardoc left just as quickly as he'd come. Silvine assumed he hastened back to his insufferable wife's side. She tried not to let pangs of jealousy and heartache show on her face.

A servant from the quaestor's house stepped beside her, offering a bowl and towel to clean her bloodied hands. Drops of blood were on her gown, but that was to be expected. In fact, it was considered a sign of strength. She closed her eyes. Liquid courage could only carry her so far.

Silvine opened her eyes when she realized Fluellen was beside her, thrusting a golden goblet of wine into her hands. "Now, drink one, drink all," he said.

Everyone was drinking, so Silvine drank, too.

The servant who offered her a bowl helped her back to her chair while others hauled the boar away to be burned. The blood had already been scrubbed from the platform. Time seemed to pass in vignettes.

The village bard took center stage to sing the ballad of Owain Morair and his trusty Fluellen, who settled the village of Ainmean by slaying The Silver Bear.

The Silver Bear had taken the form of a beautiful man with strange ears, a small, winged creature, and a tree, but Morair had outsmarted it and slew it with his sword of iron and gold.

At one point during the song, Silvine was quietly offered bread and cheese. She devoured it, unaware of any eyes on her, needing food to settle her spinning head and churning stomach. The song felt like it went on for hours. The cruel sun hung directly overhead, sending sweat trickling down Silvine's face and throughout her tight, heavy clothing.

When the bard concluded his ballad, stepping back into the crowd, Silvine felt more sober and settled. The worst was over. Now, it was time for some fun.

"Let the dancing commence," Fluellen roared, his face flushed. The villagers cheered, sharing his mirth.

Ana escorted Silvine off the platform. The village band began to set up their instruments.

Three years ago, following her father offstage in the same manner, Silvine had first laid eyes on Cardoc. He was new to the village and strikingly handsome. She'd woven through the crowd, finding her way straight to him. He'd asked her to dance, and they'd spent the entire night together.

In the present day, Silvine spotted Cardoc and his wife standing to the right. His wife was rubbing her swollen belly, looking up at him affectionately.

Ana jerked Silvine to the left, toward the wine booth.

"Does your mother know Cardoc's wife is *pregnant?*" Silvine hissed.

Ana exhaled slowly. "I'm sure she does, given how swollen with child she is. But she hasn't mentioned it. I'm sure she kept it from you to not upset you."

Silvine knew she didn't have a right to be upset. Cardoc had never truly been hers. He was someone else's husband now and had acquired reputation and status thanks to his marriage. She should have been happy for him.

Hoping saying it aloud would make it true, Silvine said, "I'm happy for him." Her monotone voice gave away her real feelings.

"Yes, just as pleased for him as you are for yourself," Ana remarked. "Be grateful the entire town is drunk and will not remember your ashen face."

Silvine blinked away her welling tears. She did feel sorry for herself. She hated everything about Morair family lore. The Morair family was full of power-hungry monsters. To add insult to injury, Cardoc's wife was parading around a tangible reminder of their love.

Swallowing her feelings, Silvine gratefully accepted a cup of wine from the booth's vendor. Her family had funded all the food and beverages for the day. She decided that the least she could do was enjoy herself.

Ana also accepted a cup and lifted it toward Silvine. "Cheers to finding our destinies tonight! May they be handsome."

CHAPTER 5

FATE IN FLAMES

Silvine

The dances at Festivale were highly organized and intricate, designed long ago to further promote order and unity among the residents of Ainmean. Silvine wished she could break free from the rigid, ancient choreography. She wanted to move freely.

Alas, the well-trained dogs of Ainmean cannot enjoy such things at Festivale, Silvine thought. *They must bow, stand, and twirl in unison.*

The band itself was given no room for artistic expression. The set list had been created and preserved for longer than anyone could remember. Only through rigid order had her forebears maintained control.

Silvine's partner for the past two dances was a cousin of the quaestor's wife. He came from Asturia. He wore a ridiculous, ruffled, yellow outfit and reeked of smoked fish. She suspected he was shopping for a wife.

"It is important to show the people that you are a person, while hiding human... fallibility," he told her in his lilting accent. "You have

done an excellent job of that today, Lady Silvine. No one would know you were a second born!"

Silvine resisted the urge to roll her eyes, settling for sarcasm instead. "I've been studying all twenty-two years of my life to do *exactly* what you're describing. It takes an observant eye to notice such things." Silvine's facetious tone seemed to escape the man's notice.

"You will find that I am aware of everything," he remarked, spinning her to his right and pulling her back to face him. She shuffled her feet quickly to avoid tripping. "Have you ever visited Asturia? It is my understanding your sister has Asturian ancestry."

Silvine tried not to cringe. As she prepared another sarcastic response, Ana cut in. "I think you've had plenty of time with *my* lady, sir. You must let the rest of us have a turn." She shoved him aside and whirled away with her friend. When Silvine looked back, the quaestor's cousin gaped as he patted the spot on his arm where Ana had pushed him.

"Thank you for that," Silvine murmured.

"That old rat's cousin is not the kind of suitable match I want for you. You are going to marry *up* in the world," Ana said. The wine on her breath and her loose movements hinted that she might have imbibed a bit too much.

"And who exactly is 'up' for me, Ana? I am the second daughter, the daughter with a smaller dowry. Most would not trek through these mountains to make a match." Realizing her gravity was killing the mood, she forced a smile. "Unless, of course, I can piggyback off your good match and live in your guest room forever."

As Silvine moved through the square, dancing in circles with Ana, she studied the faces of her people. They looked as though they hadn't a care in the world. They drank and ate their fill, moving to the same music their grandparents had. Though she had not seen much of the world, Silvine could not find contentment in *this* place.

If Ophelia were there, she would have basked in the glory of feeling superior to these people. She would have stepped on their toes and thrown elbows during the dancing, shameless in everything she did.

Lord Morair would have maintained his haughty expression and sharp tongue despite consuming bottles of wine. Even strong drink could not dim his air of superiority.

Yet, no matter what Silvine did, she could not tolerate this life. For both Ophelia and the Premier, it seemed easy. Silvine could not make herself feel the same way. Everything felt *wrong*. None of the pieces ever quite fit into her life's puzzle. She resented the carefree way the villagers celebrated.

Her bracelets clanked as she whirled around, laughing endlessly with Ana, when she heard a cough behind her. A glimmer of mischief flashed across Ana's face before she let go of Silvine. She took a half step toward a young man with auburn hair, threw herself into his arms, and whirled away. Silvine found herself alone, turning around to see who was behind her.

Cardoc.

He looked elegant in a long tunic of deep scarlet, his sandy blonde hair swept back. He bowed. "May I have a dance, Lady Morair?"

Silvine's heart pounded in her chest. "Lady Morair? Are those our terms now? Besides, considering that my partner has just abandoned me, it seems I have no choice. *Can* we dance?" She tilted her head toward Cardoc's wife and the elderly women fawning over her swollen belly.

Cardoc's serene expression did not match the somberness in his beautiful, brown eyes. "Silvine, come now. One dance with you won't destroy my marriage, and we both know that custom says the Morair at Festivale must honor those who ask with at least one dance. Three dances might cause minor controversy, but no one will fuss if you give me just one."

"If I *give* you one? Cardoc, I thought we would be wed someday, and here we are. You haven't spoken to me since the day you walked away from me to propose marriage to that simpleton rubbing her stomach. You wanted what someone else had to give. *I can give you nothing.*" Though the wine made her face tingle, Silvine worked to pull the muscles of her face correctly to glower at him.

Cardoc pulled her closer, his footwork graceful as always. "I had no choice, just as you didn't. And now I know I could never have been the man to hold you, Silvine. You are magnificent."

"We *did* have choices. I chose you, and you chose someone else," she bit out.

She allowed him to spin her two steps forward before he pulled her back to his chest. The temptation to accidentally stomp on his foot crossed her mind.

"Silvine, I know you don't understand. We played a dangerous game with figures more powerful than you and I were. It seems so unfair, doesn't it? You have to believe me when I say you have no idea who you are or how valuable you will someday be."

Silvine forced out a bitter laugh. "You say that, but you're the one who refused to fight for me, who bowed down to my father's threats immediately, who jumped at a 'good enough' match for him. I am still here. I will get pawned off soon, and you will be just as free as you were when we first met."

The song ended, and Cardoc bowed. "No, Silvine. You have no idea what awaits you. I just hope you will remember me when all the pieces fall into place. For the sake of my wife, my offspring, your remembrance will make all the difference in the world." He grabbed her hand, placing his lips on it. Her heart stuttered, memories of years before flashing in her mind. Before Silvine could find words, Cardoc lost himself in the crowd.

A gray-haired gentleman appeared at her side. He asked for a dance. Silvine obliged, numbly going through the motions.

She ruminated on thoughts of Cardoc. He was someone else's now, and she would never be able to ignore the gaping wound he'd left in her heart. Cardoc's guilty conscience brought him to her, trying to use flattery to redeem himself. There was no redeeming to be done; Silvine knew he was just as powerless as she was. She'd known it since her father forced him to marry someone else. Yet, a foolish part of her believed he'd yearn for her forever.

As she danced with the gray-haired gentleman, Silvine noticed Ana weaving her way back toward her. Ana's newest partner was a scruffy-bearded blonde.

"So?" she called out.

"So? Never leave me again!"

Silvine kept remembering that kiss, which weighed her hand down as though it was made of lead. Cardoc had not apologized, and it was clear he no longer pined for her. That knowledge hurt Silvine more than anything.

While she pondered the pain in her chest, Silvine realized there was shouting in the distance. She paused, excusing herself from her dance with the gray-haired fellow.

Silvine felt a strong urge to *go*, to find the source of the noise. None of her life's experiences had taught her to run toward conflict. In fact, just days prior, she'd run away from the eerie crone at the market stall. Even so, she hurried along.

As the shouts quickly turned into screams, she quickened her pace, sprinting toward the noise down the market road.

She followed the sounds to the end of the market, where a hooded figure had just finished slitting the throat of one of her favorite bakers. Her breath caught in her throat. Red blood spurted from the baker's neck, flecks of blood dripping onto smashed crates of apples, peaches, and turnips. The metallic tang of blood in the air threatened to bring back up her wine.

Ainmean had never seen violence like this. Small skirmishes between villagers were not uncommon, but they always resolved with little bloodshed or hard feelings.

"How easy this was," the hooded figure hissed. It glided toward Silvine, who glanced around, noticing the lifeless bodies of other villagers. The sight made her nauseous. All the villagers were still in their Festivale finery while their blood pooled all over the streets.

They had likely wandered back there after several cups of ale to pick up a few goods to tide them over until the evening feast.

Silvine blinked rapidly, wishing away the terrible sight in front of her. She turned on her heel, sprinting back toward the square. She struggled to move quickly with the weight of all her adornments. She had to warn someone. Someone had to help. She needed to make her way to Master Fluellen. He would know what to do. The thunderous clap of horses sounded behind her, and she dared not look back to see if it was friend or foe.

When she reached the square, everything had devolved into pandemonium. The band had fled, children were crying, and all members of village leadership had vanished from sight. Many of the villagers were gone or desperately trying to flee.

Silvine smelled the smoke before she saw it and realized there was a fire at the opposite end of the village.

The villagers' huts must be ablaze! she thought.

And Ana... Where was Ana?

Silvine's initial terror morphed into molten panic in the pit of her stomach. An attack on Ainmeanian soil was bad enough, but if something had happened to Ana...

Ana. Ana. Ana. She could think of nothing else.

Silvine's lungs burned as she neared the smoky edge of the village, where she found the majority of the villagers shouting and throwing buckets of water onto the blaze.

The galloping of horses drew nearer. She wove down the intricate network of side streets. The buildings were so close together that the streets were more like goat trails. Silvine knew a crew of horses couldn't pass the narrow spaces.

She made it to the source of the fire. Some of the smallest, most humble huts in the village were ablaze. Out of her periphery, she detected a hooded figure, its cloak the same shiny black as the one who'd slaughtered the baker, slinking through the crowd. She balled her hands into fists, determined to do something, anything. Everyone else remained focused on efforts to put out the flames engulfing entire homes.

Birds squawked as they flew away. A single raven remained overhead, watching in silence. Nene had always said ravens were an omen of death to come. Silvine's chest constricted as she tried to take in what was happening around her.

She watched from behind the stone well as the horsemen rode into the chaos. They were astride shiny, muscular horses, their riders adorned in green and silver tunics with green masks covering their faces. Everyone went still, buckets of water lingering in their arms, and the shouting silenced. No sound but the crackle of the fire could be heard. The emotions of the crowd were almost tangible, causing Silvine's breathing to quicken.

The horseman at the front drew a long, shiny sword and declared, "We have come for the heir of The Modrona. We will not leave until she is handed over to us." The other three horsemen drew their swords after their leader spoke. Fists still clenched, Silvine felt her body begin to shake.

Cardoc stepped forward from the crowd and pointed to the well where Silvine crouched. Earth below, he'd betrayed her hiding spot.

"She is there, My Lord. I entrust you with her safety. She is invaluable." He bowed, just as he had when they finished their dance. If this was his idea of safety, Silvine thought his mind may have been more addled than she'd ever realized. Against her better judgment, Silvine stood up straight, staring at them all, hardly breathing.

With a bucket still in her hands, Ana charged forward. She tossed it at Cardoc's head, the loud thud confirming she had reached her target. Ana lunged and picked up the bucket from where it bounced. "Like hell you are taking her anywhere!" she roared. "Get your rotting carcasses out of Ainmean. You've done enough damage." Ana gestured angrily at the fire behind her.

Silvine wondered how the horsemen could have set the fire from across the village, but she set aside the need to find reason in such an unreasonable moment. Her heart thumped in her chest.

Ana met Silvine's gaze for a brief moment, putting her hand over her heart. Silvine mechanically forced her hand over her own heart, as much an expression of love as a reminder that her heart was still beating.

Pulling the dirk from beneath her skirts, Ana hurled it at the leader of the horsemen. "Run, now," she mouthed.

Silvine took off toward the forest, willing herself not to look back at the clang of metal and an all-too-familiar scream. Ana. The sound drew her attention away. Sneaking a glance backward, she saw the crowd part where Ana lay bleeding out. As Silvine watched, tears blurred her vision.

She heard the crunch of feet drawing closer. Despite her instincts screaming at her to turn back, she forced herself to keep running. Over her shoulder, she saw two black-cloaked figures gliding behind her. They reeked of blood, the metallic smell wafting toward her in the breeze. It made her sick. She did her best to confuse them, looping around boulders, dodging around trees, zigzagging the straight stretches, but they stayed close on her heels—until she heard angry hisses and the sudden clap of horses' hooves on the forest floor.

Chancing one more glance backward, she watched the leader of the horsemen behead the hooded figures with a single swipe of his blade.

Keep running, she told herself, *just keep running*. She knew she couldn't outrun a horse. The odds weren't in her favor.

She charged into a thicket, where she knew a man and his horse could not navigate, and belly-crawled through the overgrowth of bushes. When she made it through the dense growth, she got up and reminded herself to keep running. "Run now" had been Ana's last command. She had to honor it.

CHAPTER 6

I KNOW YOU, AND I WILL NOT GREET YOU

Silvine

Her lungs burned, and her chest heaved. Silvine looked down and saw that her legs looked as bad as her lungs felt. Her skirts had been shredded during her flight, and various forest brambles and bushes left her exposed skin scraped and bloody. She needed to keep going, but she'd lost her way, zigging and zagging through the forest, up and down the hills.

Entirely unaccustomed to running distances, she could only sip the air, rather than take a much-needed gulp. She glanced around her. There was no trace of the horseman, and her body couldn't have continued her flight even if he was hot on her tail.

Silvine slumped down at the base of a tree surrounded by tall bushes. If she left no trail behind and kept the sounds of her breathing quiet, she could buy herself a few moments of rest. She tried to calm her racing heart. This was how she would die. They would find her torn to shreds, just like Ophelia's mother. Or the horseman in silver and green would return to slice her head off in one clean blow. Unlike Ophelia's mother, she would not leave behind a

fortune or a child to mourn her. Her demise would unburden her father of a mouth to feed and a daughter to worry about.

As Silvine pondered all the ways she might die, her breathing slowed, and her legs began to throb. Out of the corner of her eye, she spotted a figure a few yards in front of her. She had been too busy trying to calm her body to notice it earlier. It was a tall, imposing figure, covered in silvery fur. It had long, white claws at the ends of its arms, though it walked on two feet. It sniffed the air before striding straight toward her. Her knees started to wobble.

Look up, stay calm. Look up, stay calm, she told herself. Despite the heat of her flight, she began to shiver, begging her body to stop before her teeth began chattering.

Mere footsteps away from her, the animal stopped and sniffed again. The glimmer of sunlight peeking through the canopy made it shine with a silvery hue. The scent of white birch and the iron tang of blood wafted toward her.

"I know who you are, and I will not greet you," the thing said. Its voice was dark and deep.

This creature was startlingly humanoid. How could some being of the forest know her, and what had she done to make it refuse to greet her?

Despite the exhaustion that had every muscle in her body tremoring, Silvine felt the cold spitefulness she'd inherited from her father rise up within her. She refused to speak.

"Prideful, are we?" the creature spat. "That gift comes from your *human* father, and not The Modrona."

Silvine raised an eyebrow. Both of her parents were human, and The Modrona was a long-forgotten bedtime story told by wicked governesses and nannies.

"We will meet again, and *you* will greet *me*," the animal continued. "You will be glad to see me then." The creature looked capable of shredding her with its claws, but it crossed its hairy arms instead. This must have been the very thing in the forest everyone feared. Yet, in Silvine's opinion, they shouldn't have feared it. Clearly, it spewed venomous nonsense.

The knowledge that this thing was merely blathering emboldened her, if just a little. Silvine stood, legs and voice shaking, drawing her tiny, silver dagger. She blinked away tears. "I will not fear you, nor will I be ever glad of you. Get. Away. From. Me."

"As you like it, Regina, as you like it," the creature clucked.

Silvine blinked, and the thing was gone. It left before she could explain that her name was not Regina. Yards ahead, a blurry figure suddenly galloped away on a shiny, gray horse that had not been there moments before. The creature rode north.

Danger followed Silvine from the south, so for no other reason than avoidance, she traveled west, following the setting sun as quickly as she could. West would lead to Asturia, the land of Ophelia's people.

There was nowhere for her to turn, and she had no idea where she was truly going. She hoped she might have been able to find a village that would be friendly to a bedraggled, twenty-two-year-old refugee. As a female traveling alone, the odds weren't in her favor, but it was her only hope. She could flee for Asturia, or she could become carrion.

She forced herself to continue walking, her muscles protesting every step. She did her best to shut out all thoughts of what had happened, thoughts of Ana's sacrifice. She stopped in a clearing lit by moonlight. With nothing but her dagger for protection, she curled up behind a bush and covered herself under her cloak. She prayed to The Creator that nothing would disturb her there.

Willing her nerves to settle, she closed her eyes. In the morning, she would wake and find this had all been a nightmare. She was thirsty and hungry but didn't dare venture out to look for any sustenance. A familiar throbbing pain radiated from her ears.

Hoping to leave the day behind her, she shivered until sleep overtook her.

Eight-year-old Silvine snuggled closer to Ana under her bear fur blanket, in her small down-feather bed. The blanket was decades old, passed down from generations of Fluellens. After defeating The Great Silver Bear, the inhabitants of the village could not let any other bears rise to terrorize them. This remnant of the extinct bears, however, felt warm and inviting. The fireplace roared, casting an orange glow around the room. To Silvine, there could be no cozier, safer place than right there.

Nene sat in the rocking chair beside Ana's bed, knitting a stocking.

Ana pleaded, "Oh, Nene, won't you tell us another story?"

The old woman, her wrinkled face evidence of a well-lived life, placed her hands in her lap. "Yes, but you both mustn't fuss or stay up all night after this tale. Do you hear me?"

Wide-eyed and intrigued, both girls gave promises that they'd still go to sleep.

"Long ago, in the forest of Ainmean and beyond, the world was ruled by The Old Ones," Nene began slowly, obviously enjoying her captive audience.

Silvine widened her eyes. "Old people ruled the world? Like the king?"

"They weren't old like me or the king. They were ancient ones. Their lifespans were longer than any human could ever imagine. The Old Ones, the Fae, did not abide by our rules. Their world was one of trickery and illusions. Before their magic ran out, we didn't stand a chance against their cunning ways. Once, there was an especially wicked one. He was an avartagh."

Ana cocked her head. "But you've said they were all wicked."

Nene glowered. "Hush, child. No more interruptions. One day, The Avartagh killed the queen of the forest. He was greedy for all that was Life. The Creator cursed him to always walk the line of death. He

46

could never truly die, but he would never remember what it felt like to truly live. Until a powerful human girl, one whose blood sang to the magic of the forest, used her wiles to save the world from The Avartagh and all The Old Ones.

"Her singing blood called out to the forest, and she ensnared all the Fae in a great trap made of the forest's trees, streams, and caves. Using the power in her veins, she bound them all to the forest. No longer could they leave their confines to harm us for mere entertainment. They were each trapped in their own set spaces. When the powerful woman returned to her human village, they all praised her and named her queen."

Enchanted, Silvine pondered whether a simple girl could truly come to save the world and be a queen. In her own life experiences, she felt invisible compared to both her older sister, with her pedigreed Asturian bloodline, and her powerful father.

"Now, taking on the Fae like that is impractical in real life. The rest of us must wield iron and our wits to keep The Old Ones from enslaving us." Nene concluded the story with her usual warning, always attempting to frighten the girls into behaving.

When Silvine awoke, she forgot where she was for one glorious moment. The dream of the bear fur blanket, Ana's warm body beside hers, and stories too impossible to be real lingered in her mind. As she opened her eyes, it all came flooding back. The corpses at one end of the village, the fires, Cardoc's willingness to hand her over to strange men, all while conveying a message of safety, the bizarre creature who knew her name, and Ana... Silvine couldn't bear to think of her. The gnawing in her stomach demanded her attention.

That is it, she decided. She would have to find something to eat in that forsaken forest, dodge all the evil creatures, and find Ainmean's allies. She had to travel to Asturia.

With her resolve as firm as it ever would be, she snuck a peek from beneath her cloak. Something was unusual about the forest. The tree bark shimmered silver and gold between large swathes of rich, chocolate brown. The forest floor beneath her felt unbearably prickly and uncomfortable. In fact, she had slept inside a circle of dewy, red mushrooms. Besides that, the birds were not chirping; they were singing *music* in a foreign language. Silvine stood, brushing off bark and dust, slinging her cloak around her shoulders.

A small voice called, "I am utterly delighted! So rare I get company!"

Silvine started, looking all around her.

"I'm up here, fair lady," said the small voice.

Sitting in the branch of one of those unusual trees was a small man. If he were standing, he would have been no taller than Silvine's hip. His skin was a sickly gray, his hair and beard dark and unkempt. His facial features were as gnarled as the bark on an ancient tree. *This creature is not a man*, Silvine decided.

"Now, dance," the imp commanded. With a snap of his fingers, a harp appeared in his lap, and he began to play.

Silvine's body started to move within the ring of mushrooms. She resisted, but something propelled her limbs, her hips, her *everything* to dance while the little man played his harp.

"Show me how happy you feel," the creature said, tapping his foot on the tree branch while he strummed on the harp.

Silvine could think of several gestures she'd like to make to show how happy she was, including lifting a finger no lady of good breeding should have used, but her facial muscles betrayed her. She shot a cheesy, toothy grin at the wicked, little creature. There was nothing to be done but dance to the fast, urgent, all-consuming music. Silvine lost herself, lost her name, lost it all.

The birds sang along with the music the little creature played. He hopped down from his branch and began to dance inside the ring with her. "This is much better. You'll dance until the bitter end!" He let out a whoop.

The bitter end. *Is it truly possible to dance oneself to death?* Silvine wondered. Her whole body was numb, and her brain felt hazy. Though she wanted to resist, her body was powerless to the imp's magic.

"I see you've found a new plaything, Anaras," remarked a vaguely familiar, deep voice, cutting through the fog of Silvine's mind. She fought her own body to move her neck toward the sound as her feet kept moving. She smelled a lingering scent of white birch.

Despite the familiarity of his voice, Silvine was certain she'd never seen him before. He was a few inches taller than her, with unremarkable long, dark hair. His ears protruded from the sides of his face, long and pointed. Silvine realized all at once that this person was no mere *man*. He was a being from one of Nene's bedtime stories. A Fae.

Anaras dropped his harp and cringed. The birds went silent. "Don't stop dancing," he said, avoiding the heat of the other man's stare.

The Fae male didn't glance in his friend's direction. Instead, he bowed to Silvine, a faint smile on his lips. "I know who you are, Regina, and I will not greet you." Immediately, Silvine realized that this Fae had the voice of the silver-furred creature she'd met the day before. Yet, there was no way they were the same being. The numbness set in again, and Silvine lost herself in dance.

"Would you like me to rescue you?" the Fae asked. "I can make the dancing stop. I can even make the numbness in your body and brain cease. Your pride will not serve you right now. All you must do is say yes." Amusement colored the tone of his voice.

Anaras shuddered. "Don't say yes," he said, his words sounding more like a weak observation than an order.

Silvine begged her body to do as she wished. It was just one word. Her lips, tongue, and mouth could not betray her. The Fae's silver eyes met hers, and the fog in her brain lifted a little.

"Y-yes," she whispered.

"That's more like it," the Fae purred, gazing at her as though he knew every thought in her head and sentiment in her heart. He snapped his fingers, and everything stopped. Silvine's shoulders sagged. She wiggled her fingers and toes, thrilled to be able to control her own body again. She looked up at the sky, which had once been the most beautiful shade of blue. Now, it was a dusky gray with brushstrokes of pink and orange. She looked down at her shoes. Blood was dripping out of them. The pain in her feet felt unbearable.

Before she could contemplate what to do, two solid arms yanked her out of the ring of mushrooms.

"Now she's left the Faerie ring. You have no claim over her, Anaras," the Fae growled. "I suggest you not let me catch you at your antics again."

Anaras whimpered. "I just want someone to dance with until the bitter end."

"We're all just looking for love in the wrong places, I suppose," the dark-haired male said, leaning against the tree. "It will be *your* bitter end next time. And should you see this lady again, you are to aid her in any way that will prevent *her* from meeting a bitter end."

"I will aid this lady in any way that will prevent her from meeting a bitter end," Anaras repeated, his body going limp.

The male released one hand from Silvine's shoulder, snapped his fingers, and Silvine found herself beside a river. Her stomach clenched, reminding her of its emptiness.

The water looked like ripples of glass, painfully beautiful. The stones in the riverbed glowed like the candlelit jewels. Silvine concluded she must have been close to the Asturian plains, which were reputed to be a place of great beauty. Her memories of Asturia were not this beautiful, but then again, she'd never explored much of it.

"There are berries and mushrooms behind you, which are safe to eat," her rescuer said brusquely. "I don't suggest you eat the glowing ones, unless you wish to spend the night in darkness. You may wash and heal yourself here." He gestured at a bush behind her, filled with the biggest, roundest, purple berries she'd ever seen.

Silvine reached for a handful and nearly swallowed them all in one gulp.

"Pace yourself," the Fae laughed.

"Why do you assume you know my name and yet refuse to greet me? My name isn't Regina," Silvine said, wiping juice from the corners of her mouth.

"You should know your name and refuse to greet *yourself* in these woods, Regina. Regina isn't who you are. It's *what* you are."

Silvine narrowed her eyes. "My real name is perfectly fine. Are you, I mean, you are Fae, right?"

"As are you."

She rubbed her temples, slowly shaking her head. Refusing to fall for further Fae trickery, she said, "I am sure that is meant to be some kind of confusing Fae axiom, but I'm not indulging you. What is your name?"

"You may call me Cian, The Enduring One. I have helped you, and you seem to be accustomed to Fae tradition. What will you give me in exchange?" he asked, smirking.

Silvine glanced down at her mother's necklace. Her silver bracelet and ring were long gone. Only one golden bangle and her gold chain with the Morair insignia remained. She breathed, trying to choose her offering carefully.

"I accept payments in gold. That bracelet would be a fine way to compensate me," Cian said.

"I am not compensating you. I am paying back a debt you forced on me," Silvine clarified. If Nene's stories about the evil Fae were true, Silvine needed to choose her words very carefully. She took off the bangle and tossed it toward him.

Cian caught it in his hand. "Consider your debt paid, Regina."

Silvine was about to make a sharp retort about having no choice, but the man had vanished, so instead, she opted to glut herself on the ripe berries and bland mushrooms around her, not caring about her blue-stained fingers. She ripped her corset off and flung it into the bushes to make more room for food. When the all-consuming hunger dissipated, she stopped to take off her shoes.

The balls of her feet had been the source of the blood. It felt as though there was nothing but bone left. Her feet resembled raw stumps. She cupped the coolest water she'd ever felt in her hand and gently washed off the blood. Like magic, her feet began to heal, and the pain reduced to a dull throb. *The berries and mushrooms must have special healing properties,* she realized. She only needed one or two more layers of skin to cover the pads of her feet.

Half-curious, she cast a hesitant glance at her reflection in the water. The glow of the mushrooms gave her a yellow pallor. The image revealed a woman who was worse for wear. Blood was splattered on her face, along with dirt and berry juice. Scrubbing vigorously, she removed as much grime as she could.

She turned her head and tucked her hair behind her ear. The top of her ear, always bumpy with scar tissue, was now one smooth line. It was far from a rounded ear, but it was as though the ear was attempting to regrow what was lost years ago.

Her thoughts were racing, and her limbs were heavy. She checked to make sure she wasn't in a ring of mushrooms. She wasn't convinced she wouldn't meet her demise in some other mystifying way, but at least she wouldn't dance "until the bitter end." With a groan, she lay down and closed her eyes.

CHAPTER 7

HOSTILE WATERS

Silvine

The birds roused Silvine from sleep, singing strange songs. She jumped to her feet and surveyed her surroundings. The water and its stones were still breathtakingly beautiful. No visible danger presented itself. Placed beside her head was a crown of flowers, made with wild daisies, deep purple lupine, and a single yellow rose. It was more beautiful than any crown she'd woven with Ana. Its mysterious creator hadn't bothered to stick around or leave a message. The previous day's mishap still clear in her mind, Silvine left it on the ground.

Keep your wits about you, she reminded herself.

Inspecting her feet before putting her boots on, she discovered that they had completely healed. There was not even a scar to remind her of her dance with Anaras. There was something so strange about this place, so otherworldly, so beautiful and yet so terrifying.

If she was to get help for Ainmean, though, she was going to have to keep her wits about her. Cian told her saying her name was dangerous. Rings of mushrooms and creepy little men were another

risk, apparently. Nothing in her twenty-two years of life could have prepared her for the physical and mental demands of surviving this forest.

She searched for patches of sky and sunlight through the canopy of lush green leaves. The sun rose from directly upstream. She could follow the stream and travel mostly west. She hoped she'd make a quick descent and find herself in the Asturian plains.

Walking gave her ample time with her thoughts. A lump formed in her throat as she processed her last moments in the village. Ana's short life was given so Silvine could flee. None of it made sense. The men in green and silver were far more skilled and cold-blooded than the bronze-clad soldiers from Creon. This could not have been a simple skirmish over trade agreements.

The men had identified Silvine as the heir of The Modrona. Silvine knew the term from Nene's bedtime stories, where she described The Modrona as the most powerful Fae in the forest. Even the trees waged wars on her behalf.

Only the mages believed those stories, though. They claimed to call upon the magic of the three Fae courts for their abilities to heal and cast minor defensive spells. Silvine's father had always distrusted such people, refusing to allow mages to work for the government of Ainmean, even though they held such positions in other provinces.

As her mind turned over every aspect of Festivale, she couldn't fit the slithering, cloaked figures into what happened or why the horsemen slew them. Perhaps they were assassins who served out their purpose.

For the first time in two years, she no longer ached for Cardoc. The love that once made her stomach flutter and her heart yearn imploded into burning hatred. She wanted to use her bare hands to tear his throat out.

Rage bubbled up within her until she thought she'd burst. Her fury spanned from Cardoc's betrayal to the fire and Ana's last moments to her father's convenient absence during those wretched events. She let out a guttural screech and picked up a stone from the riverbed, chucking it into the water as hard as she could.

It felt satisfying, so she did it again. And again. Her screeching quickly turned to sobbing. She threw herself against a tall tree. The world around her faded away as dark memories consumed her.

At the sound of a glittering voice, she lifted her head. "I let you eat from my banks and my cousins make you a crown, and this is how you treat me, child?" Silvine blinked through tears in time to see a wave of water headed straight for her. She braced herself against the tree, resenting the tears that kept falling. The wave smacked her chest, knocking the air from her lungs.

"How do you like it?" demanded a shimmering female, slowly emerging from the water.

The creature could be considered a beautiful woman from a distance. Closer inspection, however, revealed blue gills where her ears should have been and an iridescent glow on her skin. *Not skin,* Silvine realized. *Scales.*

"I-I didn't know you were in the water," she stammered. She had never spoken truer words in her life. As a matter of fact, she did not know *anything* right then.

The shimmering female bent down, her face inches from Silvine's own. The creature smelled faintly of algae and fish. She opened her mouth, revealing rows of knife-like teeth. "Poor, ignorant dear," she cooed, her slippery hand brushing across Silvine's tear-stained cheeks. "Has this been a hard time for you?"

As her sobs subsided, Silvine found herself shuddering with every inhale. "Yes," she said.

The creature slid a single, slimy index finger down Silvine's cheek, wiping away single tears. "Look at me," she insisted.

Silvine looked into a pair of yellow, cat-like eyes.

"I can forgive you for this tantrum you've thrown. Wouldn't that be nice?"

"Y-yes," Silvine breathed.

"Very good." The beautiful creature twisted her face into a

pleasant expression, her voice melodious. "I think what you're really searching for, what you've always sought, is a mother. And my home is always open to daughters. Do you want to be Mother Ondina's?"

Silvine knew that her true mother, Pulchra, would have loved her. Had she lived, there would have never been a void deep in Silvine's soul. Pulchra, known for her gentle spirit, would have loved her in such a way that her now-jagged edges would have formed to be as smooth as glass. The sharp tongue forged in the fires of her father's house would have been blunted by her mother's care.

The creature ran a cold, slimy finger along Silvine's jawline. She shuddered in response.

"You would have me?" Silvine asked, narrowing her eyes.

The creature's eyes flashed, and her teeth gleamed. "Indeed, child, indeed. I have great use for a creature like you. It is all quite simple. I need your name."

Cian had warned her about this. *You should know your name and refuse to greet yourself.* His words served as alarm bells ringing loud and clear in her mind. Her heart began to pound, adrenaline racing through her veins.

Understanding dawned on Silvine. Ondina was an *undine,* a water spirit. Nene had told her about these creatures. They were reputed to be wicked, ravenous monsters. Their sweet voices and enchanting looks led many away from the safety of the forest and into the water. They promised whatever one's heart desired most. In exchange, the undines received a hearty meal. Everyone had been cautioned about the water spirits, who were not opposed to using any manipulation or seduction necessary to lure their next meal beneath the water's surface.

This was her first test of survival. Silvine slowed her breathing as she searched within herself for a source of strength. The portrait of Pulchra flashed in her mind, the person her heart longed for the most.

"I just need you to tell me your name," Ondina repeated.

"I-I think I've forgotten it. I've wandered so long," Silvine lied, slowly smoothing out her skirts and reaching for the dagger at her thigh. In a flash, she drew it. Metal made contact with the flesh of Ondina's leg. Ondina shrieked as Silvine pulled it out, inspecting the blood on her dagger.

"You evil little *thing*," Ondina spat, rising to her feet.

Silvine stood just as quickly and shoved her. The water spirit fell backward into the river. "Evil little thing I may be, but your dinner I am not. Next time we meet, I will not hesitate to gut you like the overgrown fish you are."

The undine seethed in the stream, her dark blue blood staining the crystal water. Silvine stood her ground, a lifetime's worth of Wrath yearning for release.

Out of the corner of her eye, she watched an emerald vine race across the riverbank. The rush of the vine whipped her hair around her face. She leapt backward, out of its path.

The vine glided across the river's surface until it reached the water spirit. It wrapped around Ondina's neck, slowly tightening. She went deathly still and gasped out her words. "I had not realized. I did not know. The blood of The Modrona speaks. The Earth loves its own. I am not an enemy of the Earth, so let me not depart as your enemy." She lifted her hands up from the water in a gesture of goodwill.

Tingles traveled up and down Silvine's skin as she processed what had just occurred. She shoved aside thoughts of The Modrona, for whom "the very trees waged wars," and channeled her father's authoritative presence. "You decide if we are enemies. I will not hesitate to fight back, but I am happy to bring peace between us. I think you have seen what being my enemy will mean for you." The words, the assertive voice, hardly felt like they belonged to her.

"I will not earn your enmity, child. Eat from my banks and throw rocks all you like. I will not fight you. So let it be promised from my heart," the spirit replied.

Nene once taught Silvine that the phrase "*So let it be promised from my heart*" bound its speaker's life to the keeping of their promise. In the fairytales, trickster, wordsmith Fae did not take such oaths lightly.

The vine unwound from the creature's neck and slithered back across the forest floor.

"Very well. Depart from here," Silvine said, finally lowering her dagger. She slackened her arm. Ondina bowed her head and sped upstream.

Silvine washed the blood from her wing-handled dagger, hands shaking uncontrollably. Though Master Fluellen had taught her and Ana how to use their weapons, she'd never thought she'd need to. She hoped she could slash her way through the rest of the forest if danger arose again. Judging by the past two days, she did not doubt that more danger would find her.

As soon as the dagger was cleaned, dried, and strapped back onto her thigh, Silvine tried to gather herself and keep moving. The shaking spread from her hands to her jaw. Within moments, her legs became as wobbly as a newborn foal's. The constant adrenaline rushes had finally caught up with her.

A few stray tears slipped down her cheeks. All of Ainmean needed her to carry on. Still, she could not move.

Something trampled in the bushes behind her, making a beeline for the river. Silvine yelped as a magnificent, massive bear emerged from the brambles. Her small dagger would do no good against this creature of the forest, both due to its size and her lack of training. Bears were supposed to be extinct.

Willing herself to stand, Silvine used the tree to pull herself up. The bear ignored her as it splashed in the river. Cupping her hands around her mouth, she yelled, "Go away, bear! Beware, I am a loud human."

At the words "loud human," the bear paused to snort. It opened its jaws and clamped down on something that writhed in its mouth: a shimmering, rainbow-colored river trout. With a great twist of its neck, the bear tossed the trout at her feet. Silvine swooped to the side, clearing a path for the bear to retrieve its catch. Her eyes remained glued to the big, soaking-wet bear in the river.

It did not so much as glance at its catch. The tremendous jaws clamped down again, and another fish was tossed at her feet. She moved a few steps away, watching the creature in fascination. A third fish landed at her feet moments later.

The bear crossed the river to the opposite bank, ambled out, and paused to stare at Silvine. Two gleaming silver eyes met hers. She blinked. The bear bowed its head and meandered back into the thick bushes.

These are mine, Silvine realized. The bear had intended the fish for her.

She gathered the fish, which were slimy and weakly flapping, into her arms. Finding her second wind, she trudged farther downstream. Leaving the forest as soon as possible needed to be her priority. If bears, water spirits, and little men with harps hadn't killed her, something else might have.

When the sun sank low and the sky turned purple, she decided to stop for the night. She found dry sticks and a circle of rocks arranged neatly at her feet: the perfect setting for a fire. The mechanics of making the fire, however, were foreign to her. After arranging her sticks in a neat pile, she sat down and began to rub the sticks together frantically.

She tried over and over to create enough friction to spark a flame. No luck. She groaned, the growing darkness making it impossible to see her hands.

The wood gave off a sudden crackle, and sparks flew. The humble pile of sticks inside the rock circle became a blazing fire.

Sensing danger, Silvine leapt to her feet and drew her dagger. A hand brushed against her arm. Steadying her racing heart, she whirled around, lifting her dagger to the neck of the creature who had snuck up on her.

Cian's eyes glowed in the flickering light of the fire. "I suspected you were in need of assistance, Regina," he drawled.

She continued to hold the dagger to his throat. "Once again, that is not my name. Did I need assistance, or are you here to manipulate more treasures from me?"

With a snap of his fingers, Cian threw Silvine's wing-handled dagger from her hands, and it landed at her feet. She backed away slowly, slumping to the ground in defeat. Cian would not be bested as easily as the undine had been.

"You have no need to use weapons against me, Regina," he said.

His eyes danced with mischief as he seated himself beside the fire and withdrew a small knife from his belt. He began filleting the pile of fish, which Silvine had dropped beside the fire. "Let's return to lighter topics. You mentioned treasures. What kind of treasures are you offering me?"

Silvine plucked her dagger from its spot on the ground. "I am offering you nothing, and I asked you for nothing. I guess you can take the fish as a consolation prize for your efforts to cheat me out of something."

Cian continued his work silently, amusement radiating from his face. "It's all right to accept help." He began roasting the fish over the fire.

"In this place, I trust no one. Even the air is unearthly."

"You truly don't know, do you?" he asked, his tone serious.

"Know what?" Silvine asked, tired of the Fae's antics.

Cian turned over the fillets. "When you went to sleep in that mushroom ring, you left the human Realm. Nothing here is as it seems there, even if you're in the same spot on a map. You will see things and feel things here that you could never see or feel there. That's why the forest is so bewildering to your father's kind. They experience things they can't explain. They cannot perceive the events and the creatures around them."

Not sure how she'd ever reach Asturia if she couldn't trust her senses, Silvine blinked back the tears that threatened to well up. The past two days suddenly made more sense, and no sense at all.

Cian thrust the fish into her lap. "Eat, Regina."

Silvine glanced down at the fish and felt her mouth grow dry. The sight wasn't exactly appetizing, but she needed to eat. She took a bite of the fish. Its charred skin left a burnt taste in her mouth.

When she finished, Cian said, "It's best not to keep the fire ablaze while you sleep." He snapped his fingers, and her cloak wrapped itself around her. With a single breath, he blew the fire out and disappeared. Silvine stared at the spot the Fae had been standing, her mouth agape.

CHAPTER 8

ON A PRECARIOUS LEDGE

Silvine

Survival in the forest took precedence over analyzing the extent of truth in Cian's words. Silvine knew she needed to make it out of the forest to get help for her people. *Just get out of here, and then we'll think about whether Nene's stories have come to life*, she told herself.

The next day, she decided she'd need a sack to carry her things. She would not walk with armfuls of dead fish again. After drinking deeply from the stream and devouring berries, she ripped the skirt from her chemise and grabbed a large stick to make a knapsack. Plucking a few berries and placing them in her sack, she continued onward.

She remained on edge, jumping at every sway in the trees and snap of twigs underfoot. Death lurked around every corner. Cian seemed intent on showing up at the strangest moments, and she didn't dare trust a Fae. Nene always said, "Human lives are nothing but a game to The Old Ones. Interacting with humankind is their sport." Cian's amused grin flashed through her mind. She refused to be anyone's source of entertainment.

She wondered what was happening in Ainmean. Her heart sank

at the thought of the Fluellens. The consequence of Ana's brave act would probably crush both Gilla and her husband. Silvine hoped the fires were put out and the horsemen were in pursuit of her and not destroying the village.

The only thing she could do was keep moving forward. Hopefully an emissary would be riding on horseback, heading to alert her father. A village attack had to trump whatever the king needed. She wasn't sure Lord Morair would rush to find her after her disappearance. Coin and power were his two great loves, and she provided neither of those things.

Silvine traveled for days, following the river in hopes of reaching Asturia. Birds in the distance continued to sing a song in a language she didn't understand. Fragrant flower crowns were left for her each morning, and each time, she left them behind to wither. She slept curled under her filthy cloak. She couldn't afford to be finicky when it served as her only source of warmth and comfort.

Each horror had left its imprint on her through smell: smoke, blood, and sweat clung to her. She was undoubtedly losing weight with each day. Food was scarce, and she was more active than she'd ever been. At night, she went to bed with blisters on her feet, but she awoke to healed skin each morning.

The evening of her third uneventful day, she heard the ground rumble in the distance. The low rumbling grew to the thunderous clopping of horse hooves. She was hopelessly, utterly defenseless. If it was a foe, Silvine would have no options. She took a hard turn away from the river and fled uphill. The riders were on the opposite side of the river, and the effort of crossing would take them time. Time she would use to run and find a place to hide. She darted upward through the tree line until she saw a rock outcropping.

Jade-green moss dotted the gray boulders. She'd never seen moss look so pretty before. *Nothing here is as it seems there*, she reminded herself.

From below, it looked as though there was a small ledge between rocks, which would be perfect to hide behind while she spied on the riders. She leapt up, grasping at the rocks. Her nails scraped down the side until she was able to grip her feet down below. She pushed, pulled, and gripped as she worked her way toward the alcove. Rock climbing was never something she'd contemplated, let alone done. Under the circumstances, she was more focused on speed than keeping her skin and nails intact.

With a final grunt, she swung her legs onto the ridge of the ledge and pushed herself up. To her surprise, it was not merely a place where flat rock made a shelf. She beheld the mouth of a cave. The entrance was aglow with the same mushrooms that grew along the river. She paused, wondering if this was another trap.

The sound of splashing from down at the river echoed up the hillside. Horses neighed and riders shouted words of encouragement to their beasts, clearly hoping to ford the river quickly. She stepped past the barrier of mushrooms, deciding she'd rather fight a single Fae than a crew of men on horseback.

She forced herself to keep breathing in and out as she drew the dagger from her tattered, dirty skirts. The image of a silver blade neatly beheading creatures in one blow played in her mind. The splashing ended, and the clopping of hooves grew louder.

It sounded as though a single rider was darting back and forth, looking up the hillside. Silvine was safely concealed within the cave. She heard everything down below, but she could not see past the lip of moss-covered rock. If she hadn't seen the cave's mouth while she fled up the hill, the horse riders certainly couldn't either. The hill was steep and covered in brambles and trees. No horse could make it up. She hoped they did not have a supernatural ability to smell her blood, which she had smeared on the rocks in her frantic climb.

Finally, a rider called to the others in an accent Silvine did not recognize. "There is nothing here. Let us go back." Several men emitted groans, but the thunder of hooves began anew as they splashed back across the stream bank. She exhaled slowly, releasing tension in her shoulders and jaw.

She inspected her bloodied, scraped hands. Though the injury stung, the blood was quickly drying, and new skin was growing over her gashes. Her torn nails were not, apparently, going to magically heal.

Accepting that she had no way to file her nails, Silvine was ready to rest for the night. The cave seemed like a secure location. It had saved her from meeting someone with ill intent on horseback. She turned to inspect the cave behind her.

The cave was a small, closed stone room. Glowing yellow mushrooms lit the entirety of it. At the center was a stone table with settings for five. There was a roast in the middle of it, with a plate of potatoes, a loaf of bread, and a glass bottle of burgundy liquid. A tall candle, resting on a stone candelabra, flickered.

Silvine sighed. She had climbed up rocks, scraping every bit of her epidermis possible in the process, only to realize she was trespassing in someone's home. Her dagger was still out, and she clutched it tightly. There was no turning back now. As long as she kept her wits about her, she felt confident she could outsmart whatever wicked Fae awaited her there.

Breathing in and out, in and out, she worked up the courage to sit at one of the stone chairs, where she waited. Patiently.

A creature with black wings flew into the cave. Silvine tensed as the familiar trembling in her limbs started again. Inspecting the creature's face, she decided it must have been male. He had chin-length, stick-straight black hair, a well-groomed black beard, a pointed chin, and dark eyes. He was at least a head shorter than Silvine and bedecked in a dark tunic with leather pants and boots. He moved as though he swam through the air.

"I am glad to have you as a dinner guest," the male purred, his black eyes narrowing.

"Were you expecting someone else?" Silvine asked, gesturing at the table setting for two.

"Hospitality is of the utmost importance. I often set my table for at least one more than I am expecting," he replied, casting a sidelong glance at her. His nose crinkled ever so slightly before he smoothed his facial features. "Before we eat, I would imagine you would like to clean up."

The male gestured to the cave wall behind her. Glancing over her shoulder, Silvine realized there was a side room behind her, lit by candles on the walls. Three small, crimson-winged females bounded toward her. They looked similar to the male but only reached Silvine's knee.

"Allow us to offer you a hot bath and a change of clothes," the male said.

The three females, murmuring in a melodic language, tugged at Silvine's skirts. They seemed to be just as in awe of her as she was of them. As she rose to follow them, she realized she was still clutching her dagger.

"You may keep your weapon at hand, should you feel you need it," the male added graciously. Tension she had been storing in every muscle of her body released. "Just don't wield it upon my females."

"I will only use my weapon in self-defense," Silvine said as she followed the females into the small side room. A jade-green curtain, identical in color and texture to the moss outside the cave, hung at the entrance. When Silvine entered, the females swung the curtain shut.

Steam rose from a bathtub carved of stone. Hasty, tiny hands, eased Silvine out of her clothing. Being freed from her filthy dress felt divine. She was eased into the tub, its steamy waters smelling of mint. She had once heard that the ladies at the king's court were bathed by servants. To her mortification, she realized she was receiving the royal treatment in this cave. Holding onto her dagger awkwardly, she tried to think of other things besides the dirt being scrubbed from her body. The creatures gave both her dagger and her jewelry a wide berth.

Once Silvine had been patted dry and lathered in an herbal lotion, she found herself being slipped into a loose, sapphire blue tunic with matching pants and slippers. She had never worn such comfortable clothing. Her Festivale dress was the height of luxury in Ainmean, but comfort was not synonymous with style at home.

She padded out of the small room and back into the main part of the cave. The male raised his dark brows at her. "Now this... is much better. I can have my attendants try to repair your clothing, but I'm afraid it was quite ruined. Now, eat with me."

Silvine took a seat at the table once more, tucking her dagger into the waistband of her pants. "Thank you," she replied.

"Do you feel my hospitality is owed to you?" the male asked, a sudden coldness in his tone.

Taken aback, she realized her mistake too late. Nene always said The Old Ones did not take kindly to the phrase "thank you." Thanking the Fae implied that you expected their kindness, or worse, established a contract. The shift in mood was as startling as a sudden rainstorm in the middle of a sunny day.

Silvine straightened her shoulders, bracing for what would come next. "No. I was expressing my gratitude."

"Our people do not appreciate the phrase you just used. Do not utter it again," the male commanded.

"I will not. I forgot myself."

"It is no great matter." The male poured crimson liquid into two stone goblets. He put the bottle down and gestured. "Please, dine with me and drink my wine."

Nothing bad had happened there yet. Silvine had been bathed and clothed. Despite the verbal misstep, her host forgave her. There was real, warm food in front of her, and it smelled delicious. She was too hungry not to eat, even though the food at this creature's table may have been poisoned.

She took a sip of the wine and let out a small hum. It was the best she had ever tasted, with notes of cocoa and sweet berries.

"I see you enjoy the wine. It is from my own vintage," he said. "Please, do eat."

Silvine picked up the bread and began to devour it. The man heaped soft cheeses onto her plate. She devoured it, too. The world began to shift, the glowing mushrooms spinning, shrinking, and growing on the walls in front of her. It must have been the bliss of eating real food for the first time in days that gave her slight delirium.

"And now, you are mine," the male said.

"I'm—what?" Silvine stumbled over her words, begging her head to stop spinning and the world around her to stop sparkling.

"You ate at my table and drank my wine. Thus, I claim you. Such is the way of Fae to human hospitality."

Silvine shook her head, finding some mental clarity. "No man has claimed me yet, and I will not let you be the one to do it."

"Fortunately for you, I am not a mere *man*. I am *Fae*. You were so hungry and dirty out there on the riverbank. I will never let you hunger or thirst or want for anything again, for even a moment." He stared intently at her. "Look at you. You are an absolute treasure. Now, you will never see harsh things—things you would've otherwise seen. Here, you are safe."

Her thoughts raced as her heart pounded. She'd fled into the forest to save her people and promised herself Ana didn't give her life in vain. In her desperation, she'd fallen into a Fae trap. Strolling through her catalog of memories, she thought of blood sausage at the dinner table, horse manure on Ainmeanian streets, and bitter medicine from Gilla's spoon. Bile worked its way up her throat until she vomited on the floor. The male crinkled his nose.

Gesturing at the puddle beneath her feet, she asked, "Have I still eaten your food now?"

With a clap of the male's hands, more small, winged creatures appeared, and the floor returned to its original cleanliness. "It is not so bad, pet. Most creatures in a cave are most... uncivilized. This place, however, is a genteel dwelling. You shall come to love it. I will take the best care of you. You shall want for nothing. The things to be seen outside this cave are distasteful, but the life I will give you here is a gift."

All she could do was seethe while she plotted her escape. She wasn't sure if his claim of ownership was physical or a strange magical bond. She would have to quietly observe for now, until she could make her escape and run for Asturia. There was danger at every turn in The Faerie Realm. It was no wonder so many unwitting humans wandered into the forest only to meet gruesome ends.

The world was still aglow and wobbly. The male ate quietly, his face a mask of calm. Silvine stole a glance at him, but he seemed to ignore her. Slowly, imperceptibly, she reached for her dagger.

As she went to raise it, her arm stopped midair. She swung back and tried again. Still, she couldn't force it down. It was as though an invisible wall of stone met her every time.

Finally, the male glanced up from his meal. "I think you have forgotten your words. You said you would not use your weapon for any purpose besides self-defense. As no one is actively seeking to cause you bodily harm, you *cannot* use it."

Silvine fought off her drowsiness and narrowed her eyes. The male returned her gaze, appearing nonplussed.

"Exhaustion is making you behave poorly. I think you'd benefit from rest." He clapped his hands once more, and attendants appeared. They clutched at Silvine's sides, pulling her back to the small room. She was too tired to resist.

A swarm of small hands helped lay her down atop a bed of stone. Wincing, she expected the impact to hurt. Instead, the stone seemed to flex to the contours of her body, as easily as clay molded in warm hands. A weightless, silky blanket appeared on top of her.

The luxury of her cave bedroom was so unlike her own bed at home or Ana's bear blankets and cozy fire. She thought of telling her best friend about this place, the bed of gossamer and stone. Ana would have thought her insane. Maybe Silvine *had* lost her mind.

Even so, this was the coziest she had ever been in her life—and the loneliest and most desperate.

CHAPTER 9

DELIVERER

Silvine

Over the course of several days, Silvine found her life as luxurious as her captor had promised. Her captor, who did not identify himself, ate dinner with her each day. He made small talk before disappearing at each meal's conclusion. She occupied her time with his attendants, who lavished her with books, pastries, and endless grooming. Each night, her sleep was plagued by her recurrent nightmare. When she woke up screaming, she'd find a small berry tart and water placed beside her bed. No one mentioned it to her in the morning.

She felt as powerless in the cave as she had as a five-year-old girl. Her dagger remained useless. All means of escape evaded her.

One evening, Silvine and the male shared a dinner of pheasant, roasted potatoes, and a fruit mousse. As always, the food was the best she'd ever tasted, and as always, she refused to reciprocate her captor's polite conversation.

Silvine shot a few glares in his direction. He continued to disregard her dirty looks. Emotional warfare was useless, but she found comfort in refusing to be pleasant.

Out of nowhere, her captor's face lit up, and he slapped a hand on his knee. His attendants brought in an additional stone chair and place setting. Silvine swiveled her head around.

"My friend, you come to join my table," the host said warmly.

"Luc Ollam, Oathkeeper, I come to ask if you have lost all those good senses of yours. But, I would never decline a meal at your table," a mirthful, deep voice responded. Silvine's stomach dropped as Cian strode into the room.

Always irreverently smiling, she thought.

Luc Ollam, her captor and self-proclaimed host, heaped generous servings onto Cian's plate. "Let us discuss whatever the concern is later. We should not sour good pheasant with the troubles of The Realm. There are enough troubles to spoil every meal for the rest of our immortal lives."

Cian chuckled. He began inhaling his food and taking great gulps of wine.

Silvine could not decide if Cian was a friend or foe. He rescued her, only to leave her to struggle to survive on her own. Given the way he disregarded her in the moment, seemingly without a care in the world, she decided they were enemies. If she could have, she would've plunged her dagger into his chest and ended his irksome existence forever. The fact remained, spell or not, that she was unlikely to be able to fatally stab anyone, let alone Cian. She felt like a mouse, toyed with endlessly by a silver-eyed cat.

Once the meal concluded, Silvine tried desperately to avoid staring at Cian. Her breathing grew unsteady as the anticipation built.

"Shall we go to my study to discuss whatever my alleged loss of good sense is?" Luc asked.

Cian shook his head and gestured toward Silvine. "No, this conversation must be within the lady's hearing. It does involve her, after all."

Luc's brows knit together. "Oh, her? I have been keeping her safe for you. Although I certainly wouldn't mind keeping her here. She's just my guest."

"Just your guest? More like just your captive!" Silvine retorted.

"That"—Cian smiled humorlessly— "is precisely what I'm here to address."

Luc placed his palms on the smooth stone table. A few attendants scurried around him, clearing the empty plates. "I *was* acting within my rights. Besides, I assumed you would want to know what wandered in the forest," he said.

Silvine glowered at him. What about *her* rights? If she ever made it out, she would implore her father to lead Fluellen's men back there to set the cave on fire. Burn it down like the straw houses of Ainmean had been.

"Did you take time to... assess the impact of the situation... before deciding to make her a more permanent guest? Surely if you had, you would know your folly." Cian's tone implied something Silvine couldn't discern.

Luc surveyed Silvine. He paused on her face for a moment as a revelation seemed to dawn on him. He jumped up from his seat, wings flapping, mouth open. Silvine glanced back and forth between the two of them, trying to make sense of their exchange.

"So, you see now," Cian remarked, leaning back in his chair and crossing his arms.

Silvine's palms grew sweaty. She hoped this meant she would be released. "What does he see?"

Both men ignored her. "I was merely offering my hospitality," Luc argued, gesturing at the table before him. "I could sense you in her blood, so I knew you would come around. I just hadn't realized the magnitude of the situation. Will this... change anything?"

"No, we shall keep this between us. You old scoundrel. You were so eager for a pretty, new ornament that you didn't even see who you'd snared. You thought I'd congratulate you?" Cian stood and patted Luc on the back. Silvine narrowed her eyes at him.

"When you put it that way, I sound like pure trouble. I am

nothing but chivalrous." Her captor clapped a hand over his mouth, and the two men stood, patting each other on the back.

Luc turned to Silvine. "I release you from the bonds that tied you to me. Though I hope someday you will dine at my table again. Please pardon my mistake, and do not hold it against me. I had no idea."

"You had no idea of what?" Silvine asked.

The two males exchanged glances before shaking their heads.

"Give her time, and she'll come around to your charms, Luc," Cian said, ignoring Silvine's question once again.

"Excuse me. There seems to have been confusion. Why am I being released?" Silvine demanded.

Cian patted her head. She swung to bat away his hand. He tucked the arm attached to it behind his back. "Disappointed to be let go, I see. You're simply the wrong type for Luc, Regina." He turned to his winged friend. "Is there anything we need to do before we depart?"

Luc bowed. "No, she is released. Although you *are* welcome to stay a while. I was going to enjoy a pipe in my study. I feel proud to have offered one such as her my hospitality."

"I am afraid I don't have a moment to spare. Next time I pass through, I will stay a while. I would say the same for her, but she seems just a wee bit irritated with you for keeping her here," Cian said. In one graceful motion, he stepped closer and slipped his fingers into Silvine's. She straightened her fingers to resist his touch.

"You know, he may be charming, but he is not nearly as refined as I. Nor does he have a parcel of attendants ready to wait on you hand and foot. It is all peace and pleasantry here. With him? Not so much," Luc said.

Silvine rolled her eyes. "Your cave is splendid, and your attendants are some of the loveliest creatures I've ever met. Using trickery to make me your captive, however, will forever taint my memories of our time together, *Luc Ollam.*"

His cheeks colored in response. Silvine puffed out her chest, but Cian led her away before she could say anything further.

When they reached the cave's mouth, Silvine braced herself to be dragged down the rock outcropping. She closed her eyes.

When she opened them, she found herself on a mountain trail. It wound gently down a mountainside to a green valley below. Dizziness and nausea struck her the minute her feet touched the ground. She blinked, realizing she'd just moved through The Realm as if by magic. Cian stood a few feet away.

"You found me. Again," Silvine said.

"I have a knack for that."

"You know, he never told me his name."

"I wouldn't expect him to. Names are currency and power among our people."

Silvine studied Cian's face. His sparkling eyes made up for the averageness of the rest of his features. He returned her gaze.

She continued, "I think you have me confused for someone else. I'm human, and I come from a painfully ordinary mother."

He brushed a tendril of hair from her face. She flinched at the intimacy of his touch. "You may be confused, Regina, but I am not. No one in your line has been *painfully ordinary*, especially not you."

She shuddered, sick of the Fae speaking to her in riddles. "I would like to leave this forsaken Realm and forget all of you deceitful monsters." She kicked at a boulder beside her foot, stirring up a cloud of dust.

A look of amusement spread across Cian's face while tears of rage streamed down Silvine's.

"*This* deceitful monster just saved *your* inept carcass again," Cian said. "And, as you know, I accept payment in gold." He lifted his palm up.

Reaching around her neck, Silvine found her mother's obsidian pendant. It had somehow warmed to the point where touching it felt nearly scalding. She separated it from the chain that held the Morair insignia. Without hesitation, she ripped her father's heirloom from her neck and flung it at Cian.

"I'll settle for the chain," he responded, picking up the necklace and nonchalantly tossing the insignia into the bushes.

"I'll settle for you vanishing like you always do."

"And what if I don't?" He took a step closer.

A low grumble was her only response.

"As you like it," he murmured, vanishing into the evening air.

Silvine exhaled. She took a step forward on the trail but tripped over something at her feet. Her long-lost homemade knapsack appeared. *More magic*, she thought. She picked it up and cautiously peered inside. Her cloak was neatly folded and clean. A new water skin was placed on top of it, along with a loaf of bread and a bit of cheese wrapped in cloth. A pair of new boots had been tucked into the bottom. Unable to avoid rolling her eyes, she hoped Cian wasn't watching as she slung the sack over her shoulder.

The mountain trail was sparsely dotted with trees, unlike the dense forest she had struggled in for days. The sun was low in the sky, painting the hills with its golden glow. Tall, purple mountains lined the horizon. Silvine decided she could make it to the bottom before darkness fell. The leveling of the land told her she was drawing closer to the plains of Asturia.

If she could find an Asturian mage, perhaps they could undo whatever spell she'd fallen under that first night in the forest. She would never have to see these scheming Fae again. She would get aid from Asturia and make it back to save Ainmean. After what she had seen of the world beyond, Silvine vowed to never take the peace and small-scale schemes of her home village for granted. She hoped Ophelia's suitor decided a match with her was agreeable and that her father was already returning to save their people.

Trying to hold onto hope, Silvine made it down the mountainside, where a fire pit had been dug and a freshly lit fire burned. Neatly filleted fish were speared through with a stick. Resentfully, she held the stick over the fire and ate the provisions. Although she knew it was likely another of Cian's schemes to keep her indebted to him, she was too hungry to resist.

Just a few more nights of this, she promised herself, hoping to see the walls of Asturia soon.

CHAPTER 10

ASTURIAN DREAMS

Silvine

The walls of Asturia remained just beyond Silvine's reach. The valley below the mountain was peaceful with majestic, purple mountains in the distance. However, no matter how far she walked, the mountains never seemed to get closer.

Occasionally, the strange Faerie birds would sing an eerie song in the distance. It seemed to be a long, mournful epic. The more she listened, the more words she could discern. The birds were singing of a Fae queen "who wasn't." Nene once sang a similar ballad, in Ainmean's common tongue, about a queen who had lost her mind. The depressing lyrics were at odds with the jovial tune. Silvine couldn't remember how the song ended, only the juxtaposition of the joy of the melody and the tragedy of the lyrics.

The sun's path, rising in the east and sinking in the west each day, and the changing landscape assured Silvine she was drawing nearer to Asturia. Although she hadn't been there in a decade, she remembered the way the topography flattened as it descended from the mountains of the province of Ainmean toward the southwestern edge

of The Realm. The land crossed one final mountain range before descending toward the sea.

After days of trekking across the valley and relying upon surprise gifts of food and water set near resting places, while tiny, twinkling voices faded away into the distance, Silvine found herself startled to a skidding stop. A great rift separated one end of the valley from the other. At the edge, the valley gave way to a steep, red cliff.

I'll just walk south until I reach the end of the fissure, Silvine thought. Each time she paused, the memories came flooding back. Her hands shook and her heart raced whenever she took a break from the endless walking. The burdens of what she'd seen grew too heavy to make her body carry her forward. Resolving to follow the rift's edge, she continued for what felt like hours.

A few dusty pebbles finagled their way into her boots, and she could bear the discomfort no longer. She stopped to shake them out, unrolling her dirty stockings to look at her feet. They were dirty but uncalloused, without a single blister. Silvine was unblemished by her journey. There were no scars to prove she had suffered.

Although a source of shame and confusion, the scars on her ears reminded her that she had survived. They were tangible proof to the world, namely her father, that her suffering had truly happened. She thought of trying to explain the horsemen, Anaras, Ondina, and Luc to her father. It would sound like the ravings of a woman whose time alone in the wilderness cracked her mind. Imagining her father's response, she involuntarily clenched her fists.

"Earth-forsaken—*damn!*" she shouted at the cliffs. None of this was fair. The familiar thump in her chest warned that the feelings were returning. Silvine's curse echoed back at her, as though the cruel world was mocking her frustration.

"My, that is foul language for a lady," sneered voice from behind her. Reaching for the dagger at her thigh, Silvine whirled around to face three men.

The tall, muscled men, who were wearing black tunics and black leather breeches, formed a semi-circle behind her. Gleaming metal decorated their bodies, from twin blades at their backs to daggers on their belts. These men looked trained and ready for a fight.

Immediately, Silvine knew she was trapped. She could not run past them, and the cliff behind her spelled certain death. Resigning herself to the situation, she tried to breathe through the tightness in her chest. "Who are you?" she asked, her voice cracking.

The man who had called out to her first flashed his teeth, revealing sharp canines. Gripping the pommel of the sword at his hip, he tipped his head toward her. "I could ask the same of you. What is a pretty little thing like you doing all alone?"

Fair question, Silvine thought. She had been wondering the same thing since this wretched experience had begun. Torn between fabricating a story and giving a kernel of truth, she opted to say, "I don't know. Honestly, I don't." She showed her palms to them.

The three men looked at each other. Their side profiles revealed long, pointed ears. Fae.

Reminding herself to choose her words carefully, Silvine steeled her resolve and braced for a fight she would likely lose. "One thing I do know is this," she continued, "I am utterly done with dealing with Fae men. Is there any chance you'd like to just leave me alone and go crawl back into a hole?" The words fell out of her mouth before she could filter them through the logical part of her brain. She braced for whatever consequence was going to come as a result of her radical honesty.

With more grace than any human possessed, the men glided closer.

"I'm afraid we won't be doing that," the leader said, his voice silky smooth.

Before Silvine could flinch, the men were within arm's reach of her. She straightened her shoulders defiantly, bracing herself for whatever was to come.

"Do you know who I am?" she asked. Who was she, anyway, that would deter an attack from Fae men? Her father was merely a human schemer, not an immortal warrior.

The three men grew closer, so close she could feel their hot breath against her skin. There was a sharp pain as she felt a tremendous crack to her skull. She tried to cry out. She saw stars, and her stomach lurched. Then... nothing.

"Try not to be an embarrassment to us all," her father cautioned. He was smoothing out his blue velvet coat and adjusting his coronet.

Ophelia crinkled her sharp nose at Silvine. "I think the very nature of your existence is an embarrassment. Remember, we're visiting my mother's people, not yours. Asturia is a great realm with advanced learning and civilized lands. Asturians have conquered the wilderness. Your mother came from a little, uncivilized village in the forest. Don't forget your place while we are there."

Silvine's bottom lip began to quiver, and she willed it to stop. Letting the tears fall in front of Ophelia was as dangerous as letting blood in front of a wolf. Blinking back tears, Silvine glanced over at her father. He was reviewing a scroll in preparation for their arrival. She knew that nothing passed his sight and understanding, but he selected his words carefully. Defending his youngest child was never a priority.

"I'll try not to be so outstanding that I make you look average," Silvine replied sweetly. Ana had helped her come up with a few retorts to fire back at her sister. She wished her best friend could be with her then. This long journey to promote political goodwill with their allies had worn her down before they'd even arrived. The only reason she was even attending was to show Ophelia's Asturian relatives that their father took great care of his motherless children. Faith in his abilities to parent both girls would keep their alliance strong and keep any Asturian warriors from sneaking to Ainmean in the night to abduct Ophelia.

Her older sister reached across the seat, likely to pinch her, when they were all jolted to the sides of the carriage. There was a great sound, like the clap of thunder, and a plume of gray smoke trickled through.

"Ah, finally," said their father. He was the only one with an ounce of calm; Ophelia was screeching, and Silvine found herself shivering involuntarily.

The carriage came to a sudden halt, and the door was flung open by a young man, clad in a bright, patterned tunic. "Ah, Cousin Ophelia," he exclaimed, extending his hand to help her out of the carriage. She batted her lashes in response. A servant in the distance announced her name. The Morair footman helped their father out of the carriage, and his name was announced. Silvine stumbled out on her own, surprised to see clear, blue skies and no trace of the smoke from moments earlier. Her name was also announced, albeit with less enthusiasm.

She looked around her at a crowd of people in an imposing courtyard fenced in with a massive gray stone wall. All the faces were tan and cheering in lilted accents.

I hope they like me, Silvine thought to herself.

Seeming to read her mind, Ophelia crushed her hopes in an instant. "They won't like you here, so don't get any ideas," she whispered in Silvine's ear while continuing to wave pleasantly at the crowd. "You'd be better off running away to live in the woods, heathen."

Silvine stared down at her hands, finding particular fascination with the nail on her pointer finger. In that moment, she decided she wouldn't like the Asturians, either.

Silvine spent most of her time hiding in the garden of Ophelia's great aunt, Her Ladyship of Asturia. The grounds were lined with impressive, gray statues of lean, feline-faced Fae, posed with drawn weapons and outstretched palms, fountains that spurted water into ponds with rainbow-colored fish, and ancient trees that provided ample shade. The solitude of the garden was far better company than that of the Asturian people.

At mealtimes in the great hall, Silvine kept her eyes down, ignoring comments comparing Ophelia's tall, imposing Asturian form and great elegance with Silvine's "common constitution." Their father made no attempt to defend her. He simply basked in the praise of her older sister while enjoying late nights in Her Ladyship's strategy room.

Her Ladyship was cordial to Silvine, calling them "political allies," but Silvine could hardly stand her loud, overly coiffed, heavily perfumed presence. At just twelve years old, Silvine decided visiting foreign courts was not meant for her.

Lord Morair never invited her again, either. During their last supper in Her Ladyship's great hall, Ophelia was snickering with an Asturian cousin. When Silvine got up to leave, she thrust a foot out in front of her. Silvine tripped, landing sprawled across the stone floor with a great thud. Her whole body stung as she got up, all eyes glued to her. Her sister let out a great cackle, the Asturian cousin beside her joining in. Silvine bit her lip to keep the tears from flowing, trying to block out the whispers disparaging the "weak, little forest creature."

CHAPTER II

TARAN DANDO

Silvine

Silvine was dreaming of that thud across the great hall in Asturia when she jolted awake. Her body hurt in the same way it had all those years ago.

The world was cold, hard, and tilting back and forth like an oxcart that hadn't been secured. Through the fuzz of her mind, she heard the rush of water in the distance. She opened her eyes, rubbing the sleep out of them. Her head was pounding.

When her eyes were finally able to focus, she pushed herself up from a clammy stone floor. There was no sun, just a few torches throwing light into the room. The walls were carved of misshapen, ash-colored stone. The room's furnishings consisted of a straw mattress and a wooden door with a peephole.

This was a dungeon. She was in a cell.

Silvine stumbled onto her feet, swaying a little. She'd received head trauma from... something. Though she wished to understand how she'd come to be there, she struggled to connect the dots. Her head swam as she willed the world to grow steady again. The memories came flooding back: Festivale, Ana, the painfully beautiful and dangerous forest, a Fae male with an unbearable smirk, and the three assailants who rendered her senseless. Her knees buckled.

Were they associated with the same people who had destroyed her village and pursued her into the forest? She felt a sinking feeling in the pit of her stomach. On the other hand, maybe the Fae didn't concern themselves with human political affairs. Nene only ever told stories of forest mishaps with The Old Ones, not political intrigue. Silvine wanted to believe she'd found an ally, although the blow she'd sustained dimmed her hope.

Metal clanked outside her door. With little warning, the door flew open. The Fae who had called to her beside the cliffs walked in, holding a tray with bread and a chunk of cheese. His face was youthful and tan—his cheekbones, chin, and nose all sharp points.

"I see you have regained consciousness. I apologize for how hard the pommel struck you. Most unfortunate," he said.

She blinked back tears, trying to focus through the pain reverberating through her skull. "What do you want from me? Why am I here?"

"You trespassed on royal lands. Surely you knew the consequences." His tone was flat.

Royal lands? She must have reached Asturia.

She straightened her posture. Surely, these people would help her. "I came to seek royal aid. Your leader's allies in the mountains have been attacked while Lord Morair was away. You would assault a suppliant?"

The male scoffed, looking her up and down. His nose was pinched, highlighting the sharpness of his face. "I would hardly call *you* a suppliant. Our mountain neighbors are mere humans, but that is insignificant. You will soon face my lord, and he will deliver justice." He wrinkled his nose. "I will give you a moment alone to prepare for your reckoning. Pray to The Creator." Without another word, he turned on his heel and clanged the door shut behind him.

Silvine's head throbbed in response to the sound.

None of what her assailant said made sense. The lord of Asturia was a squat, little man, who offered next to nothing to His Ladyship. She was the ruler. Both of them were definitely human. The logical side of her brain screamed that this could not be Asturia. The pommel-addled side of her brain begged her to calm down and find an ally.

She wondered how long Her Ladyship had been employing Fae in her guard. The statues in her garden seemed to indicate a reverence for them, although Silvine could not fathom how she'd managed to tame them into serving anything but their own interests. In her mind's eye, she envisioned Cian in Her Ladyship's brightly patterned livery, bowing and acquiescing to her every wish. One insolent smirk and Her Ladyship would have him flogged. Publicly. The thought brought Silvine a glimmer of joy.

A faint look of amusement was still on her face when her attacker returned. "Most unusual," he muttered under his breath.

She threw her shoulders back and looked up at him. "I could say the same of any man that assaults a defenseless woman."

He marched over and hauled her to her feet. Arm in arm, they made their way out of the dungeon and into a narrow hallway, which was illuminated with the same style of torch from the cell. She contemplated wriggling out of the man's grasp, but there was nowhere to run. It would only hurt her more if she was recaptured.

The hallway was eerily quiet, except for the sound of rushing water overhead. It was as though they were beneath a rapid river. Silvine tried to focus on the light on the stone walls, ignoring the way the shadows moved underfoot and the fear that she would soon find herself on the shores of an angry river.

Another Fae male, clad in the same all-black outfit, walked briskly toward them. Silvine kept her eyes trained on the torches, in case he was another thing borne of the shadows swirling through the hallway.

"The king has received a full update. There is to be no court audience for her," he announced when he reached Silvine and the guard.

Silvine glanced around, looking for a place to flee. If they wouldn't let her speak to the court, her hope for either escape or getting help for Ainmean was slim.

"Then what is to be done with her? Back to her cell?" her guard asked, yanking at her arm for seemingly no other reason than to exert force. She took her heel to his boot. Her captor appeared unfazed by the contact of her heel with his toes.

His bushy-eyebrowed colleague looked over at her, curling his lip. "She's a bit of a wild cat. She is to have a trial. It is ready, in compliance with the king's wishes. Our task is to take her to the trial location."

"A trial? Very well. In that case, I hope the gravedigger will be available this evening," Sharp Face said. "Lead the way."

Silvine let her body slacken. The familiar feeling of outrage was her only constant in this topsy-turvy world. She planted her feet, lurching the guard backward as he tried to move along the hall. "Oh, no, no. A trial? I would love to know the crimes for which I am being tried."

The two males paused to look at her, both appearing slightly puzzled. Finally, the sharp-faced one answered. "This isn't some *human* court of law. You are to complete a trial to show your mettle."

"My worth is where I am *from*. I need to send aid to my province. My worth is that my father and his men will burn to the ground those who make an attack on his blood." Silvine's voice rose, all of her control thrown out the nonexistent windows of the dungeon corridor. Even though she knew the words she spewed weren't true, she couldn't manage to stay quiet.

"That may be," Sharp Face responded, "but you will complete the trial nonetheless."

Silvine straightened her shoulders and marched down the hall, trailing the second man. Her head continued to throb. Accepting that there was no place to run, she knew she had to keep going. She resigned herself to her fate as she tried to ignore the growling of her stomach and the pains wracking her body.

They made their way through the dark, stone hallway with the dancing shadows until they reached expansive stone stairs. The second man trudged up first. The stairs were wide enough to accommodate both Silvine and Sharp Face. His grip on her arm tightened as they ascended. The sound of rushing water grew closer with each step.

Her heart began to race, and her breathing grew uneven. As the rushing water grew closer, she took a mental stock of the things that would weigh her down if they threw her into it. Her sack was long gone, and she'd left her cloak behind in her cell. The dress she wore was from her stay with Luc, as light as the gossamer blankets she slept in. The fabric surprised her with its durability.

This dress is as enduring as the winged scoundrel's trickster friend, she thought. Assessing the water, she found comfort in knowing the only jewelry she had left was her mother's necklace, and her little dagger was featherlight. The greatest hindrance would be her well-worn boots, which would undoubtedly take in water and weigh her down. Unfortunately, she had no experience fighting for her life against the force of great rapids.

The last stair gave way to a great cavern, aglow in violet light. A foaming river rushed through the cavern. Off in the distance, there was a great stone bridge connecting the river's margins. Silvine froze, but her captor yanked her along again. Her feet moved mechanically as they approached the roaring water's edge. She could hardly breathe as she pictured the cold, brutal plunge.

"Scared of water, are we?" Bushy Eyebrows taunted. She fought the urge to say something back. Razor-sharp words would not save her.

On the other side of the river, there was a hallway carved into the cavern wall. Just like the one they had left, it was illuminated by torchlight. Another Fae in all black approached her two captors, who immediately bowed their heads. He was a head shorter than the other two males, and Silvine immediately recognized him as Cian.

"Taran Dando," the guards acknowledged.

"I am here to take our competitor to her trial," Cian, or rather, Taran Dando, replied.

Sharp Face relaxed his grip and bowed his head.

"Watch your toes with this one," Bushy Eyebrows warned.

Taran Dando, standing at the opening of the hallway, turned to face them. His face was awash in the purple glow of the cavern and the light of the hallway's first torch. His eyes shimmered in the light. "I look forward to whatever challenge she may throw my way."

Silvine's gut lurched. Apparently, this impudent Fae male was also a liar—a liar named Taran Dando. She was already fighting against her gnawing hunger and the relentless pounding of her head, and this new development felt like a punch to the liver. In their encounters in the forest, Cian seemed to be the most candid of the Fae. Although he irritated her endlessly, she never felt unsafe with him. Here was evidence that he was just as slippery as the rest.

Nothing here is as it seems there, she thought.

Taran dipped his chin in acknowledgment. "I will not require further assistance." He dismissed them with a wave of his hand. Sharp Face shoved Silvine toward Taran before gliding across the bridge with Bushy Eyebrows.

Silvine schooled her features into a look of calm, trying to hide her hurt.

Reaching out, Taran gripped her hand in his calloused one. She winced. Dizzyingly fast, he whipped his head to look at her. She'd never seen his expression so serious. "Are you hurt?" he asked.

"Just take me to this challenge, *Taran*, and mind the matters that concern you," she snapped.

A look of understanding brightened his face. His voice, however, remained deadly smooth. "I would argue your injuries do concern me, but as you wish, Regina. By the way, you are correct. You will call me Taran here. Taran Dando." He said it with such authority that Silvine felt bound to abide by his words.

Cian, the bemused trickster of the forest, was now clad in all black and going by a ridiculous name. Cian was dead to her. The loss took her by surprise. More than anything, his lie stung. He had been her one constant. He, however, had never existed. As she tried to process this, his words came back to her.

Names are currency and power among our people. Deceiving her in the forest likely gave him some kind of power over her.

"So Cian is dead," Silvine said.

His smirk failed to reach his eyes. "I could see how you would come to that conclusion. Come, we waste too much time talking. Let me take you to your trial."

He kept a gentle grasp on her hand, leading her down the corridor and up a winding stone staircase. At the top of the stairs, a wooden door with a massive gold lock forced them to pause. Taran pulled a golden key from his pocket, thrust it into the lock, and swung the door open with his hip, never lightening his hold on Silvine.

"Regina, your challenge awaits you," Taran announced, whirling her past the threshold. He turned on his heel and left, closing the door behind him. Silvine reached for her dagger, bracing herself for the chance to break free.

CHAPTER 12

TRIAL BY PUCA

Silvine

The flood of light in the room she entered was so blindingly intense that Silvine had to close her eyes. Her inability to handle light was further testament to the damage she had endured at the hands of her black-clad assailants. *Blink,* she commanded her eyes, *blink until you can tolerate it.*

When she was able to open her eyes and focus, she gasped. The room was made entirely of white marble with unnatural purple veins. Beautiful, hand-carved pillars depicting detailed heads of mythical creatures held up a balcony that curved around the second story.

Looking up, Silvine realized this room was the interior of an expansive tower. By her count, there were five stories' worth of windows. Never before had she seen a space so sterile and unnatural. Although the dungeons aligned with the way Her Ladyship of Asturia would deal with her adversaries, this design—barrenness juxtaposed with the stale white marble—was nothing like the color-ful, ornamental style of the Asturians.

"You have finally arrived, Trespasser," a silky voice called from the balcony.

"I am not a trespasser. I am a suppliant, begging for help. Is this not the court of Asturia?" Silvine swiveled her head around to spot whoever was speaking.

The silky voice called back, "This is not the court of Asturia, Trespasser, or any human court for that matter. I would be glad to provide you with succor, should you succeed in this trial. Now, the terms of the trial are quite simple: survive."

"That's incredibly vague," Silvine called back to the unseen speaker. The awkwardness of her words made her cringe inwardly. With the throb of her head and the blinding whiteness around her, she could barely string together sentences.

"You will understand soon enough. I hope I shall see you on the other side," the silky voice responded. There were two sets of footsteps padding away and the clang of a door somewhere overhead.

Silvine fought back the rage and confusion that made her want to beat her hands against the cold, white marble walls and floors. Something sinister was certainly on its way to her. Maybe this would truly, finally be the end of her struggles. It would be the end of all—in a foreign land with cruel Fae plotting against her. No one would know what happened to Lady Silvine of Ainmean. Her mortal death would be mere entertainment for these cunning creatures.

Despair began to take over when black bunnies came bounding out of the shadows and began to make sibilant noises. *Hissing bunnies?* Silvine tried not to scoff, but she couldn't believe her impending doom was at the "hands" of hopping, black rabbits.

The tower went dark. It was just Silvine, standing beside the expansive whitewashed door, dodging the bounding creatures. A shrill shriek resounded from the center of the room. The ugly cacophony of sounds, reverberating off the marble walls, made her head hurt so badly that bile rose in the back of her throat.

Don't vomit, don't vomit, she told herself. *I am not my powerful father. There is no escaping this. I am the daughter of Pulchra, who even in death held her grace and dignity. I will die with as much dignity as I can. That is my only power.*

She hadn't realized she was saying the words aloud until she heard the echoes of her whispers resounding through the tower.

In response, the shrieking grew louder and louder. Out of the darkness came images, flashes from her own memories, all around the walls of the tower. Though the pictures were hazy, the feelings were unbearably strong. Silvine saw her ears burning, Fluellen rushing to get her treatment, Ana's scream cutting through the crackling of the burning huts, her inability to even raise her dagger against Luc.

The memories served as a highlight reel of all her failures. She did not fight back when her flesh was burned from her body. She ran away while her best friend gave her life up. Cian, or whatever his name was, had to save her too many times in the forest.

Useless. That's what she was. She'd wandered the forest for days, pretending to have a purpose, thinking she was going to find help in Asturia. She didn't even know why she was being pursued in the first place.

Her head's pounding brought her to her knees, the pain too great to bear.

One of the creatures shrieked, "You tried your best! Just rest. Just give in!" It went on for so long that Silvine wasn't sure she'd ever been anyone before the shrieking.

She dropped to her knees, palms splayed across the smooth marble. She panted, fighting her uneasy stomach. A bunny hopped onto her leg, nipping at her, and she swung it off. One nipped at her elbow, and she batted it away with her other hand. "Will you awful things *knock it off*? Get away from me!"

Cian's eyes flashed in front of her. "That's the true Regina," he whispered as he gripped her by her elbows and pulled her to her feet.

The image of Cian saving her for the hundredth time faded into darkness as the image morphed into an all-consuming vision.

Silvine saw a woman laying in Lord Morair's massive four-post bed. She was drenched in sweat, wearing nothing but a white shift. Her long, corn silk hair was plastered to her face. Her blue eyes were bloodshot. The woman was a dainty, elegant version of Silvine. Pulchra.

Two female attendants were pushing down on her bulging stomach as Pulchra strained.

"There, keep going, my lady," Gilla soothed from somewhere out of sight.

After several groans and pushes on Pulchra's abdomen, a baby began to mewl.

Lord Morair appeared beside Pulchra, one hand on her shoulder. She panted, "How is the baby?"

"A perfect, healthy girl!" Gilla replied cheerfully.

Lord Morair wrinkled his nose as Pulchra murmured, "Cherish her. Daughters are a blessing."

His face changed as blood stained Pulchra's white shift and bloody-handed maidservants gripped her tighter.

"My lord, I need you to move!" Gilla shouted. Pulchra's eyelids fluttered before her eyes rolled back. "Stay with me," Gilla called, gently shaking her.

Visibly struggling to keep her eyes open, Pulchra whispered, "My lord, you must let her fulfill her purpose. Let us name her Silvine, like the beautiful forest."

"Of course. We will do whatever you wish. Please, please do not close your eyes," Lord Morair pleaded, his tone frantic. This was not the icy, calculated Premier that Silvine knew. "Don't leave me."

Gilla and the maidservants worked frantically on Pulchra, blood everywhere, while a baby cried in the distance.

Finally, exhausted, Gilla put her hand to Pulchra's wrist, and her face fell.

Everyone stepped away from the bed.

"It is done," Silvine's father said. "Pulchra is killed by a girl. My lovely wife lost to the labors of birthing a useless girl." He padded *away, the door slamming behind him, as the baby wailed louder and louder.*

The vision faded, the hideous sounds resuming. Silvine knew she had been born useless. She'd killed her mother. Her entrance into the world was marked by sorrow. She felt her soul begin to shrivel at the weight of it all.

"Just give in," called the shrill creature. "Find the peace that comes from surrender. Come here."

Silvine took a step toward the center of the floor, but Taran yanked her back.

"Look at me," he whispered, so close her chest touched his. "You have all the power. You cannot trust whatever is being shown to you. These creatures feed off your despair, but *you—you* are more powerful than you know. Will you trust me?"

Her chest heaved, crashing into the solid wall of his own with every ragged inhale. "*Can* I trust you?"

"Regina," he whispered, running a finger along her jaw. Her pulse quickened and warmth spread across her body. "You could trust me in the forest, and you can trust me in this tower. The only weapon that useless father of yours ever let you wield was your tongue, but your very blood has the power kings would lay waste to whole armies to possess. The power to change the world is inside you. Be still and listen to the music in your blood. Step into your power."

Taran opened his other palm, stepping back. In his hand, a small leaf glowed a brilliant hue of green. It hummed. The humming felt like the most familiar melody Silvine had ever known. Though it was no louder than a whisper, it drowned out the awful shrieking.

"But—but I'm not a mage or an Old One or—" She braced to kick at the rabbits, but they'd given her and Taran a berth of a few paces when he'd opened his palm.

He shifted his hand from her cheek and followed the curve of her ear with his pointer finger and thumb. Initially, she'd cringed, waiting for him to find her marred skin. It wasn't there. His nimble fingers moved up and down along her ear, following a pointed shape.

"Do you see now?" he asked.

"Y-yes," Silvine murmured, realizing Taran's meaning. She was a Fae, like him. "But I don't even know what to do."

"I shall help you. But as you know, I never offer my services for free."

"I don't have any more gold." Silvine's heart beat wildly in her chest. As her mind began to shut down, the only clear thing that remained was shrieking and hissing. She broke her focus on the hum radiating in her weakened veins.

"I take other things as payment. I will have your firstborn child." In the glow of the leaf, his teeth gleamed. He was smiling irreverently, as always.

Silvine shook her head, trying to process what she'd just heard. "You want *what*?"

"I said, 'I will have your firstborn child.'"

Her mental fog lifted as she realized what he'd just said. Silvine threw her hands in the air. "After all I've endured, I don't think marriage is in my future. I'm not exactly the most suitable match in The Realm. You will have my firstborn child in exchange for you getting me out of this nightmare, so let it be promised from my heart."

"In order to make our bargain official, you must give me your hand," Taran said.

Silvine thrust a shaky hand into his. His rough one gently caressed hers before he lifted the back of her hand to his lips. He smiled, his eyes meeting hers in the radiating glow of the leaf, shadows cast around his cheekbones. There was a faint thrum between Silvine's hand and Taran's, and the slightest zap of electricity between them. Ever so quietly, it sang to her, just as the leaf did. Her ears rang.

"That's it. Just close your eyes if you can't face it with them open," Taran whispered. "Now, *sing to that leaf, and make Life abound around you.*"

She let herself close her eyes, taking a deep breath and pushing all thoughts of the horrors around her to the recesses of her subconscious. She chased the humming sensation, her body straining to join the call. At last, her body began to hum in response, and a melody developed between whatever was in her blood and the call coming from the glowing leaf. If a body could be off pitch, hers certainly was. It wasn't harmonizing with the tune.

"Slow down, Regina. Reach deep within. You have to relax, or it won't work as well."

Silvine peeked down at their hands, and sure enough, a brittle, yellow vine was sprouting all around them, falling down by their feet. She opened her eyes wide and closed them again.

She thought of the way she fought off Ondina. She had taken on a sinister river Fae and won. She thought of the warmth of the Fluellen household and the love they always gave her—how she fought, every step of the way, to survive The Faerie Realm. Although her mother had died, Silvine was still living. She thought of *life*. A warmth took over her body, and her own humming began to harmonize with all of the life around her.

The rabbits began to hiss as she envisioned thorny vines and vibrant yellow flowers forming a circle around them.

"Vines are a good start, but you'll need something bigger to fight these puca off. Can you summon something to you? Try it," Taran said.

Summoning the vines, she willed them to morph into branches and then snarling dogs. She began to ache from the effort, but she pushed on. The hissing began to dissipate.

"More," Taran coaxed, his thumb rubbing the side of her hand.

She pulled from something even further within herself, something primal. The sounds in her blood turned into a shrill whistle, and she felt a ray of power pass through her body, radiating from the hand Taran held all the way through her other hand. Though she kept her eyes closed, she felt a beam of light within her, growing from her connection to Taran. She opened her eyes and with one final push, one last song, the beam poured from her and radiated through the tower.

There was one more ghastly shriek and a thud as something hard crashed to the marble floor. It was done.

The whole tower became awash with the glow of Silvine's light. The once-barren marble floor now looked like an otherworldly garden, with glowing leaves and flowers covering it all.

"There's that power," Taran whispered.

Silvine panted, feeling physically depleted. She felt him let go of her hand and spun to face him. He had left. In a split second, the hope she'd been holding onto faded. She blinked and could have sworn she felt lips brush against her forehead. But he was gone. As always, he'd gotten what he wanted, proven she needed him, and vanished.

As Silvine walked toward the source of the thud, her exhaustion made each step more difficult than the one before. A wrinkled, charcoal-colored stone the size of her fist was all that remained of the unearthly creatures she had vanquished. *They must have been creatures of darkness and Death if mere Life and light ended them,* she thought. She picked up the rock, carefully studying it.

The wall opposite the massive wooden door began to move. It was a secret door, revealing a torchlit hallway and a tall figure with a purple cloak and hood concealing their features. Only their shiny leather boots showed.

"His Majesty is impressed with how you handled the trial, Suppliant. Trespasser you are no more. Come. His Majesty will wish to hold court about this matter once you are... properly recovered from your victory." Despite the person's encouraging words, their tone conveyed utter boredom. They thrust out an arm, revealing purple velvet sleeves and black gloved hands. Silvine balked at their offer, clutching her trophy rock to her chest.

"I don't want the thing you're clinging to, Suppliant," the figure said. "Now, if you would please allow me to be a male of good breeding and take my arm, I would be most appreciative."

Silvine ambled toward him, loosely tucking her elbow into his. She looked up at his face, only to be startled by glowing red eyes and sharp, inhuman features.

He chuckled. "I tried to wear my hood for good reason. Your kind is not accustomed to such things."

They walked down the hallway in silence, up two flights of winding stairs, before reaching a hall filled with doors. The man led her to one, thrust the door open, and gestured at it. "You will find a warm bath, a change of clothes, and a much more comfortable bed than the accommodations in the dungeon. Normally, you would have an attendant, as a guest of His Majesty's, but we will let you handle tonight on your own, if that is agreeable to you."

"I'd prefer to be alone right now." She inspected the door handle, looking for a lock from the outside.

The male shook his head. "You're not a prisoner, at least any longer. You have nothing to fear. There is a bell beside your bed. After you get some rest, ring it, and someone will attend to you."

She made her face unreadable as she entered the room, promptly whirling around to shut the door in the man's face. There was a bar that slid across the door as a lock, and she engaged it quickly before inspecting her surroundings.

The far wall of the room was made entirely of windows, revealing a tremendous, red-rocked valley below the building she was in. Beside the window was an immense marble tub with steaming water bubbling out of it. Soaps and bathing cloths were left beside the tub. A velvet-curtained bed occupied the other corner of the room with a tray of pastries and a kettle beside it.

Without pausing to think, Silvine stuffed some heavy, cream-filled pastries in her mouth, gulped down some of the bitter herbal tea from the kettle, and plunged herself into the tub. Sheer willpower kept her from acknowledging her pain from the time her surprise tower began until she reached the tub. As she sank into the warm water, her head began to pound again, and her bones ached unrelentingly.

There was no way she could carry on without accepting the food, the warm bath, or the opportunity to sleep in a comfortable bed, but thoughts of Luc Ollam, the "Oathkeeper," flashed in her mind. His hospitality, his chance at providing respite, led to her own captivity thanks to the endlessly tricky rules and deceptions of the Fae. Captivity had at least kept her alive, though she was certain Luc Ollam would never dare to cross her path again. The idea of clawing his eyes out with her bare hands brought her surprising satisfaction.

Her heart thundered as she tried to process all the fragments of recent memory. She was supposed to be saving Ainmean, finding her father's allies to come to the aid of their province. Now, she would probably become a story Nene's descendants would tell of a maiden who vanished into the forest. In time, she would probably even become a fair maiden with the purest heart. If only they knew how disturbing the forest really was. If only they knew about the monsters she would face and the dormant powers she had been carrying with her all that time.

Once she'd removed days' worth of grime from her body, Silvine allowed herself to relax in the tub. She would have to observe these strange Fae and outwit them. It was the only way she'd be able to get help for Ainmean.

CHAPTER 13

AN HONORABLE MAN

Silvine

Silvine dozed in the tub until the sun set and torches lit themselves in her room. The sudden whoosh of torches igniting startled her awake, and she crept into bed, concealing her dagger under the mattress.

While shelling peas in the Fluellen kitchen, Ana grumbled, but Silvine loved the opportunity to work with her hands. She was never allowed in the kitchens at Lord Morair's estate, let alone the orchards, but service was an expectation at the Fluellen household. Silvine had been almost gleeful when the Fluellen nurse had asked them to help. As they worked, Nene sang folk tunes.

Ana complained, "I wish I could make a bargain with an Old One to pick peas for me so I'd never have to again."

Nene shot her a sharp look. "Bargains with Old Ones are danger-

ous. Don't say that out loud or one just may appear. I swear, you never listen."

Silvine perked up. "Why are bargains dangerous, Nene?" In the village market, bargains and bartering were more common than the exchange of coins. They sounded perfectly innocent.

Nene's age-worn hands stopped their work, and she wiped them on her apron. "The Old Ones aren't like humans. Word is law among them. Bargains magically bind you to return the favor and follow through on your word. If you don't, you die."

"Do The Old Ones kill you if you break a bargain?" Silvine asked, tossing an empty pod into the bucket on the floor.

"No, child, they don't have to," Nene answered, her tone grave. "When I was a girl, the miller's son wandered into the forest. He came across Old Ones sitting around a fire. They invited him to join them as they feasted and danced. The miller's son thought, surely The Old Ones aren't as bad as they say, so he ate their food and danced with them. The only problem was, once he started dancing, he couldn't stop. He was terrified, but The Old Ones just laughed. Another Old One came across the fire and promised to save him, so long as he brought him two sacks of the finest grain from his father's mill every full moon. The miller's son agreed, using the words 'so let it be promised from my heart' to bind him to his word."

"That doesn't seem that dangerous," Ana said.

"It wouldn't have been dangerous if the miller's son kept his promise. And he did for the first two full moons, dropping grain off at a spot in the forest The Old One had told him about. All was well, but the next full moon, he was to marry the cobbler's daughter. He thought the bargain wouldn't really affect him, so he went to the wedding feast. His nose began to bleed during the vows."

Ana wrinkled her nose. "Did the bride still kiss him?"

Nene huffed. "Child, you do worry about the silliest details. Yes, she did. At the wedding feast, everyone gave up their handkerchiefs to help the groom. The healer gave him a tonic, but it didn't stop the bleeding. The miller's son began to gasp and turn blue. As the bride *danced with her father, her groom fell to the floor. His heart gave out. His body vanished, too. The Old One he'd wronged took him away, no doubt."*

Silvine made a mental note to never bargain with an Old One, should she ever encounter them.

Crimson eyes peering above her bed startled Silvine into wakefulness. *Skies above,* his eyes were unnerving.

"His Majesty asked that I come to check on your welfare. It has been two days since the trial, and he longs to congratulate you."

Silvine sat up. She couldn't believe she'd slept for two days. "Why now?"

"It is not your place to question." He looked her up and down. "I presume you don't call that proper clothing, wherever you come from."

She returned his comment with a glare. "Considering the unimaginable things I have survived in recent weeks, I could care less what I'm wearing. I'm glad to be alive."

Those eerie eyes narrowed in on her, a look of disapproval spreading across the man's sharply angled face. "I will send an attendant up to remedy... this. Fresh clothing and food will make you more presentable."

Moments later, a slender female entered, carrying a cart with a tray of food on it. "I brought a sample of everything from the kitchens, since I haven't been told what your tastes are. Help yourself." She gestured to the plush bench at the end of Silvine's bed, where she had placed the tray.

The female strode to a wardrobe in the corner, throwing open the doors and rummaging through its contents, offering feedback to herself about the items she grabbed. Silvine nibbled on a crust of bread, bites of cheese, and some exotic purple fruit she'd never seen before.

"Time to rise, so I can get you presentable for the king," the female said, practically forcing Silvine to her feet. She slipped her into light, thin undergarments before throwing a dress over her head and smoothing it out. "Come have a seat at the mirror, so I can get the rest of you fixed up."

"What's your name?" Silvine asked.

"Names are currency. My attendance is all I am required to give you. You may refer to me as your attendant."

Even the servants in Lord Morair's home went by their first names. It felt wrong to not have something to call her by. "Do you have a nickname, at least?" Silvine asked.

"Attendant," she snapped.

In the mirror, Silvine was startled by her reflection. Her eyes shone bright, and through the tangles of bedhead, pointed tips of her ears peeked out. The attendant frowned at Silvine's locks. Seemingly unburdened by a need to be gentle, she tugged at every rat until the hair was smooth and wavy. Silvine sucked in a breath with each aggressive yank. Faster than any human hands could, the attendant braided thin strands of the front pieces of hair before twisting them into a crown around Silvine's head.

"Best get up and be on your way," her attendant said. Silvine stopped to pocket her trophy rock.

She entered the torchlit hallway, at the end of which was an empty stone courtyard. Her red-eyed companion from earlier was waiting for her. "Well done," he remarked to the attendant, who let out a grunt.

He offered his arm to Silvine. "Suppliant, it is time for your presentation to His Majesty. I must warn you that he is the most powerful king in all the world, and he has no time to trifle with nonsense."

Silvine held in all the retorts that crossed her mind about the trifling Fae she'd been dealing with for the past several weeks.

Though she was content with him calling her Suppliant, she wondered what his name was. Most of the men she'd met who wielded authority by serving a powerful man flaunted their names and titles. The power of names was so different here.

They walked the length of the stone courtyard and entered through a stone archway into the longest hall Silvine had ever seen. The hall was made of the same sterile, white marble as the tower. At the end of the room was an expansive dais with a massive throne. Notes of eerie music, coming from a flute and a stringed instrument she didn't recognize, drifted lazily throughout the room.

Silvine trailed behind her escort, peering into the alcoves as they walked past them. In each alcove, a unique brand of Fae debauchery could be observed.

A long-limbed female in a flowy dress lifted her skirts to relieve herself in the first alcove. Silvine hurriedly looked away. At another, two rotund males were hastily gulping from the biggest flasks she'd ever seen.

At the next alcove, Silvine froze. Cardoc was inside, *her* Cardoc, kissing a petite, winged Fae. The mirror behind them reflected his face back at her. Too late, she remembered. He wasn't *her* Cardoc. He was the quaestor's niece's Cardoc. Somehow, he'd made it here, in this castle far from home, cozied up to a female who definitely wasn't human.

"Cardoc," Silvine said, accusation in her tone.

He pulled away from the winged female. There was something harsh in his eyes, something Silvine had never seen before. He flashed a mouth full of sharp teeth at her. "Not Cardoc, but if you recognize me, you ought to be worried for him." He wasted no time resuming his business with his alcove companion.

Nothing here is as it seems there, she reminded herself. Not Cardoc's warning made her chest tighten, dredging up old tenderness.

The weight of it all threatened to break her. Silvine stood frozen, slowly exhaling out her feelings, staring straight ahead at Not

Cardoc. The spell was finally broken when her red-eyed escort cleared his throat and pulled her away.

"Don't concern yourself with what any of His Majesty's court does," he said sharply. Silvine obeyed, keeping her eyes fixed on the dais ahead.

The most beautiful creature she'd ever seen was approaching the throne from the opposite side of the room. In the dimly lit hall, he shone like a gilded statue. He had a mane of red-gold hair, a muscular figure, and a cloak of purple and gold. His very walk oozed charm. This was, undeniably, the king of the castle. A gaze up at the golden circlet atop his head confirmed it.

Tears streamed down Silvine's face as emotions warred in her mind. She shoved away her mental images of Ana, her mother from the vision during her trial, and all the other horrific things she'd endured. She lowered herself to the floor, curtsying deeply.

The king took a seat on the imposing, golden throne. "Rise, Suppliant, and cry no more." His silky voice reverberated throughout the room, and the eerie music halted. Without turning back, Silvine could feel the heat of dozens of eyes on her back. Collecting herself, she stood.

"Morair, come forth," the king called.

Silvine started when she saw her father enter, escorted by guards in black. She cried, "Father, I have been looking for you!" He raised his eyebrows and glared, indicating that she had better hold her tongue or face his wrath later.

"As you promised, your daughter *is* powerful," the king remarked.

"Indeed, Your Majesty, I have always known," he responded gravely. The urge to roll her eyes or laugh at her father's outright lie was strong. Perhaps she had died at some point in her travels, and this was a dead woman's delusions.

For good measure, Lord Morair added, "Silvine is more powerful than any woman has a right to be." The edge in his statement, a sharp jab only she could detect, brought her back to reality.

The king shot a lion's smile down at Silvine's father, seeming ready to pounce. "She is a magically gifted female, and she proved it at her trial." He gestured a ring-filled hand toward Silvine. "I would like to see the trophy from your pocket, Fair One."

Feeling the heat begin to rise in her body, Silvine reached into her pocket, pulling out the wrinkled stone. She studied it for a moment—its hideous appearance—before placing it in the king's open palm.

"The heart of a vanquished puca," he surmised. "It is the largest one I have seen in quite some time. Did you enjoy your trial?"

"How do you want me to respond to that kind of question?" she asked.

"Honesty would be my expectation. In fact, I will tolerate no less," the king said.

Lord Morair cleared his throat, casting another icy glare in his daughter's direction. Silvine longed to tell him about the destruction of their village, the way they cut Ana down, the warning about Cardoc, and all the other horrific things that required his attention. Instead, she was discussing fantasy creatures and handing over rocks to a man who clearly held more sway than her father did.

"*Honestly*, Your Majesty," Silvine said, "I was struck in the head by strange men while wandering the land alone, awoke in a dungeon, and was immediately marched off to face a trial. I suppose the trial wasn't the worst thing I endured, but I would be content never having to battle one of those creatures again." She ignored her father's sharp look.

The king shook his head. "It is unfortunate you met some of my border guards under such circumstances. I do not stand for that kind of violence. Lord Morair hoped we would find you sooner, but you have proven yourself to be... more than I had anticipated. I am rarely surprised."

Lord Morair nodded. "She's surprising at times." He narrowed his eyes at Silvine. "Once you get used to her, though, I'm sure she'll become quite predictable. Boring, even. I imagine, after all the years you've seen, you don't want too much *excitement*."

All at once, Silvine realized what was happening. She put a hand up to her forehead and took a deep breath. Her father claimed the king had seen plenty of years, but to her, he looked to be no older than thirty, much younger than her father was.

A small voice in the back of her head reminded her of Cian's words around the campfire. He'd said nothing was as it seemed for humans. *They cannot perceive the events and the creatures around them.* A logical part of her wanted to conclude that this was what he'd meant. But the mere thought of Cian, of *Taran*, made her blood boil.

An attendant brought her father a chalice of bubbling wine. It buzzed faintly, like the leaf in Taran's hand had. The call for her body to respond, however, was absent this time. Lord Morair accepted the chalice and took a large swig.

"In regard to our new alliance, I would be pleased to make that official, Lord Morair," the king said.

Lord Morair took another giant gulp. "While I have always been your loyal servant, I am humbled to accept this proposal. Silvine will be the perfect consort for you."

The whole situation was odd, to say the least. Silvine interjected, "Um, I need clarification from Your Highness and my father. What do you mean by 'consort'?"

Lord Morair gazed dreamily over at her, appearing to be in a complete stupor. The king, however, looked unfazed. "I heard that you, Lady Silvine, were quite remarkable. You survived an attack from the enemy on your village and overcame the trial. I require a gifted wife to help overcome threats from the enemies of The Realm, and you shall be the perfect match for me. Your purpose is to restore The Realm to its original glory. Only your power can do it, and with you as my bride, we will bring about a new era."

Her jaw dropped. "You want to marry *me*?"

The king nodded. "I do. Since your father agreed prior to your trial, it is done. It will be a long betrothal. In the meantime, you will be an honored guest at Court."

Lord Morair gave a sweeping bow. "We are honored, Your Highness."

Silvine shoved her clenched fists into the folds of her dress. There was no "we" in this agreement at all. "I hope your hospitality matches your manners, Your Highness," she said. The thought of Luc Ollam made her shudder. Unable to think about the way her father had just signed her life away, she jumped to other topics. "I thought I was traveling toward Asturia. Where am I?"

"My hospitality is unmatched, Fair One. I am Guval, King of The Realm. You are at my castle. We call it Court, as I am told most of my people do." The king rose from his throne and strode toward Silvine. With more charm than anyone had a right to possess, he beamed as he took her hand. He slipped a gold ring with a large, purple stone onto her finger. The stone was unlike any she'd seen before, with whorls of purple and a splotch of black in its center. The black spot made the stone resemble an eye.

It seemed to be a reminder that she had been transferred from the watchful eye of her father to the supervision of another man: the king. Never, in her wildest dreams, had Silvine thought she would find herself engaged to the most powerful man in The Realm. *At least he's beautiful*, she thought.

King Guval whirled her around to face his court. "Now that this matter is settled, let us enjoy a feast in honor of our betrothal."

Lord Morair cheered. Silvine studied him closely. The wine must have been too strong for humans. She'd never seen him unable to hold his drink before. An attendant rushed toward him while Guval linked arms with Silvine, the two of them flanked by black-clad guards.

They walked down another long hallway, which was lit by torches. Silvine tightened and relaxed her fists. This had not been the audience with the king she'd hoped for. Her father and Guval seemed to be aware of the threat presented to Ainmean, but she wasn't sure the extent of their knowledge. She hoped the people of the province were safe.

Now, she was realizing that her father was more of a liar than she had thought. Why did he think she had powers? Lord Morair never treated his second-born like she was anything but ordinary. Her jaw tensed as she thought of the way he'd gambled with her life. She shouldn't have succeeded in the trial. He was lucky that she had.

Silvine avoided thinking about what would have happened if she had failed. She would have likely died if Taran hadn't helped her. Death by rabid hares with a funerary song of screeching seemed like an unpleasant way to die.

She was trying to determine *why* she appealed to the king when he looked at her. "So you have met my brother, Phelip, I understand."

"Have I?"

"He's as tall as me, but with more of a... wild... Fae appearance. Red eyes, strong opinions?" The king raised a brow.

The realization struck her: her escort was the brother of her betrothed. The thought of this man being her husband someday made her both deeply giddy and deeply apprehensive. "Yes, Your Majesty, I know exactly who you're describing."

"I have no doubt he was abrasive. He is quite fond of his traditions and hates to be disrupted," Guval explained. "He will grow on you. He throws the most lively parties and is far more cultured than I."

"I know nothing about Fae culture. I thought the Fae were a myth most of my life," Silvine confessed.

Guval halted, placing a hand on her shoulder. His touch chilled her. "Your level of knowledge, your fears, and your inexperience are all to be expected. I would not have chosen you, or an alliance with Ainmean, if there was anything about you that was lacking. You suit my needs for a consort perfectly; we need power, not cultural knowledge. I trust that, in time, you will come to love me, to worship me, as more than just your king." His green eyes rested on her lips for a moment.

Jarred by the contrast between his cold touch and kind words, she could only manage to nod.

The dining hall seemed larger than the entire Morair estate. Three of the longest tables Silvine had ever seen, with countless gilded chairs, were scattered throughout the room. There was a dais at one end and a stage at the other.

A guard seated Guval at the head of one of the tables and gestured to Silvine to sit at his left. Phelip took the spot beside her. Lord Morair took the seat across from her. The expansive dining hall was filled with Fae of all sizes, complexions, and interesting, unhuman features. Musicians stood at the stage—a lute player, a flute player, and a singer—telling an epic tale of a Fae girl who burned down the forest, freeing everyone from evil.

"I prefer intelligible lyrics," Lord Morair said. Silvine cocked her head at his strange words. Seemingly oblivious to her, he sipped contentedly from his goblet and mumbled about Ainmean's generous annual tax payments to the king funding talentless entertainers.

The food was excessive, all of it rich and plated opulently. Silvine ate her fill but refused to drink the strange, humming wine. Phelip seemed to ignore her entirely, devoting his attention to a crimson-eyed creature with fiery red hair sitting at his other side.

Between the bard's song and everyone's apparent disinterest in her, Silvine could not find time to broach the subject of Ainmean. A stern-faced guard walked her to her chambers once the song concluded, her king tilting his head in farewell. Her audience with the court had not brought the help she'd hoped for.

CHAPTER 14

MOTHER OF ALL MAGES

Silvine

"Rise, Lady," her attendant said the next morning. "After you break your fast, I'll need to dress you." She placed a piping-hot tray of food on the table.

Silvine, who'd dreamt of Ana's death all night, yawned and grumbled, "Why must I wake up? The sun is not up yet."

Her attendant paused her march about the room to plant her hands on her hips. "His Majesty has a full day planned for his betrothed. Lord Phelip will be here soon, and I must get you dressed."

Silvine was not eager to face Lord Phelip again, with his startling countenance and obvious disdain for her. She clung to the hope that she would get to speak to her betrothed and her father about the events that transpired in Ainmean, which still weighed on her heart. There were more questions than even a day could answer, but she had to start somewhere.

Regarding her attendant, Silvine decided compliance would benefit her, so she began to nibble at the exotic fruits and poached

eggs on her tray. Curiosity got the better of her, and she asked, "Why won't you give me a name to call you?"

Her attendant frowned. "It's for the best. Some questions aren't the right ones to ask here. Look for other truths instead. My name isn't the one you need."

The echo of Cian's... Taran's... words rang true again. Although his actions made no sense to her, she could not deny his honesty about The Faerie Realm. Nene had once told her a story of The Old Ones who could never tell lies and The Old Ones who lied with ease. Both were unreliable tricksters, but the honest ones were considered friends of humanity. Taran Dando probably would call himself a friend to mankind, but if his smugness was any indicator, he likely thought he was a gift to everyone whose path he crossed.

The food on her tray became too rich to finish. "Since there's little chance I'm going to get anywhere making conversation with you, can you please help me dress?"

Her attendant did not answer. Instead, she opened the wardrobe doors.

After she'd put on a silky, purple gown, Silvine found herself arm in arm with Lord Phelip. He had been doused in perfume, and the stifling combination of musk and floral notes made Silvine sneeze.

"I've sent word to His Majesty's seamstress in Luteche. She will create an appropriate wardrobe for the future queen consort," he said.

Before Silvine could reply, the scarlet-haired, red-eyed beauty from the night before entered the hall. Phelip bowed his head, and the woman curtsied at him in response.

"Minuet," he said.

"Husband," she replied, revealing a mouth full of unsettlingly white teeth. She turned to Silvine. "Lady, I was just with your betrothed. It is our pleasure to have you at Court."

"This is your wife?" Silvine asked, astonished that something so lovely would be tied to a man so... *unlovely.*

Phelip laughed darkly, and Minuet shot him a venomous look.

"Don't let him fool you. He adores me," she said. "As the Court mage, I'd like to take you to my study to ensure no spells or bargains from the forest are tied to you."

"I was once told mages were frauds. They look to the stars, wave their arms around, and gain power with sleight of hand. Is that untrue?" Silvine asked.

Minuet linked her arm with Silvine's free one. Her lips formed a flat line. "The mages are my children. Any *true* mage can trace their lineage back to me, although many say I'm a myth or a goddess. Some of my children simply have *stronger* gifts than others."

"How exactly do you plan to check me for spells and bargains?" Silvine asked. She thought of her last agreement with Taran and wondered if Minuet would find evidence of it.

Would a promise like that end her betrothal to Guval? Would Guval free her from the agreement? Nene's warning from years ago stuck with her: breaking a bargain with the Fae was fatal. Thoughts of losing her beautiful king made her nervous for reasons she couldn't explain. He undoubtedly wanted heirs. If she gave away their first child, she'd be exiled from Court.

"It will be quick and painless," Minuet said. "It's a matter of analyzing how your vapors respond to mine." Minuet used her free hand to squeeze Silvine's shoulder, her sharp nails scratching Silvine's flesh. She winced.

Phelip cleared his throat and began tapping his foot.

His wife remained focused on Silvine. "It won't take long. Welcome to my study." She stopped in front of a large, black door. She thrust a black key into the door handle and pushed it open.

The study was unlike anything Silvine had seen before. The room's torches cast little more than a dim glow on the deep crimson walls. Scrolls and bits of bones were scattered around. The room smelled of incense and must. It was a foreboding place. Silvine's feet grew leaden with each step.

Phelip sighed the moment they entered the room. Minuet

ignored him, setting things up, checking scrolls for references, and gathering items.

After a great deal of building anticipation, all Minuet did was fan the fumes from a cauldron of boiling liquid at the center of the room in Silvine's direction and mumble to herself. Silvine's own body released an odorless, forest-green mist in response. It made her deeply self-conscious, especially under the heat of Phelip's stare.

Minuet led them out of her study. Silvine twisted the purple ring on her finger, waiting for the verdict.

"Congratulations. I shall be able to give a good report to the king. You are bound to no one and nothing." Minuet winked. "Except, of course, to your betrothed."

Silvine's shoulders sagged. Perhaps Taran Dando was a liar. She wasn't bound to him after all. Unless, of course, the opposite was true. Minuet could've been a fraud, like all her "children" in the human realm were. Silvine shoved aside the small voice of doubt and focused on her freedom. She was free of Taran and engaged to *the king of The Realm*.

As Silvine continued her errands with Phelip, she waited to see her betrothed or her father. Instead, they bustled from place to place, meeting minor figures of Court. They assessed Silvine's musical abilities (lacking), Fae dance training (nonexistent), and palate (woefully human).

Seeming pleased with the completion of his itinerary, Phelip escorted her back to her room. Silvine leaned against the door, pausing before she entered.

"You seem exhausted, Suppliant," he observed.

"What a profound observation, Lord Phelip."

He shot her a sharp look. "I would not advise showing any weakness here. Carry yourself as though you are powerful, since you've proven that you are. It will keep the royal piranhas at bay. They are always eager to take a bite out of those who are vulnerable. Show them the side of you whose powers will right all that is wrong in The Realm."

Narrowing her eyes, she studied him. His words came close to sounding helpful. "I appreciate the advice. When will I see my father? Or Guval?"

The king's brother swung her chamber door open. "After you remove the look of exhaustion from your face and prepare for dinner. Make yourself presentable."

CHAPTER 15

VERDANT FOLIAGE

Silvine

The dining hall jarred Silvine's senses as much the second time as it had the first. Strange stringed music, with eerie Fae lyrics and the same performers from the night before, reverberated through the stone walls. Everything was a blur of laughter and bubbling wine. The Fae inside seemed enchanted with everyone they crossed paths with. Everyone, that was, except Silvine.

Phelip had seated her at the end of the table opposite Guval, giving her no chance to engage in conversation with her husband-to-be. He was engrossed with Fae who were debating something about governing, and Silvine's father had trained her well enough to know the political musings of the opposite sex were to be left alone. Lord Morair always said ladies needed to be merely observant of politics in public. Her father seemed engrossed in the company of a host of Fae ladies at a table across the hall.

Despite the fact that Phelip had introduced Silvine to her neighbors, all of them had merely smirked at his introduction, sniffed, and then took to ignoring her.

The rich food felt too heavy. The spread was delicious—the most delicious Silvine had ever consumed—but more than a few bites threatened to make her ill. Not wishing to show any sign of weakness, she took to mindlessly stabbing at her plate.

A gentle thrum in her ears shook her from her stupor. It grew louder and louder until she could hear nothing else, and her left palm began to tingle. She looked down to see a single, delicate yellow flower whose verdant vines wrapped around and caressed her fingers. Her eyes followed the source of the sound all the way to the wall, where a smirking figure was leaning, his own palm aglow with green light. Crossing her arms and clenching her fists, Silvine willed away the growth of the flowers. When she opened her palm, all that remained were yellow petals in her hand.

Taran beckoned her toward him and disappeared down a hallway. She decided to follow him. No one looked up from their conversations as she rose from the table.

She followed him down the narrow, torchlit hallway. He stayed twenty paces ahead the entire time, seeming to sense her presence no matter how slowly or quickly she walked. Out of spite, Silvine tried to both quicken and slow her pace, and yet, he remained the same distance away. They went down flights of stairs, twisting and turning, until they stopped abruptly at a heavy wooden door.

Taran rested his arm against the door as she finally caught up to him. "You followed."

Silvine narrowed her eyes. "I'm a pariah here. I was bored."

"Ever willing to use that sharp tongue of yours. After all we've been through, you repay me with nothing but cruelty."

"What do you want?" she demanded.

He took a deep breath, and silver eyes met hers as she felt the buzz again.

"I want you to remember your power. You are in the midst of some of the most powerful Fae in the entire realm, and you could decimate them. Don't let *Guval*"—he spat the name—"placate you with pretty dresses and food. Keep your wits about you."

"You think I'm being placated with finery? I'm the daughter of a lord of a province. I know what this is. This is how all the nobles behave," she hissed back. The hum grew louder. The angry little girl within her—whose ears were burned in Ainmean, who was mercilessly mocked in Asturia—threatened to come unglued.

Taran winked. "Do you remember our agreement?" Silvine blew out a loud breath as the humming grew deafening. "Don't lose control. Breathe, Regina."

She wrung her hands in response. A flash of green-white light shot out from her hands, hitting Taran's chest. He wobbled a bit and gasped, and the faint music stopped.

"I'm sorry!" she blurted, stepping forward to check on him.

Taran's face lit up, and his hand met hers as she reached out for him. He spoke between coughs. "There's—that—power. I want—to see—more of this—from—you. Just maybe when—I'm expecting it."

"How will the king ever tolerate this?" Silvine nearly sobbed, yanking her hand out of Taran's. "My father always warned me I'd overpower a husband."

"There is much you have to learn. Every lord in The Realm would desire this, desire *you* for a wife. Your power is something you need to learn to control so that it can never be used against you."

Silvine shook her head. "I don't understand any of it."

Taran bowed. "As a service to such an awe-inspiring lady, I will help you try. You must simply remember my name."

"Taran Dando? I'm aware," she snapped.

"That one... and the other, which you must only remember for *yourself*. That name, that person, is not a memory to share with anyone else." Taran's eyes bore into hers with an intensity that didn't match his perma-smirk. It was the closest thing to vulnerability she'd seen in any of the Fae.

"I won't tell them your name," Silvine whispered. It was as though she couldn't stop herself from agreeing. Even if she'd wanted to use her biting sarcasm, she couldn't have. Her words felt final, binding even.

"Consider that a bargain, Regina."

There was a brief, hopeful note, and a flower sprouted from the neckline of her dress.

Taran turned on his heels without another word, marching further into the bowels of the castle, leaving Silvine to find her way back to the dining hall.

The whole walk back, she toyed with the magic within her, creating threads of vines and leaves from the flower that Taran magicked onto her collar.

By the time she reached her table, unnoticed by everyone who seemed to be intrigued by everyone's company but hers, she was hungry enough to eat the rich food.

She crushed the little flower in her palm, stuffing its petals in her dress to hide the evidence. A quiet shame that she couldn't quite place drove her to it. It felt as though she'd done something that would disappoint Guval.

CHAPTER 16

FAREWELL

Silvine

After a long night left with her thoughts and grief, Silvine woke to find Minuet sitting at her table the next morning, tapping rhythmically on the smooth surface. Silvine rubbed her eyes before confirming that she really was seeing Minuet in her room. Her attendant was notably absent.

"My Majesty wishes to dine with you today," Minuet announced in her sultry voice. Minuet's red eyes burned into Silvine's soul, and she sucked in a breath. This woman was just as unearthly as her husband, although she was fiercely beautiful, unlike Phelip. Silvine wasn't sure if Minuet was there to help her or hurt her.

Silvine arose and walked to the wardrobe, where her new gowns from the seamstress had been tucked away in her absence. Minuet stared at her, unblinking.

"Do you mind?" Silvine asked.

Minuet stared. "Not at all."

Breathing through her shakiness, Silvine avoided returning Minuet's gaze as she slipped into a gown.

As soon as she started smoothing out her skirts, Minuet was by her side.

She raised an eyebrow, hairbrush in hand. "Allow me?"

Her unnatural stillness and intense gaze felt predatory to Silvine. Helpless to do anything else, she watched as Minuet drew nearer. All of her instincts were telling her to flee, but she needed to embrace these strange people. She was to be their queen consort, and before she began stumbling socially, she'd need to get her bearings in this strange Faerie realm.

"I believe you'll also have an audience with your father. He is soon to return home. My Majesty has been negotiating how many troops will be needed to put down the cute little coup that is in the works." The way Minuet said "My Majesty" grated Silvine's nerves. It was, in all likelihood, merely one of the Fae's strange rules for words and names, but it left her unsettled nonetheless.

Finding her tongue, Silvine spoke slowly. "It is of the utmost importance that my father— that Ainmean—receives the support of Court. Radicals burned our town, and they... they killed my friend."

Minuet yanked at a knot in Silvine's hair. "My Majesty has faced far worse foes than those. You shouldn't worry so much. Nothing fades beauty faster than worry."

Silvine wrinkled her nose. Fae women sounded as vain as human noblewomen.

"You don't need to worry about Highness's thoughts of your beauty," Minuet said. "You will be bound to him for eternity, and your worth is more than appearance to him. It's merely a tool at Court. Being half-human, you'll have to be so very careful."

"Half-human" stuck in Silvine's mind. Was Minuet saying what Silvine thought she was? That her mother, a strange, woodsy foreigner, had been Fae? It appeared so. Everyone in The Realm could see it but Silvine herself. That's why her ears had been mutilated by someone trying to rid The Realm of "forest nonsense." It threatened everything about the safety of humans to be in the presence of a Fae-human hybrid. Silvine wondered if Morair himself knew or if Pulchra had merely been a shiny, rare item he'd collected.

With an art Silvine had never managed to master, Minuet arranged Silvine's hair into shiny, wavy locks. Silvine felt almost obliged to compliment her handiwork, but she was frozen, half-afraid, half-mesmerized.

Phelip breezed in, stiff and imposing as ever. Lord Morair followed on his heels. Both men bowed, and Minuet returned the gesture.

"Your lord father wishes to speak with you," Phelip said, gesturing back at Lord Morair, who looked small and approachable compared to the Fae male.

"I am relieved to hear that's the reason the two of you have barged into my bedchamber. I would not have known any other reason for your visit to such a private place," Silvine snapped. Morair shot her a look of displeasure.

She added, "Thank you." Only the slight curl of his lip gave away Phelip's irritation at Silvine's forbidden expression of gratitude. "Thank you" implied expecting the gift or help received, and Fae hated presumption. Minuet took her husband's arm and led him out of the room, the door closing behind them of its own accord.

Lord Morair gestured at the table, seating himself. Silvine joined him, hoping he would take her concerns about the safety of Ainmean seriously.

"I leave for Ainmean today." He cleared his throat. "You will remain here."

"Father, we must talk."

He arched a brow. "I don't think I must do anything my daughter demands of me."

"I think this is the smallest demand I should get to make after all of this. I have had no choices in life. Can't I go back and help you restore peace in Ainmean at least?"

"Silvine, the most powerful person in our entire continent wishes to have your hand in marriage. Through the invasion of our lands and your success at the trial, your powers have been discovered. With King Guval's troops, I will stamp out any rebellion and any coup d'état. Your presence here establishes Ainmean and our family far more than journeying home only to return back here. I am aware that his age makes him rather unappealing, but you will marry the king." Morair's tone was firm.

She gaped at her father. "His age?"

"Yes, of course. We know King Guval is ancient. But he is a rather charming fellow for his age and quite spry. You will be the most powerful woman in all the land, and that is surely something worth falling in love with," Morair said. "Besides, he can't possibly live forever. Being a young, powerful widow wouldn't be so bad."

Realization dawned on her. Taran, when she'd known him as Cian, told Silvine that she had crossed into The Faerie Realm, where reality was both more muddled and far clearer. Those who had not entered The Faerie Realm could not perceive the Fae as they truly were. Morair was blissfully unaware of the true nature of the creatures he was interacting with and receiving aid from. They always said the king of The Realm was ancient. He must have seemed that way to humans, but he was incredibly beautiful, undeniably youthful, to Silvine.

Nothing here is as it seems there.

Thoughts of Guval's beauty vanished when Silvine thought of that insufferable smirk that would have come across Cian's face to be proven right. But Cian wasn't a real person, wasn't her true rescuer, just like Cardoc wasn't hers anymore and her only friend wasn't alive. Silvine was alone.

"Was my mother powerful?" Silvine decided to ask.

Lord Morair's face went slack for a moment before his signature cold determination returned. "If you're asking about the source of your own power, fate saw fit to give it to you. Ophelia will be sick with envy at the thought of your powers and new position."

"And yet, you're pawning me off just like you're doing with her. I'm just your bargaining chip," Silvine said. Despite the fact that she was marrying a beautiful and powerful man, she could not ignore how she felt about her father's choices.

"Everyone has a role to play. A servant's is to do the mundane so the great may do their part. The horse's is to carry us along our paths. *Yours* is to rein in your tongue and make the king delighted that you're his wife. The day you learn that your perceptions and feelings have no bearing on duty will be the day you find peace. Ophelia is quite pleased with her family-to-be. Start looking for similar sources of joy."

"Will you at least attend my wedding?"

"Today is the day we sever our ties. His Majesty may not deign to invite any of his vassals to attend his wedding. I can make no promises that I can leave my province. Your betrothal is as strong a commitment as any ceremony. You must push aside these worries about Ainmean. It's no longer your home," Morair said, his ever-present tone of reproach becoming stronger.

"I hope you are just as callous when you give Fluellen condolences for the way they severed Ana's life from her!" Silvine shouted, unable to contain herself anymore.

Morair smoothed his tunic. "A most unfortunate loss, I know. Let her death be a reminder to you to know your place and do what is right for all of us. If you care about Ainmean and the sacrifice Fluellen's daughter made, do your best here." He wouldn't even say Ana's name. Silvine slammed her fist on the table.

Morair glared. "Try to limit your outbursts to the privacy of your own chambers. I will not be able to save you if the king grows tired of you. Your lack of restraint will be your death warrant."

"I will do my best here, but I will never, ever allow myself to grow as callous as you are!"

Her father jerked his arm across the table and grabbed her hand. He squeezed until it hurt. As Silvine inhaled deeply, she realized her obsidian grew ice-cold in response. Odd.

"It is my greatest wish that you never have to be *callous* like me, but I have a duty. Just as you do. That hardness has kept our family's status for generations. I must go to finish preparations to leave."

Silvine yanked her hand away. "Tell me this one thing. Did you know I had powers before you agreed to set me up in a trial?"

Morair shrugged. "It was a difficult game, and I played my hand well. My gamble paid off, did it not?"

Her father wasn't a conspirator, just a power-hungry fool making promises to the king. He had no idea how his promise would play out in the end. Silvine studied him closely. For so calculating a man, it seemed ridiculous to wager with his daughter's life in such a way.

The conversation ended abruptly as Morair walked out the door and Phelip breezed in again. He offered Silvine his arm. "Come, you must be present for the send-off." He looked her up and down. "It is a relief Minuet has improved your appearance. You are far more... tolerable now."

"I was concerned you would never approve of my appearance. Almost as concerned as I have been that you might leave me alone for a few minutes," Silvine replied sarcastically.

Phelip simply said, "I am your Court escort. I am doing my duty."

He led Silvine wordlessly through silent hallways until they reached massive, purple glass doors. With a twirl of Phelip's finger, they sprang open, revealing a white marble balcony with the same purple veins that had been in the trial tower.

Beyond the balcony were red cliffs and a dark sea far below, white foam crashing against the cliff's edges. The sun beat down upon them already, even though the morning was young. Guval stood regally at the balcony's edge, Minuet stood closely beside him, and an array of colorful Fae with various wings, gills, foot adornments, and feathers surrounded him.

Guval pivoted to offer Silvine a smile. "My betrothed," he murmured. "Come, stand beside me."

Below the three-story balcony, Lord Morair handed a goblet to a servant and mounted his steed with a host of purple-clad soldiers. A few wagons were loaded with supplies.

Once astride his horse, Morair looked up at the balcony-goers. "My eternal thanks, Your Highness. Ainmean will continue to prosper thanks to your aid."

Guval nodded. "Offering you the service of my men was the least I could do in exchange for your daughter as consort." He patted the hand that wore his charoite ring.

"The only other thanks you could offer is a cask of some of that delightful vintage!" Morair called up. Wincing at the memory of her father's changed behavior under its influence, Silvine hoped her father would never drink Faerie wine again. Clearly, that hope would be futile.

Guval called back, "I am afraid my vintage does not travel well. It would spoil." His entourage tittered at this comment, sharing knowing smirks.

Morair responded with an attempt at laughter. The sound came from his lips so infrequently that it sounded wrong. "Indeed, Sire. Away I go, for my court and for Ainmean!" He urged his horse onward, leading all the purple-clad soldiers and loaded wagons away from the cliffs toward a thick woodland.

At the same moment, several purple-winged Fae females stepped to the edge of the balcony and began singing in voices that sounded at once like a lake as smooth as glass and the sharp point of a knife:

"Farewell, farewell,

Human man.

Flee from us fast as you can.

Farewell, farewell,

Delicious one.

For now and later, we've had our fun.

Farewell, farewell,

Human man.

Say goodbye to your dream and plan."

Silvine cocked her head as she listened. The lyrics were odd, to say the least. Unaccustomed to Fae culture, she brushed aside her feelings, assuming she was just ignorant of tradition. When the song concluded, Guval's people shared knowing looks, cracked jokes, and murmured things in hushed voices to one another. The smirks all around made Silvine feel like a joke had just been told, but she'd missed the punchline. They meandered off the balcony in small groups until only Guval remained. Silvine stared at the forest, unable to move.

An inexplicable ache grew in her chest as her father dug his heels into his horse's side. She longed for him in a way she never had before. A naïve little girl, deep within her, hoped Morair would turn back for one last wave, one acknowledgment of his youngest daughter, but he never did. Was it duty that made him so hard-hearted, like he claimed? Was there a loving man in there somewhere? It hurt Silvine to think she'd never know.

"The moment has passed," Guval said gently. His green eyes, so knowing, stared into hers. "It will be a change, but you will be better because of this new chapter of your life. Come with me." He took her hand.

A tall, red-eyed servant led them through tunnels back to the underground river Silvine had crossed before her trial. The river itself had a faint purple glow, but it was the roaring torches on the stone walls that truly lit it.

Guval and Silvine sat at a great crystal table beside a waterfall at the abrupt end of the river. "The river continues in smaller underground tunnels," Guval said, noting Silvine's stare at the roaring water. "One would have to be a fish to follow it to its end, but it is rumored to be an everlasting flow."

He stopped to take a sip from a purple goblet. "Now, tell me about what you went through to get to me."

"I wasn't trying to get to you," Silvine blurted before realizing what she'd said. "I mean, I was just trying to save my people."

Guval snorted. "No offense taken, my future queen. I would love to hear about what you went through to save your people." Guval's amusement startled Silvine. No one ever found her amusing. She was either fearsome or almost lovely or too sharp-tongued. Guval's reaction warmed her chest, a stark contrast to the pendant that had been stone-cold against her skin for hours.

Silvine gave him a summary of her experience. She recounted Festivale, finding fire in the village, Cardoc's betrayal, her flight into the woods, the mushroom ring, the undine, staying in the cave, and the violence of the guards at the red rocks. The words flowed out of her like they never had before—a beautiful, epic story of a maid taking on the world and surviving. Her honesty stopped at Taran and any names of any of the creatures she'd met. Even if she'd wanted to, her mouth couldn't form the words that would name Cian, Luc, Anaras, or Ondina.

When her tale was done, Guval placed his hand on hers. "My Silvine, you are brave. Thank you for your candor. One of the greatest challenges I am facing in The Realm is the evil of the woods. Fae and humans alike have lived in terror of the woods for too many generations."

Silvine sipped the frothy, warm beverage beside her plate.

"Will you help me, as my consort, make our realm's forests a safer place? Your powers and your strength make you the perfect assistant in this important work. As The Seelie Court, the court of the good Fae, it is our duty to drive out the evil of the forest. The Morair line has done well starting the purge, and now, we must continue what was started long ago when The Great Silver Bear was slain." Guval's speech was a call to action.

"Of—of course," she answered.

"You will have to work hard and continue to show me the powers you revealed in your trial," Guval said, his voice firm.

"Yes, I will," Silvine promised, a small pit growing in her stomach. Would she be able to be as powerful without Taran leading the way? Was she cut out to be some kind of magical heroine to all The Realm? Silvine concluded that she simply had to figure out how to do it or her place in Guval's life would be in jeopardy.

While her father was a weak, power-hungry man, it was true that his ancestors had slain The Great Silver Bear. Perhaps it was the blood, with her mother's hidden Fae heritage, that made her so special. Her father would have never deigned to recognize it, though.

Lost in contemplation, Silvine hardly noticed Taran Dando's approach. The king stood. "My Silvine, I was glad to have your audience this morning. I must attend to security matters with my General of Intelligence. He handles all matters of intelligence for Court, so he is often out roaming for the good of the kingdom. Allow me to make proper introductions. Taran Dando, this is my betrothed, Lady Silvine of Ainmean. Silvine, Taran."

Taran's face was unusually blank, his eyes looking past Silvine. He didn't wear a hint of a smirk.

"Pleasure, I'm sure," Silvine said, attempting to bridge the gap.

Taran remained silent.

Phelip approached, extending his arm to lead her back to her chambers while Guval and Taran walked toward the waterfall to have more privacy. *Why is Taran acting so strangely?* she wondered.

CHAPTER 17

THE URSINE MAN

The Ursine Man

The Ursine Man, the bear within him unleashed, galloped along the red cliffs of the coast. He needed to run somewhere, run anywhere, and yet, his heart was tethered to one place. It was like being caged in a pen of his own heart's making.

I can't fight fair. I won't fight fair, he thought to himself, over and over again. To win this war, to fulfill the prophecy, he would do whatever it took. He would cut down any of them, cut down himself, all for her.

She made it abundantly clear that she resented him. He could sense it every time he got near her, but he knew it was necessary. If she had to hate him to save The Realm, it would be worth it.

And yet, that jasmine and petrichor scent, those ocean-colored eyes, entranced him. He wanted her to love him. He wanted her to see him in a way no one else dared, to bare his soul to her and drop the facade of nonchalance.

The Modrona had prepared him in his boyhood for what lay ahead. For centuries, the Eurons had worked alongside the Modronas, Eurons

at the heart of natural forces while the Modronas were the queens of all Life. When The Old Ones flourished and all was right with the world, before The Invasion ruined everything and sequestered everyone to shattered domains, the Eurons empowered the Modronas, who kept the order of Life. After The Invasion, the Eurons hid with the Modronas, forced to bide their time as they watched the destruction of all the good in the world. Every generation was precious, every descendant an opportunity to right the wrongs and injustices of the world. This Euron just happened to be born when all of the stars were aligned and the fulfillment of the prophecy was to happen.

When he reached his private cave above the raging seas, more like a little alcove than a true bear's den, he reached for the ancient parchment he'd hidden underneath a rock and dusted it off. Noticing the spidery, faded, blood-red writing, he read the prophecy:

When the blood of the hunter unites with the blood of the cultivator,

Power will blind the world in its light.

All will seek her,

But only when *he* wins her,

Will victory occur.

As life leaves the one

Who loved her first

Will she shake The Realm from The Curse.

Every Fae in the land knew that bit of the prophecy. What most didn't have was the final bit, given from the last Oracle of Phythia, Macha. It was the last prophecy ever given before she fell to the invaders. While they cut down her husband, she frantically wrote her final words. Macha lost her life in a place where so many had come to find answers to improve their lives. Her younger sister, called Fair Anella by the humans, was rumored to have vanished the same night. No one knew for sure. All The Ursine Man had left of them was the prophecy. The final part of the message read:

The appellation of The Euron will save The Modrona,

Who doesn't know her own name.
But The Modrona will save the whole world.
If she can see truth with her own eyes
And rid The Realm of its lies,
Modrona and Euron will end Death's game.

The color of the ink foretold of the dear cost it would take to see the prophecy fulfilled. If the Fae were to ever be free of the blight upon them, it would take many great sacrifices. So many had already been paid, but many more were to come. The Ursine Man had known the steep price his entire life.

What he hadn't known was that it would feel like his heart was being ripped from him at every moment—that he would yearn to tell her everything. Those lovely eyes, oblivious to their own magnificence, had to see the truth for themselves, or it would never work. The mouth that could only spew venom at him, the mouth he wished would do other things, would have to speak truth on its own.

She had no idea the power that thrummed through her veins. The world had beat her down from her very birth, and yet, she was magnificent. He wanted to fight her battles for her and take her away from all of this. He wanted to sit back and watch her blind the world with her might. He wanted to reach out for her. He wanted it all at once.

He could have nothing at all.

The bear was teetering on a ledge, not only the ledge of his cliffside cave, but his heart and the fate of all Fae. The Ursine Man, once a lone bear cub, had learned so much of it all for himself by fighting to survive, traveling all over The Realm to befriend those who still held the old torch and clinging to that tattered parchment. Nothing had truly hurt since he had seen the price of the prophecy.

It hadn't even hurt when he'd sold himself away, hiding the fabric of his very soul, because he knew he served a purpose. He'd tucked everything that made him himself away gladly. He'd given himself up for the cause. He'd never been bold enough to contemplate that there was anything else to do. The Ursine Man was a servant to his very core. No torture could reach him anymore.

*And yet. The way his heart had thawed and melted so quickly in so short a matter of time felt deeply unnerving to him. He needed an outlet for the turmoil within. He wanted to drag his claws along the trees and toss boulders at the mountains in his rage, but the forest belonged to his people—*her *people. For their sake, he held it in.*

CHAPTER 18

RAPPING, TAPPING AT THE CHAMBER WINDOW

The wind howled against Silvine's chamber windows in the dark night. The sky was starless, the moon solitary and haunting. Pacing the floor, she wished she was the kind of person who could experience something horrific, deal with it one time, and never think of it again. Her mind, however, hoarded the bad memories until her thoughts were so cluttered she could do nothing but bounce from reliving one trauma to the next.

All of this idle time spent alone chipped away at her, bit by bit. Thoughts of all she'd lost and all she'd survived made her heart race. It felt like she was frozen beneath a glacier of worries.

She was now living in the mystical world Nene had spun yarns about. The things that could never be real or true *were*. And yet, she could not shake Taran's words in the forest that nothing was as it seemed. Her mind could not erase the sounds of Ana's screams or the sensation of full body tremors as she fought for her life in the forest.

She'd never reached Asturia after all. She had magical abilities that had lain dormant until now. Her idiot father had gambled with her life, and by sheer luck, he'd won.

Could she truly become a powerful consort to the king of The Realm? For a fleeting moment, she wondered if Guval himself was a mere illusion. Maybe she'd lost her mind, hallucinating after eating the wrong mushrooms. It seemed like something Taran would have done to her.

A scratching at the window startled her. It sounded like tree branches scraping with the movement of the wind, but the red-rocked valley beyond the glass had no foliage to speak of, let alone an ancient tree that could reach the height of her window. She saw the white gleams of a claw. Sucking in a breath, she reached for the dagger hidden beneath her mattress and continued toward the window.

The claws turned into pale hands, glowing under the moonlight. *My eyes are deceiving me*, she concluded. Perhaps she really had lost her mind. The hand was immediately followed by its match and a gleaming smile with silver eyes. Silvine sighed and opened her window, and Taran swung his legs through.

"What are you doing here?" she whispered.

Taran looked her up and down.

"I could have been indecent. Not even my betrothed comes barging into this room," she hissed.

"Have you ever been truly indecent?" Taran asked.

Silvine resisted the urge to roll her eyes. Visible signs of annoyance would have only continued the game the two of them played, in which he irritated her, and she gave him the upper hand by showing her frustration.

"Besides," Taran continued, "Your attendant and that... mage... have come traipsing in here as they've pleased, and you haven't so much as said a word about it. Are we just such good friends now that you can truly make your feelings known to me?"

Silvine's tone grew sharp. "You may be General of Intelligence for Court, but you don't have to concern yourself with comings and goings in my private chamber. If you work for my king, I assume you can intelligence your way to all the golden bargains your evil heart desires. I have nothing to offer you."

Taran smirked. "It doesn't suit you to be so cruel to me. We're old friends, after all. And I came to invite you to go roam with me for the good of The Realm."

"I'm not sure I can leave this chamber. I get escorted everywhere and leaving could be dangerous." She chewed her bottom lip.

"I am the king's favorite escort. Phelip is an untried milksop in comparison. I have slaughtered more beings than you have seen living, my Regina. You are most safe with me, unless you desire a bit of danger. I'm good at finding that, too." Taran gestured toward the starry sky and red valley below. "You must be incredibly bored going from meal to chamber to dress fitting to chamber to meal. You were not made for such a dull existence. Besides, we can practice some of that magic of yours."

Silvine couldn't say no. She gave a brief nod, deciding she needed to be freed from the prison of her memories. She hoped it wouldn't make Guval unhappy. Going out to work on her powers with the king's General of Intelligence certainly wasn't the worst thing she could do. Taran offered her his hand, which she took, and they climbed out through her window.

She teetered on the edge of the window frame.

"How did you get up here?" she whimpered, looking down at the six-story drop beneath her feet. A gust of wind blew upward, chilling her through her thin nightgown. Nothing in Ainmean was this tall. A fear of heights was a new yet unsurprising development, given her sheltered upbringing.

Taran's eyes glowed in the moonlight. "I climbed, of course, Regina. I'm quite a skilled climber. All my people are."

Silvine's heart began to race as she studied the drop below. She was quite certain none of her people were skilled climbers. Her last foray into climbing had left her bloodied, battered, and held against her will in Luc Ollam's cave.

Taran yanked on her hand, and she braced for the freefall. Instead, there was a whirl, and her feet gently landed on the dusty red rocks she'd seen from a distance. She looked up and realized they were at least a quarter mile away from the imposing castle, which looked purple and black under the night sky.

She shuddered from a mixture of chills and overwhelm at this new form of travel. Nausea hit her suddenly, and she bent down to breathe, hands on her knees, willing it away. Taran whipped off his cloak and wrapped it around her. Silvine looked at him, ready to protest that he'd need his cloak.

Taran waved her away. "My line runs particularly warm by design, allowing us to survive some very harsh elements. That thin nightgown you're wearing won't do for tonight's adventure."

"How did you do that?" she asked, motioning at the castle behind them.

"You don't become General of Intelligence for the most powerful ruler in all The Realm without a touch of magic," Taran said nonchalantly. "Now, let's go. The night belongs to us, but it won't last forever, I'm afraid."

There was another tug on her hand, and she found herself at the base of the purple mountains she thought she'd never reach.

Taran grunted a bit. "Just one more."

He jerked on her hand for a final time, and she found herself sitting atop the purple mountain's summit. They sat on a rock outcropping, where Silvine could see everything. She saw the red-rocked valley below, the castle, and the raging sea beyond. There was little life or flora and fauna below them, but the purple mountain buzzed with the glow of flora and fauna in the quiet vibrance of night.

Silvine breathed, taking in the smell of the mountains and listening to the sounds of owls calling, insects buzzing, and dogs baying. All around the rock outcropping they sat atop, flowers and mushrooms glowed in phosphorescent colors of greens, yellows, oranges, and purples—a stark contrast to the general darkness of the night. Taran crouched beside her on the rock.

"It's beautiful here," Silvine said. "Really, though, how did you do that? Was I—was I too heavy? I heard you grunting."

Taran laughed. "I can shift from place to place. I'm not used to shifting with a partner, but your mass had nothing to do with the exertion. I'm simply out of practice at traveling with someone." His fingertips touched Silvine's, and in a whirl, they were at the base of the rock outcropping.

Silvine stared up at the rocks she'd been sitting on moments before. The world around her was magnificent.

"Have you ever gotten to simply exist like this?" he asked.

"No," she said. She'd come close at times with Ana, but to be atop a mountain with endless open sky was a new experience altogether.

Three glowing orbs, the color of the hottest blue flames, floated up to them, thrumming a familiar melody. The music in Silvine's blood echoed a reply, emitting its own new melody. Taran took her hand and outstretched her palm, and the orbs hovered above her. They let off a warm breeze that put her at peace. Euphoria rushed through her veins as her blood continued to sing, and she closed her eyes, soaking it in.

"Will o' the wisps. They recognize you," Taran whispered. "*Do something with this moment.*"

Silvine reached deep within, pushing the song outside of herself, and a phosphorescent little sapling sprang up at her feet. The song within her grew quiet for a moment, but the will o' the wisps seemed to sing louder for her.

"Do something—anything—with it. Listen to your blood and what it tells you," Taran instructed.

She closed her eyes again and had the saplings' branches reach out like arms to grab Taran. Using her magic, she reached out for him and found only empty space.

"Everything that lives is at your disposal. You need only listen to the song of Life that flows through your veins and use it. You will meet Fae who thrive on Death and sorrow and suffering. Your power is the opposite, and it can blot out all of the destructive forces. You are the restoration of the balance that has been lost."

Silvine stopped to pant, hands on her knees.

"Weak," Taran taunted, mischief lighting up his eyes in tandem with the flame-blue glow of the will o' the wisps. In a flash, he was in her ear repeating his words, then he was atop the rock outcropping, then he was behind the rocks. "Keep up!" he called.

Silvine sprinted toward him, but in a whirl, he was out of her reach. She was fast—faster than she'd ever been before—but not fast enough to best someone who could move in the blink of an eye.

Taran stopped in front of her. "Your power is the cultivation of Life. Sense my Life, sense what it's doing, and you'll beat me every time."

She closed her eyes once more, trying to pick apart the chords each life was singing. A melancholy song stood out. It was Taran. Not an irreverent song, nothing bawdy, nothing like the mischief promised on his face. It was so heartbreaking she gasped.

Taran's eyes locked with hers in the phosphorescent glow. He disappeared, but Silvine focused on the music pulsing through his veins and spun around to point at where he'd stopped.

"There's that power," he purred, and in a flash, he shifted in front of her.

"This place is... This feels... It feels *right* with my very being," Silvine breathed.

"That's because it *is* right. This is where you belong. I wanted you to see the beauty, the wonder, the Life that abounds on this mountain. In the King of Donadais's kingdom, you will not see much of this, so you must cling to memories of the beauty and not submit to the loud voice of all the decay." Taran's tone was suddenly quite serious.

"I've heard no one else call him the King of Donadais since I arrived. Why?"

"Well, Regina, only mortals like to issue names so freely. Nor does the king appreciate being called that name, one of the few surviving words we have from the language of The Creator."

Two bear cubs cut across the mountainside, and a small cry escaped Silvine's lips. The mother bear followed, ambling across the mountain peacefully. The three creatures stopped and looked up at her. Silvine could have sworn the mother bear gave her a reverent nod before shoving her cubs forward with her snout.

"These are the things we fight for. These are the things I hold most dear," Taran said. "The king abhors these things and prefers the lifeless red plain and the cruel sea, but you and I are different."

"Is that because of your work in intelligence or your desire to deceive me with more of your Fae trickery?"

Taran barked out a laugh. "My Fae trickery? If you think *I* am a trickster, I think you've forgotten some of your woodland acquaintances. Besides, you'd say far different if you were allowed to roam Court freely. The actions of Donadas's courtiers would be abhorrent to your mortal-raised sensibilities."

All of the things Silvine had once thought to be evil—a threat to the fabric of society and creatures deemed to be mere ancient myth—coexisted on this mountainside beneath a starless sky in peace and beauty. She wondered if she'd even see Luc and Anaras and Ondina differently under the moonlight, bathed in the glow of otherworldly phosphorescence.

"Are will o' the wisps really trapped souls?" she asked.

Taran shrugged. "You would know a trapped soul if you encountered one."

He reached for her hand and yanked her back to the confines of her room. The king's intelligence man had grown suddenly quiet.

Without so much as a goodbye, he left her safely beside the window of her chamber and fled into the night.

She hugged herself tightly after shutting the window, realizing she was still wearing his cloak. It smelled of him, a smell of summertime in the mountains: morning dew and crisp air and white birch sap. She decided to tuck the cloak away with her dagger beneath her mattress, wanting to keep this moment, this cloak, her own little secret.

CHAPTER 19

LORD CREON

Silvine

Over the next several weeks, Phelip's sole goal seemed to be to teach Court etiquette to Silvine. He told her that good manners were of the utmost importance, and with a sniff, he insisted they were the only way she would ever secure an invitation to one of *his* parties. Silvine had yet to go anywhere that wasn't the dining hall or a place to receive instruction from Phelip. His parties seemed like a far-off notion.

Phelip's training involved tedious hours of learning about various perfumes (all of which were exceptionally overpowering—courtesy of Silvine's newly discovered Fae sense of smell), proper ways to consume a meal (rather than the human standard of forks, spoons, and knives, there were seven different implements at a refined Fae table), appropriate ways to make eye contact, and the best Fae dances.

Silvine surmised that her time would be better spent trying out her powers and learning how to play the game of Court rather than learning to be a pretty ornament, but her desire to avoid listening to any additional Phelip lectures kept her from sharing her thoughts.

Several times, she tried to pick up the song of his blood, tuning in

141

for the faintest sounds, but all she detected were a few flat notes. When she concentrated on her nameless attendant in the morning, all she could make out were notes of dissonance. None had as clear a song as the song in her own blood or the way the creatures on the mountain spoke to her or Taran's mournful melody. She didn't understand enough of her magic to know why she could sense the differences, but there was a clear line between those whose blood sang and those whose blood did not.

On one such occasion, Silvine had stared off into the mirrors of the vast ballroom where Phelip was providing a dance demonstration. She watched her face change in the floor-to-ceiling, gilded mirrors as she wove in harmonies and changed the dynamics of her blood's song.

During this day's lesson, Phelip, in his silken dance slippers, seemed utterly entranced with himself, directing his own dance with no music accompanying him. Minuet glided into the room and clapped.

At the interruption, Phelip stared icily at his bride. "Yes, Wife?" His tone was sharp.

Minuet seemed unfazed by neither his tone nor his stony glare. "We have a guest who requires our audience." She sashayed toward Silvine, taking her hand and leading her out of the ballroom. Phelip cleared his throat. His running footsteps caught up to them quickly.

The glacial temperature of Minuet's hand was startling. In response, Silvine's pendant grew just as cold.

The hallway led to the throne room of Court, where Guval sat atop the dais. His beauty took Silvine's breath away. She'd felt chemistry with Cardoc, certainly, and had seen attractive males before. There was something magnetic about Guval, though. He was the most beautiful creature she'd ever laid eyes upon. Golden and powerful and *hers*. Glancing her way, he offered her a charming smile. A younger version of Silvine would have probably blushed at that point, but she got hold of her twenty-two-year-old self and gave him a flirtatious look.

Minuet took the spot to Guval's right, fingertips lightly thrumming on his arm rest as she gestured for Silvine to stand at his left. Phelip stood by his wife's side.

Avoiding stepping in front of His Majesty, Silvine reached her assigned post by walking behind the throne.

Unlike her first visit to the throne room, the vast space was dead silent. All the Fae lords and ladies, who had been making merry in the alcoves the last time, stood solemnly lining the walls, watching.

Finally noting who stood in front of the dais, Silvine's breath caught in her chest. An enormously fat human man, whose body bulged out of his bronze armor, stood with dozens of stone-faced, bronze-clad soldiers. She immediately recognized him as Lord Creon, the aptly-named Premier of Creon. Originality was not known to be important in his province.

Lord Creon appeared to have the same moment of recognition as he jabbed a sausage-shaped finger in her direction. "What is that Ainmeanian baggage doing here?"

Guval raised a brow. "Baggage?"

Creon bowed. "My apologies, Majesty, if my language is too coarse. I am just wondering why Lord Morair's child stands beside your throne."

"*Silvine Morair* is my betrothed," Guval declared. A few of the Fae lords and ladies exchanged looks, which Silvine tried to ignore. She worked to make her face bland, bored even, but knew she was likely showing her displeasure.

"You—you so blatantly show preference for one of your provinces then, Your Highness?" Creon demanded.

"Not that my marital affairs are your concern, Creon, but she happens to be one of the most powerful creatures The Realm has seen in a very long time. Her allegiance is not just to Ainmean, but the whole realm. You will recognize her as your queen." Guval punctuated every syllable with great emphasis.

"My apologies, Majesty, but that second-born bitch of Morair will never be my queen. I will not bow down to such a creature. Any power you think she has is her bastard father's deception. I'd sooner snap her neck and stick it to Morair than snap my old knees recognizing her as anything but worthless. Maybe my men can handle her for you, and I'll find you a better match."

Silvine's cheeks burned. Although she hadn't heard those harsh words since leaving Ainmean, they were a stark reminder of the criticism she'd heard her whole life. She was a lord's second-born daughter—no one of worth.

There was a flash of black out of the corner of her eye. In an instant, Taran was in front of Lord Creon, grabbing him by the neck. For an average-height and build man, Taran managed to lift the obese lord off the floor effortlessly. Silvine clapped a hand over her mouth as she watched Taran take on Creon. *Fae strength*, she surmised.

The bronze-clad guards all drew swords in response but stood still, some of them casting glances in the direction of the king.

"I will give you two choices, *Lord Creon*," Taran sneered as Creon choked and gasped. "You can choose to never speak a word against her again, in your thoughts or out loud, or you can continue to demean her, and I will choke the very words and life out of you. And rest assured, I have the ability to know if you even think them. I will find you, and I will extinguish you."

He dropped Creon with a thud. Creon's guards remained poised with their drawn swords.

"Withdraw your weapons in my court, or I shall have you all executed," Guval said. "It is an executable offense to kill without my permission."

Creon clutched at his throat. "Control... *your*... guard, M-Majesty."

Straightening his shoulders, Guval said, "That was the only entertainment I've had all day. I am not sure if anyone wiser has ever taught you this, Creon, but it's best to know when you're up against a more powerful opponent and submit. You left my party early last time I hosted all the Premiers here, otherwise you would have already heard the good tidings."

A few more coughs and splutters were the only sounds Creon made in reply. Taran remained right beside him. Silvine listened for the melancholy music in his blood; this time, it emitted tones of anger. Everyone remained deathly silent, but the sound of Taran's music crescendoed.

Arms crossed, Taran demanded, "Which choice are you going to make?"

Still seated on the floor of the throne room, Creon looked to Guval, who stared at his ring-adorned fingers in apparent boredom.

"I choose life, but only on one condition. I demand to know what powers we speak of and how this daughter of Morair is an asset to The Realm. I want to see with my own eyes."

A growl escaped from Taran, who appeared ready to pounce on Creon once again, but Guval's words halted him. "I will oblige your request. You *should* get a glimpse of my court's power. We will arrange a trial to be held here, in the throne room, tomorrow. Silvine will show you just how valuable she is. Hopefully your insolence does not resurface, otherwise you will leave Taran with no choice but to make your position of Premier *vacant.*"

Silvine pursed her lips. *Don't say something you'll regret,* she told herself. Thoughts of another trial sent her pulse racing.

One of the bronze-clad soldiers helped Lord Creon to his feet.

Taran swiveled away from Creon. He sauntered toward the exit door behind the dais. A few of the courtiers began clapping for Taran, who bowed dramatically while smirking. It was then that Silvine knew this was the sort of thing the court thrived on: violence.

Warmth replaced the pit in her stomach. No one had ever come to her defense like that before. It was gratifying. If she could just focus on that sensation, she knew she might have been able to push aside the anxiety about her public trial the next day.

"Taran, I'll see you in the strategy room," Guval said. "Minuet, help Lord Creon and his men to the guest wing. We want to make sure we offer them our *best* hospitality. And Phelip, ensure Silvine makes it to her chamber without incident."

"I thank you kindly, Your Highness. I hope I have not stumbled on my words. I just didn't think a man of your age would take a wife, let alone a girl from Ainmean," Lord Creon said.

A man of "your age," Silvine scoffed to herself. *Guval must glamour himself to appear old to humans.*

Minuet gave Guval a knowing look and strode to Lord Creon, hips swaying as she walked. Creon leered at her, hunger in his eyes. A river of rushing bronze slowly trickled out of the room, following their leader.

Silvine froze, the thud of her heart's racing deafening her to whatever Guval had turned to say to her. The sound of Phelip clearing his throat broke the spell, and she took his arm reluctantly, allowing him to lead her from the throne room as she lost herself in her thoughts.

CHAPTER 20

THE EARTH LOVES ITS OWN

Silvine

Phelip sniffed as they strode down the winding hallways toward Silvine's chamber. "We can all sense it, you know. It's most unrefined."

"Sense what?"

"Your fear. It *smells*."

Silvine stopped abruptly, yanking her arm out of Phelip's. His eyes widened.

"You know what I think is most unrefined? I think it's absolutely beneath my dignity to kowtow to the wishes of that *scum*. If I am the king's wife-to-be, I should have nothing to prove to his ilk."

Phelip reached for her arm again, but she whirled it behind her back forcefully.

"Silvine, you must see reason and stop being obstinate. It is time for all of Court to see your power, to know why the king is so intent on marrying you," Phelip said. "Why would you expect a group of powerful people to simply accept you? It is a mere bonus that Creon will be silenced, at least for a while. He is useful, you know."

"I can't see why. He's a fat, lecherous fool. Isn't deceiving a stupid mortal like him the kind of thing the Fae thrive on?" Silvine felt unwilling to back down, rage replacing the fear within her.

Her future brother-in-law crossed his arms. "I refuse to continue this ridiculous conversation. My brother ordered me to ensure you make it to your chamber without incident, not to argue with you."

Silvine clenched her fists. "I'm not going anywhere with you right now. Go get your wife before she has to use her mage vapors on Lord Creon and his men."

Red eyes met her glare. Silvine's blood began to sing as her anger grew, its melody fast and deep.

"It isn't like I don't know the way to my room at this point," she continued. "I don't need to endure your snobbery before I have to go take on some horrible creature, all for the amusement of His Majesty's courtiers and a man who likely killed my father's first wife."

He gestured ahead of them. "A compromise, for the half-human with iron will. You walk in front of me. I will keep my thoughts to myself about your glaringly obvious human feelings so long as you keep your naïveté to yourself."

Silvine stomped in front of him, the contrast of his measured pace with her rapid one putting greater distance between them with each step. As she reached for the golden doorknob to her room, rough hands grabbed her from behind. She let out a shriek as a blindfold was fastened around her eyes and two sets of hands dragged her down the hallway.

She threw her elbows and kicked wildly. Rasps of male laughter filled her ears. "You think you'll get away from us? No, we have a plan for one as valuable as you." A cloth that reeked of salty seas and stale fruit was clapped over nose and mouth. Brineweed, she thought to herself as she drifted from consciousness.

A woman in a loose, white linen gown strode toward Silvine. The moonlight shone overhead, highlighting the beauty of the woman's pale skin, light-colored hair, and mesmerizing indigo eyes. The two women were beneath a sky with so many stars it was hard to distinguish where one star began and another ended. As a result, the sky was a haze of whites, silvers, blues, and purples.

"Rise, Daughter," the woman said. Her voice was gentle, but she spoke with an authority Silvine dared not defy.

"Mother?" Silvine whispered.

The beautiful woman reached out her hand and pulled Silvine to her feet. "I am." A sorrowful smile spread across her face. "I wish you could have known me, but it was not written in our stars." She gestured up at the sky. "Macha told me long ago that it would be so."

"Macha? The Oracle?" Silvine had heard the stories of Macha from Nene. Macha was yet another fictional character, rumored to preside on the mountains of Phythia. She supposedly answered questions about the nature of Life and the future of those who dwelt in The Realm.

Pulchra put her arm around her daughter's shoulder. They began walking the perimeter of the treeline. The trees towered above them, ancient giants in their own right, probably as ancient as the stories of Macha.

Silvine's mother laughed. It was sweet music, a song that sounded so much like the innate buzz of Silvine's own. It wasn't like any of the songs she'd heard from others. It was pure peace and Life.

They trod on in silence before Pulchra finally answered. "Yes, Macha, The Oracle. She was slaughtered long ago by those who did not understand the order of our realm."

"You knew The Oracle?"

"Yes, Daughter, but I don't have the time to tell you of those things. Time is a precious currency, and you will wake any moment."

"I will?"

Pulchra continued walking. "You are bewildered, I see. I knew growing up in Morair's house without me would do that. I need you to understand that you have the gift of Life within you."

Silvine looked down. She, too, was wearing a flowing, white gown, and her pale skin glowed in the moonlight.

Pulchra smoothed the hair back from her daughter's face, her touch warm and loving. "You can wield the bits of your father in you in a better way than you are doing now, but do not mistake being gentle and using the gifts of Life for tolerating atrocities. Your purpose is to fight."

Silvine nodded, wishing she could live in this dream world with her mother forever. She yearned to know her mother.

Pulchra seemed to read her thoughts.

"You must awaken. We cannot stay in this dream much longer, I'm afraid. You have a great purpose to serve, one foretold long before you were born. You must restore the balance that was destroyed one thousand years ago. The attack on Ainmean will seem small compared to what is to come, but you are brave enough to overcome it."

"I don't feel brave. I feel like I am constantly carrying around heavy stones that weigh my chest down. Sometimes, I can hardly breathe because of the panic," Silvine replied.

Pulchra squeezed her hand. "Bravery is not defined by a lack of fear. Lack of fear is just the pretense of fools who enjoy their folly. Those who are brave are those who can acknowledge their fears, their traumas, and their worries and do what must be done anyway. You can do what must be done. I've always known it."

Silvine desperately wanted to believe her mother's words, but she reminded herself that Pulchra did not know her, had not raised her, and was not alive. This was merely a dream.

"The brineweed is almost gone from you. It is time for me to go. Remember: the Earth loves its own, and the Heart sees the Earth for what it truly is."

Silvine's sight grew hazy, and she felt herself falling backward. It was as though her body was plummeting down a depthless pit.

CHAPTER 21

LIGHT IN THE DARKNESS

The Ursine Man

The Ursine Man, in the unremarkable Fae form he'd bound himself to decades before, paced the marble floor of the usurper king's strategy room. The tension in his core was a strange juxtaposition to the calm demeanor of the rest of the advisors.

The usurper's brother had come flying into the room, faster than the man had ever seen Phelip move. "They took Silvine, My King," Phelip said. "Three men in brown cloaks snatched her from her chamber door. I was too late."

A feral expression lit up the usurper's face. "Now we shall see just how clever and powerful she is." The Ursine Man stopped in his tracks, a shadow of fury flickering across his face.

After endless pacing, he could take it no more. "Your Majesty, you are correct that your betrothed is both clever and powerful, given what we've seen from her. However, are we certain she does not require some degree of protection?"

The usurper raised a brow. "Is she not protected?"

The Ursine Man ran his fingers through his hair. He exchanged a

brief look with Phelip. The usurper's brother, he thought, did not seem to exude the same aura of peace the other Court advisors did. He was wringing his hands in his lap.

"If it makes you feel better, you could collect intelligence on her whereabouts," Guval said, returning to the papers laid out across the table.

"I already have my suspicions," he drawled. "However, it may be worthwhile to confirm where she's been taken."

There was a creak as Guval rose from his high-backed chair. He held up a single finger. "Taran Dando, I noticed you stepped beyond your scope of authority in my throne room today. As I'm sure you know, that kind of misstep cannot go unchecked. It would destroy order and decorum here at Court."

The man's stomach tightened in knots. The remaining shreds of his dignity begged him to fight back against the pain and humiliation he knew was coming. Thoughts of breaking his bargain with the usurper and its deadly repercussions locked him in place. The act of submission to the false king sickened him, but he knew he had no choice. He reached for the knot around his neck, slowly untying it and allowing his cloak to fall to the floor. He pulled his tunic over his head and clutched it in his hands, waiting.

The usurper's measured footsteps promised agony to come. The Bear Man closed his eyes and withdrew inside himself. As icy shadows wrapped themselves around his back, Death delivering its steady punishment on his flesh, he transported his mind elsewhere. He bit his lip until it bled, blocking out the icy burn of the usurper's magic as it carved him open. Though his body suffered, in his mind, he was with her.

He went back to the night on the mountain. She'd glowed under the light of the will o' the wisps and the full moon. He pictured her eyes, sometimes blue and sometimes green, changing color like the waters of the sea. Her wonder at the beauty of a world she'd never been allowed to enjoy took his breath away. When she'd laughed at the sight of the bear cubs, he thought his heart would burst. Every word she spoke to him, especially the ones that showed the fire inside her, replayed in his mind.

She'd become his beacon of hope in the darkness. The usurper could batter his body, but he could never truly break him. His mind—his soul—were entwined with the beauty of hers. His soul was with hers, wherever she'd gone.

Working together, as two sides of nature's balanced coin, had been the expectation for The Euron and The Modrona since the dawn of time. Yet, he had been surprised by how instantly he felt connected to her. Being around her felt like more than a mere fate-ordained working partnership. It felt like the sum total of his entire life's purpose.

A soft touch on his arm pulled the man back to the reality of the strategy room. Phelip's red eyes were fixed on his face, which had crumpled in pain while he'd let his mind wander to more beautiful places. He spat the blood he'd drawn from biting his lips onto the white floor.

"Shall I walk you to your quarters?" Phelip asked.

The offer of kindness threatened to dissolve The Bear Man's carefully curated mask of calm. "No," he said, his voice cracking.

Wincing as he pulled his tunic over his head, The Ursine Man straightened his posture. He could feel the skin of his back mottling and blistering beneath the thin fabric. The flesh would die over the course of the night, blacken by morning, and heal within the course of two days. Guval's favorite methods of punishment involved use of his Death magic. Every courtier endured such treatment at least once every few full moons.

Guval clapped. "This is why Dando is my favorite among you. He understands his place and takes punishments with dignity. The rest of you all whimper and scream like newborn babes. It bores me to listen to it."

The Ursine Man suppressed the Wrath simmering beneath his skin, forcing himself to bow. "Your Majesty."

He did not allow himself to limp until he reached the relative safety of the dungeons.

Once there, he willed his body to heal faster, his mind spinning in a million directions as he hatched a plan. He needed to find her, find the shining light in the shadows, before her betrothed's cavalier attitude caused her any harm.

CHAPTER 22

A RECKONING TO COME

Silvine

The pungent scent of ammonia brought Silvine back to her senses and away from the comfort of her mother's presence. She jerked her arm to swat away the source of the smell but found that she couldn't move. Her arms had been restrained by her side. Taking in her surroundings, she realized she was in a dark, dilapidated cottage littered with furniture in various states of decay. Beside her, a man in a grimacing bronze mask, held a vial of smelling salts.

"Finally awake, eh?"

Her lip curled. "Obviously." She looked to see if his ears were round or pointed, but the mask obscured her view. Yanking on her arms once more, she realized thin strips of fabric held them. She could remedy that.

"You think you're a fighter, don't you?" the bronze-masked man asked.

She looked him up and down. "I've faced much, much worse than a man hiding behind a hideous mask. You're with Creon, aren't you?"

"Your charade as the future queen has you confused. I don't owe you an explanation. You're here to send the message that we won't let trash from Ainmean receive a place she doesn't deserve. *He* will be here soon." The man turned on his heel and slammed the wooden cottage door behind him. The force sent dust billowing throughout the cramped room.

Oh yes, he's definitely with Creon, Silvine thought. The other provinces all had relatively positive relationships with one another. However, her father's refusal to import his gold and iron to Creon, who charged exorbitant import taxes, had caused decades of bad blood between them. The province of Creon settled for bronze everything, making it a mark of provincial pride, rather than a sign of failed foreign relations. What began as a trade war turned into full-on hatred over time, the small offenses on both sides snowballing into mutual loathing.

Silvine knew she would die if she didn't escape. Creon would stop at nothing to send a message to her father. Knowing how the schemes of the provinces worked to curry favor with the king, Creon would probably frame someone else and make himself the hero. She would not allow that to happen.

She thought of Taran, who'd insisted she practice wielding her powers. If he were with her, he'd say she needed to use her powers to save herself. He'd be right.

She listened to the music in her blood. The sound had grown familiar in recent weeks. Then, she turned inward to find other sources of Life around her.

Soft melodies, loud singular notes, and tumultuous symphonies flooded her senses. She felt them in every beat of her heart, every fiber of her being. It was too much. Breathing deeply, she severed the connection between herself and her magic. An image of Taran's taunting face flashed through her mind. She assumed he'd be disappointed in how easily she'd given up, but this was so new to her. Power may have been granted to her by The Creator, but she didn't know how to wield it.

She busied herself with the fabric binding her hands. Her

captors' choice of material spoke to how weak they assumed she was —the useless, spoiled second daughter of Lord Morair. The urge to prove them wrong lit a fire within her.

Running her fingers along the restraints, she felt the knots. A measly two of them. She twisted her wrists back and forth until she had an angle to grip the first knot with her fingers. With surprising ease, she undid it. Her restraints loosened, and she undid the second and final knot.

Her legs shaky, she stumbled out of the wooden chair and surveyed her surroundings. Through dingy windows, she saw the pinks and blues of the sky. It was either dawn or dusk. She hoped for the cloak of protection that nightfall would offer as she sought her escape. Navigating The Realm had proven to be a weakness of hers. She didn't want to be there when "he" arrived.

She patted her thigh and found that her wing-handled dagger remained at her side. If they'd checked her while she was unconscious, they'd done a terrible job of it. As she unsheathed her dagger, the cottage's door groaned and swung open.

Her bronze-masked captor stood in the doorway, hands clenched in tight fists. "What in the Skies-damned Earth do you think you're doing?"

Although Silvine's heart began to race, she forced herself into the only fighting stance she'd ever been taught. The inheritance of her father's sharp tongue was a gift in this moment, giving her the ability to bluff her way through the roar of her fears. "Showing you what trash from Ainmean can do." She lifted her blade above her head and prepared for a downward swing.

The bronze-masked man gripped her wrists in one bulky hand. He tightened his grip until she screamed and released her hold on the handle of her silver dagger. It clattered to the floor beside her. He let go and took a step back.

Rolling his shoulders, her captor braced himself before swinging a still-clenched fist. It collided with Silvine's temple, knocking her down. The other side of her head crashed against the dirty, wooden floor with a thud.

"As I thought," her captor muttered. Silvine heard the rustling as he dug through the drawers of a small, dilapidated cabinet against one of the walls.

Wet, sticky blood pooled in the space between Silvine's head and the floor below. Never before had she felt so close to death. Life was a beautiful, precious, fragile thing. She had just come to learn she had potential beyond her wildest dreams. Now was not her time to die. Now was the time do what needed to be done, as her mother had said.

As her captor fumbled around the drawers, grumbling under his breath, Silvine tuned into the magic in her blood again. A song of Life played with the beat of her heart. She reached her powers out, searching for something small and helpful. Although the multitude of tunes threatened to overwhelm her, she focused on the individual strands of Life and their distinct songs.

Isolating a soft, upbeat melody, she called the music toward her, harmonizing its song with her own. A sapling sprouted from a crack in the floorboards, an answer to her call. She played her own song to the music of the sapling, amplifying it as the young tree grew. Its branches reached out, scraping along the limbs of the man in the grimacing mask.

He gave a shout. The branches wound around his legs until he could not move them. Silvine stretched her arms outward, beckoning the limbs of the sapling to wind upward.

"Having troubles?" she asked in her sweetest voice.

Her captor lifted an arm, revealing a rusty blade. He began to hack away at the sapling. It blackened with every swipe, slowly retreating back to whence it had come as its music stuttered and died away.

With it, Silvine's hope began to wither. The music in her blood grew frantic as she sought another strand, another ally, in the symphony of Life outside the cottage.

The man lunged toward her. The blade remained firm in his hand. "None of that mage nonsense is going to work here, Lady. I can wield the blades your people cannot."

Silvine wanted to say she didn't believe in mage nonsense either, but she held her tongue, her heart pounding as she took in the sight of the rusty blade. Only iron oxidized that way. Iron, it was said, could significantly weaken the Fae. It had just destroyed the sapling she'd called forth. *Nene's right about some things*, she realized.

Stealing a glance at one of the grimy windows, Silvine saw nothing but darkness. Night had come. Thunder rolled in the distance. A flash of light illuminated the sky through the window.

Silvine called her powers out farther and farther, analyzing the magic of all the beings around her. A melancholy tune, one she'd heard before, grew nearer and nearer. She wove her own song into the tune, calling it closer. "Do your worst," she said.

The man in the mask sliced his blade through the air, landing it on Silvine's forearm. The cut burned as blood spurted from her arm. She hissed in pain. She tried to staunch the bleeding with the sleeve of her free arm, waiting for the reckoning that would come when the source of the melancholy magic arrived.

CHAPTER 23

VICTORIA DE FELIPENTĒ

Silvine

A figure in a dark cloak stepped through the doorway, pulling the hood off their cloak and shaking the raindrops from their mane of brown hair. Taran.

"Am I late to the party?" he asked. Thunder crackled in the distance.

The bronze-masked man pivoted to face him. As he spun, Silvine caught a glimpse of a round ear, affirming her conclusion that he was a human. The burning sensation in her arm continued. She pressed down firmly on her wound, but her efforts to stop the bleeding were in vain. Blood continued to spatter onto the floor beneath her.

Wordlessly, the man lunged at Taran, wielding the blood-stained, rusty blade. The masked man was a head taller than Guval's General of Intelligence, who had yet to move or draw his own weapon.

Unsure if she was shaking from blood loss or fear, Silvine felt her tongue grow heavy, and words became hard to form. "It's iron," she managed to say.

A look of amusement lit up Taran's face. "So it *is* a party. I'm afraid

I missed my invitation." Faster than any human could, he shifted to stand behind his attacker. He reached up, grabbing his assailant's wrist. With surprising ease, he yanked the man's arm down, tucking it against his back, putting careful distance between his body and the blade.

The bronze-masked man had both mass and height to his advantage. He jerked backward with the full force of his weight, throwing Taran's back against the cabinet. Taran let out a groan before rushing toward his assailant. The impact sent dust falling like snowflakes through the cramped cottage.

Numb to the melee in front of her, Silvine felt her knees begin to buckle. Little black stars framed her vision as she struggled to continue pressing down on her wound.

"Have a seat, Regina," Taran called out. A chair slid across the floor, stopping against her legs. Silvine collapsed into the chair, resisting the hazy black dots that threatened to pull her from consciousness.

The crack of flesh colliding with bone jerked Silvine out of her stupor. She looked up to see blood pouring out of Taran's nose. He'd taken a vigorous blow to the face. The iron blade lay on the floor between Taran and the masked man's feet.

While Taran wiped at his nose, the bronze-masked man took the opportunity to bend down and retrieve his blade. The copper tang of blood, flowing from two bodies, filled Silvine's nostrils. "The blade," she murmured.

Taran lifted his head in time to block the man's downward swing with his forearm. Lightning-fast, he locked his assailant's blade arm between his wrists, forcing it downward. As if they were dancing, Taran twirled backward, taking the man's arm with him.

"This has been so much fun, but I'm afraid it's gotten tiresome," Taran said.

He gripped his attacker's wrist with one hand, yanking it toward him. There was a sickening crunch, and the man cried out. The blade fell from the bronze-masked man's grasp as his hand hung limp. Startled by the unnatural position of the man's bones, Silvine let out a shaky gasp.

"For good measure," Taran murmured, reaching for the man's other wrist. "Let's make sure you never touch her again." Another crunch and cry of pain quickly followed. Taran had snapped both the man's wrists. Raising a foot, Taran kicked him to the ground. The man reached his hands out to catch himself and screamed in pain as he landed on his broken bones. Taran lifted a finger upward, and the man's body vanished.

Silvine's breath began to slow, and the black dots in her vision morphed into clouds. Rough hands peeled hers from the hold she'd kept on her gash. She tried to protest. "No, no, it's bleeding," she whispered.

"I know it is, Regina," Taran said softly. "Let me help."

A cool, viscous substance made contact with Silvine's open wound. The burning faded, and the black clouds in her vision subsided almost instantly. She peered down, noticing Taran was holding a small, green vial. He tilted it, letting a silvery substance work its way down to her injury.

"Silver counteracts iron. Any metal that isn't magnetic will do, but silver is fastest. These are selkie tears," Taran explained. He pulled a green handkerchief from his pocket and began to dab away the blood from her temple.

"How does one collect selkie tears?" Silvine asked.

He winked, which Silvine thought looked absurd, given the battered state of his face. "One asks very, very nicely. It's particularly helpful if they already owe you a favor."

"You collect favors like a lady collects fine ceramics. Do you need help?" Silvine gestured at his nose.

Taran reached for his handkerchief and wiped away the crusted blood. His nose had turned purple, swelling to twice its normal size. "No, it'll set itself and heal before we have time to do anything to fix it. We're Fae, remember?"

"After that iron blade set me on fire from the inside out, I don't think I will ever forget. Can you shift us back to Court?" she asked. Her body grew weary. Although the iron had been counteracted by the silver, she felt as though she'd run for miles. She wanted nothing more than to return to her bed.

His brows furrowed. "I am afraid I don't have my normal reserves of energy at my disposal. It's an inconvenience that delayed me in coming to find you. Were you waiting long?"

Legs wobbling like a newborn foal, Silvine took a few unsure steps forward. Taran reached out to catch her when she stumbled, scooping her into his arms. As she sank into the comfort of being held by someone, anyone, she studied his face, which was covered in the green and yellow blotches of fading bruises. "I didn't know if anyone would come for me. I just knew I couldn't die. That man was with Creon, and—they want me dead."

"I know, Regina," Taran said softly. "But you're not dead. It may be a bit of a journey back to Court, but we will get there. Safely."

He carried her out of the cottage and into the embrace of the night.

The storm had passed at some point during the altercation with Creon's masked man. Silvine inhaled the fresh scent of petrichor as Taran wove through the trees, carrying her the whole way. The stars above and sliver of moonlight lit his path.

His breathing grew labored, and he paused. Silvine slipped in his arms. Trying to secure herself, she clutched at his back. He sucked in a sharp breath as he shifted her weight around.

"Does it hurt to carry me?" she asked.

Taran scoffed. "No, I've carried far heavier burdens in my life."

Silvine wriggled away from him. "Allow me to take away one of your heavy burdens, then." Tightening his hold on her, he pulled her closer. She'd decided she wanted him to let her go, and he *would* let her go. She reached around to smack his back as hard as she could.

He yelped, dropping her on the damp forest soil.

Rising to her feet, she dusted the sticks and mud from her dress. "Something is wrong with you. Did that filth hurt you somewhere I can't see?"

"A human gets one good shot at my nose, and you assume I've been gravely wounded. No, he did not hurt me somewhere you can't see."

"But you're hurt. You said you can't use your magic to shift us back to the castle," Silvine said.

"By morning, I will be back to my usual self."

She frowned, studying his face. He flashed her his signature, irreverent look. There was no use in trying to get any further information out of him.

"I can walk now," Silvine said.

He gestured grandly. "Follow me, then, Regina."

Leading her out of the forest, Taran took her to a red hill. The stillness of the night engulfed them. Taran climbed up the mound, reaching out his hand to help her climb up. The soil beneath her feet felt dry, unlike the moisture in the forest after the rainstorm.

As they crested the hill, Taran jumped. He pulled Silvine downward with him as they sank through the earth and landed with a thud on a stone floor. She surveyed their surroundings, taking in the torchlit tunnel. It looked like the halls of Court.

"What in Earth's name did we just do?" she asked.

His teeth gleamed in the torchlight. "Faerie kingdoms are always linked to mounds, even the corrupted ones. We entered through Court's mound, and we'll roam the hallways until we arrive in the throne room."

Shaking her head, Silvine accepted yet another bewildering aspect of Fae life. Taran delivered his information, from selkie tears to Fae mounds, which such nonchalance. She was thankful for the way he made it all easier to process.

They made their way down the corridor, just as they had before when Silvine faced her first trial. Knowing what she knew now, she hoped Guval would not entertain Creon for another minute. She would not participate in another trial.

Silvine and Taran reached a place where the narrow hall expanded into a vast rectangular, stone chamber. The darkness made her eyes fuzzy, a contrast to the well-lit hallways they'd just walked. Crumbling stairs marked the left hand side, with unlit torches lining the remaining walls.

"I will go make contact with the king," Taran said. "You can rest a moment."

Before she could protest, he was bounding up the stairs, two at a time. A yowling, screaming noise echoed in the distance. Silvine held her breath, hoping whatever was coming her way wasn't as sinister as it seemed.

The yowling grew into a caterwaul. *Am I facing off against a great cat?* she wondered.

Her blood began to hum, and she reached within herself as a glowing, white light of power emanated from her palms. The caterwauling creature was illuminated by the glow. Silvine's opponent was not just a feline. It was a feline-headed serpent, a chimera of the worst kind. It was known in the human realms as a felipentis, dwelling in the darkest caves and haunting the nightmares of mortals. Not only was its wailing overwhelming to the senses, but its bite contained some of the most powerful venom in the world.

It slithered toward her, scales scraping along the dark, stone walls while it hissed and tossed its gray mane around.

Please don't bite me, Silvine thought.

She remembered the light she'd shot out at Taran when he'd lured her away from her dinner. Wishing she'd used it in the cottage, she reminded herself that she could do better now. She channeled her rage into a beam of white light that struck the serpentine chimera in its abdomen.

The felipentis let out a hiss, slithering backward against the wall to Silvine's right. In the glow of her palms, Silvine saw extinguished torches lining the stone walls. She knew her power came from Life, however vague that term was, so she cast her song out to the old sticks along the walls.

Dead, silent, dead, silent, she mentally panned each torch along the wall.

The caterwauling grew louder until... *snap!* The felipentis lunged at Silvine. She dodged to the left just in time, its rough scales slicing across her legs and drawing blood.

She sucked in a breath from the pain. Fighting against the throbbing in her legs, she kept calling out to the torches until finally, she found one with a hint of Life left in it. It sang back at her. She concentrated, sending out a song that would call the stick toward her.

Once again, the felipentis lunged. Drawing up her pent-up emotions, Silvine shot another beam of power at it. It hissed, slithering away again. She could hear its hunger, the desperate song of starvation within it. The creature seemed eager to eat, to return to its full strength. Silvine could not let her carcass be what it fed upon. She *would* not.

Finally, the torch skittered across the floor, stopping at her foot. She picked it up, singing, singing, singing in her blood to bring out the slightest hint of Life. A little green spark sprung from the side of the torch, and she let it blossom into a vine.

Rather than willing it to grow into something beautiful and delicate, she made it sprout thorns. *Let it be the mightiest, sharpest thorns ever known,* she said to herself.

Slowly, she built a wall of thorns around her, which grew from the torch in her hands. The torch was now humming back at her, growing louder by the moment.

She braced herself as the felipentis let out a great hiss, ready to pounce, as it opened its jaws and ate a mouthful of thorns. Sticky, foul blood spurted from its mouth. It shook its gray mane back and forth in the green-white light of her glowing palms, seemingly trying to get the thorns out of its mouth.

Silvine was exhausted. She hoped the beast's consumption of the wall of thorns would earn her a few moments' reprieve. Her blood continued its song, frantically growing more thorns.

Once again, the felipentis lunged at her. This time, she shoved the vines out at the creature before it hit her. The great thorns embedded themselves in the monster's sides. It shrieked and yowled, and more blood began to trickle from the beast.

The torch had given her the last of itself. Holding the stick, since cut off from its home tree, Silvine knew its life force was limited. She reached out to the Life that had sprung from the torch itself, all the green-thorned vines that were now embedded in the mouth and flank of the felipentis.

Singing the song in her blood, she implored them to grow and wrap around the monster, tighter, stabbing into it. The only game she could play was the game of endurance, hoping she could slowly bleed the felipentis until it had no more strength. As the thorns hit their mark, the creature yowled pitifully, writhing and smacking into the stone walls.

Creeping closer, Silvine made her song grow louder and louder. The thorns springing forth were bigger than her head. A few skittered to the floor, but most of them landed in the scaly skin of the felipentis.

With a sudden jerk, the felipentis' bloody face twisted to meet Silvine's. It sank its teeth into her right arm. Its hot venom stung as it coursed through her. The song in her blood grew quieter, weaker, as though she was listening to music through a wall. The felipentis's jaws latched onto her arm, appearing ready to shred away the skin at any minute.

Her knees buckled, threatening to give way.

In her mind, she grasped for the vines all around her—sang them up through the floor. They wiggled ever so slowly, seeming to respond to her quiet song, until they burst through the skull of the felipentis. Gore splashed all around, coating Silvine in a foul smell.

With one last gasp, the monster sighed and fell over. Silvine fell with it, her arm still in the clutches of its jaw. There was endless shrieking, screaming, and burning. Removed from herself, Silvine knew deep down that the shrieking was her own.

Her song was gone from her blood. She was dying, giving up her life before she lived the purpose her mother called her to fulfill.

With one final scream, she closed her eyes.

A thud, followed by a quiet hum, brought Silvine back to awareness. The dissonance hurt her head. Yet, the more she leaned into it, the stronger she felt. She opened her eyes to find herself on the floor of the throne room, Guval's lips hovering above her arm. Taran hovered behind him. She struggled to breathe as she realized the king was sucking her blood.

No, no, he was *pulling* the felipentis venom from her. Tendrils of dark magic wafted between his mouth and her arm, a yellow liquid oozing from her wound.

Guval removed his mouth from her arm as the familiar melody in her veins returned to its normal cadence. He reached into his pocket and pulled out a violet handkerchief, dabbing away yellow liquid from around his mouth. An attendant rushed up with a chalice for Guval. He drank deeply before clearing his throat.

Taran lifted Silvine to her feet, steadying her before letting go and retreating out of sight. His melancholy song threatened to buckle her knees again, but she forced herself to focus on the soothing music within her own veins.

Guval took her good hand—the visible muscles and skin knitting themselves back together before her eyes—and raised it to the crowd.

"I present to you the victor. Bow before your future queen, Silvine, Victoria de Felipentē," Guval called to his people.

Victor of the Felipentis, Silvine thought. She wondered why

Taran had left her to fight alone. Gazing around for the first time since awakening, she noticed they'd all crowded around an opening in the floor. Casting a glance to the side, she saw the corpse of the felipentis in the chamber below.

All the Fae fell to their knees and bowed. Not one hesitated. No one dared defy their king. Even Creon and his men had fallen to their knees.

"You may return to your alcoves," Guval said to his courtiers. He walked Silvine up the dais, seating her on his throne. Minuet raised an eyebrow and then wrapped her fur-lined coat around Silvine's shoulders. She bent to look at Silvine's damaged arm before gently massaging it with her fingers.

After providing Silvine with refreshments, Minuet led her to the study. Silvine stumbled, barely able to lift her feet. The mage made her drink a concoction that tasted of boiled dirt and grass. After gagging it down, Silvine felt her strength return.

"Lady Silvine," Minuet said breathlessly, "How did you manage to generate all of that Life magic with no Life to draw from down below you? I have not seen such power in so long."

Silvine sighed. "What do you mean? I nearly died due to the venom of that creature."

"I have seen people contain those beasts, the beasts that are condemned to dwell in the depths of My Majesty's dungeons, but we do not ever see them slain so easily, especially at the hands of a single female," Minuet insisted. "My Majesty has a knack for dealing with the poisons and treachery of the world. I knew he'd save you from death. It is more a question of your ability to draw from Life out of nothing and slay great monsters."

"I just—did," Silvine said numbly.

"Of course. Of course you did. That's why My Majesty chose *you*. While his subjects now know who they are dealing with, you must be extra careful. Those who are jealous will wish to strike you down at every turn. Your power is rare, unseen among our people."

"When can I see His Majesty?" Silvine asked. She felt small tremors begin in her limbs.

Gliding in from behind a curtain, Guval said, "I'm here."

He traced a finger along Silvine's jawline. She flinched, ever so slightly. "My Silvine, you never need to fear me."

"Do you know what happened today?" she whispered, unable to control the shaking that grew increasingly violent.

Guval's hand, as big as a lion's paw, gently swept her hair out of her face and tucked it behind her ear. "Today was your first acclimation to the blood that must be shed in order to subdue the Unseelie wild. All of it was so unsavory, my Silvine, and I hated every moment for you. But I knew you could handle it, and we shall not hear another word of disrespect from Creon."

Silvine's teeth chattered so hard she could barely get her words out. "C-could I h-handle it? I f-f-felt myself dying. My m-magic almost left me, and it b-b-burned. And C-Creon is so m-much w-w-worse than—"

Minuet cleared her throat. "She's going into system overwhelm, My Majesty. I gave her my strongest remedy, but I don't think her magic has ever been spent like this."

Guval frowned and nodded, leaning close to Silvine's ear. "We can discuss this later. You shone brilliantly today. When you have healed, we shall talk more. Know that I shall never, ever let you succumb to everlasting darkness. I only wish to illuminate how dazzlingly powerful you are so that all will fear you." He scooped her limp form into his arms, Silvine leaning her head against his solid chest. She inhaled his spicy, subtly sweet smell.

"Come. Once you have rested, I have much to show you."

CHAPTER 24
IS BLOOD THICKER IN CRISIS?

Silvine

The next morning, Silvine was forced to gag down another of Minuet's bitter remedies. The sluggishness in her body, remnants of her great struggles from the day before, left as she drained the chalice of its contents.

After Silvine was hurriedly dressed in several layers, Minuet and Phelip exchanged a knowing look as they escorted her from her chamber.

"You shall get to witness Court justice today," Minuet said, prancing down the corridor.

Silvine narrowed her eyes. "What exactly does 'Court justice' look like?"

"My Majesty," she began as Silvine winced at her nickname for the king, "is going to show The Realm what happens when someone crosses him."

The trio made their way outside the castle's drawbridge and into a flat space. A crowd of courtiers, along with Lord Creon's host of bronze-clad soldiers, formed a circle around Guval's imposing figure.

Phelip cut through the crowd, Silvine trailing behind him and Minuet.

Taran stood beside Guval, his arms tucked behind him. In the center of the crowd were three men, kneeling with rough sacks covering their faces. Silvine took in the scene and the anticipation that hung thickly in the air. Creon stood across the circle from the king and his entourage, sneering at Silvine.

"We have come here," Guval shouted, "to right the wrongs committed against me. I have chosen my bride, and it is not a matter for my subjects to manage." He motioned toward the three men, and Taran strode toward them, uncovering each man's face one by one.

Silvine shaded her eyes with her hand, blocking out the morning sun, and identified the three kneeling figures. The first was Sharp Face, the second figure resembled her bronze-masked captor, and the third was an entirely unfamiliar human.

"You three have conspired against the wishes of the king of The Realm," Guval said. He sauntered toward the men. "You are now condemned to die."

Taran locked eyes with Silvine and winked. *That Earth-forsaken tattletale*, she thought, *told Guval all about what happened.* A part of her was relieved. She hadn't found the words to tell Guval about the scheme, but Taran had. Nonetheless, she wished she'd been the one to explain how harrowing her kidnapping had been.

"Your Majesty, what evidence do you have?" Lord Creon called out.

Silvine pointed a finger at the man in the middle. "I cannot say for certain who conspired with this man, but I was taken." She shook aside her cape and lifted the sleeve of her gown, revealing a jagged scar that had nearly healed. "He attacked me."

A collection of exclamations of surprise and gasps rang out from the crowd. Lord Creon's face reddened, and he began mumbling to himself.

"I believe I said we would have a trial to show her power. Not only did she have to survive the kidnapping, she slayed a felipentis by herself. Now, Creon, you should hold your tongue." Black tendrils of magic wafted from Guval's fingers to Lord Creon's mouth, twisting past his lips. He yelped and began to spit onto the ground. His tongue turned black.

The crowd grew silent. In reflex, Silvine clapped a hand over her mouth.

"Dando, please hold them still," Guval said. Taran nodded, placing his hands on Sharp Face's shoulders. The same black magic emanated from Guval's hands as he placed them on Sharp Face's temples. Silvine kept her hand clamped on her mouth as she watched the Fae who had once attacked her and taunted her splutter and fall to the ground. Dead.

Guval and Taran moved to the next man, a glimmer of mischief on Taran's face. He reached for the man's wrists, murmuring something in his ear. The man cried out, his face crumpling in obvious pain. Silvine coughed to conceal her laughter.

In a matter of moments, Guval executed the remaining two men, leaving their bodies where they'd fallen. Silvine thought Lord Creon looked like a caricature of himself, his swollen, black tongue hanging from his mouth as he shifted weight from one foot to another.

"Let this serve as a reminder to you all. I will always have things done as I wish," Guval said to the crowd. He turned to face Lord Creon. "You are dismissed from Court. Do not return until you are invited."

The crowd dispersed, wandering back through the gate of the castle. Guval made his way to Silvine, taking her hand in his. He rubbed his thumb along her charoite ring. "That was my first surprise for you today," he whispered. "I have one more. Wait in the courtyard while we prepare." He left her standing beside empty barrels while various courtiers and servants bustled around her.

Silvine hadn't particularly enjoyed the first surprise, although Taran's small act of vengeance on Creon's man had been satisfying. She braced herself for what was to come.

After Silvine spent a great deal of time watching the servants of

Court pass through the courtyard, Guval rode in on his surprise for her: a gilded chariot, drawn by two horses.

"These are the finest bests in all The Realm," Guval said, rubbing the neck of a shining black stallion. Beside the stallion was a strawberry mare.

Silvine thought both of them looked menacing, almost hateful. Perhaps she was just unaccustomed to such finely bred animals.

"Have you ever ridden in a chariot?" Guval asked, eyes glowing.

Silvine shook her head, tossing around her fur-lined bonnet. She wore a black cape with a shimmering, violet dress beneath it. Guval's outfit matched hers.

"It's one of the most thrilling things one can do," he said. He lifted her into the chariot effortlessly.

After a few months of eating Court food, Silvine's figure had returned to its average size, with her generous hips and thighs. She was shocked by the way Guval carried her as though she were a most delicate, dainty creature.

He climbed into the chariot. "Here, these are handles. They're enchanted, so if you simply touch them, they'll keep you in place." Guval snapped the reins, and the chariot sped down steep red rocks. It plummeted down the cliffside, dropping hundreds of feet.

Butterflies fluttered in Silvine's stomach as they went. Guval chuckled, the wind ruffling his russet hair. He looked exhilarated. Silvine contorted her face into an expression that mirrored his.

They rode on. The road flattened as they reached a black, stone gate. It looked so out of place among the barren, red rocks. Two black-clad guards stood, spears crossed, blocking the entrance. At the sight of their king, they lowered their spears and dropped to their knees. Guval snapped his fingers, and the gate groaned open.

"I wanted to show you my city," Guval said. "It is not a place for Fae nobles or kings to dwell, but I want you to see the might of what I have made."

They crossed a bridge high above a purplish river and dropped once more. Their descent revealed the biggest city Silvine had ever seen. It was nestled in a valley of red plateaus.

There were endless rows of white stone buildings, a few columned buildings Silvine took for temples, and a teeming population that buzzed around on foot, on horseback, and in wagons.

As they descended into the city, Silvine was struck by the smell of sewer, livestock, and something that reminded her of death. With so many people in such a small space, it was an unsurprising smell. She pinched her nose.

"*That* is one of many reasons why we reside at Court, beloved," Guval said.

The chariot rode along smooth, white-and-purple brick roads. Fae ladies in fine dresses walked along the roadside. Human men rode the streets on well-kept horses.

"I've never seen anything like it," Silvine breathed.

"Just wait," Guval replied. "The city of Luteche has more I want you to see."

The road led to a massive plaza. To the right was a fountain, glowing purple. A statue of Guval occupied the center. He held a sword in his hand, reaching for the sky, muscles bulging in his arms. Aside from the statue, there was no sign of life to be found.

"Welcome to the Platea Regium, or Guval's Square," Guval said. He pulled the reins to a halt and hopped off the chariot, offering Silvine his hand to help her do the same.

"I think Her Ladyship of Asturia would be sick with envy if she were to see the grandeur of what you've created," Silvine said.

"She's seen it. She wishes she had the kind of power to reach the pinnacle of creation and beauty that I have. Luteche is a rare jewel, one I have spent centuries cultivating. The lords and ladies of my provinces can only aspire to such heights." If anyone else had made such a declaration, it would have sounded like a nauseating brag. Guval, however, said it quite matter-of-factly.

Silvine, slowly walking toward the statue, stared up at it. "I've never seen a structure quite so tall."

Guval threw an arm around Silvine's shoulders, pulling her close. "This is what I have built on my own. With you as my consort, think of the things we can do."

She shuddered, thinking of the way she'd nearly died taking on the felipentis and Creon's men. Guval seemed to view her as his personal assassin of monsters. She didn't want to build an empire of Death. "If I survive, that is."

"You will only grow stronger with each obstacle you overcome. I can sense it." Guval gripped her chin gently and placed a kiss on her lips. Her obsidian necklace went ice cold.

Her chest tightened. *Safe, you're safe,* she reminded herself.

A man, bedecked in jewels and a shining black suit, strode into the square. A female in a shining black cloak and full-skirted dress trailed behind him, similarly adorned. The man kept his eyes trained on the ground, no doubt in reverence for the king who stood in his midst.

"Silvine," called a familiar voice, dripping with contempt.

"Ophelia."

"I told you I had a surprise for you once you were rested," Guval said cheerfully. "I thought the sight of your sister might be a balm to your soul."

Ophelia scoffed but seemed to catch herself when she realized her male companion had dropped to his knees, prostrating. She imitated his gesture.

"Rise," Guval commanded. He gestured at the dark-haired man who was hurrying to his feet, eyes fixed on the ground. "This is the Duc de Luteche, and this is his new wife, the Duchesse de Luteche. He keeps my city running, just as his father and grandfather did before him."

"Your Grace, I had not realized it was you. My sincerest apologies," Ophelia said. "Silvine, dear sister, what are you doing here?"

Guval took Silvine's hand into his, revealing the massive charoite ring on her finger. "She is to become Queen Silvine, Victoria de Felipentē."

Ophelia blanched. "The people of Luteche say you have a sense of humor, Your Majesty, but certainly this is too great a jest even for you."

The fear that this was all some great joke had been lurking in the back of Silvine's mind since her betrothal to Guval had begun. Despite the fact that she'd destroyed the puca and slayed the felipentis, she still could not fathom why Guval wanted her.

The king narrowed his eyes.

The duc put a firm hand on Ophelia's shoulder, his eyes still trained downward. "I hope you will excuse the duchesse. We have just returned to society after our nuptial time. She has forgotten her social graces. Won't you join us? We were just sitting down for afternoon tea." The Duc de Luteche gestured at the grand, white marble building behind him.

Guval approached and took the duc's hand in his own.

"Allow me to show you my home, dear sister," Ophelia sneered, leading the way into one of the large, marble homes in the square.

The males retreated into a room to the right of the entrance while Ophelia ushered Silvine into a parlor. Everything was gaudy, lined with gold and velvet and festooned in the brightest colors. A servant brought in a tea kettle, placing it on the table beside them before bowing and hastening out of the room.

Ophelia poured tea into two cups, doing a poor job of concealing the way she seethed. She shoved a cup into Silvine's hands.

"How did you manage to ensnare the ancient king of The Realm?" Ophelia demanded.

"Our father arranged it. There was nothing I could do either for or against it," Silvine said.

"It's not proper." Ophelia slammed her cup of tea on the table, spilling it all. The servant rushed in, dabbing at the water.

"Would you like to say that to His Majesty or Father first?" Silvine asked. "I'm sure both of them simply forgot to consult you before making their choice about *my* future."

"Do not think I am displeased to be married to the duc. It is a good match, and city life suits someone like me. I am just not sure what the king sees in a second daughter... especially *you.*"

Silvine frowned. "Do you know what I have had to endure?"

Ophelia shrugged. "No?"

"His Majesty's troops have just returned to Court. I'm assuming some of them have returned to Luteche as well. Do you know where they went?" Silvine placed her empty cup down, and the servant rushed to collect it.

Ophelia waved away her servant. "I have never cared for war games."

"I'm glad to see you're still tormenting the help." Silvine sighed. "Ainmean was attacked."

Ophelia went still.

"On Festivale, cloaked men came, and after slashing our citizens, they set fire to the village. We went from dancing and ceremony to death and screaming. The only Morair there was me. Cardoc tried to give me up to men who wanted to take me captive, but Ana bought me time." Silvine's voice faltered. "She—they—they cut Ana down. I fled into the woods. I thought I was fleeing to Asturia, but I got mixed up somehow. I wandered for weeks before being attacked by some of the king's guards because I had trespassed on his lands. I ended up finding Father the same moment I met the king."

Ophelia snatched Silvine's hand into hers. It was a rare moment of sisterly solidarity, although her touch was far from gentle.

Despite all of her flaws, Ophelia's patriotism ran deep. Silvine knew the great pride her sister felt for both Ainmean and Asturia and assumed she had likely grown to feel that same fierce pride for the city of Luteche.

"Did they find the bastards?" Ophelia asked.

"By the time Father and the king's army reached Ainmean, the fires had been put out and whoever attacked had fled. It took me weeks to get here. Reports say they were pursuing *me* in the forest. Guval knew something was wrong and already sent some of his men to find me. Ana was the last one to die. The only hunch they have to go on is that Cardoc is gone." Silvine's voice cracked, and she could not hold the tears in any longer. "It is all my fault."

Ophelia looked around her then leaned in. "It is *not* your fault," she whispered. "My Lady Aunt thinks Ainmean is cursed, and that the curse stems from Father himself. Women suffer and die wherever he goes, even if not at his hands directly." She wiped away the tears on Silvine's cheeks.

"I'll never be able to go back or make it better for our people. We never cared about them, not really, and they died because of *me*." Sobs racked Silvine's body, sobs she'd been holding in for so long.

Ophelia patted her sister's back awkwardly, seeming to make an earnest attempt to be comforting but falling short. "I think you've earned the right to marry that wrinkly old king."

Silvine laughed at the thought, letting Ophelia believe her sister was marrying an ancient, powerful man. She threw her head back as she thought of the absurdity of it all, knocking the bonnet off her head. Only by magic had it managed to endure the chariot ride. Only by Silvine's habitually poor luck did it fall off in her sister's parlor.

Silvine felt her ear poking out, felt the heat of Ophelia's gaze as she reached out and pinched her ear. "Your ear is... healed." Her sister's voice trailed off.

"Yes," Silvine said, her heart pounding.

"What *are* you? You survived in the woods for weeks. Your ears that once were scarred are healed. You are engaged to the king. That is not normal." Ophelia's voice shook.

"I'm—I'm not sure," Silvine stammered.

Guval and the duc walked in, breaking up the tension. The duc continued to stare at the floor. Silvine concluded that he must have had great reverence for the king.

"This has been a most pleasant afternoon, Duc," Guval said. "I am sure the sisters enjoyed catching up as well. We shall do it again, but I must get my bride-to-be home."

The Duc de Luteche bowed, and Ophelia stood to curtsy. Her

eyes did not leave her sister's. Silvine felt the heat of her stare even as she was lifted into the chariot.

As they exited the Platea Regium, Guval said, "I apologize."

"For what?"

"I thought seeing your sister would be a welcome surprise. I hadn't realized she was as serpentine as the felipentis, and I was sending you to face another opponent."

"Well, if we could spend more time together, you might have come to learn these things. Lord Morair exerts a strong hand over his subjects, and they respect and fear him. Our family is more an extension of his rule than a group of people who care for each other," Silvine replied.

"I wish to spend all my moments with you, every single one, but the weight of the Unseelie threats and the petulant human Premiers require my attention. I will do better," Guval promised, jerking the reins of his chariot.

Silvine nodded.

"Never doubt that you are the most special, most important, feature in my life. Aren't you glad I interrupted before you had to give some kind of explanation for the fact that you're a wildly powerful Fae to your mortal sister?" The king raised a brow.

She found herself grinning. "She would have thought I was unwell."

Only once she had returned to her chamber did she realize Guval had been eavesdropping. She wondered how much he knew of her past and why he hadn't asked about it.

CHAPTER 25

THE BIRTHDAY FEAST

Silvine

Shortly after Silvine fell asleep one night, her attendant woke her. She couldn't imagine what would have required her to wake up at such an hour.

"Come now. You must come to Princess Minuet's chambers. There isn't a moment to waste," her attendant insisted, throwing a silky violet robe over Silvine's nightclothes.

"To her chambers?" Silvine asked groggily.

"Yes, yes. His Majesty likes all of his court to be there for these things."

Phelip was waiting outside Silvine's chamber door. He looked unusually rumpled, and his red eyes were rimmed more crimson than usual. "Come, all of us must attend this *glorious* moment."

Still sleepy, Silvine followed him down corridors, upward into a wing of the castle she had never explored before. She played with the music in her blood, reaching out, but nothing sang back to her. This wing, like many other spaces at Court, felt barren.

They reached a room with a great red door, and a footman let them inside.

In the center of the expansive room was a gilded four-poster bed. Minuet lay in the center in a birthing position, panting and moaning delicately. Several females in traditional red mage robes attended to her. Guval watched intently from the foot of the bed. He seemed intrigued by the show.

Some of the most prominent nobles of Court stood off to the side, witnessing Minuet's vulnerable, private moment.

Silvine stood beside Phelip. "I didn't know you were an expectant father," she whispered.

"In all candor, neither did I. I am still not convinced that *I* am," he muttered, more to himself than her. He crossed his arms, frowning. Silvine didn't know what to make of the comment and wasn't entirely sure she wanted to know about the paternity of Minuet's surprise baby.

"Why are we all here for this?" Silvine asked.

"This is how His Majesty prefers all births at Court to happen. There can be no question of the legitimacy of the birth or any Fae trickery." Phelip paused to gesture at Silvine. "No Unseelie changeling allegations will be made if we are all here witnessing it."

"Politically, that is a sound call, but doesn't it feel weird that the king is so involved in your wife's birthing affairs?" Silvine asked between clenched teeth.

Phelip leaned in closer. "Don't fret. This will be you someday, too. Minuet is an expert at this kind of spectacle. She thrives on the drama. She and Guval do their very best work together."

Silvine shoved away her petty jealousy and focused on the "spectacle." Minuet was the picture of delicate, motherly exertion. This was nothing like the births Gilla had described or the vision the puca had shown of her mother's death.

Her mother. Moisture threatened to well up and drop down her cheeks, but Silvine breathed the tears back inside her. Minuet's display was nothing like her mother's final exertion, where she gave her life up bringing Silvine into this dark, confusing world.

Minuet continued her breathy pants and moans. Silvine caught the ghost of a smile on the woman's lips each time the mother-to-be looked at Guval. It wasn't hard to believe Phelip's accusation that his wife enjoyed the performance and the attention. If she had done this repeatedly, Silvine wondered where all of their offspring were. She hadn't seen a single child since her arrival at Court.

Within ten minutes of Silvine's arrival, a mewling babe with glowing red eyes had been born and placed atop her mother's chest. Guval clapped with delight at the sight, his blood emitting a loud bit of clanging music in the process, and he uttered some type of Fae blessing for both the mother and child. The volume of his expression made Silvine queasy.

"Do not forget our celebratory measures," Guval's voice boomed in the chamber.

The rest of Court accepted their king's words as a dismissal. Phelip strode toward the bed, reluctantly greeting the newest member of his family. "Here goes another week of parenting," he grumbled. "Then it'll be sent away to torment some poor province with the antics it's learned from its mother." Silvine raised an eyebrow. A week of parenting?

Guval and Minuet both sighed before turning their attention back to the miracle of life that had just occurred.

A silent guard entered the room, nodding at Silvine before escorting her away. Guval stayed, clearly enjoying the moment.

Silvine wondered what it would be like to give birth so openly, in front of others. Most did not bring forth children into the world with the grace and gentleness that Minuet had just gone out of her way to show. She pondered how giving birth would go for her. Would she bleed out like her mother?

She challenged her thoughts to shift, focusing on Guval's joy instead. If he felt such joy about the arrival of a niece, surely he would be the world's most doting father with his own child. Since Minuet had not detected any bargains on Silvine, surely she would be free to have a child, and Taran wouldn't be able to interfere.

The prospect of taking on the responsibility of raising a *human* child, let alone a Fae one, felt daunting. She knew Taran couldn't stand up against an ancient king and his entire mighty Court. They would all rise up against him before he took away her firstborn child, she was sure. Satisfied, she pushed away the small voice in the back of her mind.

When Silvine returned to her room, there was a knock at her window. Before she could get off her bed and decide whether or not she cared to see Taran, he appeared beside her massive bathtub.

"Regina," he said in greeting.

"Did I invite you in?"

Taran leaned against the empty tub, arms crossed. "We're such good friends that I assumed you just hadn't had the chance to say, 'Come in, oh savior of mine.' Why *wouldn't* you want me in here, after all?"

"Shall I start listing off all the reasons? Number one, you make me engage in ridiculous bargains that may or may not be real. Number two, that look on your face is insufferable. Number three—"

Taran broke in, "Court is doing nothing for refining that tongue of yours. You continue to wound me with your vicious words. Our bargain is very real and rather precious to me." He clutched at his heart, pantomiming being stabbed.

"What do you want?"

"You," Taran drawled, "to stay in your bedroom tonight."

Silvine's jaw dropped.

"Not for *that* reason. You dishonor me with assumptions. His Majesty asked that I come in and check on your welfare. The milksop and your attendant are both unavailable to do their usual duties. I want you to stay here for your own safety." Taran's eyes darkened. "Tonight, there is a witching hour feast you cannot partake in."

"You're not partaking in the feast, either? What happened to being my betrothed's Commander of Intelligence?"

"Our kind, yours and mine, can't consume what they are feasting upon tonight. We aren't made like they are. We aren't made for…

that. And it's *General* of Intelligence. I cannot command knowledge. I steer and direct it."

Curiosity got the better of Silvine. "Tell me what it is they're doing that your kind and mine, whatever that means, aren't made to consume."

"We don't drink the hot blood of our enemies." Taran laughed darkly.

Silvine stared at him. "My—I mean, Guval, wouldn't... Would he?"

"*Your* Guval is the leader in partaking. You and I are garden variety Fae. We engage in trickery, maybe a little harmless deception. Our morals are a little murkier than humans' are, and we have magical powers. Guval and his people are what they call avartagh." She detected a bitterness in his tone she'd never heard before. "They thrive upon the fear, the energy, the life force of the others. Their blood."

"And why can't I go down there?"

"You would see unspeakable horrors, and there is no telling how they would respond to the human part of your blood. They are uncivilized and bloodthirsty on a quarterly basis in order to be more... civilized... the rest of the time."

Silvine gaped.

"What, have I finally struck you silent?" Taran purred. "I think I like it more when you wield that tongue of yours against me."

She crossed her arms. "Guval would never put me in harm's way like that. You're more likely to go around feasting on blood than he is, since you're more than comfortable bargaining for people's *firstborn children.* This is yet another one of your deceptions. What's the real reason you're here?"

He prowled closer to her. "I have no reason to deceive you. You're here for your own protection. Your precious powers are too important to the king to risk you being attacked by his courtiers in the height of their blood lust. He's quite a monster when feasting.

"And I may add," he continued further, "I have zero desire to consume the life force of anyone, let alone your firstborn child's. Have you noticed the red eyes around here? They unsettle you to your core. Their kind and ours are ancient enemies."

Silvine backed away from Taran until the backs of her knees rested against her bed.

He sniffed the air, smirking insufferably. "Nervous?" he whispered. "What will this knowledge of your king's true nature do to your pending marriage?"

"I hate you!" she seethed.

"Hate me? I'm your one true ally at Court, Regina. What if tonight was the night you finally got the courage to break free from your cage, and you turned into someone's meal? There are fates worse than public childbirth at the King of Donadais's court."

Silvine glowered at him. He stepped closer, so close she could smell white birch and the Faerie wine on his breath. "You hate me?" he whispered, eyes fixed on her.

"Yes," she breathed.

She sensed his shift but couldn't move fast enough to intercept what was coming. He whirred past her and produced his cloak from beneath her mattress. He swept it over her shoulders, smug victory on his face. "Oh, look at how you hate me. You could have easily tossed this old cloak into the fire. Admit it. That night was the most alive you've felt since you've been here, maybe ever."

"Y-yes," she murmured. Taran had the most infuriating ability to pry the truth from her lips.

"I'll be back tomorrow night to open your eyes a little wider." He studied her velvet robe and the black nightgown underneath. "Dress appropriately for the occasion this time."

CHAPTER 26

THE WEIGHT OF DREAD

Silvine

Dread for the following night's plans with Taran hung on Silvine like wet clothes after a rainstorm. He hadn't given her room to refuse the invitation, but nonetheless, she wished she could have turned him down. She wasn't eager to verbally spar with him for hours, and it felt wrong to sneak around in the middle of the night.

Even worse, this was the day Guval had finally decided to make good on his promise to pay more attention to her.

With a few guards trailing behind them, Guval had shown her around his art gallery. There was a collection of rare jewels, including an ancient pendant containing what he called "crystalline blood of the enemy," endless statues of Fae warriors, and a few paintings of sneering, haughty Fae families.

Following that adventure, he took her to his personal library. It made her father's study look humble in comparison.

Lastly, Silvine had gotten to tour Guval's chambers, complete with its own pool. Guval led her out to his veranda, which had been built over the edge of the red cliffs with a view of the roaring sea

below. The table and chairs on the veranda looked as though they'd never been used before.

With a flick of his wrist, Guval cleared the dust from the table before seating himself and gesturing for Silvine to follow. A servant brought out a covered tray. One of the guards stepped forward to sniff it before giving Guval a gesture and retreating.

The king offered her a flute of sparkling Faerie wine. She froze, studying the bubbling glass. He chuckled. "Afraid you'll handle your Fae spirits as well as Lord Morair?"

"That is one concern, yes."

"You are not merely your father's daughter, you know. You lived as a human for almost twenty-four years, so it is understandable you still see yourself that way. You have the unique gift of being able to live as human or Fae, to walk between two worlds and know what is real in both. Choose to be Fae in this moment and share this delightful vintage with me." Guval raised his flute.

Silvine clanked her glass against his, daring a small sip. The Faerie wine tasted sweet, like moonlit dances and wild revelry. Yet, it also tasted bitter, like rivalries and wicked games. This was the heritage she'd been denied for so long.

She downed the whole glass on the next gulp.

Despite Guval's insistence that if she simply chose to be Fae while drinking she would stay quite sober, Silvine simultaneously felt quite Fae *and* quite intoxicated.

She stood up, unable to resist the music in her veins that called to her. *Get up. Move, move, move. Dance. Revel.* The way she moved, so free, following the rhythm, was nothing like Phelip's regimented waltzes or the routines of Ainmeanian group dances. This was pure liberation.

Guval hummed to himself. His golden features in the sunlight were blindingly beautiful. He took Silvine's hand in his, gently placing the other hand on the small of her back, seeming ready to join her reverie. The minute Guval's hands made contact with Silvine's body, the music within her changed. It became screeching and dissonant.

"I need to have a seat," Silvine said, putting a hand to her temple. "The wine has gone to my head."

She watched his face beneath lowered lashes, wondering if he sensed the lie on her lips. If he had, he didn't say a word about it.

He gently lowered her to her seat. "Phelip is hosting one of his balls soon. You shall have to work on building up your tolerance for Faerie wine to truly enjoy the occasion. I can't wait to hold you in my arms and show off your magnificence." Guval eagerly pulled up a chair beside her.

Desperate, she thought to herself. He was just as desperate as she was to connect, but it felt awkward. She had been at Court for months but spent most of her time with his brother or alone in her chamber. It was no wonder they hadn't built a true connection.

Even his magic sang the wrong notes to her. It was the only magic she'd encountered that left her reeling in a way she could not understand. She'd had a sense of the magic of the less powerful Fae at Court, but their magic was so small it was a single, clanging cymbal to her blood. His magic was a symphony of notes that played at the wrong time, simultaneously too deep and too high.

Silvine resolved to try to connect with Guval. The awkwardness had to be caused by her disbelief that he would want her, her hesitation to let anyone in after Ana.

She resolved to change the subject. "Congratulations on the birth of your niece. I have never attended a birth quite like it, or any birth for that matter."

A broad grin lit up his face. "Minuet is a magnificent and prolific mother. Her pregnancies come on suddenly, and the babies reach maturity in a fortnight."

Despite her efforts to make her face neutral, her eyes widened.

"It is strange, isn't it?" Guval said. "It is not natural for Fae. Most struggle to conceive and give birth, and pregnancies are traditionally the same length as those of human mothers. It is her unique mage essence, the way she can call and speak to the elements of the world. She is truly invaluable."

Visions of him drinking blood with Minuet, feasting upon mortals, flashed across Silvine's mind. She knew her tongue had been loosened by wine, so she worked to control her words before speaking.

Despite her mental effort, the words fell out awkwardly. "Is that —? What will our future be like?"

Guval took her hand in his, tracing the charoite on her finger. The galaxy obsidian necklace went icy in response, as it always did, on the bare skin of her chest. He kissed the tops of each of her knuckles, which made her toes curl.

"Eyes will watch you and I even more closely than Minuet and Phelip. We will have the same public child-bed practices, and there will be the initial Blooding Ceremony. It is unlikely you will have the same quantity of offspring as Minuet. Our heir will age normally. Raising them to continue my Seelie cause will be priority. Minuet says the mingling of our bloodlines will create a power the world has never seen."

"So our match is made with the goal of breeding powerful children?" Silvine asked. The wine had stolen all her tact.

"Fair One, I have waited centuries for the birth of a woman whose powers will complement mine. Ours are opposite powers, and both are incredibly strong. I expect you to bear powerful children, but I am thrilled at the prospect of having *you*." Guval slowed the circles he rubbed around her ring.

"I suppose that does make you better than many of the human lords, who marry solely to breed." Silvine paused for a moment, thinking. "What's The Blooding Ceremony?"

"It is a sacred ceremony that will solidify our union, one heart in two bodies. It will happen the night of our wedding, according to custom. It will bind you to me forever." Guval's voice had grown soft.

"That's... incredibly vague."

"You said that to me once before, Silvine, before I ever laid eyes on you, before I claimed you as mine. Do you regret the way things unfolded that day?"

Silvine laughed until hiccups set in, and she held her breath to stop them.

Her betrothed, her king, raised a red-gold brow in response.

Brutal honesty would not help. "My king, I do not regret becoming your betrothed."

Guval shook his head. "You're holding back. Elaborate."

"Despite the benefits I just listed, defeating both the puca and the felipentis aren't fond memories."

Guval squeezed her hand once more. "Watching you face off with some of the deadliest creatures in The Realm, things of nightmares and horror stories, is not my favorite thing. There will be more bloodshed, but all for the good of our people. The bards shall write ballads about your victories. And, one day, I will blood you and claim you for my bride."

"So, I'm your assassin-bride?" Silvine asked.

In a heartbeat, Guval appeared on his knees before her. He took her hands into his soft, uncalloused ones. The attention felt good, but her chest constricted uncomfortably. Slowly, painstakingly, Guval kissed his way from the tips of her fingers all the way up her arm. His mouth found its way to her neck, and he planted countless kisses there. She felt as though she couldn't breathe, and tingles ricocheted throughout her body.

"Silvine, allow me to show you what kind of bride you will be," he murmured. His hands began to shake.

The dissonant clanging of his magic unsettled her. She willed herself to remain calm. This man was going to be her husband. "Are you sure?" she asked breathily.

He sighed. "You aren't making this easy. I am quite sure about you. You—you're going to be my redemption." Guval cupped her face as he kissed her with urgency. His mouth persisted until Silvine gave in, kissing him back. She ran her hands through his lion's mane of hair, the one she'd been dying to touch since the day she first laid eyes upon him. It felt coarser than she'd imagined.

He reached for her hips as he kept his lips on hers, forcing her mouth open with his tongue. Rising, Guval lifted her by her hips as she wrapped her legs around his waist. Her heartbeat began to slow. He pulled his head away, letting out a loud gasp.

He loosened his grip on her, allowing her to slide to her feet. "I cannot take this further, and it kills me because I want to claim every bit of you as *mine*," he murmured. He wiped at his nose, pulling his hand away to reveal droplets of blood.

Silvine took a step back, filling her lungs with air she'd been missing. "Did I hurt you?"

Guval squared his shoulders. "No, not at all. I think I may have breathed in too much of the salt air. I will have Minuet attend to me. It is nothing, I am sure. We will have many more passionate moments."

She cocked her head, wanting to press him further, but thought better of it. The thought of ardent love that left her breathless sounded hopelessly romantic, but the experience had jarred her. Guval called for a guard, who returned her to her chamber.

Her day with the king only made the dread heavier. Silvine tried to brush it aside. Rather than gleaning answers or even comfort from Guval, she had added public birthing, the mysterious Blooding Ceremony, and whether or not her betrothed drank blood to her list of concerns.

A part of her fumed at the way Taran Dando had successfully planted seeds of doubt in her mind. Just as he planted little flowers in her palms, so too were his words taking root in her head.

Nothing seemed amiss during supper at the dining hall. Silvine was seated at the left of Guval for the first time ever. Ever since she defeated the felipentis, she was no longer treated as invisible, but she inspired hushed whispers when she passed. Perhaps, after she lived at Court for a decade or two, they would accept her enough to have a conversation.

Phelip, Minuet, and the new baby were notably absent, likely resting in their chambers, making the most of their two weeks together as their child grew.

On any other night, Silvine would have been elated to be moved to a better spot. All she could think of, though, was a blood feast in celebration of that new baby's birth the night before. She scanned the walls, the floors, and the tables for signs of leftover vital fluids. None were to be found.

A red and green scaled Fae, with delicate wings at his back, was seated to Guval's right. Silvine had seen him a few times in the dining hall and the alcoves of the throne room. Guval referred to him as Lord Tylon.

"Tell me, Consort-to-Be," Lord Tylon finally asked, once their plates had been cleared in preparation for dessert, "do you have the power to bring back the dead?"

Silvine's jaw dropped. "Lord Tylon, are you asking if I'm a necromancer?"

Guval paused in the middle of his sip of wine, studying the lady on his left and the lord to his right.

"You can call the power whatever you'd like. The rules of magic, for every magical being I've encountered in my centuries of life, insist that magic and Life cannot be created out of nothing. Yet, you managed to spring forth Life out of torches. You brought long dead branches back to life. Can you do it with living creatures as well?" Tylon doubled down, staring at her in a way that made her shudder.

Silvine paused, avoiding the mental picture of him feasting on blood the night before. This man, while a lord, would someday rank beneath her if he didn't already. She had been forced to give away so much of herself to so many people.

It felt wrong to explain how her powers worked or admit that one of those branches had the tiniest grain of Life within it.

The silence grew heavier. Guval put his cup down, waiting for his betrothed's reply.

"That sounds quite unsavory. I am uninterested in corpses," Silvine said with feigned boredom.

"You will have to get over that kind of backward thinking soon. Bloodshed abounds around here," Tylon sneered.

The king cleared his throat.

Tylon bowed his head. "War is coming. Learning to bring Life to that which has lost it would make you truly *useful* to the cause."

"Are you saying she does not already have use?" Guval asked, his tone sharp.

"I cannot lie, Your Majesty. She has use, I am sure, to you. She does not have much use to me unless she increases the power of Court and defeats our enemies."

Gleaming, white teeth were bared at Lord Tylon in response. Silvine started, picturing Guval sinking his teeth into the necks of his enemies.

"I will be retiring to my rooms now," Lord Tylon said, rising from his chair.

A predatory smile spread across Guval's face. "I am glad to see your wisdom has returned."

Silvine didn't speak a word the rest of her time in the dining hall. Mercifully, Guval was called away to attend to something, and no one objected when she pushed away from the table to walk to her chamber alone.

CHAPTER 27

TRUTH IN CAVERNS

Silvine

After sunset, Taran appeared in Silvine's chambers. He took her by the hand and whisked her away to the base of the mountains.

"You'll find that appropriate attire changes your entire experience," he said, nodding at her outfit in approval.

"You sound like Phelip," Silvine said. She tried to ignore the nausea from the rush of moving through space at a sudden pace.

He rolled his eyes. "Phelip is nothing more than a court ornament. Wearing clothing with a useful purpose is life-changing. His opinion on appropriate attire revolves around whether or not the fabrics and colors align with his made-up rules."

Taran took her hand once more. "We must go. There's so much I want to show you before dawn."

"Would Guval approve?" Silvine wasn't sure why she'd even asked. Being around her betrothed had made her feel so *weird*, every interaction adding to the growing heaviness that weighed her down.

That irreverent smirk found its way back to his face. "Would you like to go ask? I don't hold my breath in anticipation of his approval, nor should you."

"But you're his *General of Intelligence*," Silvine said. She hated the way she let her words slip out so hatefully sometimes. "I assumed the two of you were as thick as thieves."

"All my position means is that I am in the business of secrets. Most would say I'm quite good at it. Some secrets are useful to the crown; some I keep locked away, just for me."

Silvine wanted to mock him, but he interrupted before she could. He tugged at her with impatience as the world slipped away in a blur.

The nausea she'd fought the first time caught up with her the second time. She clutched her knees and vomited the moment the world became lucid again. Even though she'd been on the Fae side of reality for months now, she still found her heightened senses jarring. It felt impossible to comprehend how clear the world was, how defined the sounds were, how keen the scents were. The human realm, with its mortality, lacked sensory beauty, but it was easier to understand.

She looked up at Taran, expecting him to smirk at her, but a look of something like concern crossed his face as he studied her hunched form. He gestured at the puddle of vomit between her feet, and it vanished.

"My, my," he said, "you must become more accustomed to my methods of travel. A powerful queen such as yourself can't be felled by something as minor as traveling through the fabric of The Realm."

Silvine glowered as she steadied her breaths. Looking around, she realized they were at the entrance of a cave. The moon and stars bathed the stone around them in white light. The drop-drop-drop of trapped moisture in the distance was the only sound she could hear. She rose to her full height. "A powerful queen such as myself should kill the kinds of creatures who can manipulate reality like that."

Taran slapped a hand over his heart. "Come now. When you threaten me, you sound like your precious king. Are you intimidated by my power, Regina?"

"No." She had a variety of feelings about Taran, but she'd never feared him.

"It's time you learn a truth the ancients held dear. The best of the Fae are those who embrace others' gifts and work together. If we slaughter those who scare us, rather than working with them, we only feed an endless loop of Death and destruction."

"So, what did you just do with my mess?"

"I sent it elsewhere."

"What does that mean?" Silvine demanded. "You didn't simply... vanish it?"

"Oh, *Little Queen*," Taran drawled. "The laws of The Realm dictate that we cannot create or destroy things. We can simply change their form. In this case, I sent it somewhere else. I didn't give much thought to where it went."

"Is someone going to just wake up to find vomit on their floor?"

Taran chuckled. "Perhaps."

Silvine dipped her chin. She pitied anyone who experienced the horror of finding a puddle of vomit on the floor. A small part of her hoped it would end up on Ophelia's bedroom floor in Luteche.

Taran took her hand once more, and Silvine winced, anticipating the indescribable, nauseating blur of traveling with him. The playfulness left his tone. "I hope you never flinch again when I touch you. Take my hand and walk with me, Regina. I am trying to lead you through this dark cavern. I would never willingly cause you pain."

She wasn't sure what to make of his words. Taran seemed to be in the mood to impart truths, to be understood. He'd transformed from the most irritating, irreverent person she knew to a sage sharing wisdom. She hated the way he could read her, the way he called her out, the way he just knew things.

"Wonderful, *Taran*. Where are you taking me?"

"Back to your usual attitude, I see. You really should spend more time in my company instead of with avartaghs and mortal vultures. You wouldn't have to point your verbal daggers at everyone so much if you *felt* as safe and powerful as you truly *are*," Taran said. "Now, come, we don't have a moment to waste."

Silvine allowed him to hold her hand, the callouses from where he held blades at odds with the gentleness of his touch.

They walked in silence, farther into the dark depths of the cave. Silvine was reminded of Luc Ollam's home. *Luc was a gracious host,* she admitted to herself, *even if he was a kidnapper.* This place was nothing like Luc's. It was damp and dark.

A light flickered in the distance. They made their way toward it. Silvine resisted the urge to ask if it was safe to walk toward the light, knowing Taran would either make a joke or share more philosophical ramblings.

"You know I can withstand all the verbal blows you send my way, but tonight, please try to approach others with a more open mind than you give me," Taran whispered in her ear. She squeezed his hand in acknowledgment, a little more firmly than she had meant to.

Her obsidian always warmed around him, most likely a physical representation of the irritation he stoked within her.

As they approached, the flickering light grew, showcasing all the illuminations around the room: individuals holding torches, a glowing female, and a will o' the wisp. A quick head count told Silvine there was at least a score of people.

"It is the queen," the glowing female said. Although her skin was a rich sepia, she emitted a green glow from head to toe. The crowd fell to their knees in response to her announcement.

"The Earth loves its own!" the crowd shouted.

"The Heart sees the Earth for what it truly is," Taran cried. He gestured with the hand that wasn't holding Silvine's, and they all rose to their feet.

Silvine remembered the words of the crone in the village of Ainmean, an eternity ago. The same words Gilla used to comfort her. *The Earth loves its own.*

"I am not a queen *yet,*" Silvine corrected.

"Our queen is obstinate." Taran winked. "Are we ready for our night's labors?"

A slight male with dark eyes and dark wings stepped forward.

Luc. "It is a pleasure to meet again." He tipped his head in Silvine's direction.

"You," Silvine growled. Before she had a moment to think, she found herself launching at him, drawing the dagger from her side. Her white light flared at her fingertips.

In his smooth, unfathomably quick way, Taran managed to wedge himself between Silvine and the male. "Now, Regina, you may not stab Luc."

"He held me captive," she argued.

"I was a gracious host who kept you *safe*," Luc corrected. She lifted the hand that held her dagger in response. All the air in the cavern disappeared in a breath, and everyone went deadly silent.

Taran grabbed her wrist before she could swing downward, and in the same swift movement, he stepped so close she could feel his breath in her ear. "Luc is a friend. There is so much you do not know. Stop letting your human feelings rule you."

She exhaled sharply.

"Have I ever let harm come to you?"

"No."

"That's my Regina," he purred. "Now, sheathe your dagger and play nice. I'd hate to have to return you to your room. You belong out here, not in there, but I won't let you do this."

Begrudgingly, Silvine decided it was best to comply. She was vastly outnumbered and didn't know where Taran had taken her. While she had powers and keen Fae senses, she had no doubt this band of Fae had been honing their skills for longer than she'd been alive. She also didn't want Guval to know she had threatened one of his subjects.

Luc peered over Taran's shoulder. "It is unfortunate that you hold a grudge against me. I assure you, it was for your benefit. You wouldn't have survived much longer on your own. It is a pleasure to cross paths under better circumstances."

The glowing female strode up to them, and Luc retreated with a sweeping bow. Silvine was still seething, wondering how Luc could be a friend or believe his actions had benefited her. She was starting to think of the best ways to berate him when the glowing female spoke.

"I served alongside your mother for many years," she said. Her voice was rich and earthy.

"*My* mother?" Silvine asked.

Taran, now back at her side, laughed. She wished she could stomp on his toes, but that was, unfortunately, probably an unwise choice.

"Yes, I served Pulchra, the last Modrona. It is an honor to serve you now."

Pulchra, the last Modrona. No longer surprised by the new developments that changed her understanding of the world, Silvine was coming to accept the truth of who her mother had been. "I'd like to learn more about The Modrona. I've only ever heard tales of her from my—my friend's nurse as a child." Her stomach twisted at thoughts of the Fluellen family.

The glowing woman's face lit up even more, defying what Silvine would have thought possible. "I'd love to—"

Taran cut her off, "But time is of the essence. On to Luteche." He cupped his hands around his mouth. "We are all met. Onward, friends!"

The band of Fae formed neat rows that reminded Silvine of a military unit. Their steps echoed through the cavern. The glowing female fell back, walking to Silvine's left. Taran remained close to her right side, although he didn't touch her. He surely sensed her irritation.

"I'm Phos Lumos," the glowing female said as they walked.

Silvine tilted her head. "I'm Silvine. No one ever introduces themselves with their full names here."

Phos winked. "In The Faerie Realm? True names are currency here. I know. I will gladly pay my dues to The Modrona. Any true servant to the Earth would."

Taran watched Phos intently. Silvine could feel the intensity of his gaze and heard the melancholy song in his blood speed up. Phos's blood sang a sweet, uplifting song. While completely different in mood, the tempo was identical. Playing around with her ability had allowed her to start picking up on the music of others without being overwhelmed by so many sounds all at once.

Silvine wondered if there was some kind of attraction between Phos and Taran. If so, it would certainly make for an awkward march to Luteche.

Phos flashed her white teeth. "You know, Silvine, you couldn't have a better companion as you adapt to the endless complexities of Fae life. I don't know anyone as loyal, and he is such an accomplished fighter."

Yes, Silvine thought. Her suspicions were correct. There was definitely something going on between the two of them.

She snorted. "I would hardly call him a companion, and Taran seems only to enjoy irritating me. If I had more sense, I would tell him to leave me alone."

Taran remained silent.

The atmosphere grew serious, and Phos's glow dimmed. "I understand why you want to murder Luc. You couldn't possibly understand his motives, and he bothers me, too. But you must never, *never* turn away from him. He's The *Euron*. Your powers and his are meant to work together. It is in your f—"

Silvine was about to retort that Taran could be considered a *moron*, but he was certainly *not* whatever -ron word Phos had just used. Before she could share her clever comment aloud, the scenery stole her attention. Ahead, the glow of moonlight lit the cave. They had reached the other side.

"May the work we do tonight serve the Earth and its Heart," Taran called out. All at once, the Fae drew their blades and repeated his call.

CHAPTER 28

THE DARK SIDE OF LUTECHE

Silvine

"No matter what occurs, no matter the *feelings* that pop up, I need you to stay by my side," Taran said, quickening his pace to catch up to the rest of his crew. "I'm going to make sure everyone knows their roles. For now, stay by Phos's Earth-irritating side and ignore anything she says about me."

His words felt like a challenge. Silvine hoped that she could stick by Phos long enough to hear some of Taran's secrets.

Everyone in the group followed Taran's orders without question. Silvine found it difficult to reconcile Taran the leader with Taran, the Fae who irritated her endlessly, but the evidence was laid bare. Every fiber of her being wanted to defy him, but these people recognized him as their leader. She wondered if Guval had made him the leader of this group or if this was one of the secrets he kept for himself.

Phos cocked her head. "Oh, Silvine. You don't realize it, do you?"

The immediate familiarity and friendship was new. Ana had been a built-in friend, their bond's foundation formed when they were infants.

"Realize what?" Silvine asked, half-focused on watching Taran clasp Fae males' shoulders and give what she presumed were instructions, complete with dramatic hand gestures to illustrate his point.

"Nothing. I'm just being a mysterious Fae right now. It doesn't appear you fell for my tricks." Her eyes glimmered conspiratorially. Silvine didn't know how to respond. "Congratulations on your betrothal to the King of Donadais."

"I—thank you."

"Are you ready for all that a marriage to the king entails?" Phos raised a brow.

Silvine lowered her voice to a whisper and asked the question that had been eating her alive all day. "Do you know what The Blooding Ritual is? It sounds rather terrifying."

"You *should* be terrified of it. If I were in your place, I'd use all my wiles, magic, and *resources*"—Phos tilted her head toward Taran —"to get out of that particular ritual."

Silvine sucked in a breath. Phos's warning only amplified her preexisting fears. She, however, wasn't sure how the king's General of Intelligence could possibly be a resource that would free her from whatever the ritual entailed.

Taran appeared beside her again before she could ask more questions. He hefted a large sack over his shoulder. "Our work tonight is distribution. Phos, you're with Luc. He'll share the details with you." Phos gave Silvine a radiant grin and walked away. Silvine frowned. She'd wanted more time with Phos.

"Where are we going? What are we distributing?"

"To the dark side of Luteche. The side you weren't shown on your first visit," Taran said, grabbing her hand once again. "If you exhale when the world first gets blurry, you won't retch when we arrive. Inhaling gives you air to take from one part of the world to another, which your body will think is *wrong*. Don't do that. Ready, exhale."

She narrowed her eyes. That information would have been helpful to receive weeks before.

In a whir, they'd gone from the cave entrance to an empty,

narrow street. Four-story buildings, made of crumbling stone and rotting wood, towered over them on either side. The buildings seemed ready to collapse from exhaustion.

"Hood up," Taran whispered. Silvine covered her head with the hood of the cloak he'd given her.

The largest rats Silvine had ever seen scurried through the gutters, chirping to one another, carrying morsels of old food they'd pilfered from some unfortunate soul in their paws and mouths. The combined stench of human waste, rot, and desperation made her stomach clench.

She reached out with her magic to see if there were any traces of magic around this part of Luteche. She heard the hum of her own melody, the melody she knew now was an echo of the last Modrona's, and the quiet of Taran's melancholy one in the distance, but otherwise, the area was devoid of magical creatures.

The silence was broken by the squalling of a babe from one of the houses and the drunken yelling of a man across the street. He'd come out of his house, filthy and stumbling, and started yelling and waving around a bottle.

"Come on out, Etienne. Ye took my woman. Come ou' an' fight me like a proper man would," he taunted.

Silvine cast a glance at Taran. One side of his mouth curled upward. "Are you afraid, Regina?"

"I'm a little nervous for myself, but more worried for Etienne."

"If he so much as looks at you the wrong way, I will deal with him. And although I've never needed to put you through a trial to realize it, you and I both know you can summon your tremendous power and deal with him yourself." Taran patted her shoulder in mock condescension.

"Now you're willing to defend me. For weeks in the forest, you left me to suffer," Silvine muttered. He jutted his chin out, ignoring her, and strode toward the drunken man. Etienne, wherever he was, had wisely chosen to stay out of sight.

"Is something the matter?" Taran called out.

Swaying, the drunk made his way over. Silvine stayed safely behind Taran, ready to watch him get clobbered by a man toting around a brown, glass bottle.

"Iss somethin' you may be able t' hannel for me, Fae!" the drunk shouted.

His acknowledgment of Taran as a Fae piqued Silvine's interest. While it was an unspoken belief in Ainmean that the forest contained Old Ones, none of the humans she knew would have acknowledged one, let alone asked for their help. Most of them knew better than to entrust the Fae with anything but the cruel work of tricking them. *Or entrapping them into promising their firstborn*, she thought.

"Is that so?" Taran murmured, crossing his arms.

"I wan' you to find the man what's taken *my wife*," the man pleaded. "Etienne's his name, an' I wan' you to swap him out for a changeling. My wife'll come back to me. Etienne'll be a right good changeling, I know 't. Truly, I need the help of The Old Ones."

Taran stroked his chin thoughtfully. "I will offer you a bargain."

"You 'ill? I knew you would." The man hiccuped. "What iss 't?"

"I will give you a feast from this sack over my shoulder." Taran tilted his head backward. "If you give me that bottle of liquor you're carrying. You'll find that Etienne's charms pale in comparison to the promise of a full belly."

"A'right." The man shook his wobbly head up and down. To Silvine's surprise, he handed the bottle over to Taran, who had already reached into his sack and grabbed out a smaller sack within it.

The man pawed open the sack, and his face lit up. "Iss a feast! My woman'll think we're the finest folk on the block. I'll no' forget the graciousness o' the Seelie court." He lifted his chin toward Silvine. "Th' Earth loves iss own." He stumbled back into his home.

Silvine gaped at Taran. His gesture was kind, taking drink away from a man who clearly didn't need it. With a twirl of his fingers, Taran whisked the bottle away to another part of the world.

Before Silvine could say a word, a door creaked open. Two sets of eyes peeked out at them. Taran whirled around and softened his gaze. He looked gentle and friendly. "You can come out, little ones. We bring gifts."

Two small, thin children in tattered clothes crept outside. Taran lowered his sack and knelt. "Regina, can you give these two plenty of supplies?"

Silvine's throat went dry, choked up at the sight of the children. She reached into the bag, pulling out a sack for each child. She could smell the fresh bread, salted meat, and a hint of citrus.

Their eyes lit up. "We will not forget the graciousness of the Seelie court." They each bowed.

Taran reached out to tousle their hair. "Now, remember, don't make bargains or accept gifts from any others of our kind. I'm friendly, but the others—"

"Are not," the tallest child finished.

"Very good. I am glad you remember my words of wisdom." Taran laughed with a softness Silvine had never heard before. "Now, back inside. These streets can be dangerous."

For at least an hour, Silvine and Taran made their way down the filthy streets, giving out supplies to elderly women, beggars, children, and anyone else who dared approach them. All the people seemed to know not to say "thank you," something even Silvine struggled to remember, but they all promised to remember the "graciousness of the Seelie court."

The two of them reached a dead end in the narrow street at the same time their sack emptied. Pausing for a moment, Taran studied the street. Silvine took the opportunity to reflect upon what they'd just experienced. She'd never seen so much hunger and suffering in a single place. This truly *was* the dark side of Luteche.

Taran sneered, "When you first came to Luteche, I imagine you saw the picture of perfection, a testament to Guval's might. Beautiful, immaculately clean white stone at the square erected in his honor, complete with a statue as a testament to his greatness."

"I thought—I thought the people must live a better life than the commoners in Ainmean. My father takes better care of his people than this. This is—" Silvine felt hot tears streaming down her face.

Taran was before her in a heartbeat, wiping the tears from her face. "This is not what it should be."

Silvine sniffed, glancing up at Taran. "Why?"

"Why is it this way? Well, because—"

"No," Silvine murmured. "Why did you wipe my tears away?"

"I can't have people knowing their Regina cries. I love the vulnerability, but our relationship is special, after all."

She looked down at her feet, avoiding eye contact. "Why do you call me that?"

"It's what you are to me. Haven't you studied the language of The Old Ones? You really ought to *study* it."

Taran snapped his head to the side before he could continue waxing poetic about studying The Old Tongue. Something seemed to have caught his attention that was beyond Silvine's perception. He put his hands on her shoulders. "Time to go. Exhale."

Silvine blinked and found herself atop a grassy knoll. A million stars lit up the sky. A silver sliver of moonlight dangled off to the side. She had never seen so many stars.

Taran's eyes glowed in the moonlight. They were the most unique eyes she'd ever seen, and though she hated to think it, they were the most beautiful.

"Why didn't you tell me to exhale before?" she breathed.

"I didn't realize I had to advise you not to bring air from one part of the world to the next, but I am glad it came to mind. Aren't you?"

Silvine felt a primal urge to snap back at him, but before she could say anything, a glow appeared behind Taran. She braced herself, putting her hand on the dagger strapped to her thigh.

The phosphorescent glow laughed as it turned into Phos, followed by a dozen other Fae who had taken form beside her.

"Well met, *Taran*." She put heavy emphasis on his name.

"Well met, Phos. Well met, all," Taran said. All the Fae bowed in response.

Turning to Silvine, Phos gave a deep bow. "Well met, My Queen."

Before she could bow awkwardly in response, Taran grabbed her arm, firm but gentle. "Just say well met," he whispered. "The Regina does not bow."

"Well met," she murmured.

"How many were saved?" Taran asked, donning the demeanor of a leader.

A male voice replied. "We were able to free fifteen. Luc is routing them through his caves to safety in—"

Taran held up his hand. "Well done," he said. "Now, shall we revel? The night is ours!"

"But it will not last forever!" they responded.

Someone snapped their fingers, and a fire ignited at the top of the knoll. A few Fae grabbed instruments and began to play. Silvine heard a lute and some kind of wooden flute, but the other instruments were unfamiliar to her human ears.

Phos's glow provided the lighting for their festivities. Taran's sack, which had been empty in Luteche, was now filled with silver flasks. He reached in and handed one to each of the revelers.

The Fae began to dance around the fire to the strange, ethereal music. Their dancing was unencumbered by choreography or social mores. It reminded Silvine of the urge her own body had felt to simply move when she'd drank the wine with Guval. It felt like a lifetime ago she'd been on his veranda, yet it was no less than a day.

She thought of the abject poverty the king's subjects lived in. He'd hidden it from her, showing only the most beautiful parts of town and forcing her to endure a surprise reunion with Ophelia. Silvine wanted to believe her betrothed was oblivious. What she knew of her father as a leader, however, made her certain that Guval was completely aware of his people's suffering.

Why is Taran running interference, she wondered. It made no sense that the General of Intelligence would organize an aid party to provide relief to Guval's subjects and "save" fifteen people, whatever that meant. Taran hadn't wanted her to hear many of the details. None of the puzzle pieces fit.

Taran danced his way back around the fire to Silvine. "Why aren't you partaking?" he asked.

She shrugged. "No one asked me to."

"In any space I bring you to, it is implied that I want you to partake. I opened your eyes to some harsh realities tonight. Allow me to open your eyes to the simple pleasures of being a garden variety Fae. This is what you were made to do. The ancients reveled under the stars every night."

He thrust a silver flask into her hands. "Drink," he commanded. She threw the flask back and took a gulp.

To her surprise, the liquid burned her throat. This was nothing like what she'd drunk on Guval's veranda or in Luc's cave. She coughed as it went down.

Taran raised an eyebrow. "Expecting Faerie wine?"

"I wasn't expecting to drink *fire* tonight."

"I brought whiskey. I didn't think you'd be up for more Faerie wine anytime soon. Won't you dance?" There was a hint of vulnerability in his eyes as he searched her face. It made her forget that he knew about what had transpired between her and Guval that morning.

"I don't know this dance." What she meant was, *I feel self-conscious and unsure of myself.*

Taran gestured toward the sky. "Look up at the stars." The stars sparkled throughout the sky, more lovely than any she'd seen before in the human realm. Nothing there was as beautiful as even the most mundane things in The Faerie Realm.

Silvine gasped, watching a star shoot across the sky, leaving a trail of silvery fire in its wake.

"Listen to the music," Taran said. Silvine cocked her head, puzzled. "I know you can hear it, but I want you to truly listen."

Her hips began to sway of their own volition. The song, one she'd never heard before, felt like home. She fought the urge to take Taran's hand and join the others in dance.

The ghost of a smile crossed his lips. "The Great Silver Bear wrote this."

"The what?" Silvine's eyes widened.

"Yes, The Great Silver Bear was once an accomplished musician, philosopher, and king of the lands your father holds a Premiership over. I am sure you were told he was a *literal* bear who terrorized humankind and that you've celebrated his death every year with your people." A humorless laugh fell from his lips. "He was slaughtered senselessly by a power-hungry traitor."

Although it threatened her worldview, Silvine believed what he was saying. The story of a man called The Great Silver Bear made far more sense than celebrating the death of a mere bear, which meant her ancestor had slaughtered a king. It made her the descendant of a usurper.

"You come from a line of the most powerful females this realm has ever known," Taran murmured.

"I don't know my maternal line. I know I come from a father who put my life in danger in the hopes that, by some chance, I had some kind of powers that the king would find desirable. I come from a man who does not care."

The song took a sudden, tense turn. The dancing picked up, the people growing frantic in their movements.

"Does it ever strike you, Regina? Great men have lived and died. Lesser men have done the same. Art has been made, people have suffered, people have loved, people have survived. This very moment we're experiencing? Others have lived a thousand moments identical to this one, and yet, it's a paradox. There will never be another moment like this one. It's a beautiful contradiction, a reminder to *live*. We are not just sums of our ancestors. You have the potency of two lines with great power. Only you can decide what to do with this moment. Use your potential."

Silvine studied his face in the moonlight. "Have you ever thought that you have the potential to mind your own business?"

Before he could give a response, Phos twirled up to them with outstretched arms. "Let's dance," she cried, taking Silvine by the hand.

Silvine complied, her feet moving before her mind could catch up.

As they danced around a fire under the starlight, she lost herself to the music. Her body moved as though it had spent every night before with these people, in this moment beneath the stars. The rigidity of Ainmean and Court fell away. She felt alive, deeply so.

CHAPTER 29

A BLOOD SPORT

Silvine

The following weeks felt unusually boring for Silvine. Without Phelip's daily lessons and tours, there was little to do. Paternity leave took him away from his normal Court duties and insistence upon educating Silvine in all matters of Court life.

Guval had told her at dinner one day, with softness in his voice, that he was quite busy with politics and would be spending most of his days in the strategy room and would have to travel for a few days along the coast. She was escorted by Phelip to the dining hall for dinners, where none dared speak to her after Lord Tylon's spat with the king. She only socialized with her attendant, who avoided conversation whenever possible.

Someone had placed a musty, yellowed tome entitled *A Treatise on The Old Language* on her table while she dined one night. She found paper and a quill in one of her drawers and spent most of her hours studying the language. Language was meant to be shared, however, and studying it in a vacuum was a harsh reminder of her isolation.

Taran was undoubtedly the one who had gifted her the book. He was so good at leaving her crumbs of hope and then failing to be part of the big picture. Silvine wanted to taunt him with the new insults she'd learned in The Old Language, but she didn't even spot him at dinner.

The air in the castle was stale, like the stillness of water before a great rapid. Change was imminent. Silvine was simply unsure of what changes were to come.

Finally, at the dusky end of a dull fortnight, she decided it was time to go exploring. She put on a loose, gauzy pants set and delicate slippers, both of which she'd found in her wardrobe. Strapping her dagger to her thigh, awkwardly bunching the loose fabric of her pants in the process, she crept out of her room.

She had no idea why she felt the urge to leave her chambers on this night, at this particular moment, but she refused to acknowledge the *what ifs*. She reminded herself that she was the king's betrothed, a protected position even if everyone at Court snubbed her, and she was powerful enough to defend herself.

The entire castle was eerily silent. No humming in another's blood called to her own. She traipsed past the wide entry to the throne room, noting movements and sighs in a few of the alcoves, declining to think of any activities that may have been occurring within their partial enclosure. The dais, surrounded by torchlight, glowed in solitude. There remained only one throne.

She crept through the barren courtyard, through another hallway, wandering aimlessly. Nene would have cautioned against young ladies wandering anywhere, let alone in a castle controlled by The Old Ones. What Nene had failed to realize was that Silvine herself *was* an Old One. She had the gift of a clever tongue and could wield her bright, white light against any enemies who threatened her.

Overt rebellion and self-assuredness were new for Silvine. She embraced it as she continued, not knowing where her path would lead.

By a stroke of luck, the hallway she'd chosen led to a hefty wooden door. As she opened it, she felt fresh, cool night air. It smelled like the salt of the angry sea below. The stars above didn't shine as brightly as they had when she was with Taran, but she didn't care. The air felt like freedom. She took off in a sprint.

The humidity made the dusty red rock cling to her pant legs and useless slippers. She kept running. Her lungs ached from the exertion. While her body begged her to stop, she used her willpower to carry on. Beneath her feet, she felt the sharp stones. Before everything she'd endured, before she'd channeled her Fae nature, she would have flinched with every painful leap. She was different now. Feeling the rocks beneath her feet reminded her that she was alive. She felt connected to the earth and all the beings whose Life forces were tied to it. Though she couldn't sense their individual threads, individual songs, she felt a great harmony of Life. The burning in her lungs subsided.

She stretched out her arms, still running, soaking in the sounds of the waves crashing below her and the hum of Life throughout The Realm. Even if she couldn't feel it in the castle, she was reminded that Life was truly present. A euphoric hope made her soul feel lighter.

Caught up in her reverie, she didn't notice the dark figure rush out from behind a boulder. She didn't realize anyone was coming toward her until strong arms grabbed her from behind. Those arms wrapped around her chest, squeezing her tightly and lifting her feet from the ground. A scream caught in her throat as a hand clamped around her mouth. Her obsidian went ice cold against her skin.

She tried to kick backward, but the person swung her forward, avoiding the brunt of her kick. Their body towered above her, their firm, muscled torso nearly as long as Silvine's entire body. They easily overpowered her. Thoughts of all the ways she could come to physical harm sent her heart racing.

You have powerful magic. You can fight back, she assured herself.

A voice that was not hers whispered in her mind. *The Earth loves its own.*

Worries about being carried away to yet another land made

Silvine's heart pound, but she tried to redirect her thoughts. She would never be a captive or bargaining chip again. She would rather die in the fight than relinquish her autonomy.

She squirmed one last time, attempting to jab an elbow into her captor's ribs. They tightened their hold on her instead. She struggled and wriggled, unable to make any contact.

The Life within her veins thrummed, and she let it wash over her, building and building and building. The presence of the Life all around her, in all The Realm, seemed to sing in support. Finally, she felt her chest warm, and she sent a jolt of light backward.

Her captor gasped as the wind was knocked from their lungs. They let go of her, and she heard them crumple to their knees. Silvine whirled around to identify who had held her.

Golden red hair hung limply over a beautiful face. *Guval.*

"M-my King, I apologize. I—I had no idea."

Guval let out a raspy laugh. "None who have had *any idea* and dared harm me so brutally have lived to tell the tale. Be at peace, Fair One. I know you did not intend to harm your king and future husband." He rose to his feet and took Silvine's hands into his own.

"Why did you grab me like that?"

"I was curious what you'd do," he said, showing her his palms.

Although the adrenaline had worn off, Silvine found her breathing and heart rate had remained elevated. No matter how her mind willed it, her body was never as fast at returning to normal as she'd hoped. The threat of being snatched away, once again, had been too real.

Guval studied her before pulling her close to him. Silvine's hands went to his chest as she braced herself, and he wrapped his arms around her. This embrace was much gentler than when he'd pulled her back against his chest to see what she'd do. Now, he was pure action, showing her what *he* would do. His lips met hers frantically.

He kissed her more thoroughly than she'd ever been kissed in her life. She opened her mouth to him, letting him explore. He moved with urgency, pulling her close, running his hands all along her torso.

There was a trace of Faerie wine in the way he tasted and something coppery.

Silvine knew she should have felt the same urgency that he seemed to, should have run her hands up and down his body the way he was doing to her. He somehow suddenly tangled one hand in her hair as he traced his tongue up and down her neck, inching up the lines of the ears that had once been a hideous reminder of her trauma. He paused to cough.

It felt *wrong*. With Cardoc, even though his kisses were decidedly *less* than Guval's in every possible way, Silvine's heart and body had felt at home. She'd been at ease. He had felt like *hers*. Guval's passion was undeniable. Any female should have felt honored to be the recipient of that kind of kiss.

Yet her heart and mind didn't want it.

Breathless, she pushed herself backward. Guval's eyes fluttered open, and he gasped, the same way he had the last time they'd kissed. *Skies above.* For a moment, Silvine thought she saw crimson mingled with emerald in his irises. It must have been the illusion of the dark night because they once again began to glow in their rich, dark green shade. It illuminated the sculpted lines of his face.

He cocked his head. "Was that too much for you, Fair One?" he asked, grasping for her hand once more.

Silvine gave it over limply. "My senses are on edge after you... apprehended me."

He bowed his head apologetically. "I forget just how magnificent and delicate and full of Life you are. You must forgive me. Finding you here made me give in to my baser instincts, and I simply had to have a taste of you. I promise that we will not go farther than this until The Blooding Ritual."

Silvine silently chided herself for being so foolish. Women alone in nature at night were certainly at the mercy of those they encountered. She'd been fortunate her betrothed had found her, but his show of desire left her feeling unwell. Was it any wonder she didn't know what to do with the king of The Realm?

"You have passions for me?" she asked, trying to steady her breathing.

"That is putting it mildly. I cannot wait to claim you as mine, to blood you, to let the world know your powers and mine have mingled and joined for all eternity. However, we have something more important to discuss." Guval frowned. "Why are you running outside the castle grounds, in your finery, with a dagger strapped to your thigh?"

Skies above and Earth below, the dagger is out, she thought. Silvine had hidden it from him in Court, and now he knew.

"I wasn't aware I was forbidden to leave my chamber," she muttered.

"I never forbade it," Guval said. "I am curious why such a powerful lady would feel such a simple, old dagger was going to protect her. Why did you come out here?"

Silvine pulled her dagger from her thigh and studied the wings on its handle, avoiding his question. "I carry my weapon in case strange men attack me in the darkness. Do you favor the new to the ancient?"

Guval kissed her cheek, leaning away from the dagger. "I favor progress and improvement. The smiths in my forges could make something far more fitting for my consort, my queen, than that old scrap of metal."

Silvine set her jaw. "That old piece of metal is an heirloom more precious to me than most things."

"You are adept at changing the subject, Fair One. *Why* are you out here?" The edge in his voice grew sharper.

"I am out here because, as you said, it is not forbidden."

"You're my future consort, not my prisoner. I would prefer you at least notify me or one of my trusted ones if you are leaving, and ideally, you should bring one of us along. Right now, the Unseelie creatures are more active than usual."

The words had no sooner left Guval's lips than gray clouds had concealed the moon, and an unearthly moaning reverberated behind them. It seemed to shake the very mountains. Silvine jumped at the sound.

"We stay together," Guval said, setting his shoulders. "That is a troop of bananach. It is well that I found you when I did. Your powers are needed."

Silvine spun around to see three floating, ragged creatures wailing in the distance, probably forty yards away. A sickly, purplish aura shone from their tattered forms. All three of their mouths were open, wailing, as blood dripped from them. In the claws of the middle bananach was a black-clad guard, his body twitching and mangled.

Guval strode forward, arms outstretched as if he meant to draw in the dreadful creatures.

The biggest of the bananach screeched, "It... is... Death... come... to... see... the... death... we... give..." Where eyes should have been, gaping black holes homed in on Guval. The sound of Silvine's heartbeat boomed in her ears, and she froze in place.

A breeze blew by, wafting the acrid scent of carrion to her nostrils. She willed herself to breathe through her mouth. Guval needed her powers, not her retching.

"You have slaughtered one of my guards, I see," Guval said, his voice carrying across the darkness. "You fail to see that I am not merely Death anymore."

"You... have... The... Modrona..." the middle bananach shrieked. "But... soon... The... Modrona... will... have...*you.*"

Silvine's throat grew dry. A montage of her father's warnings about overpowering a husband, along with her mother's call to use her powers, played on repeat in her head.

The far left bananach snatched the shredded guard's body from its companion, took one last, bloody bite from the corpse, and threw it to the ground with a sickening thud. The squelch of blood and organs hitting the dusty ground made Silvine gag.

A whir of motion beside Silvine startled her. She let the power in her blood flare. The whir turned into Taran, whose gaze remained

218

focused on the screeching bananach in front of them. He seemed unfazed by both the stench and the ear-splitting sounds.

A cackle left the lips of the left bananach as they hovered closer. Its gaze shifted to Taran. Silvine felt herself draw closer to him, protectively.

"Only... when... *he*... wins... her... will... victory... occur."

Black mist drifted from Guval's fingertips toward the bananach, who shrieked in response. The head of the middle one crunched grotesquely as it fell off. When it hit the ground, the creature continued moaning with its brethren. Their endless shrieking and wailing was deafening.

Ten stealthy, black-clad guards sprinted forward from where they'd been hiding behind a hill, spears at hand. The air buzzed with various forms of magic. Light, blood, and smoke were launched at the bananach. Six deft claws reached out, unfazed, and decapitated each guard.

The sudden silence that followed startled Silvine. The three figures glided closer and closer as a head regenerated from the neck of the third. This was the most fearsome group of monsters she had seen yet.

Guval's posture tensed as he looked back at the figures. His tension made Silvine's muscles clench. If he was frightened, she had even more to fear.

"Dando, guard your future queen," he said.

Taran's eyes glowed in the dark night. "*My Regina*," he whispered, low enough for only her to hear. He turned toward Guval and called out, "At your service!"

The momentary distraction was all the bananach needed. In one swift blow, moving as one body, they knocked Guval aside. He went flying across the flat, desolate terrain. A mere human would have died from the impact.

Silvine's body, muscles still drawn taut, began to quiver. A loud sniff from Taran suggested that he could smell the fear that consumed her.

"Regina, Regina, Regina," he whispered in her ear.

A flower with brilliant, verdant leaves blossomed in her palm. She knew who had summoned it to her, knew he was reminding her of how powerful she was. She stole a peek at Guval's crumpled form. He was pure power, the power of Death, and he had been crumpled into a mere heap.

"His magic cannot possibly defeat the bananach. It's the wrong *kind.* Time to take action."

The blood in Silvine's ears began to build into a roar. The smell of rotting corpses grew closer, ever more sickening, as she thought of all the good and all the beauty in her life: the love at the Fluellen house, dancing with Ana, Guval picking her, and... Taran. Cian. Taran. Dancing beneath the moonlight with him, utterly free. The roar settled into a powerful, steady song.

She opened her eyes, which she hadn't realized she'd closed, to find herself face-to-face with the bananach.

"At... last..." The middle one seemed to sigh. Silvine would have found its tone endearing in any other creature. "A... Modrona... comes... back... to... this... ill-starred... battlefield."

Jutting out her chin, Silvine shot two white beams of light from her palms. The beams struck true, one to the heart and one to the head of the middle bananach. With the most ear-piercing shriek, the being burst into flames. Whatever it was composed of must have been highly flammable. It had combusted to nothing but ashes in a matter of seconds.

The bananach's companions took to squawking, flapping their blood-soaked claws in mid-air.

"We're not done. Keep going," Taran murmured in Silvine's ear.

"The... Modrona... and... her... Wrath... once... more... reunited," the left one howled out. "A... shifting... tide..."

The bananach glided forward and stretched out its bloody claws, so close they nearly scratched Silvine's face. Taran twirled his finger, and a crack of lightning struck the creature. It let out a terrifying yowl, ignited into flames, and was mere ash within moments.

Wrath, Silvine realized. The Wrath of nature itself had been called down upon the head of the bananach that dared come for Silvine, come for the powers of Life. Taran *was* Wrath incarnate. His smugness came from the knowledge that he was retribution itself. He had the right to be so irreverent when he had the power to bring reverence forth at his very fingertips. Silvine felt as though she was seeing him for the very first time.

The smell of ether from the lightning lingered on the breeze. The last remaining bananach went eerily quiet, seeming to be weighing the gravitas of its impending doom. Its black hole eyes honed in on Silvine. "We... were... once... guardians... of... Life... now... chained... to... this... battlefield. Free... me... from... this... existence." It let out a pitiful howl. "Please... Modrona..."

The Modrona within her obliged the request of her subject. Silvine channeled the purest moments in her life, calling forth the deepest light within her, and shot it out at the bananach. It breathed in a final, audible breath before disintegrating to ash.

The chorus of joyful music in Silvine's blood felt as though the very Earth was thanking her for the mercy she'd given—the mercy of using her powers of Life to grant a quick and easy death to creatures who may or may not have deserved it. A crackle of thunder shook the ground at her feet, finally catching up to the flash of lightning Taran had summoned.

Silvine found herself breathless and lightheaded from the exertion. She swayed before falling backward into Taran's arms.

"I've got you. Let the sleep consume you," he murmured softly.

Any thoughts of concern for Guval or what she'd come to see on this barren plain, a land the bananach had called an ill-starred battlefield, vanished.

CHAPTER 30

VENTUS ET ARBOR

Silvine

"Wake, Fair One," a voice murmured in Silvine's ear.

Silvine swam back to the surface of consciousness. She rubbed the sleep from her eyes. Guval's handsome face slowly came into focus. Behind him, Phelip and Minuet's crimson gazes focused on her, unblinking and emotionless.

She groped around her, realizing she was in the comfort of her bed. Words escaped her as she tried to clear her throat. Her tongue felt heavy, and her mouth was dry. Guval produced a goblet, raising it to her lips. "Drink first, then talk."

Silvine took a greedy gulp from the goblet, realizing at once that it must have been Fae wine mixed with one of Minuet's concoctions. The earthy, herbal taste made her stomach lurch. Her attendant breezed in at that moment, bearing a tray with breads, cheeses, and fruits. Guval took the tray, waving the attendant away with a single gesture.

"Eat," he implored, thrusting a piece of crusty bread into her hands. Minuet propped some pillows up, scooting Silvine's body into

a more upright position. Silvine munched on the bread before greedily snatching cheese from the tray her king held.

Guval smoothed her hair. "I told you once before I would never let you succumb to the everlasting darkness. I meant it."

Silvine glanced Guval up and down, assessing him for injury. "Were you hurt?" she asked.

He grinned broadly, flashing his sharp teeth. "I haven't been handled that roughly in centuries, but recovery was easy enough." He rubbed Silvine's arm, which was covered in the long sleeves of a silken sleeping gown. "You, however, have slept for two full days. To have slaughtered three bananach in a matter of seconds is an unheard of feat, and it expended a great deal of your energy. We have all watched over you in shifts to ensure that you didn't take a turn for the worse."

His remark made Silvine thoughtful. "But... aren't the Fae immortal?"

Minuet slithered to the other side of the bed to grasp Silvine's free hand. "I would say you are *quite* immortal. I haven't felt a force of Life this strong in... well, as many centuries as it's been since My Majesty was well and truly knocked out. However, Fae are not impervious to death, sometimes in childbirth, sometimes due to magical overwhelm. Immortal just means that you're harder to kill. My Majesty may be the hardest to kill of all."

Guval's eyes narrowed for a fraction of a second. "Magical over-whelm can be lethal for young Fae, so it is important to ensure that the restoration of energy is a smooth process."

Silvine studied the three of them. She wanted to know how they could watch her so intently, full of concern and care, while the common people of Luteche struggled. They were certainly aware of what went on. Perhaps it was the constant threat of puca, felipentis, bananach, and Skies knew what else that kept them from focusing on the well-being of the commoners.

Phelip cleared his throat. "I am glad to see you've awoken. I am planning my ball, and I could not have our newest member of Court absent. It would be most improper, and you would miss the new dance I have choreographed."

Silvine rolled her eyes. Was that really what he was focusing on? "What about your child?"

Minuet's face grew animated. "A new mage child arrived in Ainmean, to live with a family we honored. Lord Tylon and his wife were gifted the human child that came in the exchange. Its mother had died in childbirth."

Before she could think about her response, Silvine realized she'd curled her upper lip. Phelip coughed politely to cover what she was almost certain was a laugh, while his wife seemed unfazed.

"You haven't heard of the changeling practice?" Minuet asked. "It is a great honor to have your human child spirited away as you are gifted a mage child in exchange. It is growing to be a rare practice these days, but it is a privilege I still like to bestow upon the mortals of The Realm."

As if childbirth itself was not dangerous enough for women of any species, there were actual Fae swapping out children. It did not seem like an honor at all. Silvine tried to block out all the thoughts that would make her spiral down dark paths.

Nothing here is as it seems there, she reminded herself. The sense of honor and code of morals she had grown up with did not apply to the Fae. No matter how she tried, though, she could not shake her human sensibilities or her horror at some of the things they did.

"My father does not believe in mages. He will not allow a changeling to live in his province," she said.

Minuet smiled broadly. "The Premier has changed his mind about the *political advantages* of having a mage in his land. Our child will prove most useful to your dear father."

Silvine felt her throat tighten, unable to swallow. Of course Lord Morair's morals were for sale. Just as he'd wagered an impossible bet on her powers, even now, he was bringing a mage into Ainmean.

Minuet tilted her head in a silent signal and glided across the room. Phelip followed. They slipped out the door wordlessly.

Guval took the opportunity of having Silvine alone to plant a kiss on her lips. "I am in awe of you, my Silvine. Are you sure you are feeling restored?"

Silvine nodded, taking another sip from the goblet. She had to force it down. "I was not injured, so I had nothing to recover but my energy."

He inclined his head. "The Unseelie movements are increasing. Both the creatures of the darkness and the Fae who plot against me are emboldened with each passing day. I have taken to patrolling, which is why I was fortunate enough to meet you when I did. Tell me, are you bored?"

His question felt like a trap. Answering honestly seemed dangerous, but Silvine had never been the best at holding her tongue. The buzz of the Fae wine, which had grown pleasing, loosened her tongue. "I'm glad you asked. I do not enjoy sitting in a bedchamber all the time." She cringed inwardly as the words artlessly tumbled out of her mouth.

Guval took a seat on her bed. "On nights that Phelip and I are off duty from patrol, you and Taran will be on patrol together. He is exceptionally talented at fighting the Unseelie monsters, and I trust he will return what is most precious to me safely. You will fight. Will that satisfy your boredom?"

"Yes," she said. Silently reminding herself that being chosen by the king of The Realm was a privilege, she accepted her fate. If, in exchange, she had to partake in blood sport to keep the very Realm safe, she would. She hated how weak and afraid she often was, how easily triggered her nerves were, and how, even now, she wanted to beg for a life of entertaining adventures and not dangerous ones.

Her father used to say that good alliances came at a price, and one should have always been willing to pay for the most valuable ones. Silvine doubted he imagined her marital alliance would require her to be prepared to fight the creatures from the nightmare stories told by Nene.

"I am so pleased to hear that." Guval kissed her again, tangling his fingers in her hair. "I am sending you to Taran in the dungeons to train."

Knowing the reward her honesty had earned her, Silvine decided to smile pleasantly rather than make a comment about the strangeness of the future queen training in the dungeon.

"One more thing," Guval added as he rose to his feet. He pulled her sheathed dagger from a pocket of his breeches, inspecting it. "While I think it inferior to my future queen, I understand its sentimental value to you. I had it removed from your person when Minuet was attending to you. Now, I return it. I will not keep you away from the small baubles that delight the human half of you."

An ancient dagger that had once belonged to The Modrona hardly seemed like a "small bauble," but Silvine didn't bother to correct the king. Nor did she correct herself, knowing deep down that *she* was now The Modrona. Her husband-to-be gave her one last, charming look before leaving.

Returning to the dungeon through underground tunnels and the bridge across the eerie, purple river, Silvine was reminded of how she'd arrived at Court. As she fought off a concussion, half-starved, Guval had thought it best to thrust her into a trial to prove her power. Proving herself came easier than expected, revealing a power she hadn't realized she'd had—a power she wouldn't have used if Taran hadn't been there to show her the way. She simply wasn't certain she wanted to play assassin for the king.

Amidst screams, groans, and the clanking of iron cell doors opening and closing, Taran sat at a long, wooden table with iron restraints welded onto it. Silvine wondered if the secrets he dealt in were pried out of people on the rough, wooden surface. The wall behind him was lined with numerous metal implements with various sharp edges, gears, and other menacing facets. As she pondered what those implements must have been used for, she struggled to maintain eye contact with Taran Dando, General of Intelligence.

A dark chuckle rumbled across his chest, perhaps realizing what caused her to avoid looking at him. "Have you forgotten who I am?"

"I know who you are, and I will not greet you," she mimicked, training her gaze on her boots.

"It seems you will not make eye contact, either."

His challenge roused the stubbornness within her. She lifted her gaze, catching his irreverent smirk. *Taran is Wrath itself, a promise of retribution to come*, she thought. Although he'd manipulated her at every turn, his Wrath had never been used against her.

"We are to train, I am told," Taran said, "so that we can work together to take patrols around Court's plains."

Silvine crossed her arms, finally able to face him fully. "I was given full credit by the king for slaying the bananach. Care to explain why?"

"*Didn't* you slay them?" Taran countered.

"We both know what happened."

"We are the only two." He pushed his chair back from the table, rising to his feet and swaggering toward her. Although he was one of the most average of the unbearably beautiful Fae, his graceful movements and unshakable arrogance were that of a king—the confidence of someone who could call forth nature's retribution. "We shall remain the only two.

His words bound her to compliance once more. She murmured her agreement, feeling the way her blood sang a little louder. There were so many secrets she kept for him: his Cian alias, the nature of their alleged bargain, and now his power to call forth lightning.

Her eyes darted back to the table. A few drops of red liquid were spattering the ground near the iron restraints. He snapped his fingers, and the table flipped itself over to a smooth, black glass surface. With an additional snap of his fingers, a plate of pastries appeared.

He took a bite of one, offering her another. She shook her head, her appetite gone at the sight of the red splotches.

"You don't need my training in magic," Taran said, his tone infuriatingly casual. "Nor do you need me to chase you around. You did a spectacular job running across the plains in those pathetic little scraps of fabric the other night. We want to preserve your energy for patrol."

"How do you manage to know absolutely everything?" Silvine asked.

"My sources." He shrugged. "So, what shall we do with our time together so that your precious king feels we're being good little subjects?"

She dug into the pocket of her leather pants, producing a small, umber tome. "*Impudens es!*" The English translation of her words was, "You are shameless."

The melancholy melody she was so used to turned into a playful tune, its beat matching Taran's peals of laughter. "Earth below and peace within. You have no idea just how *shameless* I am, Regina. Is that all you've managed to learn from that volume? Insults?"

Silvine shook her head. "*Maxima debetur puero reverentia.*" The greatest respect is owed to a child.

"Ah, so you've also learned some proverbs? That's some of Macha's oracle drivel, no doubt. Have you learned how to speak to the trees yet? The wind?"

"*Ventus et arbores?*" The wind and the trees?

"You're just listing off nouns. Language is best learned through conversation and interaction. I'm glad you've got some vocabulary, although it is disappointing to see your tongue is just as intent on wounding me in The Old Language as it is in your native one." Taran clucked in mock outrage. "We shall work on language during our allotted training time together. It is an invaluable skill, just not exactly the skill the king was assuming we would work on."

The thrill of getting to learn with someone, anyone, filled Silvine with warmth. She tried to ignore the setting of her classroom, where quiet songs of desperation mingled with the stench and bleating of the prisoners that filled the space. The heavy wooden doors, obscuring each cell's contents from her view, were truly something to be thankful for.

228

CHAPTER 31
A QUEEN ON PATROL

Silvine

Nothing exciting happened at Court during daylight hours. Nighttime was the time for sneaky trysts in hidden corners, secret plots in bedchambers, and endless parties that Silvine was not invited to attend. Court slept most of the day and schemed all evening. It made sense that Taran Dando thought it best to make his visits to her at night. Everyone else was occupied with matters of copulating, imbibing, fighting, or a combination of the three.

The first night of their patrol duty, Taran led her through passages of Guval's castle she'd never seen. They traipsed past suites hosting raucous private parties. Taran interrupted a duel between two black-clad guards, the two men exchanging blows over the affections of a scullery maid.

Silvine suspected Taran's detour was meant to show her the lay of the castle. She stole a glimpse at the strategy room in passing. The room had a great table, with a raised-relief map and stone figurines atop it. A head of beautiful red locks sat in a stone chair, back to the doorway, while a svelte figure with scarlet hair leaned in close.

Minuet and Guval must be discussing strategy, Silvine told herself.

She caught a glimpse of Minuet's slender hand, absentmindedly tracing circles along the king's bicep. Silvine mentally compared her own less graceful hands, her less-than-svelte figure. A heaviness settled over her. Minuet had been in Guval's life far longer than she had, and Silvine could not begrudge the mage's expertise. Besides, she'd always been told that a jealous wife was easily discarded.

Taran quickened his pace, as if sensing that Silvine needed to move forward. He didn't speak as they ascended a winding staircase and emerged from a great wooden door, which opened up to the bailey.

The bailey of the castle lined the front side where the gate stood. Every twenty feet, an archer was posted, ready to exterminate any possible threats, their gazes fixed on the arid, red plains below. A stone trench, burning with otherworldly purple flames, lit the perimeter. Threats by sea were a laughable thought. Few living creatures or ships could have survived the rage of the seas below or the half-mile climb atop the dusty, red cliffs.

"Why do we need to be out here if it's so well-guarded?" Silvine asked, surveying all the crouching figures.

"These guards keep watch in case any of the humans get ideas or members of Court wish to flee back to their estates. We're here for a different kind of foe," Taran said, leaning against the white stone behind him. "The creatures whose souls are bound to this land have an insatiable thirst for Death. It takes powers like yours or mine to truly stand a chance."

"Or Phelip and Guval's?"

He patted Silvine's shoulder. "Their powers are Death. They push it away temporarily, like two objects made of the attracting metals repelling one another, but Death cannot stave off more death permanently. Only the powers of Life and nature can end these creatures."

Silvine pursed her lips. She was beginning to feel more and more

230

like she was merely a useful tool to her betrothed. Where Guval's powers could dominate his Court, her powers dominated the world around him. He expected *her*, however, to face off with the true darkness in The Realm and conquer it for him.

"Time to exhale," Taran purred, placing his hand in hers.

As soon as she complied, he whisked her away to the grounds outside the gates of Guval's castle. It glowed eerily under the cover of moon and starlight. Taran waved up at a guard.

He then led her across the dusty, red plain. The desolation was in stark contrast with the abundance of forest Life Silvine knew lived in the mountains, which kept watch over the barren lands below. It was jarring to think of why one area so close to another could be so empty and lifeless.

"An ancient battle was once waged here," Taran said. "These grounds used to be the King of Donadais's vineyards, but nothing grows here anymore."

"It feels... wrong," Silvine said. She scanned the land all around her. To the west was the steep incline that led through the mountains to Luteche. To the east were the majestic purple mountains. The music within her veins was duller here.

"All the inviolable laws that made up the very fabric of The Realm were violated here," Taran replied. "When the world as The Creator intended it to be is altered like that, it changes the very fabric of this piece of The Realm. Traveling through it like I do also feels *wrong*."

"Do you really believe The Creator intended the world to *be* at all?" Silvine asked. She gestured at the barrenness around them. "I can't fathom why The Creator would make a world where people would battle, where the humans are at such a disadvantage, where the very act of bringing life into the world often means death."

Taran crouched down, reaching for something in the dust, before thrusting it into her palm. It was the tiny, angular skull of one of the smaller Fae, perhaps a pixie. Out of instinct, she felt for even the faintest hum of Life, but of course, there was none.

"The creation of The Realm is an entirely separate conversation than the ills of the beings who now live in it. The corruption of people does not take away the irrefutable beauty of Life itself." He took the dainty skull from her palm before sending it elsewhere in The Realm with a flick of his wrist. She imagined he sent it to a sacred place to rest eternally.

"Those who gave their lives on this battlefield believed in fighting for the good of The Realm. They did not give in to a tyrant who wished to manipulate reality. It is only thanks to their fight and The Modrona's great sacrifice that you and I stand a chance. Those who fought here thought Life in our realm was worth dying for, and I'm inclined to agree."

Taran's vulnerability made the words flow out of Silvine's mouth before she could stop them. "How am I ever going to be able to change it all?"

Taran scoffed. "No singular being is going to restore order and Life to The Realm. As long as you allow me to remain by your side, though, we can accomplish so much."

For the first time, Silvine realized she trusted him. More than that, she wanted Taran to remain by her side, to banter with her, to show her how to be a "garden variety Fae." She wanted to go wherever Taran led her.

At the same time, her heart had become a traitorous thing. The king of The Realm had selected her to be his bride, his consort, and she could barely muster the gratitude to return his affection. She traipsed off into the night with the General of Intelligence, sometimes with Guval's knowledge, sometimes without. She thought of Guval and Minuet in the strategy room, and she felt her mindset shifting. Guval's loyalties, too, seemed limited.

The blare of a trumpet somewhere along the parapet echoed across the plain. A few shouts rang out from the guards as a sickly, shimmering yellow figure rose up from the dust ahead of Silvine and Taran.

In response, Silvine's palms tingled and emitted their iridescent glow. Taran set his stance beside her, casting a quick glance of approval in her direction.

The shimmering yellow figure, initially a blob that glowed in the night sky, began to take the form of a horse and its rider. The rider was missing something crucial: its head. This disadvantage did not seem to hold the headless horseman back, however, from shouting out garbled battle cries. In The Faerie Realm, silly things like tongues and vocal chords were unnecessary for speech.

The horse galloped toward them, its eyes glowing red.

"*Regrediate!*" Taran called out to the rider. Retreat.

As the horseman drew nearer, Silvine drew upon the song of love that she knew within herself, drawing up so deep that her palms began to burn. She shot her beam of light out at the horseman. It struck the figure in its chest, and the horse it rode stumbled back.

A neigh resounded all around.

Appearing undeterred, the horseman collected itself and galloped toward them again. Silvine panted. Her beam of light had never before seemed so weak. Typically, the very light of Life itself did most of the work in destroying undead creatures.

She reached deep within her soul for the strongest feeling of love she'd ever known. A white-clad woman, with flowing blonde hair and a voice like delicate bells, spurred her on. Silvine built up and up, a rising crescendo of the music within her, until the beam glowed from her chest instead.

Taran's power mingled with hers, his sorrowful tune louder than ever as he helped launch the beam of light from within her. The beam struck the headless rider in his chest, knocking him off his ghostly horse.

"Don't get distracted. He's vicious," Taran whispered.

Silvine planted her feet, just like they'd practiced in the dungeon, preparing herself for whatever further viciousness brewed from the horseless, headless figure. It was beginning to feel as though she had been selected to be Guval's high-powered pest control system, but rather than combating noxious weeds, she had to cut down the monsters even her worst nightmares dared not conjure.

The smell of carrion wafted toward them across the dry air of the plain. The preternatural horse neighed again as its rider strode toward Silvine and Taran.

Taran jumped in front of her protectively, shoving her behind him with his arm. "Let it rest, Lain," he called out to the rider.

Silvine tried to calm herself as her heart raced and her chest tightened.

"You have not wandered this plain for a millennium. Your soul is not entrapped like mine. May this new one be a worthy opponent!" Lain's voice boomed.

Silvine thought about what it'd feel like to be stuck on this plain for a thousand years, but Taran's hand on her shoulder reminded her to stay focused. Long ago, he had been the one to warn her that nothing was as it seemed in The Faerie Realm. They were fighting against a creature for whom death was of little concern.

She focused on the thrumming in her ears, the pounding of her heart. Although they were initially frantic, she wove them into a love song instead. For the very first time, she was in full control.

"Regina, a little faster," Taran hissed.

Breath that smelled of death blew in her face. It was simultaneously icy and infernally hot. Lain lifted his palm, and Taran went flying across the dirt, landing with a thud. The carrion breath wafted closer and closer.

Silvine took the symphony pumping through her veins and pushed it out, out, out. An immense beam of light shot forth from her body and blasted Lain's chest at point-blank range. The impact of the force sent Silvine reeling backward, landing beside Taran, who had risen to his knees and begun to dust his leathers. She found herself gasping for air, the force of her fall having knocked all the air from her lungs.

"There's that power, Regina," Taran whispered. Something in

her chest warmed at his obvious approval. Beneath his usual sad song, she heard a hint of awe.

Gathering herself, she looked to where Lain had stood. The stallion's hooves beat in the distance, galloping away. Empty space remained where the menacing creature had been moments before.

Arm in arm with Taran, Silvine strode forward. She expected to see a corpse. Instead, there was just dust, and upon further inspection, the tiniest, glowing yellow flower.

"There hasn't been Life here in a millennium, Regina. Do you see how magnificent you are yet?"

He twirled her close to him. The smell of white birch and morning dew steadied her racing heart. They stood chest to chest, barely an inch of space between them. Silvine felt tempted to draw him closer, run her fingers through his shaggy locks, put her mouth on his.

The shouts of the guards above and the blaring of their warning horns interrupted them before temptation took over. Silvine commanded control over her body, taking slow breaths until her heart stopped pounding and the air fully filled her lungs. Taran let go as footsteps from royal guards drew near.

"Wait until His Majesty hears of your victory, Lady," a voice called out. The guards rushed toward them. Taran disappeared into the darkness of the night as a dozen Fae, who had never so much as cast a glance at Silvine, appeared fascinated by her accomplishment.

"Life has returned to the plain," they said.

Their chatter followed Silvine throughout the castle and the dining hall. Many of the courtiers, who had once turned up their noses at her, now gazed upon her with reverence. Lord Tylon eyed her hungrily at every instance. It was clear he craved what he believed her powers could do.

Taran, however, must have kept to the shadows. He didn't so much as speak to her for days after the slaying of Lain. Though her limbs were heavy, Silvine marveled that this time, she had saved Taran, brought Life back to the plains, and managed not to fall into a days-long slumber. She knew she was growing stronger with every challenge she faced.

Guval, however, remained absent. He insisted that war strategy and a pending fight with the Unseelie were unavoidable.

Praise surrounded Silvine from those who had previously turned up their noses at her very existence. Yet, she could not deny the pangs of longing in her heart.

CHAPTER 32

THE FIRST IMPRESSION UPON THE HEART

Silvine

The silence between Silvine and Taran ceased on their next assignment of the watch. Guval made a rare appearance in her chambers shortly before dusk. His green eyes appraised her hungrily, but he kept his distance.

"Fair One, I require you to stand watch tonight," he said. The authority that emanated from Guval's pores was irrefutable. All Silvine could do was agree, which brought a grin to his face. Her betrothed tucked his hands behind his back and departed her chambers without another word.

She'd assumed the man she married would require her to run his household, bear his children, and behave with decorum in public. The sacrifices Guval required her to make were far more sinister and left her lonelier than ever. Taran's appearances were the highlight of her days.

Silvine's attendant prepared her for her shift in silence. Unlike the clothes Taran had given her, these leathers had endlessly intricate lacing systems that required at least two people to put them on.

Her nameless attendant seemed to sense the longing in Silvine's heart. She squeezed her shoulder gently after pulling her long hair into two braids down her back. Silvine cleared her throat to say something, make a bid for connection, but a knock at her door interrupted.

Taran let himself in. He exchanged a bow with Silvine's attendant, who swiftly exited. "Are you ready to continue to crown His Majesty again and again with the light of your glory?" Silvine detected a hint of bitterness in his tone.

"What am I to do?" she snapped. "When I was born a female, rather than an heir, my fate was sealed. I was destined to be fodder for my father's attempt at an alliance. I never thought my power would be the ability to slay dark beings, so you'll have to excuse me. I thought the best thing I'd ever be able to offer my future husband was how well I held my tongue."

Taran shook his head, shifting a few stray brown locks over his eye in the process. "Have you not yet seen that the impossible is very much in the realm of possibility for you? Why content yourself with letting him take all the credit for saving The Realm? It's you." He clenched his fists.

Silvine was not sure she'd ever seen Taran this ruffled. His casual irreverence had been replaced with feelings she could not quite name. She blinked at him for several seconds.

Finally, Taran smoothed his hair out of his face and shook his hands, as though casting his frustrations into the air. "I am not quite myself. I just can't help but think the creature who sought to put me, and even the Queen of Undines, in their place in the forest is so eager to please the king. He's done nothing to earn your devotion."

"And you have?" she bit out.

"The gold I've earned in the process of saving your life would favor that assumption, yes. Unlike the King of Donadais, however, I do not require your devotion to survive."

Silvine wondered if Taran wanted her devotion. She had always thought of him as nothing but a trickster. What had motivated him to save her in the forest, time and time again? His high rank in Court entitled him to far more jewels and gold than she'd had in her possession.

Taran grabbed her elbow, dispelling any softening thoughts Silvine was developing toward him. "Let us go complete our shift. The night is ours once again."

It had begun to feel as though the night was their special time. Guval was occupied, and the rest of Court went about their own seedy traditions. Night was the time Silvine felt most herself.

With her sleep schedule so disrupted by changing night shifts and lazy days, it meant she hadn't experienced her recurring nightmare in ages either.

As Taran and Silvine made their way to the parapet for their normal patrol, a guard in violet approached. "Taran Dando." He bowed his head. "We have word of an intruder attempting to infiltrate the grounds."

In the glow of the torchlight, Taran's signature facial expression looked sinister. "Is that so?"

"The winds say so, General."

Silvine had been studying the way the Fae, her people by blood but not upbringing, danced around their words. When words were not necessary, they did not use them. They played games with their words. Taran was a rare exception.

"Of which species is our intruder?" he asked.

"The species that does not have a magical signature. His Majesty's mage did... one of her 'tests' of the environment and detected nothing."

Taran's eyes flashed wildly in the dim light. "Perhaps it requires a different sort of magic, then. We shall find it."

He gestured for Silvine to follow him. Taran was her teammate in these endeavors—this blood sport for Guval.

As they walked away from the guards, Taran's voice dropped low. He willed a rickety rope ladder from somewhere in The Realm, dropping it from the edge of a battlement. "I think we should split up. We can handle a mortal on our own." He gestured at the ladder. "After you, Regina."

Silvine gaped. "Can it hold me? I'm not exactly light."

Taran shushed her. "The entire Realm does not need to hear your qualms. It will hold you. If not, I'll shift through space to catch you. This is the best way to move swiftly and not deal with nosy middle management."

He left her no room for argument and continued to gesture. Silvine sighed as she made her descent. The ladder did not even sway in the breeze as she clambered down it, although she found herself resisting the urge to close her eyes. No sooner had her feet met with the earth than Taran appeared at her side.

"Why did you make me do that?" she demanded.

Even in hushed tones, the smugness in his voice was undeniable. "I feel like you should do something challenging every day to build character. I could tell you didn't enjoy a moment of that. Before you decide to wound me with that vicious mouth of yours, let's split up and find this intruder."

Taran flashed a yellow flower in his palm. "If you're in need of me, make vines grow from this. I'll be there. No need to pay me for my services this time."

Silvine exhaled sharply. Before she could find the words Taran probably wanted to avoid hearing, he had disappeared.

She found herself wandering the "ill-starred battlefield" alone. It was far less haunting and more pathetic this time, now a field with glorified weeds. There were no eerie creatures, and nothing called to her blood. There was not so much as the faintest sound, except for the notes of Taran's melancholy magic as he grew farther and farther away.

The wandering grew boring. As she'd been prone to do at long ceremonies in the village square as a young child, Silvine found herself tracing artwork in the dust with her boot.

She nearly completed a rendering of the planets and prominent constellations in the dirt when a yank on her arm interrupted her. *Skies above*, she thought, cursing herself for getting distracted.

Jumping at the touch, she sent a pulse of white-hot energy down her arm. There was a distinctly male grunt as the hand gripping her let go.

"I told you that you had no idea how valuable you would be," rasped a voice Silvine couldn't quite place. "Or that someday, your power would sting as much as a cruel word from your lips."

Her heart sank in her chest as she turned to face the owner of the voice. "*You.*" It was Cardoc.

He was shaking one hand and holding a glove in the other. "That really *did* hurt, Silvine. Can you heal me? You burned clean through my glove, and it's beginning to blister."

Silvine balled her fists. The rage she'd suppressed for days, months, and maybe even years pumped through her veins. It threatened to burn her up entirely. She looked down at her clenched fists, which were glowing under the dark sky.

The hooded figure stepped closer to the glow before slipping off the hood. Warm, honey eyes met hers.

Her fury bubbled over. Without thinking, she swung a shaking, glowing hand through the air and struck his cheek. There was a hiss as Silvine's hand made contact. The air smelled of burning flesh.

Cardoc's wide smile did not falter, although she sensed pain in the way he held his body. She could not believe that this man, the one who had betrayed Ana, the one who had offer to give her over, would reappear and try to talk to her. To try to tell her of her value.

"I came to save you," he said, throwing his charred glove to the ground. It disappeared beneath the bits of brush Silvine had restored to the once-barren plain.

"Save me? It seems a little bit late for that." Her chest heaved. Her whole body began to glow. She braced herself, vines crawling from the reaches of the forest, slithering toward Cardoc.

He shook his head. Most people would have had the good sense to cower or back away from a woman so angry she glowed, but Cardoc lifted his good hand for a moment as if to reach out. A younger part of Silvine, buried deep within her, wished he'd reach out and touch her like he once had. Grown-up Silvine, however, was ready to choke him with the vines that began to latch onto his boots, crawling up his legs.

"You went off course." He didn't even flinch as the vines wrapped around the sword at his hip. "Those of the silver and green are your true people. You were not on the right path when ours crossed. I am still trying to steer you where you need to go. After all of that, you still fell into the wrong hands."

Someone's breath brushed against Silvine's ear as she braced to do further damage to her first love.

"Easy, Regina," Taran said. "You've found the mortal. Don't murder him before I can take him in for questioning."

She whirled around to face Taran, who lifted his palm to reveal that the once-yellow, beautiful flower was now covered in thorns and thistles.

"General of Intelligence, remember?" Taran smirked. "Taking lives will take a toll on you. The greatness of your power lies in the preservation of Life. My power? Mine is the Earth's very Wrath. Let me handle it from here."

She was certain she heard the crackling of thunder in the distant purple mountains.

"Breathe, Regina," Taran said. As Silvine breathed deeply, the glow beneath her skin receded, and the vines released their grip on Cardoc.

Taran put his hand on her shoulder, settling the music in her veins to what might have been considered a lullaby to humans. He looked at her, and his irreverence was gone.

"But you don't understand, Taran." She hadn't meant to finish her thought out loud.

"I understand more than you think I do. I understand more than you yourself apprehend. And that's the first time you've called me by my name, in case you hadn't noticed."

She hadn't.

Silvine looked at Cardoc once more. He continued to stand resolute between two powerful beings. It no longer stunned Silvine to think that *she* was a powerful being. Perhaps Cardoc could not perceive The Faerie Realm and the frightening things around him the way she now could. For a brief moment, she pitied his naïveté.

"This man wronged me. He wronged my only friend, Ana. He let Ainmean burn around him and did nothing as I fled for my life. Ana bought me time." Silvine let a single tear fall. It slid from her face to the earth below.

More tears came, but rough hands wiped them away. "I know," Taran said. Crinkles formed near his eyes.

"Look," Cardoc gasped, gesturing at Silvine's boots. "See! I said you were valuable."

Where her tear had fallen, a single yellow flower bloomed above the other foliage.

"Simply beautiful," Taran murmured. "*That* is why I will be your Wrath and vengeance wherever I can. You are Life. You are at your best when it flourishes."

He turned to Cardoc, crossing his arms lazily. "Do you understand that you trespass at Court, at the stronghold of the king?"

"I do, Silver-and-Green One." Cardoc bowed. As he rose, he gave Silvine a pointed look. He must have been suffering from some kind of delusion. Maybe he'd been the victim of a Fae on his journey there.

"Do you understand that your actions leave your life forfeited?" Taran continued.

"I do."

"Very well. Regina, I will be taking our guest to my domain. In the meantime, I need you to breathe out."

That was the only warning Taran gave as he placed his hand back on her shoulder with lightning quickness. In a blur, Silvine found herself folded through the realms and deposited in her chambers.

Cardoc's appearance unsettled her, dredging up all of the trauma she'd tried to suppress. Sleep evaded her that night as she struggled to get a grip on her thoughts and her racing heart. He'd given no explanation. He seemed unfazed by her magic. None of it made sense.

While her girlish affection for him had long since faded, there was a fondness that would always linger for the first boy she'd ever cared about. Nene always said the first impression upon the heart left a permanent indent, one neither time nor circumstance could fully undo. She'd been right.

CHAPTER 33

THE VALUE OF LIVING

Silvine

It wasn't long before the day of Cardoc's trial. In the throne room, Guval declared, "There has been a... rare bit of entertainment that has arrived at Court for our amusement." Silvine, standing at his left, glanced around.

The courtiers had abandoned their usual alcove debauchery to listen to their king's announcement. The fascination of the crowd of assorted, colorful Fae was tangible. Though she was largely disengaged from the goings on of Court, Silvine knew their glee matched those of human commoners about to witness a particularly gruesome execution.

The king clapped his hands together. "Taran!"

The heavy door, concealed to look like part of the wall behind the dais, swung open. Silvine had discovered this was one of many entrances to the dungeons: Taran's domain. There was a muffled grunt and a scraping sound as Taran dragged a writhing body to the front of the dais.

Minuet cheered as she stood at Guval's right side. Several members of the crowd joined her. Her husband gave her a sharp look.

No doubt, Silvine assumed, laughter was some sort of faux pas according to the rules of Phelip's Courtly Code of Conduct.

Taran removed the burlap hood from the body he'd dragged in, revealing the bloodied face of Cardoc. Silvine's heart sank. His golden hair was matted in his blood. The sun-kissed glow of his skin had paled, and his warm, chestnut eyes were dull. Even though he was not *her* Cardoc, would never be *her* Cardoc again, it hurt to see him brought so low.

"A human?" Lord Tylon shouted.

"Astute observation," Taran retorted.

Lord Tylon ignored the snide remark from his majesty's General of Intelligence, pushing his way forward. Courtiers hastened out of his way. Silvine heard Phelip muttering imperceptibly under his breath.

"Your Majesty, with all due reverence, you have called us all here to show us a bloodied mortal." Lord Tylon bowed his head slightly.

Taran crossed his arms. "You continue to point out new and exciting information, Tylon." The lord hissed between his teeth, focusing his gaze on the king.

Guval, acting unbothered, took his time appraising the situation before responding. "Tylon, I find you have recently taken to greatly testing my patience."

Tylon gestured at Cardoc, who was struggling against Taran's tight grasp. "I mean, we have the opportunity for entertainment with whichever humans we please, whenever we please. I am certain you have a grander plan in store, but curiosity makes me wonder why we are all here for a single human. He looks... and smells... as though Taran Dando has already received quite a bit of entertainment from him. Time is so precious, after all."

The king rose from his throne with the grace of a predator. He raised an arm, tightening his fist as he did so. Lord Tylon began to gasp, clutching at his throat.

"I grow tired of you, Tylon. Perhaps a long nap will make you less tiresome." Guval flicked his wrist, and Tylon fell to the floor. Minuet giggled sinisterly as a guard hurried to collect Tylon's unconscious body and drag it away.

"Now that I have a moment to finish a thought without impudent questions, I come to share with you this entertainment. Tell us, human, what gave you the courage to trespass at Court?" Guval glided down the steps toward Cardoc, gripping him by the jaw when he reached where Taran held him up.

Though his eyes were nearly swollen shut and several hideous shades of purple and green colored his face, Cardoc did not flinch as he met the Fae king's gaze. "I came... to steer Silvine on the right course. I came... to save her."

Laughs rang throughout the throne room, echoing into the alcoves. The cacophony of their cackling, so unnatural, made Silvine shudder. The blood raced in her veins as she watched the mortal man, presented before the very embodiment of Death.

Guval gestured at Silvine. A host of Fae eyes, so many of them that unnatural crimson, followed him.

"Does my lady look like she needs a human man to save her?"

Cardoc wheezed and straightened himself against Taran's hold as best as he could. "Silvine... can save herself, but she needs me... to fulfill my purpose. She needs... to know... what you really are."

The sound of Guval's hand colliding with Cardoc's face rang out through the room. Silvine cringed. She'd struck him herself, but for good reason. Watching her betrothed strike the man who'd broken her heart and betrayed her multiple times should have felt satisfying, but a sinking feeling in her soul told her Cardoc was right about the king.

Blood dripped down Cardoc's face as barely-healed wounds reopened. Silvine tried to get Taran's attention, hoping he'd do something to end this. He was too busy watching the bloodbath from his front row seat to pay her any mind.

Cardoc shouldn't be here. A true Fae king shouldn't feel threatened by a human, Silvine thought.

Her stomach twisted in knots as she watched helplessly.

Another smack rang out through the room as Cardoc grunted, crumpling into Taran's outstretched arms.

"Please," Silvine found herself calling out, skipping steps as she hurried off the dais. Guval whirled around, his eyes wide.

"The humans were my people. *Are* my people," Silvine explained. "Traitor or not, I can't stand to see senseless violence against an already broken man." The words tumbled out before she could think to stop herself. She was not sure how Guval would respond to the challenge she was posing.

She detected clanging notes, the musical equivalent of annoyance, ringing out through the crowd. A few sighed, seeming disappointed that the bloodshed had been interrupted.

A softened expression shifted onto Guval's face as he reached out to caress Silvine's fingers. "My lady's power is Life. It does her heart harm to see it extinguished. We should be reminded of the value of living." Past Guval's shoulder, Silvine caught brief looks of admiration on both Taran and Cardoc's faces.

She knew she was right to speak, no matter the ire it drew from Court or the king. Although he praised her publicly, she worried about his private feelings. Lord Morair had been an expert at being a gentleman in front of his subjects, only to unload his displeasure at home. Minuet sighed, which kicked off a chorus of similar noises. Phelip cleared his throat reproachfully.

Before Silvine could find words to temper Guval's response, a black-clad guard advanced toward the king and whispered in his ear. Even Silvine's Fae hearing could not detect what had been said.

"Very well." Guval nodded, dismissing the guard away. "This will have to wait, my beloved court. Go back to your debauchery. I must meet with Taran and my lady immediately."

Another cloaked guard, appearing out of nowhere, approached Taran to take custody of Cardoc. Guval tilted his head, gesturing that they should follow him. Phelip, Minuet, and the usual guards rushed over to join, but the king held up his hands. "I must meet with them alone. Bring in some other *entertainment* while I attend to this matter."

When Guval took a seat in the strategy room, Silvine flinched. Her mind flashed back to an image of his coziness with Minuet. Perhaps as Guval's mage, Minuet's magic required some kind of physical contact when strategizing. Silvine tried to shrug off her lingering jealousy. Despite reminding herself of her duty, her purpose, and the wifely art of looking the other way, she could not shake her unease. The memory of what she'd seen left a bitter taste in her mouth and notes of discord in her blood.

The king gestured grandly at the other chairs around the table. Taran took a seat.

Forcing herself to move, Silvine followed suit. The tabletop had been crafted into a map of the known world. Figurines of humans and Fae as well as towers representing strongholds were littered across the table. Only the Isle of Rafflesia lay bare. Rafflesia, according to the myths, was the land of dwarves, which had been burned from the inside out millennia ago.

Guval reached his hand across the table, placing it atop Silvine's. The gesture was likely meant to be affectionate, reassuring. Her obsidian chilled in response. "Fair One, I need you. I need your powers. The Unseelie have unleashed their monsters in the northern reaches of the forest. Hordes of bananach and felipentis have been spotted entering the forest from the coastal plains. It will not take much for them to reach Alivon and then Ainmean."

Pausing his study of the map, Taran lifted his head. Guval gestured at the northeastern corner, where the small province of Alivon lay. Rumored among the humans to have once been a glorious northern province where sheep roamed in droves and amber-colored liquor had been distilled by The Creator, it was now sparsely populated. Its only value to The Realm was the convenient location of its port. Transport by sea was easier than crossing the forests.

With a flick of his sinewy hand, Guval conjured all manner of fearsome figures and moved them toward Alivon. The figures hovered dangerously close to Ainmean. Silvine wondered if Master Fluellen's militia would stand a chance against such creatures, but a small part of her accepted the grim answer.

"Taran, I trust you can equip yourself, select discreet men, and keep my lady safe," Guval said. "In fact, I expect it."

No words passed Taran's lips, but he bowed his head. His calm demeanor stunned Silvine. A part of her wanted to save The Realm, save the people of Ainmean, but another part of her refused to blindly accept Guval's orders.

"I have concerns," she said.

Her betrothed raised an auburn eyebrow. He was clearly not used to being questioned. He said nothing, which she took as encouragement to continue.

"I have hardly any training. I don't know how I could possibly save Ainmean from these creatures. I've handled three at a time at best. The most intense training I've had is fighting for my life alone in the woods when no one could find me, when no one saved me."

Something stormy flashed in Taran's eyes, but it faded quickly.

Silvine jabbed a finger at a figurine meant to resemble a felipentis. "And now I am to be the king's personal mercenary for ancient creepy-crawlies? You're in no rush to 'blood' me, and yet you're willing to send me off to fight the Unseelie. I feel like I'm a tool you're using. This is confusing. Concerning, even."

Guval frowned. "Taran, leave us," he said. "This shall take just a moment." He winked at Taran, who chuckled in response. Silvine glowered at him.

Without a word, the General of Intelligence left. He closed the heavy door with a thud. Silvine wished he'd stayed and said something, anything. She wished she wasn't alone with Guval. She hated herself for not wanting this king, this betrothal, this future, but it made her feel empty.

The king rose and made his way to her chair. He leaned down and planted a wet kiss on her lips. Silvine grew stiff. He grabbed her hair and yanked, pulling her closer.

"Don't you see, Fair One?" he whispered, tracing the length of her ear with his tongue.

Her fists tightened. "I see a great deal, Guval."

His hand slid down her shoulder while his mouth hovered on her neck. Ever so slowly, he moved his fingers lower. Silvine suppressed a shudder. Every inch of her body screamed at her to stop this. It felt wrong. Her chest tightened in a vice, leaving her struggling for air. It was as though her very Life was leaving her.

There was a sudden zap of energy between the two of them. Guval flew backward, his chest heaving. Blood trickled out of his nose, just as it had when they'd kissed in his room.

"This is most strange. I must consult Minuet," he said.

"Is—is it necessary to ask the mage?" Silvine asked, her breath returning to her.

He straightened his jacket. "Yes, this has never happened before. Minuet and I will ensure it *never* happens again."

Silvine cringed and wrapped her arms around herself.

After placing a chaste kiss on his betrothed's cheek, Guval said, "This wasn't how I intended for this to go. I do want you. Perhaps I've been cursed. We will resume on our wedding night. The world won't be all Death forever. Once we have The Blooding and the marriage, things will be the way they should have always been."

Despite his words of reassurance, he wouldn't meet Silvine's gaze. He left her alone in the strategy room. She did not know where to begin unpacking everything that had occurred. She didn't think physical connection should have felt anything like dying, but it had.

CHAPTER 34

KING OF DONADAIS

The Avartagh, 1000 Years Before

Macha's warning that further scheming would corrupt The Realm could not compare to the need for retribution The Avartagh felt. He and his people went to war. With every province that fell, he installed one of his highest-ranking officials as a lord and intermarried them with the humans of The Realm.

He made The Old Ones, the true Fae, out to be creatures of nightmares. He commissioned the bards to write horror stories about the Fae and the forest. He glamoured himself in the presence of humans, appearing as an aged, benevolent king.

After The Great Betrayal, all the grapes began to rot. The women and children of his court were tasked with preserving as much as they could ferment while the rest shriveled away. The land itself dried out and became barren.

As his paradise slipped away, all his thoughts were of The Modrona.

She was all he wanted. With her Life force, he could restore the crops, improve his people, and heal his heart. She had so fiercely rejected him that he was determined to take her by force.

Years of battles throughout The Realm only agitated him further. Finally, the great clash culminated in a battle along the cliffs of his now-barren province.

The naiads and dryads fought valiantly for her. The river and ocean spirits drowned his men where they were standing. All while she stood atop a mountain summit, hurtling endless thorns and fierce creatures down to where he fought along the cliffside.

She was so powerful. She had the absolute advantage in the battle being waged. She was magnificent.

The Avartagh cut his way up the mountain, leaving a path of destruction in his wake. Long after the adrenaline had worn off, he drove himself onward by yearning alone.

In blind fury, he even cut down a few of his own men, cleaving their heads from their bodies. His only thoughts were to get to her, to reach her, to claim her. Anyone that got in his way would fall prey to his rampage.

His ascent came to a screeching halt when one of the dryads reached out spindly arms and scooped him into the air. He hovered on the mountainside, up so high he was taller than the jagged outcroppings of boulders.

"Unhand me at once!" he commanded, voice hoarse from the rages of battle.

The tree man chuffed at him before hurtling him down the mountainside. The Avartagh landed on a sharp rock. It pierced through him, narrowly missing his lungs and damaging a kidney.

He shrieked and pried his body loose. The pain was excruciating, but he forbade himself from thinking about it. Such a wound would have killed a mortal, but he was no mortal. He was a man with one mission. He would claim The Modrona for himself.

The power that swirled around her was breathtaking. Between his awe at the magnificence of her abilities and the endless bleeding from his wound as he made his way back up the mountain, he was dizzied and could hardly think. The Modrona exuded pure Life and light. She glowed with the exertion of battle. She was his.

As his throat burned from screaming and grunting in exertion, she did not break a sweat. He would make it to her. She would be his salvation. She would complete him and make him whole in a way he had never been before.

When he made it within fifty feet of her, she gave a great cry. The pendant at her neck shot out icy, white light at him. It struck him in the chest, throwing him backward.

Gasping for air, he forced himself to his feet and continued the climb.

Every muscle, every bone, every part of him was screaming. His ears rang from all the sounds of battle. He would not give up. He would reach her.

She had fallen by the time he made it to her side. Even The Modrona's magic had its limits. No magical being was immune to magic overwhelm.

Delicately, in a way he'd never touched anyone before, he gathered her into his arms. His whole body was shaking, and he couldn't feel his legs anymore. She gave him a final look, curling her lip, before shutting her eyes tightly. He could almost taste the bitterness of her disdain.

The Modrona had used up the deepest dregs of her power. The fierce creatures she had forged with her very blood continued to fight, creatures forged from a tangle of branches and pure might. They continued on while life drained from her. Each of her breaths grew fainter until they finally stopped. The Avartagh's legions were falling in droves on the plains below.

The sounds and smells of battle, the heavy tang of iron, fell away. All The Avartagh knew was that his chance to rule this realm and become whole was gone. His chance to save everything he'd worked so hard to establish, that he'd murdered to gain, was slipping from beneath his fingers.

"No, I need you," he whispered. A strange warming sensation crept through his body. It felt like what his warriors described in their final moments as Death overtook them. He tried to ignore the thought that maybe he was dying, too.

In the battle to win her, he'd lost her. The Modrona, the great Life force he so desperately craved for himself, had been extinguished. There was none other with those powers.

He decided he would drink from her Life force before it disappeared. If he consumed it, surely it would become his. He ignored the sensations of Death in his body and drew upon his last ounce of strength. He bit into her neck, drinking from the blood in her veins. Neither his people nor the Fae of The Realm drank blood, but he could think of no other way to gain the powers he sought.

When he had drunk his fill, he fell back. A heavy darkness filled him, starting in his chest and consuming him until his body was too heavy to draw breath or hold his eyes open. Eventually, even retaining consciousness became too heavy. Everything went black and ceased to exist.

Dead. He was dead.

There was nothing. He had no dreams, he did not breathe, and his heart did not beat. The Avartagh welcomed Death. For the first time, he felt no thirst as his life slowly ended.

A painful jolt of his heart brought him back from the void. Everything hurt, and the return to life was wholly unwelcome. His heart beat in his chest, painfully and slowly, nothing like the steady beating he'd known before. He succumbed to a secondary darkness as his body was consumed by pain and rot.

Macha was standing over him in the twilight when he returned to consciousness. "Was it worth it?" she asked bitterly. He could only study her, his tongue too heavy to use.

"You are dead, but you cannot truly die. You have twisted all the laws of Life, and now you will forever thirst for it. Violating the laws of hospitality was a grievous sin, but you did not listen to me. You continued to sin against the order of our very world, the order our Creator set forth for us. You will need blood to maintain even a semblance of the Fae form you should have. You and your people will be monsters until your day of reckoning comes. You have ripped apart the very fabric of The Realm."

The Avartagh felt it then: thirst that gnawed at him, rushing through his core. This was a need he'd never felt before: a need to feed upon the Life force of others. He had become a monster.

"The—The Modrona?" he rasped.

Her body was gone.

Macha cackled, its echo ringing down the bare mountainside. "The Earth loves its own, and the Heart sees the Earth for what it truly is. You took her, but her heir has taken her rightful place far from your clutches. You took The Euron, but another one rose in his place as well. That part of the balance remains. You won this battle, Avartagh, but not the war. You will not see the end of this suffering until you meet The Modrona who is foretold."

With that, she left him on the mountain to crawl back to his fortress.

Avartagh. A word he'd never thought was more than a myth. An undead creature whose powers and thirst could only be controlled when buried headfirst. Avartagh. A word to describe the cursed being he'd become.

The thirst he felt after dying was nothing like the thirst he'd known before. He was becoming a shell of himself, and the resulting doom touched everything around him. He launched himself upon the first living being he found on the battlefield, draining the body until it was little more than a husk of skin and bones. The Avartagh did not even remember what species the creature was.

His entire court found themselves with his same curse: the need for blood. They had fallen at the same time he had, the battle halting, and everyone awoke with an insatiable need for blood. The battle was won as they extinguished most of the remaining forces in a frenzied mess of ichor. The rest of the Fae of The Realm retreated as bloodcurdling screams rang throughout the valley.

The Avartagh was powerful, now stronger than he'd been before. To be powerful but to always hover between Life and Death was a price he would not have wished to pay. His people had no more dignity. Many of them bore the physical signs of their avartagh nature: crimson eyes, a reminder of the color of the liquid they had to consume to exist. Death was a gift denied them. The lesser subjects gave in to Death's embrace almost easily, an embrace The Avartagh himself was adept at gifting to them, but he could not access it for himself.

A stab to the heart was painful for even The Avartagh. The pain was short-lived, however, and each time he resumed his mockery of living again. Once, he'd asked a trusted courtier to behead him. Before the blade had finished its full arc, the sinews had begun to reattach themselves. Poison sickened him and kept him abed, but eventually, he rose again.

Again and again, death evaded him.

The beautiful marble his fortress had been constructed of was drained of its radiant colors. All that remained was a stark white with veins of purple, reminding him of the endless corpses drained of their blood.

The creatures The Modrona had sent to battle morphed into creatures of unspeakable horror. They terrorized Fae and humans alike, thriving on evil. Although The Avartagh blamed the other Fae, he knew deep down that he had created the darkness and horror when he'd desecrated The Modrona's body. Some of the creatures seemed to be eternally damned to haunt the battlefield. Others scattered with the winds, haunting the forests in the farthest clutches of The Realm. As provinces rose to power, many of them cut down the surrounding forests as a safety measure.

The Avartagh kept up the pretense of a good king who trusted his vassals to maintain order. He let the mortals dominate trade and industry, playing the role of an absentee landlord. He clutched his Fae courtiers closer to him, paranoid of coups as disastrous as his own.

In his mad desperation and yearning for her, he had destroyed the fundamental good of The Realm. He had broken every law of creation. The Avartagh was thirst. Thirst was the Avartagh. There was nothing else.

He bided his time, waiting for when the one who was foretold would be his salvation. He would make her love him, bind her to him, and finally, his thirst would be quenched.

CHAPTER 35

LUMINESCENCE

Silvine

Thoughts of Guval's advances and threats of Death filled Silvine's head as she marched to the dungeons. Nods of acknowledgment met her as she made her way from wing to wing, through the underground tunnels, and across the bridge.

It felt better to receive acknowledgment than the cold indifference and mistrust she received at first, but nothing about Court felt like home.

Physical love should be intoxicating, she thought. She didn't consider herself an expert at love, but she assumed physical attraction came naturally to most couples. Without passion and attraction, there was only an alliance. She clung to the hope that true connection would come on their wedding night. With Cardoc, she'd been consumed by him immediately. Their connection was instant.

His words of warning from earlier rang alarm bells in her mind again, and her heart hurt at the thought of his fate. It made no sense to her that he'd come to find her.

Thoroughly distracted by her ruminations, she stumbled into

Taran's table. A low laugh assured her that her clumsiness had not gone unnoticed.

She whirled around to glare at Taran.

He covered his mouth and coughed. "Is all well between the king and his precious little possession?"

Silvine tightened her fists. "All is *very* well, thank you for your concern. Did you use your intelligence-gathering skills to learn all about what happened in the strategy room?"

Taran smirked as he leaned lazily against a wall. "Would you like me to? I didn't know you had such tastes."

He stalked closer to her until she could feel his breath on her skin. She smelled the faint hint of whisky. "I don't always need to *see* to gain information. Sometimes, the truth is obvious to those of us who stop to observe." Taran Dando, bane of her existence, was so close that if she twitched, her lips would touch his. "Or would you like to provide me with a reenactment?"

Scooting to her left to put distance between them, she glared. Under her breath, she muttered, "Only if it ends with your utter revulsion at the sight of me."

His eyebrows shot up. "Care to explain?"

"No," she said. "Skies above and Earth below, I hate Fae hearing."

"Some thoughts should be inside thoughts then, Regina."

Desperate to change the subject, she bit out, "I can't wait to travel with you. After all, you're such a *great* travel companion."

With more grace than any person had a right to have, he walked toward her. "I am choosing to ignore that comment. I'd like to return to what you said in the strategy room. You," he lowered his voice, "were never alone in that forest. You were never lost. Not really."

Silvine clenched her fists. It was easier to direct all of her anger at him than to acknowledge how she really felt. "I find that hard to believe. Your help came at great cost and at intervals."

He seemed to disregard her comment. "We have to leave soon. I have a few of my men ready. I have a task I think you'd like to help me complete before we leave. If you can't control your temper, I'll do it without you."

Silence hung in the air as both of them refused to budge.

Finally, she let out a deep breath and unclenched her fists. "Better?"

He patted her shoulder. "I knew you'd make the right choice, Regina." Gesturing for her to follow, he led her down a tunnel. The sounds of the dungeon that Silvine had trained herself to ignore died out. He whispered, "For a woman so unable to hold her tongue, you keep so many secrets. I hope one day to know them all."

Silvine was too drained to respond. Thoughts wandered to his deception. It shamed her to think he had deceived her while playing the hero in the forest.

"You may call me Cian. Now, I have helped you, and you seem to be accustomed to Fae tradition. What will you give me in exchange?"

The tunnel darkened. No torches burned along the stone walls. Silvine pulled from a melody in her blood until the tips of her fingers glowed enough to see a few feet in front of her.

A door appeared in front of them. The end of the tunnel. The door was another of the heavy wooden ones from the castle. Strange runes shimmered along the handle.

Taran whispered, *"Volo te aperire."* I *want you to open.* The door creaked as it moved.

Silvine could hardly believe her eyes when she saw what lay beyond the door. It was a cell of some sort, but far more luxurious than the one she'd woken up in months before. The far wall of the expansive room was made of floor-to-ceiling, purple stained-glass windows. A modest bed was tucked against the farthest wall. A crumpled heap lay on the bed. A cloaked figure hovered over the edge, tending to them.

Silvine's heart stuttered. The melancholy song in her veins became sad enough to rival Taran's. Her intuition told her the crumpled heap was Cardoc.

Before she could say anything, Taran yanked her into the room and shut the door.

The upbeat, fast-paced hum in the blood of the cloaked figure was a striking contrast to everything else in the room. The room was beautiful in the same eerie way the rest of Court was. It was a somber beauty, lacking warmth. The figure seemed unaffected by either the coldness or the half-dead man.

The hood slipped off as the person swung their head around. A glowing face met Silvine's own. Phos. She squealed as she closed the gap between her and Silvine, throwing her arms around her. Her tall, lean frame dwarfed Silvine's shorter, stockier one.

Silvine thought the hug would suffocate her. She hadn't realized her one evening with Phos had forged enough of a connection to put them on a hugging basis.

"My Queen." Phos let go and wrinkled her nose at Taran. "You have not come on any missions with us since that first night. Is *he* keeping you away? He's the absolute worst, isn't he?"

Everyone else seemed to admire or fear Taran, but Phos did not hold back. Silvine rolled her eyes. "Yes, he *is* the absolute worst. He's made me guard the castle with him, on night shift no less. It's so much less entertaining than going on real missions."

For a brief moment, Taran's lips curved upward into a rare, genuine smile. It was short-lived. She wondered if he saved those smiles for Phos.

He wagged his finger at her. "First of all, both of you are being too loud. Are you or are you not here for a purpose that has nothing to do with girl time and mocking me?"

Phos sighed. Her glow seemed to dim ever so slightly. "My *charge* is sleeping soundly. It is the best I can do for him until someone else comes to relieve me."

Silvine cast a glance at Cardoc, who lay motionless in the bed.

"That should be happening any moment now. I was hoping we could offer relief to our queen." Taran's tone surprised Silvine with its seriousness.

She rolled her eyes. "When have you ever cared about whether or not I get relief?"

Taran shrugged. "Always. Isn't it obvious?"

Phos bobbed her head in agreement, likely understanding his suggestion although Silvine did not. Phos took her by the hand and led her to the bed.

Beneath the glow of Phos's beautiful skin and the ample torchlight, Silvine could see just how many injuries Cardoc had received. Her heart sank. A warm hand found its way to her shoulder. The upbeat song buzzed from Phos to Silvine. Her own magic changed, harmonizing with the notes of her friend.

"Modrona, I know you are not a healer, but you are the Earth. I can only give him feelings of comfort. You can actually do something."

Silvine made a mental bookmark of that thought. The sight of Cardoc's battered body, every inch cut or bruised, made her want to hurl her dagger at Taran's heart. When they met to train in the dungeon, he'd taught her just the right way to flick her wrist and hit her target. She could do it. For Cardoc and what they'd once had, she'd tear Taran Dando to shreds.

Yet, the magic of Phos's touch made it impossible for her to latch onto the fiery tension in her body. It was a fleeting emotion, continually washed away by joy that made no sense to her.

"I—I don't know what I could do for him," Silvine said.

Phos's vibrant, honey-colored eyes glowed. "It doesn't require knowledge. I think it's instinct. It's in your blood. I know all of these men want you to use your Life powers to extinguish Death, but you can aid the processes of Life, too."

Cardoc groaned in his sleep as he tried to roll onto his back. Phos eased him into a more comfortable position.

After hesitating for a moment, Silvine laid her palms on Cardoc. She listened for a song within him, desperately trying to find a single note. Unsurprisingly, there was nothing. Mortals did not have magic. His blood could not sing to her.

He groaned again, and she flinched. His eyelids tried to flutter open, but they were too swollen. Phos murmured something, her hand on his chest, and Cardoc settled again. Silvine stared at him. She wanted so desperately to provide him with some measure of comfort, but she didn't know what to do. If he had been Fae, she would've tried to change the music in his blood. Hands shaking, she froze. What if she broke him even more? She crouched down, rocking on her heels, hovering just above Cardoc.

"Regina, you just need to dig deeper within *yourself*. It all comes from you," Taran said softly. She didn't know when he'd come to stand so close beside her. Phos seated herself at the head of the bed, staring sympathetically at the broken mortal man she'd called her charge.

"Think of the moments where you've felt truly alive," Phos suggested.

Shaking, Silvine placed her hands on Cardoc's chest again. This time, he stayed still. She closed her eyes and tuned out the rest of the world. She listened to the beat of her heart. It was a gentle drumbeat, not the war march of so many others. She thought of her time with Cardoc. A particularly fond memory of springtime in a meadow crossed her mind.

He'd plucked asters and sunflowers, deft fingers weaving them into a crown he'd placed atop her head. Then, she'd run away from him, giggling, trailing her hands along the tall grasses and flowers as she let him catch her.

He'd swung her around in circles when he reached her.

It was perhaps the first time she'd ever felt.

Images flashed through her mind of the way she'd enjoyed dancing under the moonlight with Taran. She saw the faces of the children and widows of Luteche as she'd given them food to fill their starving bellies. The hope of sustenance for a few more days. A hope for a better future.

Something more primal took over as her heartbeat slowed.

She saw the Modronas who had come before her. She saw the way they cultivated the ground, enriching it with the essence of Life. They mourned for the dead, for they knew that where Death had won, Life could not prevail. Yet, the gifts they could bestow upon the living held firm to the balance of Llife and Death.

She saw those lovely, golden-haired women, each in their own turns presiding over a throne of silver tree branches. Life thrummed through them, flowed from their veins as everything around them flourished. Where there was Life, there was possibility.

The Earth loved its own. It still did to that day.

At this moment, the Earth loved Cardoc. Cardoc was just as much part of Life as the soil that fed the creatures of Galanthe, as the beautiful flowers, as the steadfast trees that stood watch over the forest. Every life was a part of the cycle of those who contributed to its endless possibility. Death had its place, and it was a domain that The Modrona could never conquer, only balance, but while there was still a glimmer of Life, there was hope in abundance.

Life thrummed through Silvine's veins as her heartbeat rose. She felt the vibration from her chest to her fingertips. She willed her song outside of herself, forcing a thin thread of light into Cardoc's heart. She felt the thread flow through his veins. With every beat, the gift of Life filled in the cracks of his body where decay and despair had taken over.

As soon as the thread had circulated through his whole system, she called it back to her. Phos had been right. Healing was not a skill to have. It was simply instinct. It was a calling all the Modronas had answered at some point in their journeys.

With a small gasp, Silvine felt her legs begin to wobble. Taran caught her, holding her chest to his. The three of them watched in silence as, slowly, the swelling receded. The bruises faded. The cuts turned to faint pink scars.

No one seemed to dare take their eyes off Cardoc. He sighed peacefully and rolled back onto his side. He was no longer a crumpled heap, but a man slumbering comfortably. They collectively exhaled.

Phos glided toward the table, pouring herself a glass of wine. She kept her eyes trained on her glass before turning to look at the crashing ocean waves outside the window, her back turned to Silvine and Taran.

Taran pulled Silvine closer. "Are you alright?"

"Y-yes," she answered breathlessly.

He playfully smacked her arm. "Have you realized I am always right yet?"

She pursed her lips. "If you were always right, Cardoc wouldn't have needed me to save him. *You* would have done the right thing and let the mortal man go."

Taran released her suddenly. She'd forgotten he was holding onto her, but her feet were steady enough that she didn't stumble.

"Regina, do you think those injuries were my handiwork?"

"The dungeon is your domain. I have yet to see my king ever come down here."

Taran's lips tugged upward. "*Intelligence* is my domain. I thought your friend would be able to mind his manners in a standard issue cell while I attended to my many other duties. He chose to exchange words with one of His Majesty's less refined guards, and the guard called in a few of his companions to join him."

"Since Sharp Face was taken out of the equation, I'm assuming Bushy Eyebrows got his feelings hurt and solved his problems with his fists?"

Taran raised an eyebrow. "Bushy Eyebrows? Sharp Face?"

Silvine crossed her arms. "I hardly know any names in this realm. I'm just naming people based on their attributes at this point."

Amusement twinkled in Taran's eyes. "Well, with that being the case, you're right. Bushy Eyebrows, as you call him, was the one who could not handle taunts from a mortal prisoner and chose to beat him to a pulp. He and his friends have found themselves assigned to latrine duty for the next year. I do not stand for attacking the defenseless. I moved the prisoner to safer accommodations. I knew it would please you to see him kept comfortable, Regina."

"You didn't lay a hand on Cardoc?"

"I did not touch a single hair on his head. You insult my honor to assume I need to spend my time harming mortals."

Silvine lowered her voice. "I wanted to stab you when I saw how badly beaten Cardoc was. I would have, but Phos kept her hand on me. Every time I tried to hold onto an angry thought, she overrode it with this weird upbeat emotion."

Phos called out, "I was glad to do you a favor, my queen. His vanity could have never withstood being wounded by a woman he trained himself."

"I would have dodged anything the Regina sent my way," Taran insisted. "Phos has the ability to control emotions with touch. It's one of her most vexing attributes. No one can feel properly irritated when she's within arm's reach. She gave your friend peace until you could get here."

Silvine felt the sting of tears welling up and willed them away. Too choked up for words, she gave Phos an appreciative nod as Taran led her out of the room.

Phos smiled in return. "Your friend will be in good hands and safe from the king's brutes while we're away. His companion is the most hospitable Fae in all of Galanthe."

Silvine folded her arms across her chest. "It's not Luc, is it?"

Both of her companions ignored her, which she took to mean, "Yes. Yes it is." She couldn't deny that Cardoc would be in good hands while she wandered The Realm slaying monsters for the king. She hoped to find answers on her journey that would right the feelings of wrongness she got every time she was with her betrothed.

CHAPTER 36

TRAVERSING THE REALM

Silvine

After Taran strapped a surprisingly heavy pack onto Silvine's back, he touched her hand and whisked her through The Realm. She didn't have a moment to object to the weight. They appeared in another cave. It reminded her of their night in Luteche.

"This again?" she asked.

Taran patted her pack as a glow bobbed toward them in the distance.

Phos arrived with five other Fae in tow. Silvine didn't know their names, but she recognized them from their Luteche adventures and the revelry under the stars that had followed. All of them hurried to take a knee.

"My Queen," they called. "The Earth loves its own."

Silvine struggled to find a reply. No one at Court showed her reverence like this. Taran insisted she was the Regina, but at Court, she was merely the future consort.

Taran added, "The Heart sees the Earth for what it truly is."

All six of the Fae rose to their feet.

"I trust Phos has at least somewhat explained the purpose of our mission? We must go north to deal with the effects of The Avartagh's Curse."

"The Avartagh's Curse" was a new phrase for Silvine. She filed it away in her mind to pester Taran about later. Hopefully, he would provide a meaningful response and not choose to speak to her in those irritating riddles and taunts he loved so much.

The luminescent glow of Phos's skin seemed brighter in the darkness of the tunnel they traveled. No one needed torches under the ample light.

Silvine quickly found the weight of her pack exhausting. She debated complaining, but everyone in their party had packs of similar sizes.

Taran strode beside her, quietly humming a tune to himself. It reminded Silvine of something Nene would have sang to her and Ana at bedtime.

Finally, Taran whispered in her ear. She tried not to exhale too sharply in his face, although she was struggling to maintain her breath the longer they walked. "Since you're doing so well at keeping secrets, I think it's time, Regina, I tell you something else."

She huffed, "Wh-what might th-that be?"

Taran chuckled. "Unaccustomed to carrying a heavy load, Regina?" Her sharp glare stopped his laughter. "Very well, I won't tease you right now when you're struggling to breathe and walk at the same time. These Fae you are with are the true Seelie Fae. It's strange, isn't it?"

"Pr-pronouns are r-really un-spe-cific. I d-don't know what 'it' you're re-referring to."

"I see your study of The Old Language has shown you what's wrong with the mortal language," Taran said. "The mortal language is too casual and unspecific. Anyhow, what's strange is that you've been told the Unseelie unleashed these creatures, which is true, and we are on our way to end those creatures. That is also true. What is untrue is the identity of the Unseelie. These garden variety warriors with you? As Seelie as they come. The place we just left, however, is the true Unseelie stronghold. All The Old Ones know it. The king just can't give up his delusions."

Silvine froze. Taran stopped alongside her. Phos looked back for a moment, but Taran tilted his head, a silent command for her to continue. In the bond the two of them seemed to have, it apparently took only one look for her to understand his meaning. The other six continued on while Silvine basked in the glory of catching her breath. She was half-tempted to sling her pack onto the ground for a moment's rest.

As she processed Taran's words, the truth hit her. "These aren't Guval's men, are they?"

"They are *my* men," he answered. "They serve the Seelie cause, not the King of Donadais's misguided purposes."

"Are you traitors?" It felt like everything she knew hinged on his response.

"We share the same belief that your betrothed has. The creatures of Death and horror must be ended. The bananach, felipentis, and other unsightly beings are a threat to all Life in The Realm. What we know, which the king does not publicly acknowledge, is that they only exist because someone ripped apart our realm one thousand years ago."

"Who?"

"The Avartagh. He was so thirsty for power that he violated all the laws The Creator put in place for us to exist in harmony. You can bring back the balance to The Realm, to stitch back together the fraying edges and tatters *he* tore wide open."

She searched his face for any of his usual mirth or laissez-faire attitude. This time, he appeared serious.

Phos and the others had gotten so far ahead that Silvine and Taran were suddenly in the dark. With a thought and a few notes in her blood, Silvine sent her powers to her hands. The tunnel walls became alight with her white glow.

Taran reached out and held her hand. The obsidian at her neck warmed immediately to his touch. "I want you to know that you will meet many people on this mission. I want you to approach them with an open mind. I cannot give you all the answers, but I can tell you this: what you do right now, what you do with the knowledge I'm giving you, can change life as we know it. I hope it shall change things for the better."

Her heart was in so much trouble, so much danger, but she couldn't stand to let go of his calloused hand.

When they caught up to the group, Taran let go of her and announced, "The sun is about to rise in the west. We will lay out our bedrolls here to rest. Phos and Demetrius will take the first watch, then everyone else will follow. Regina and I will go last."

Phos wrinkled her nose. "What if the queen and I wanted to take a watch together and have girl time?"

Something about her words tugged at Silvine's heart. It was an answer to her desperate need for female companionship. She'd never stop missing Ana, but to have a single friend in The Realm again would be life changing.

"That's precisely why you will not have 'girl time,'" Taran returned. "Taking watch requires paying attention. Besides, we don't need you filling her head with any of your Earth-forsaken nonsense." Taran winked at Phos as he gently removed the pack from Silvine's back and began laying out her bedroll.

Demetrius linked arms with Phos, who flashed him her effervescent smile as they prepared to take the first watch.

Taran laid his bedroll beside Silvine's while the others took the opposite side of the tunnel walls. Some of this journey reminded Silvine of her first flight into the forest and the physical demands of survival, but this time, she wasn't alone. She had adequate supplies to be comfortable. She wasn't sure what to make of the Unseelie versus Seelie truths Taran had shared with her, though. It made sense now why Guval had kept saying he needed Silvine and had waited for her.

As the next Modrona, she had the ability to reset the very Realm itself. If Taran was telling her the truth, it meant she'd have to pick a side eventually, even if she didn't understand the sides or what they meant.

Silvine fell asleep sometime later, but she soon startled awake as calloused hands shook her. A hand promptly clamped over her mouth. Her body went rigid, but before she could fight, she inhaled the scent of white birch and morning mist.

Taran whispered in her ear, "Stay quiet. Rise. Grab your dagger."

His strong hands steadied her onto her feet. The cavern was dark, and it was eerily silent, except for Demetrius's soft snores. Silvine kept one hand clutched to her dagger while the other stayed firmly in Taran's grip as he led her away from their party.

His lips brushed her hair when he whispered, "There are sluagh here."

Silvine's blood chilled. Nene had told her stories about the sluagh when she and Ana had been particularly naughty. Sluagh were said to be the souls of the unforgiven dead. Doomed to roam the earth, they snatched up humans to damn them to the same horrific fate. Sluagh appeared as ravens, but unlike the birds said to contain infinite wisdom of The Realm, the sluagh were harbingers of a gruesome death. Much like all the other nightmares come to life that Silvine had faced, these creatures were a perversion of all that was good in the world.

A chilling squawk reverberated throughout the walls of the cave, which was met by a cacophony of sinister squawking. Silvine thought they sounded like they were jeering at her.

There was a rustling of wings, and Silvine felt a biting pain on both of her shoulders. She cried out, trying to shake off the feeling. The wings flapping above her ears rushed in cold air so loudly she couldn't hear anything else. Before she could wrest her body away, she felt her feet lift off the ground.

She couldn't move or hear. *Think, think, think,* she told herself. The roar of wings and desperate squawking were too loud for her to detect the singing in her blood, the power of Life that would allow her to defeat these creatures of disorder and Death.

A sluagh bit into her right forearm while another clawed her left bicep. She could feel her heart pounding in her chest but couldn't *hear* the frantic staccato beat.

The squawking grew louder as more sluagh swarmed. They clutched onto Silvine until her body was fully airborne. She thrashed desperately, which only dug the claws and beaks deeper into her skin, tearing her flesh more.

Without her music, Silvine couldn't reach into the depths of her power. There wasn't even a low hum that she could discern. She closed her eyes and went still. She did not know how to fight this. Surrender was her only option, so she succumbed to the pain, the deafening roar of wings, and the high-pitched screeches of these accursed souls. Useless. She was as useless as she'd always been.

"Regina!" Taran shouted. In the chorus of destruction, his voice sounded no louder than a whisper.

It gave her the will to open her eyes, and shaking her head, she looked down to see a small, yellow glow. She knew it was their flower: a reminder of the beginning of her powers and the things she could do with so little.

Reaching out with her mind, she felt the rhythm of the flower's song. She couldn't hear it, but something in her magic knew it was there. In that tiny flower was the promise of Life anew. She hummed the power back to herself, quickly willing it into her body until a burst of white light shot from her chest.

Agonizing screams came from the sluagh. Claws and beaks released their grip on her in a frenzy. Silvine fell to the cave floor with a sudden thud, which knocked the air from her lungs.

Wind rushed past as the sluagh flew toward the campsite. Silvine felt the music of the flower fading away as Taran followed the creatures.

Hating her own weakness, she struggled to get her body to take in air again. She retched as she stood, and then, she made herself run back toward the sluagh.

Their people were surrounded. Taran appeared to have been trying to lure the sluagh away from all of their sleeping companions. In Silvine's Earth-forsaken weakness, she'd let herself get swept away and hadn't kept anyone else safe. This was the very weakness that had killed Ana and allowed Ainmean to burn.

Rage fueled every step she took.

The Earth loves its own. The Earth loves its own. Skies above, Silvine *did* love her own. She had watched enough of the creatures of her realm suffer and die. She would not tolerate another moment of it while she still had air in her lungs and a song in her veins. She was the Earth and its Life force. She was *The Modrona.*

The song in her blood fueled a death march song that crescendoed within her. Her senses were heightened. Something within her knew the chaos she was about to meet, knew the battle ensuing between unforgiven souls and still-living ones, and yet, the only thing she heard was the song within her soul, containing the rage of all the Modronas who had come before her.

The light of Life flowed from her palms out at the mayhem in the cave. Bedrolls were flung everywhere. Swords and wings and claws clashed and clanged. The metallic smell of blood filled the air.

The green glow of Phos illuminated Silvine's fight with the squawking sluagh. Holding her twin blades in her hands, she sliced through the air and hacked away at them. Meanwhile, Phos resembled a goddess of war and light, expertly dancing on her feet as she took down each unnatural bird that flew at her.

As Silvine's eyes adjusted to the sight, she realized most of her companions were faring far worse than she was. Quite a few were airborne and struggling. Those Earth-forsaken birds were relentless in trying to drag them away. Taran, relying on his ability to move through space itself, dodged the creatures and popped up from place to place trying to free each person from the worst of it.

Silvine pushed her hands forward, shooting the essence of Life out at the monsters. Birds and Fae alike flew to the floor and against the cave walls.

"This will cease," Silvine said. She found the voice of a queen somewhere deep within her. All the creatures, both malevolent and benevolent, paused and stared.

The surge of power deterred the sluagh for a few moments, but the Fae needed more time than she'd bought them.

The fight resumed.

More of her companions were forced into the air. Phos struggled against five sluagh, desperately kicking her feet to stay aground.

On instinct, Silvine called upon her power and listened for other Life in the cave. She found exactly what she needed. Another blur of wings rushed by her, tinged in a greenish glow. A colony of the biggest bats she'd ever laid eyes on descended upon her. She adopted the stance Taran had taught her, bracing herself.

The bats made quick work of the sluagh, slaughtering the creatures that were too dumb to flee and chasing the rest out of sight. One by one, each member of their company fell back to the cave floor with resounding crashes.

Taran appeared beside Silvine, eyes fixed upon her as one solitary sluagh flew toward them. It hovered just in front of Silvine. Its crimson eyes shone. "You shhhhall never undo what'sssss been done," it hissed.

"Oh, it speaks," Taran crooned as he flicked his wrist in its direction.

There was a roll of thunder, a flash of light, and the metallic smell of ozone as the remaining accursed bird burst into flames. Taran smirked at Silvine, who stared at him agape.

"I couldn't let you take all the credit, could I?" He pulled a handkerchief from his pocket and began dabbing at the bites and scratches on her arms. "On a more serious note, never scare me like that again. Never forget that you are the Earth, and I am your Wrath."

Before they could begin to tend to the rest of their party, a wail interrupted. Silvine's heart sank as she found her glowing friend hunched over a bloodied, motionless body.

"Demetrius," Phos sobbed. "Demetrius, come back to me."

Silvine had found her power too late. Though the sluagh hadn't carried Demetrius off, they'd taken his life. Silvine ran to Phos, wrapping her arms around her. If the embrace could absolve her of the guilt of inaction and take away the pain of her friend, she'd hold Phos forever.

ENTER INTO HIS ARMS

Silvine

The light of day did nothing to lift their spirits. Carrying Demetrius's lifeless body over his shoulder, Taran led them out of the cave with great haste. Silvine withdrew into her thoughts. She was sick of senseless, preventable deaths.

Her jealousy of Phos seemed silly now. In her preoccupation, she'd failed to realize Phos was in love with someone who was not Taran. In a matter of moments, her true love had died. If Silvine had used her powers sooner, the sluagh wouldn't have been able to peck at his heart—a heart that would never again beat for his wife.

Phos's glow took on a sickly, jade-green hue. She stopped crying and marched with a brave face, but Silvine could feel her grief. Losing your true love was something you could never recover from. She wondered if her father would have been a different man if Pulchra had survived Silvine's birth.

The group's wounds had healed by the time they entered the sunlight. The only reminders of the battle they'd waged were their bloodied, shredded clothing and Demetrius's corpse, which was slung over Taran's shoulders. The mood remained somber.

Silvine had never witnessed a Fae funeral before. They stopped beside an imposing oak tree outside the cave's entrance. The mouth of the cave opened to a clearing amid the thick forest. Rays of sunlight illuminated the forest in a wash of green and yellow.

Taran laid Demetrius's body atop the roots of a tall tree. His gloved hand reached for a fistful of earth and gently spread it over Demetrius before stepping back. Phos, still emitting a sickly hue of phosphorescence, knelt beside her husband's body. Her shaking hands gently smoothed his hair to frame his face. She reached into her cloak and pulled out a sword, laying it on Demetrius. Then, just as Taran had, she reached for a handful of soil and scattered it.

One by one, the rest of their group knelt to pay their respects, leaving behind small trinkets and sprinkling earth upon Demetrius's body. This was nothing like the showy funeral pyres for the wealthy or the hastily dug graves for the peasants in Ainmean.

When the last of their company had finished, they all turned expectantly to Silvine. Acting on an ancient instinct, focusing on the memories of all the Modronas who had come before her, she found her blood singing to the abundant Life in the forest. Her power had grown stronger with every trial. The obsidian at her neck warmed so much it almost vibrated against her skin.

Calling forth all the Life that beckoned to her, Silvine grew vines until they covered every inch of Demetrius's body. The music in her veins was soft and somber as she sprouted a small sapling out of his heart. The sapling grew rapidly, winding its trunk around the older, stronger tree.

She didn't have a moment to pause and see if she'd made a grave misstep. When she turned from her work, all of the company had bent their knees and were murmuring, "The Modrona, cultivator of Life and love, the Earth who loves its own." The reverence expressed made her throat tighten and her eyes water.

As one, the company rose and sang a song that Silvine knew in her soul. This was not the music of Nene and the humans, nor was it the eerie and haunting music of Court. Rather, it was the music of the forest—the music of The Creator.

"May the sun shine upon you,
May the darkness turn its back from you,
May the rainfall be gentle to you,
May The Creator smile upon you
As you look upon His face and enter into His arms."

Taran flicked his wrist, and a gentle rain kissed the earth. It was an offering equal to Silvine's own—nature and its forces, working hand in hand.

The mood lifted as soon as the funeral ended. Even Phos's glow returned to its usual brightness. The thought of her partner returning to The Creator's arms seemed to give her a peace she could not otherwise attain.

Their company trudged on through the dense woods for hours. Unlike Silvine's last foray into the forest, this felt peaceful. Squirrels, birds, stags, and foxes went about their business, seeming unafraid of the group's presence. Silvine's muscles ached, and her heart felt heavy, but she found the strength to continue.

Taran kept his distance from her for hours, leading the rest of the Fae onward.

She remembered one of the dusty tomes in her family library at Ainmean. Inside, some long-forgotten scholar had written, "A true king must never ask his followers to do that which he himself is unwilling to do. A true king is a warrior, a servant, a comrade, and a confidante." Guval may have had a great castle and terrifying Death powers, but Taran's humble leadership seemed to embody a true king.

With a gesture at Phos, who seemed to instinctively take the lead, Taran fell back. Silvine stayed at the rear, taking in the sights of the forest. The peace she felt was what she had yearned for her entire life. These woods felt more like home than any place she'd been before. Taran stopped to study her. "Do you know now why I call you Regina?" The sunlight trickling in from the trees made his teeth gleam and caught the twinkle of smugness in his eyes.

"In The Old Tongue, it means 'queen.' So, I'm led to guess that through your General of Intelligence wiles, you have apparently always known I would come to belong to Guval." The words felt wrong, but she'd always known that daughters were property to be given to their husbands. The idea should not have felt so unwelcome. She was going to be Queen Consort of The Realm.

A humorless laugh spilled from Taran's lips. "Your title of 'Regina' has nothing to do with the King of Donadais. Do not believe that because I am pinned under his thumb I desire to see the same fate for you. Regina is as much your true name as the one of mine you cannot utter. You are *the queen*. He is merely... Donadas and Avartagh."

Silvine studied his face as they trudged forward, the underbrush crackling beneath her feet. "I have studied and studied The Old Tongue, and I cannot find the words you use anywhere."

Taran tapped his temple. "So powerful, and yet, you still know so little of your people. Those words come from The First Language, what they say The Creator used to speak all of this into existence. We garden variety Fae have clung to the last words that we know. The Old Tongue was just the language used to unite the provinces of The Realm, to give everyone a shared language. It was picked for its precision. There is something that feels right in the soul and in the tongue when speaking the words of The First Language."

Silvine rolled her eyes. "Thank you for that lesson. You're such a *worldly* language tutor. Care to *define* those words?"

"Regina, you need only ask me. For anything you want." He winked. "Donadas means usurper. An avartagh is an abomination, an undead being that feeds off Life."

Silvine couldn't hold in her gasp. "Is saying that treasonous?"

Taran clasped a hand over his mouth in mock astonishment. "I suppose it is. Are you going to tell your *beloved* king?"

Silvine shoved him. "Sometimes, I grow so tired of you that I really believe I should snitch. Your head would look so much better on a pike on His Majesty's parapet."

He clasped a hand over his heart. "You always injure me."

The company ahead of them halted when they reached a stream. The crystal water was so clear Silvine could see the rock bed and all the fish undulating in the stream.

The group began laying out their packs, seemingly preparing their encampment for a brief rest. Silvine dropped her pack and let out a whimper. Her muscles released a day's worth of tension in a single moment.

Taran put his bedroll beside hers. "Come. They can handle settling in. I have something to show you."

CHAPTER 38

ELSEWHERE

Silvine

Taran shifted Silvine elsewhere without warning. She clutched her knees, breathing away the nausea. "When I was fighting for my life in the forest, did you ever think about whirling me straight to the king?"

Taran bent to her eye level. "I am not allowed to interfere with your journey. I can only aid you."

Silvine exhaled sharply. "According to whose rules?"

Rather than indulging her question, he stood up and rolled his shoulders. "Regina, you would waste a century of precious daylight chastising me and miss all the wonder around you. *Look.*"

Silvine was far more interested in getting answers from Taran than taking in her surroundings. Furthermore, he was the only person she could gripe at and push away. Even when she didn't know what to make of him, he was her one true constant. The thought made her stomach tighten. She forced herself to look around instead of acknowledging the way she yearned for him when he was gone, the way she wanted to push him away just to see him return.

They had landed on a slab of granite speckled with azure. To their right, there was a pool the same hue as the blue rocks beneath their feet. In the distance, the earth rose high above them.

Silvine gazed up at a waterfall. The meager ones she'd seen before could hardly compare to this. The water fell in neat streams of blue, not the roaring tumult of white she'd seen elsewhere, and sounded like chimes as it hit the bottom.

Daring to inch closer, Silvine gasped. The pool was lined with jewels. Taran had taken her to the most beautiful place she'd ever seen. She wanted to wade in and listen to the ethereal chiming for all eternity.

Taran stayed where they had landed, giving her space to process. Dipping her hands in the water, she sighed at the warmth. This was not the icy water she'd known in Ainmean.

Nothing here is as it seems there.

She endeavored to untie her boots and submerge herself in the warm water, but the beating of wings on the wind halted her attempts. This time, she would be ready. She sprang to her feet, not sparing a thought for her loose laces, and clutched her dagger in her hand, elevating the hum of her music until her palms glowed with power.

Taran froze. Silvine worried he was paralyzed with the fear of a foe that was finally too great for him to take on. She told herself it would be fine. He had saved her often enough. The trauma of Demetrius's loss could have crippled him. The Regina would save him for once. The scourge of the sluagh would not take another precious thing from her.

The largest black bird she'd ever seen loomed overhead. Its croak reverberated across the pool. Without hesitation, Silvine shot forth the full force of her power. The glowing, white light struck the magnificent bird in the chest. Unlike the creatures in the cave, this monster seemed unfazed as it began its descent toward her.

Once more, she fired a bolt of pure power. This time, she struck a wing.

The creature continued gracefully diving until it landed at her feet. The massive onyx bird stood at attention, as tall as her knees. Summoning other Life around her and finding moss close by, Silvine began to wind the substance around the bird's thick, black legs.

The bird cocked its head and croaked as it shifted its weight from one foot to the other, shaking the moss off with little effort. Clenching her jaw, Silvine swung back the dagger in her hand. Calloused hands wrapped around her wrist, forcing her to let go.

"Silvine, this is not a foe. This is a friend," Taran whispered.

Using its beak, the bird plucked the remaining bits of moss from its clawed feet. "The Avartagh persists in corrupting everything it touches, I see," it said.

Silvine started.

Taran laughed and turned his attention to the bird. "We had a casualty at the hands of the sluagh earlier. Regina is simply a quick study in fighting the corrupted creatures."

Croaking, the bird crooked its neck in Silvine's direction. "I am a raven, not a trapped soul. To be specific, I am The Modrona's raven. You can call me Bav."

Not grasping the magnitude of such a statement, Silvine looked to Taran for reassurance. He nodded.

"What exactly does The Modrona's raven do?" Silvine asked, finally finding her words.

Bav's eyes bore into the depths of Silvine's. These were not the eyes of an ordinary raven. Where the other birds had beady, black orbs, Bav's eyes were flecked with silver. Their depths spoke of ancient truths—truths in prophecies long-since revealed and prophecies yet to come. Her eyes were galaxy obsidian, the perfect match to the stone around Silvine's neck.

"I see, and I serve," Bav said. Without offering further information, the bird began to preen her feathers.

A spark in Silvine's obsidian startled her, and her blood warmed in response.

Bav's voice continued in her mind. *Your language is tiresome for me to use. I would prefer to sing to the blood of the Earth.*

How does this work? Silvine asked.

I will come when I am needed. I see, and I serve. The Earth loves its own. So much of what you are to do has been foretold. Bav flapped her great, sable wings and flew off. In the blink of an eye, she was nothing more than a black dot fading into the horizon.

Silvine whirled to face Taran, who had barely moved since preventing her attack on the raven. He must have known what was going to happen and perhaps even planned their meeting. He seemed to know more about Silvine's situation than she knew of it herself.

"I want to know your secrets," she whispered.

Taran cupped her face. "Most of the secrets I deal with are not mine to share, Regina."

"I want to know *my* secrets, then."

Gently, Taran pulled her into his arms. The embrace had neither the hasty yearning of Cardoc's nor the possessiveness of Guval's. Taran held her as though he wanted to put all of the pieces she was missing back together.

The warmth of his body, the earthy scent of petrichor and white birch, and the sound of his heartbeat soothed away the tension in Silvine's muscles. She considered pulling him closer, lifting her head up and putting her lips on his. Mercifully, agonizingly, he broke away before she could cross the bridge between thought and action.

"I do not think I can marry Guval," she said.

Taran's eyes widened. Silvine regretted her Earth-forsaken impulsivity. This was the man who dealt in secrets, who wielded the Wrath of nature, who boldly called the king a usurper. Here she was, giving him another secret.

Taran's voice grew husky. "Have you forgotten our bargain?"

Of course, she had not forgotten. It was always in the back of her mind. "Minuet checked me for enchantments and bargains. She found nothing. Our bargain cannot be real."

Taran raised an eyebrow. "It cannot?"

Silvine shrugged. "I don't know. *Is* it real?"

He tapped his temple. "You forget much about me, Regina. I hear the whispers spoken in the wind. I see the secrets that Court wishes so desperately to hide. His majesty's mage can only detect that which comes from her people. My magic has nothing to do with their ilk."

Silvine began to wonder if the heaviness she felt at the thought of marrying Guval was tied to her promise to Taran Dando—the promise of her firstborn child. How could she marry someone and give him a child if Taran was going to take it away? Taran had to have known the end result of her success in that trial. The reward for passing the test would be Guval's hand in marriage.

If Taran truly thought Guval was a usurper, this would have been the perfect scheme to alter his plans for an heir to the throne. Silvine bit her lip. "Am I just a pawn in a scheme to overthrow Guval? Is that what this is?"

Taran shook his head. "You are *everything*, Regina. Everything. I give you my word that I do have plans for you. I hear what you are saying about Donadas. You will not be his unless you wish to be."

Silvine looked down at her boots, their laces askew. "I *want* to wish for it. I should be thankful for it. And yet, I cannot make myself want him."

Taran's fingers traced lines around Silvine's. "You are far too powerful to be contained by Death when you are the very cultivator of Life. I will always give you aid, so let it be promised from my heart. But never forget that you have enough power on your own. You are more powerful than even him."

Silvine paused, taking in the words of the oath Taran had just bound himself to. He would always help her. The magnitude of such a promise shocked her. Yet, she hesitated. This was the same man who endlessly confused her and endlessly schemed.

Taran gestured at the pool, encouraging Silvine to continue what she'd intended to do before their encounter with Bav.

She yanked her boots off and crumpled her stockings inside. Slowly, she dipped her toes into the water, luxuriating in the warmth.

Taran's smile was genuine as he watched her twirl her fingers and toes in the water. "We call this The Pool of Respite. Long ago, you could find The Modrona in these restorative waters, attended by all the females of her court. The liquid is said to heal sore muscles and sore hearts. The burdens you carry are weighty. You need to spend time caring for yourself. I will wander out of sight so you can do just that."

Silvine studied Taran as he left, ready to ask if it was safe for him to go away. A small voice reminded her that she had the power to take on any foe, any threat. Rather than protesting Taran's retreat, she gave him a slight nod, and he wove himself to somewhere else in The Realm.

Slipping off her grimy, blood-splattered clothing, she rushed to get into the waters that called to her. The chime of the waterfall created a lovely song, and her magic harmonized with it.

Breathing deeply, she let go of the loss of Demetrius, accepting that it was not her fault. She surrendered her grief over Ana and her ambivalence about Guval. Every dark thought that caught her breath and made her freeze eased away into the waters of the pool.

When she climbed out of the waters, her old outfit vanished, and a clean set of clothing replaced the old pile. She fought back her grin. Taran Dando was many things, including observant. The minute Silvine's boots were laced, Taran took her hand without another word and returned her to camp.

The rest of the group had started a fire, and four tents circled it. The smell of roasting venison lingered in the air as Phos cooked.

In true Fae fashion, they all danced and drank Faerie wine under the starlight. Even Phos, who had been consumed with grief, made merry in Demetrius's memory.

No one in the company seemed to notice when Silvine withdrew. Perhaps, they knew her well enough to recognize the thoughts that consumed her, or maybe they simply didn't care.

Her necklace warmed as she huddled outside the entrance of her tent, sipping spring water from a silver flask. The warmth of her obsidian, she'd come to see, indicated safety. When it grew cold, it served as a warning. Although she feared for the journey ahead, she chose to accept the peaceful atmosphere while it lasted.

CHAPTER 39
SILVER BEAR

The Ursine Man

Great, silver claws scraped their way up and down the trunk of a tree. The bear paid no mind to the pieces of bark that went flying with every swipe. Finding no release from his great well of emotion, he climbed up the tree until he reached its top.

Below the canopy of leaves and needles, he saw the mountains of Ainmean in the distance, the sea beside it, and the small outposts along the coast, which were invisible to all but the most well-trained eye. He bit the top from the tree, dropped it from his mouth, and listened to the satisfying crash of wood hitting the forest floor beneath him.

Seeing Bav had shaken his curated mask of nonchalance. He'd known she would find The Modrona here. She would see, and she would serve. After all, none served The Modrona quite as faithfully as her raven.

Twenty-four years ago, the bear had met the one who came before at The Pool of Respite. She'd been heavily pregnant, soaking in an emerald bathing shift, preparing for the toll birth would take on her

body. The naiads and dryads, stags, small-winged Fae folk, Fae from throughout The Realm, and creatures of the forest gathered around her.

Bav was perched atop her shoulder. The bird did not need to speak a word. All of The Modrona's attendants knew the raven was prophesying mind-to-mind with her.

"It is time," Pulchra said.

Murmurs rose in a chorus all around her. Many of the onlookers held their heads and wrung their hands.

"It does not have to be this way," the bear said. "You can leave The Great Hunter and live."

Pulchra gave him a sad smile. "You know what has been foretold as well as I do. When the blood of the hunter unites with the blood of the cultivator, power will blind the world in its light. It is time. We knew my purpose was to bring her into the world."

Bav croaked in a way that implied her agreement. The bear hated that bird sometimes. Admittedly, though, she was the least bloodthirsty of the trio of sisters that had once guided The Realm, spurring on fate and bringing on wars. Without the other two by her side, however, the lone member of The Court of Skies Above became insufferable.

A wiser Fae had once said not to shoot the messenger, but the bear wished he could summon a lightning bolt and strike down the raven.

"We cannot forget your role in this," Pulchra continued. "You, too, are the one foretold in the prophecy. You must guide her on her journey, let her see the King of Donadais with true eyes in due time and see the restoration of the true balance."

"Yes, Modrona," the bear said. He was prepared to sign himself away to see Life reign again. He was prepared to see The Court of Earth, The Court of Wrath, The Court of Skies Above, and The Court of the Waters Below take their rightful places, restoring equilibrium to all The Creator had bestowed upon them. He would give everything he had to see the true Seelie Courts rise again. He just did not want to watch The Modrona, who bravely led their resistance, fall to set those events in motion.

"I shall remember my part," he promised. He wondered how he

would ever be able to stand the sight of the next Modrona, knowing her birth brought about her mother's demise. The Euron and The Modrona were supposed to work together, but there was much he would have to do to overcome his resentment for her.

In the present day, he wondered how he'd ever thought he would've resented her. Now, he wanted to give himself up to spare all of the suffering she would have to see. Silvine had the very best parts of her mother, with her own radiant spark and stubbornness. She would claw her way out of any situation, wielding her barbed tongue at everyone who crossed her.

He loved her. He wanted to claim her for himself. He hated every moment she thought she was tethered to Guval, the lecherous avartagh. The bear knew that giving up his freedom to the king would be worth it, if only he could keep Silvine from the monster's clutches.

With the way Silvine had come to him today, at The Pool of Respite no less, knowing she could not marry Guval, the bear felt like he was losing every ounce of self-control he'd spent decades cultivating. The bear wanted to whisk her away and set up her court far away from the clutches of Death. He wanted to get into the pool with her and wash away all his sins, all his trauma, and make her his queen in every way. Her stolen touches were more than he could bear.

A great beating of wings interrupted his thoughts as Bav perched beside him on the treetop. "It is not time to take her away," Bav spoke into his mind. "You are still enslaved to him."

"If she is free of him, it does not matter what becomes of me," the bear said sullenly. He turned to look at Bav and realized she'd assumed her other form: the crone. Bav was startling as an aged woman. This version of her possessed none of the warmth of a matron but all the reminders of the harsh and bitter realities of old age.

"This is why The Euron needs The Modrona," she said. "You are quick to deliver Wrath, but she will remind you of the importance of Life. You must be freed, too."

"I hate every moment of this. Do you ever get tired of talking so much sense?"

"I think that sentiment is similar to how the young Modrona feels about you," Bav replied. She cackled before stopping to stare at him with those unnerving eyes. "You love her. In fact, you are *in love* with her. The Euron has never been in love with The Modrona before. The oracle did not speak of what such love would do."

"I don't care what it will do, nor do I care that your sister never got to weigh in on my feelings. Silvine doesn't need to return my love. I just want to see her safe and out of The Avartagh's clutches." The bear steadied his voice, noting the way his tone had grown sharp. "You, Bav, would bind yourself to her only to bring about the war you think is the way to save The Realm."

Bav frowned, multiplying her wrinkles tenfold. "You bound her to you with a fool's bargain. Is that any better?"

The bear slid his claws along a branch, avoiding eye contact with Bav. "It worked, didn't it? It has allowed me to remain close, to lead her to the truth without ever crossing the line."

"I am on her side even more than you are," Bav insisted. "I did not say this love is a bad thing. It is simply... new. Maybe new is precisely what The Realm needs. Promise you will wait. Promise you will do what you know you must, no matter the cost."

"I will wait, even if it is the worst torment I ever endure. I know my role," the bear promised.

Bav transformed into her true form, the hulking raven. Without a word of dismissal, she flew away, leaving the bear alone with the tumult of conflict that weighed on him. All he could think of was the sensation of Silvine's skin beneath his hands, the way she looked at him so earnestly, the way she laid her feelings bare to him. She had been so honest while he was harboring so many lies. She would be the salvation of them all, but what role would he play in her story?

CHAPTER 40

A SILVER THRONE

Silvine

For the next two days, their crew trekked through the woods, following the coastline. Taran said that they would stop at a few small outposts that functioned outside the control of province Premiers. The outposts were unincorporated, lawless, and disregarded by the king. Silvine's mind wandered to the worst outcomes of visiting such places, remembering how she'd felt dancing with Anaras and being captive in Luc's cave. The mischief in Taran's eyes as he shared the sordid details about the lawless outposts only deepened her worry.

They continued to encounter wildlife. Unlike the skittish creatures on the edges of Ainmean's forest, the birds, foxes, raccoons, rabbits, and deer near the outposts went about their lives without fleeing at the sight of them. A few times, Silvine thought she spied flashes of a bear with silvery fur wandering the periphery of their campground. In The Faerie Realm, perhaps, there were multiple silver bears that her ancestor did not slay.

She shivered in her open tent, hoping the bear was not as intelligent as Bav and would not seek retribution on behalf of its progenitor. An attack never came.

At the end of the second day, Silvine and her friends left the forest for open air, and Silvine was able to see the first outpost they would visit. Far off in the distance were signs of civilization: small buildings and boats coming and going from the outpost along the shore. A raven circled overhead. The buzz of Silvine's obsidian told her it was Bav.

The earthy forest smells gradually faded away, overpowered by the battling scents of fish and salt.

Taran sidled beside Silvine and asked, "Are you ready to be among the unruly Fae?"

"Haven't I already been?" she retorted.

He gestured toward the outpost ahead. "You have no idea the revels and entertainment in store for you, Regina."

Silvine sighed, bracing herself as they finished their march toward the outpost named, aptly, Outpost Unum. Taran had informed her they would also visit Outpost Duo and then Outpost Tria. When she'd made a snarky comment about the originality of the names, he'd shrugged and said there was no need for fancy names for unsophisticated places.

"An unsophisticated place" was one way to describe Outpost Unum. Despite warnings about unsavory deeds and rampant tricksters, Silvine found herself in awe of the way of life in the small traders' village. The chaotic noise in her blood from all the variations of magic made it impossible to pick out each person's song.

The outpost had been established along a grassy bit of coastline. Homes were carved into the sandy hills with gardens growing atop them, coexisting with the chaotic, tall grass of the coast. Doors were wooden, intricately carved with Old Language inscriptions. The small roads, which were more like walkways, were lined with stones, smoothed to perfection by the waves.

Fae children played outside their families' cabins. They seemed nothing short of miraculous to Silvine. The only Fae child she'd ever laid eyes on was Minuet and Phelip's newborn babe. These children, with their pointed ears and shining eyes, were more like Ainmean's children than she would have imagined. Their games were different, with mysterious winds, flashes of light, and moved objects, but the rest was much the same.

Fae women and men sang songs at their looms in The Old Language. They sent fluttering winds and sparks of flame to dry their laundry. There was a carefree ease in the outpost she had never seen in a village or anywhere else before. These people seemed entirely unburdened. No one stole suspicious glances their way.

Most clapped and whooped when they spotted Taran, who returned their greetings with smirks and winks of his own. Silvine decided she had *zero* interest in knowing what kind of debauchery earned him such reverence from the residents of Outpost Unum.

Silvine was so engrossed in observing Fae daily life that she nearly slammed into Taran when he abruptly stopped in front of the largest mound house she'd seen so far. "This is the Unum Inn. Best accommodations around." He threw his arms out for dramatic effect.

Silvine took in the sight of the inn. "I've never stayed... in sand before."

Phos hurried to her side, bumping her hip against Silvine's affectionately. Silvine welcomed the first sign of joy in Phos she'd seen since Demetrius's death. "It is the most Fae experience you'll have. Are you sure you're ready for it? This is going to be nothing like your king's courtly dining hall and lavish rooms."

"I'm not sure that's necessarily a bad thing," Silvine replied.

"I agree wholeheartedly," Phos said.

Taran threw open the heavy wooden door, and a chorus of voices shouted words of welcome. He gave a deep bow. Silvine tried not to roll her eyes in response to his display of ego.

Guval was notably absent in the affairs of the provinces, which were overseen by human lords and ladies in his stead. Silvine assumed he played the role of absentee landlord just as much with the Fae outside of Court. Perhaps the people needed "heroes" like Taran Dando to look up to in the absence of a strong monarchical presence.

"We get to host The Enduring One," a matronly voice sing-songed.

"And all of my companions, of course," Taran said, beckoning to Silvine and the others as they trickled in behind him.

A Fae with skin made of bark and leaves for hair—a dryad—turned to face them. "Any friends of The Enduring One are friends of ours," she said. There was a tray filled with pewter mugs, all overflowing with amber foam, in her hands.

Taran reached for a stein, condensation dribbling down its sides, and guzzled it greedily. Then, with speed Silvine had never seen before, he reached for another while tilting his head toward the rest of their crew. The dryad flashed her teeth at him and thrust an ice-cold mug into Silvine's hands. The rest of her companions chugged greedily and dispersed to intermingle with the diverse group of Fae, all of whom looked like rugged versions of the paintings in Lord Morair's study.

Silvine sipped daintily, bracing herself for the foamy, yeasty taste of tavern ale. Instead, she was stunned by the light, crisp froth that tasted more like earth with the faintest hint of cinnamon—far from the "piss drink," as Ana used to call it, that she drank whenever they snuck a mug from the tavern.

Silver eyes flashed with amusement as they studied her reaction. "Nothing here is as it seems there," Taran reminded her. "Drink up."

He reached for her cup, lifting it to her lips. The gesture should have felt invasive, but his confident authority spurred her on, reassured her. Gulping, she drank until the cup was empty.

With a flick of his wrist, Taran whisked the mug away to Skies-knew-where in The Realm. He grew wilder—his movements simultaneously more graceful and fluid and yet more chaotic. He whirled her hands into his, leading her in a zigzag past the bodies that filled the tavern portion of the inn.

As he led her, Silvine studied the interior of the building. Its square, upright build and strong smell of pine made her feel as though the building wasn't merely a hole in a mound of sand.

Everyone was immersed in conversations, dancing to the lutes and drums played in a corner of the room or downing tankards of the strange, earthy ale the dryad served.

It was unruly and utterly glorious. Silvine drank it all in. This did not feel like the chaos of Ainmean, where she'd always been on the periphery, or the cold mysteries of Court parties. This was where she was meant to be.

"What about our bags?" Silvine whispered to Taran.

"Trivialities. They've been sent to our rooms already." He tugged her past the final throngs of the crowd, down a narrow hallway. The walls were lined with salacious paintings of various Fae in all manner of creative embraces. Silvine forced herself not to gawk as Taran led her farther and farther down the corridor.

She realized the ale, like every drink the Fae made, was far stronger than the watered-down hops she knew from Ainmean. There was a buzz deep within her that no other strong drink had ever made her feel.

A strong, pulsing magic, radiating from a door at the end of the hallway, sang to the magic in her blood. She cocked her head. "Where are you taking me?"

"To the most unruly place of all—*your* court, Regina," Taran said.

The ale has gotten to his head as well, Silvine concluded.

As they neared a glowing, crystal door at the end of the dark hallway, Taran practically skipped toward it. The death grip of his hand on hers forced Silvine to mimic his frantic movements. The power radiating from the portal made her heart thump in her chest. She wanted to rejoice, to touch it, to absorb the powerful energy. She reached out, her palm almost flat against the carved, white quartz.

As her skin began to feel the vibration of power from the door, Taran grabbed her, spinning her until her back was against the door. He stalked so close that she could feel his breath against her lips, the firmness of his abdomen pressed against the softness of her own.

Her traitorous emotions, tormenting her with conflict about Guval and drawing her inexplicably to Taran Dando, made her heart pound. This was it. This was the moment. His fingers smoothed their way across her cheek, entwining in her unruly hair.

She closed her eyes, breathlessly awaiting the spark of when his lips would meet hers, knowing this moment would change the trajectory of her very existence.

Two heartbeats later, his fingers were still entangled in her hair, and she was still waiting, not daring to stare into his otherworldly silver eyes, which were always so full of mischief and smug self-confidence.

"Open your eyes," he commanded, his voice husky.

This is new, she thought, but she would've done anything he'd asked of her. Even if she sparred against him with her words, she'd always do his bidding in the end.

She opened her eyes. The door, with its sharp, intricate carvings, was still pressed to her back. Instead of seeing the dark corridor, however, she stared up at the night sky. The moon was low and bright, hovering overhead. The stars twinkled in the sky. The air was cool and fresh.

Taran had extricated his fingers from her hair. He was standing an arm's length from her, arms folded, smirking. His leathers were gone, replaced by a silver tunic and pants embroidered with whirls of moons and stars.

He motioned to the night sky behind him. "Is this what you were expecting?"

No, it certainly isn't, she thought. She breathed slowly, trying to orient herself to the sudden change in surroundings. It was Taran's calling card, whisking her from one part of the world to the next without warning.

"I don't have expectations when it comes to you," Silvine said.

"Lies," he tsked. "At the very least, you could tell me you are surprised by how magnificent I made you look in the blink of an eye."

Silvine looked down. Her sweaty, dusty leathers had been replaced with a gown of white linen. Silver and black threads were embroidered onto its hem, forming the silhouettes of trees and flowers. She ran a hand through her hair, realizing the tangles had been smoothed away.

"How?" she asked.

"I am The Enduring One, didn't you hear?" His eyes glimmered. "I have endured *you* for months, after all. Come."

Silvine followed, linking elbows with him. Will-o-the-wisps lit the way as they walked through a dusk-lit forest clearing. The entirety of the forest glowed in purples and pinks, reflecting the lit sky around them. The smell of the forest, of *him*, overtook her senses. A warm feeling of rightness settled in her chest.

Taran wove her through an arch made of bent aspen branches before another clearing appeared. Hand-dipped candles lit the way to a dais of green earth and a throne of silver branches. Old Ones solemnly lined a walkway leading to the throne. It reminded Silvine of the way humans arranged themselves at a wedding, with an aisle left for the bride to walk upon.

Taran's moonlight eyes sparkled as he led her down the aisle. "My Regina, my queen," he whispered in her ear. "These are your court, here to serve you."

None of it made sense, but Silvine had become accustomed to bewilderment. Now, Taran led her down an aisle lined by Fae in a variety of shapes and sizes, all of whom looked upon her with adoration in the glow of candlelight.

Time seemed to pause and fly by simultaneously. The candlelight, the moon, and the stars were the only light in the darkness of the forest—the forest Silvine had been taught to fear, the forest she yearned for, the forest that made her blood sing.

Taran led her to the dais, seating her on the throne. This court was nothing like Guval's. The Earth and its beauty enveloped them. No one had snuck into an alcove to do their business or engage in a forbidden embrace. All eyes, a rainbow of colors and myriad shapes, were focused on Silvine. Taran stood beside her as she sat on the throne of silver branches.

Silvine was their queen. This was a world outside of the human domain of her father, outside of the court her future husband ruled. She exhaled away her nerves and inhaled the purpose she knew she had. This was her birthright. All of these Fae were gathered for her. It was a mirror of the paintings in her father's study, except it was far more beautiful than she could have imagined.

Power thrummed in her veins. She could perceive the truths within the music of the crowd gathered around her: their jubilation, their anxiety, their sorrows, their boldness. If these people were here to serve her, she should first serve them. She had no riches to offer. What she could provide was hope.

Searching within her heart, she changed the music in everyone around her to share a song of optimism and love. The music told a story of home—a story of overcoming the sorrow and despair from recent centuries.

Silvine thought of the grief in her own life—the people who had hurt and betrayed her—and focused on the gratitude she felt for the heartbreak that led to this beautiful moment.

She planted a glowing, yellow flower in the palm of the dozens of Fae gathered. Murmurs of awe echoed throughout the crowd.

Taran studied his own flower before addressing the crowd. "The Earth loves its own."

"And the Heart sees the Earth for what it truly is," the crowd responded. Tall, willowy dryads and small brownies alike clapped their hands together before all of them took a knee.

Silvine looked to Taran for reassurance. He gestured toward her people.

She took a step forward. "I am... incredibly moved to be here with you." She stopped herself before using the human expression of gratitude.

The crowd and Taran continued their call and response. When Silvine was in Ainmean, she knew the song and dance she was expected to perform. Here, she had to rely upon instinct. Her obsidian necklace warmed and vibrated against her chest, grounding her in the moment.

Bav perched beside her on the throne as Silvine prepared for the most ancient of rituals. Her very bones knew them.

The smallest of The Old Ones approached, head bowed. "May I place the crown upon your head?" she asked. The tiny creature wore emerald, homespun cloth adorned with beetles.

Silvine gulped and murmured her consent before lowering her head. A crown of flowers was placed upon her before the tiny Old One retreated into the crowd.

Taran cried, "All hail The Modrona—the Earth who has come to shed light upon the darkness, to counter Death with the beauty of Life!"

In that moment, Silvine realized Taran's proclamation sounded far more regal than any of the terrifying edicts Guval boomed at his people. Mirthful, enthusiastic clapping followed. Taran's hand reached for Silvine's as he lifted her onto her feet.

On instinct, she gestured out to the people. Every Fae took a knee at that moment, their reverence moving Silvine to silent tears. She still could not believe or grasp the true depth of her power and impact. Yet, in that moment, she *believed.*

Bav's voice whispered in her head, *May you lead us in the battles to come. May you restore the balance that Death has stolen from the Earth.*

With Taran beside her, Silvine felt all of the surreal become real. Whether through glamour or scheme, it did not matter. She was a queen on her throne, taking her rightful place.

As flasks—carved in wood, forged of metal, and dipped in springs —touched her lips, she danced through the night. Silvine was truly The Modrona. She was queen of the Earth.

Every time she danced across the fire, her hands clasped in those of another Fae, she could not shake the feeling that this was exactly where she was supposed to be.

Guval would never stoop to dancing with the members of his court. He used fear and awe to hold them all at arm's length.

Silvine, ruler of the forest Fae, was his opposite. Every dance, every sip of burning Faerie brews, drew her closer to her true purpose. She danced with reckless abandon. She snuck glances at Taran, who looked lost in the moment. Reveling beneath the starlight, Silvine found her home.

Hours later, as she stumbled through the crystal door and wandering down the earthen hallway, Silvine felt her world become a blur of scents and colors. She was The Modrona, the crowned queen in her own right, drunk on Faerie wine and liquor.

Wholly embraced by her people, she tried not to let the weight of such responsibility sink her. Instead, she grounded her thoughts with Taran's warmth and his unshakable belief in her.

Her father had sold her into marriage, gambling upon powers he didn't know existed. But Taran saw her. Taran knew who she was. He led her to the most beautiful world, lit by stars and an abundance of hope.

The festivities were hardly over as Taran whirled her through the crystal doors. The tavern room in the inn was filled with raucous Fae, singing a cappella tunes of loves lost and Fae tricksters.

Phos, clearly deep in her cups, ran to embrace Silvine. "My Queen has returned," she slurred.

The world was a blur of lights and sounds. A few people struck up instruments in the corner of the room, playing a lively tune that the drunken crowd sang along to.

Taran took one of Silvine's hands in his, gently wrapping the other around her waist. "The queen must dance with all of her people," he murmured as he spun her around the pine wood floor. He whirled her into the arms of another Fae, who in turn twirled her into the arms of someone else.

"My Queen," each dance partner mumbled in her ear as they took turns whirling her around.

After what felt like an eternity, Silvine found herself in Taran's arms again. She rubbed her eyes in an effort both to clear her fuzzy vision and fight the call for sleep. Anaras had once tried to make her dance until the bitter end, a thought that haunted her.

But here, among *her* people, she understood the urge to dance forever. This was the fulfillment of the things she'd longed for her entire life. She belonged. She did not worry about how her dancing might appear or how they might interpret her actions. She simply moved her body and freed her soul.

"Come, Regina, let's put you to bed," Taran said after hours of dancing. "You've been the very best queen tonight, but it'll take you a bit to adapt to the lifestyle. We leave in the morning."

His calloused hands, drenched in all the comforting scents of the forest, laid her in a soft bed. Silvine couldn't remember if he'd used his magic to take her back to her room or led her down a hall the normal way.

He pressed his soft lips against her forehead as his strong, familiar hands pulled the quilt and down-filled blankets up to her chin.

Lazily, she patted the space on the mattress beside her. "Won't you stay with me? Just this once, I wish you wouldn't leave me alone."

Taran chuckled. "Ascending to the throne has made you bold. Haven't you learned anything about me yet? This is where I leave you."

CHAPTER 41

MEMORIES OF WARMTH

Taran's voice, gently teasing her, interrupted the nightmare Silvine was caught in. Her dream was a blur of bloodshed and screams, flashes of color, and a sense of foreboding she couldn't shake. "It just doesn't do for The Modrona to be so hungover. You lost half the day sleeping. I have already generously packed up your belongings, but I insist you rise," he said.

Her head began to pound as soon as she sat up. Moments later, nausea blossomed in her stomach. She started dry heaving. A bowl found its way into her lap, pulled from somewhere in The Realm.

"Umph," she muttered.

Taran patted her shoulder, and she smacked his hand away. "Breathe through it, Regina. For someone so strong, your stomach is weak. You'll find the innkeeper's lunchtime meal on the table."

She sniffed the food and made a face. Food sounded terrible at the moment. A pile of leathers landed beside her with a gentle plunk.

"Get dressed," Taran added. "It is time to leave Outpost Unum. Last night's experience was vitally important, but we need to continue toward Alivon."

Silvine discarded the bowl as her nausea subsided. "Can't you magic me into clothes?"

"I save that for special occasions. Being hungover is hardly special. I tried to tell you that you weren't prepared to cavort with the unruly outpost Fae."

"We can't all be masters of revelry and generals of intelligence."

Taran's chuckle echoed down the hallway. He'd woven his way out of the room with his magic, leaving her to collect herself.

When they departed Outpost Unum, memories of the warmth of his lips on her forehead and her body moving freely to the music kept Silvine going. The innkeeper's food, though she'd been reluctant to eat it, bolstered her strength. Her head still ached, and her stomach still churned, but she moved along the trail without complaint. Taran, whistling to himself, seemed entirely unfazed by the events.

The rest of their crew plodded along, looking just as bedraggled as Silvine felt. Phos, usually the leader of the pack, hung back with Silvine.

At one point, the glowing woman stopped to release the contents of her stomach into a nearby bush. "My Queen, can't you conjure some kind of healing herb or something to stop this awful nausea?" she quipped, wiping her mouth.

"What do you suggest?"

"Mint."

Silvine wrinkled her nose. "Mint? There isn't some magical Fae herb that can cure the ill effects of alcohol?"

Phos shook her head. "There probably is, but I'm not trained in herbology."

With little effort, Silvine scanned the music of the forest they were again crossing. There was a cheerful, upbeat melody her instincts said was mint. She called it forth, and a small bush of mint sprang up at Phos's feet. The fresh scent wafted in the air.

"Are you going to just... munch on the leaves?" Silvine asked.

Phos grinned. "No, I have a feeling help is on the way."

Taran cast a glance at them over his shoulder and flicked his wrist in their direction. A silver strainer and two mugs appeared at their feet.

"As anticipated. We'll brew tea," Phos said.

Silvine had never consumed tea from fresh, undried leaves, and the mint had a rich depth she'd never tasted before. The tea settled her stomach and her throbbing head, making the rest of their trek more tolerable.

The other two outposts were just as captivating for Silvine. No crystal doors whisked her away to the clearing where her throne rested, but she knew if she needed to return, she would find a way.

The residents of Duo and Tria were just as thrilled to see Taran as those in Unum had been. Silvine could not figure out the reason why he was hailed as The Enduring One, unless it was a reference to his indefatigable party habits. Although Silvine limited herself to a glass of wine or two at every tavern they stopped at, Taran could drink endlessly without so much as a hint of a headache the following day.

Their last night in Tria, Silvine sat on the bed of her room at the inn, pondering if she should go downstairs. She had aided in healing a sick Fae boy that afternoon, amplifying his Life force and weaving it with the strength of her own. From the joyful racket downstairs, it sounded as though the revelry was far more Taran's scene.

Taran whispered in her ear, "I want you downstairs. With me."

Silvine started. "First of all, are you some kind of mind reader? Second of all, you can't just pop up into my room whenever you feel like it."

He raised an eyebrow. "I am not a mind reader, but I can read you like an open book. You may not remember this, but just three nights ago, you begged me to stay the night with you. I am certain I'm not unwelcome here."

Heat flushed Silvine's cheeks. She'd tried to forget that she'd asked a man who was not her fiancé to stay with her. She'd just wanted the comfort of being close to Taran. Regardless of her intentions, it was probably treason to betray Guval in such a way. She shuddered as she imagined herself, disgraced, being executed the way her captors had been.

"So you *do* remember? Fascinating," Taran said. "Anyway, The Modrona belongs everywhere I go."

"Even on your intelligence trips?" Silvine challenged. It was a stupid question, but she could never manage to hold her tongue with him.

He winked. "Even then. We make an excellent team."

His familiar touch warmed her shoulder before he whisked her onto the inn's dance floor. The music, played with instruments that reminded Silvine of chiming bells and flutes, rang out above the chatter of happy, drunken Fae.

No one else was dancing, but Taran pulled her close and began to spin her around. The music faded away in the warmth of his embrace. In her periphery, Silvine saw other Fae begin to join them.

"What if we just escape this place?" she murmured, resting her head on his shoulder.

Taran raised a brow. "The inn?"

"No. Court. If I am queen without him, if I am The Modrona, why do I have to tie myself to someone I don't think I love?"

"As I once said, I have plans. Do you trust me?" Taran's voice grew husky. He twirled her away from him, and she worried he would let her go. Instead, he spun her closer, wrapping his arm around her waist again.

"I think I—I trust you more than anyone."

The truth laid bare between them.

Once the song concluded, a lifetime later, Silvine found herself flanked by Phos. "Care to explain why you were just snuggled up to Taran?"

Silvine's face flushed. "I don't know."

"You are the Earth, and he is the Earth's Wrath. I think it's beautiful," Phos said. Maybe Life and Death were not the match. Maybe it was the Earth and its Wrath.

The rest of their journey, through the rugged Ainmeanian mountains, was far less pleasant. The leather boots Silvine had loathed became her most valuable asset. They gripped the rocky earth as she ascended craggy, granite mountains.

The dearth of Life forms in the area was a stark contrast to the abundant Life in the lower part of the forest. Even the trees were tougher, almost barren, swaying as they dug their roots into the ground. The wind shrieked as it coursed through the bare trees and slammed against the mountains.

Silvine clutched her cloak tightly around herself. The weather reminded her of stormy nights at her father's estate and Nene's relentless warnings about the wild lands beyond the village.

Phos's luminescent glow led them forward as they zigzagged up and down mountain passes. Silvine's muscles cried out in response, but she forced herself to trudge on. Taran was distant as they ascended the mountains, opting to lead the line with Phos rather than banter with Silvine. *Skies below*, she missed their verbal sparring matches.

She'd said too much at Outpost Tria. The General of Intelligence could not run away from Court with the consort-to-be. It had been foolish to suggest such a thing. Besides, where would they have gone? Ainmean would not have welcomed her with open arms, Ophelia would have rejoiced at her downfall, and Ana had already been sent into the arms of The Creator.

Furthermore, there was the deal to think of. Taran had bargained for her firstborn child, a secret she desperately guarded from Guval. Taran would not save her from the match that terrified her. For whatever reason, he desired to have the child of their union.

Too preoccupied to notice the loose gravel sliding below her boots, Silvine slipped and landed on her rear end, sliding down the mountainside they were descending. Hoping desperately for something to stop her, she clawed at the rocks as she flew downward. The weight of her pack only increased her momentum. Her body went limp as she realized she may never get to see Alivon.

Just as she readied herself to accept death by traumatic fall, she remembered who she was. She forced her blood to sing to the trees on the desolate mountain, and they sang back. She stopped sliding, opening her eyes to find herself in the rough arms of a dryad.

She stared into his gray-brown face, the color of the bark of the leafless trees, and was stunned by his sky-blue eyes. "You—you helped me."

His deep voice was thick from disuse. "The Earth loves its own, Modrona."

Taran tapped the dryad's shoulder. "Thank you, Oreas. You've done quite enough."

Oreas turned an icy stare to Taran. "You may be The Enduring One, but she is not. Why is she traveling these mountains?"

Taran scowled. "Are you implying that I am not doing my duty to care for The Modrona? Have I not earned my birthright?"

Still recovering from the terror of her fall, Silvine thought she was experiencing auditory hallucinations. Why was caring for The Modrona Taran's birthright?

Oreas placed Silvine on the ground, keeping a hand on her upper back until she was steady. "I think there are simpler ways to travel with such precious cargo."

"You and I both know Death and its creatures fear these mountains. This is the safest way to travel where we must go. Regina just needs to grow steadier on her feet. Her upbringing did not prepare her for her calling." Taran placed an arm around Silvine's shoulder. His eyes flashed. She swore she heard the rumble of thunder in the distance.

"Understood," Oreas said. "She called, and I answered. I should not underestimate your reasoning. You know how precious she is to The Realm. You might try to exercise more caution. It's not her fault she was raised as a sheltered human."

Taran narrowed his eyes, and Silvine thought it seemed like a challenge. Oreas bowed to her, shooting a quick glare at Taran before he turned into a whirl of gray.

Following the wind, the gray streaked through the sky until it collided with a tree further down the slope. Even though the moment was not graceful, Silvine found herself stunned to witness a dryad return to its tree. Nene had once told her only females could be dryads.

Silvine asked Taran, "What exactly is it that I am going to do for The Realm?" The rest of their group kept their heads down as they passed them.

Taran waved a hand in the air before reaching for Silvine's hand. "Save it, of course. The cultivator of Life must triumph over Death by any means necessary. Anyway, I'll be holding your hand the rest of the way. I don't need to be lectured by any more dryads about your clumsiness. Impressive choice to call out to the trees, though."

No further words were exchanged the rest of the way down the steep grade.

Taran maintained his silence when they rejoined their companions at the base of the mountain. One by one, they all placed their hands on one another. Taran's hand found its way to Silvine's shoulder. In the blink of an eye, she found herself in a dark tunnel, which was illuminated by Phos's natural glow.

Silvine made a mental note to ask Phos later what powers gave her the gift of phosphorescence. Remembering their last experience in a cavern, her muscles tensed. She reached within for the comforting warmth of her powers, and her hands began to glow with white light. Her obsidian necklace warmed in response.

Phos found her way over. "This cave is safe. It's part of Luc's cave system."

"I'm not sure that makes me feel any safer," Silvine scoffed. Realizing she was being insensitive, she added, "I haven't had the chance to say it, but I am so sorry about Demetrius. I wish I could have done more."

Phos squeezed her hand. "It wasn't your fault. The best you can do is to right what is wrong with The Realm. Right now, Death rules, and there is no balance. Demetrius died doing what we knew mattered the most, and he has returned to The Creator."

Silvine found herself humbled by her friend's strength during the height of grief. "To be honest, I'm still so confused by it all."

"I would be confused, too. I am sure Donadas has dazzled you at Court. Do you think you can give up that luxury to lead us? We live a far less glamorous life than the king and his retinue do."

Silvine blurted, "No, this is beautiful. This feels right."

"It should. You are closer to home than ever," Phos said.

Silvine cocked her head. She supposed they were close to the village of Ainmean, but they were supposed to go to Alivon. Home, furthermore, was a place she couldn't really name.

Within forty-five minutes, they had found themselves walking into the light of dusk. The cave's mouth abutted a knoll with a great castle atop it, which was graying and crumbling with age.

Finally deigning to speak, Taran walked toward Silvine and asked, "What do you think, Regina?"

Holding back the urge to rehash old events, Silvine opted for honesty. "It's a beautiful ruin, full of stories I wish I knew."

"A beautiful ruin? Look past the glamour."

Accepting his challenge, she squinted as she studied the ruin. Her necklace warmed against her chest. As though a fog had lifted, she realized the castle was not crumbling. It was fully intact, formed of gray stones covered in ivy and moss. There were towers at either end of the barbican. The gate itself seemed to be knit together from foliage.

"Welcome to Dùn Falaich, your castle."

She bit her lip, taking in his words. Every queen should have had her own palace. Could this truly have been hers?

The gate of woven greenery opened like curtains being thrown back. Although it looked deceivingly flimsy, Silvine had no doubt it had been enchanted to be as strong as iron gates.

"The Earth loves its own," a chorus of voices called from the courtyard.

Silvine scanned the figures mere steps ahead of her. All of the people, who wore green and silver tunics, had taken a knee. The recognition struck Silvine like a punch to the gut. She'd seen those tunics before. Her heart began to pound. The soothing beat it had grown accustomed to drumming out was replaced with arrhythmic chaos. Ana's murderers dared bow before her. Vengeance, once a lofty, far-off notion, now felt close enough to taste.

"You need to listen," Taran whispered, holding out a yellow flower in his palm.

Someone that was and was not Silvine roared in answer, "The time for listening is over!" Her powers flared to life, her palms sparking light. Beams shot out past the gate and into the courtyard. Screaming reverberated around the stone walls.

CHAPTER 42

FORCEFUL RAGE

Silvine

The force of months' worth of suppressed rage found its way into Silvine's outstretched palms. With every step she took, she called out to the Life around her, using it to hurtle Death at the green-garbed Fae in Dùn Falaich, the hideout. Her court.

These murderers were in her presence, in the court Taran called hers, daring to bow before her. She drew forth bolts of thorns. She summoned the fiercest creature her powers could muster, reaching through her surroundings until she could detect the predatory sounds of its heartbeat. She was no longer powerless.

Wind whipped back at her face, coming from inside the court-yard, making her efforts to cause destruction increasingly difficult. The harder the wind fought her, the more thorns she summoned. Silvine would never again let herself feel the bitter pang of terror and defeat. Today, she would win. She would win for Ana, Demetrius, and even Cardoc.

A need for vengeance drove her on as she glided through the open gate. She watched as the Fae fled, ducking and dodging weapons of thorns as they ran.

She felt the predator grow closer and closer until she thrust her right palm out at her side, feeling a damp muzzle rub against her skin. *Good,* she thought. No more Earth-forsaken murderers would run free.

The wet nose left her as the creature ambled in front of her. The muzzle belonged to the most immense bear she'd ever seen. Not that she'd seen many bears in her sheltered life. The bear's size, nonetheless, seemed unnaturally large. The creature, with silver-hued fur, stood on its hind legs in front of her where Taran had stood moments before.

Was it blocking her? She had called forth a deliverer of Wrath, not a barrier to her mission. Each time she attempted to sidestep the bear, it jerked its body in the same direction. The bear was, indeed, blocking her.

There was a croak and the beating of wings. Bav landed on the bear's shoulder as it sank back onto all fours.

My, my. This is a new side of The Modrona, Bav clucked in Silvine's mind. *Are you so quick to betray your own?*

Betray my own? Silvine snapped. *These people murdered Ana, the one person who stood by my side before I had powers everyone wanted. When I was no one, she saw me as someone worth saving.*

Are you sure they're her murderers? Bav countered.

I ran. They came to take me away, and she saved me. She sacrificed herself for me.

Modrona, that is not what I asked. Are you sure they're her murderers? Did you see them kill her? Bav's raspy voice, which had disturbed Silvine at first, had become almost soothing.

They're the only ones who could have done it, Silvine insisted. Her burst of power was catching up to her. Exhaustion rolled through her limbs, making them heavy—so heavy she needed to sit. *Why are they in my castle, if it's truly mine?*

This is The Modrona's seat. He told you the truth. Remember, though, nothing here is as it seems. Would you like to see with clearer eyes?

Silvine nodded, her breathing settling while her heart continued to beat wildly.

The world turned black for a moment. Silvine wondered if she was going to pass out from exertion, but the blackness quickly faded into a vision.

She saw the village of Ainmean from a bird's-eye view. Flames crackled, and smoke billowed up toward the sky. She saw herself crouching behind the well.

Ana stood proudly, arguing with Cardoc. The crowd was gathered around them. All was silent except for Ana, Cardoc, and the green-liveried horsemen.

Tension held Silvine's chest in a vice. She grieved Ana fiercely, and she hated what Cardoc had done. At the same time, her heart broke over Cardoc's fate. She hoped he was healing, tucked away at Court.

Ana yelled out, "Like hell you are taking her anywhere! Get your rotting carcasses out of Ainmean! You've done enough damage." The water bucket collided against Cardoc's head with a thud. Silvine watched him grimace and clutch the side of his skull.

The black-cloaked creatures slithered among the crowd, undetected, as Silvine fled into the forest. There was a shriek.

Silvine wondered, watching from above, how no one had noticed the strange creatures weaving through the crowd toward Ana.

No, no, no, she wanted to scream. Someone, do something—anything.

One of the creatures snuck up behind Ana, slitting her throat. No one in the crowd seemed to be able to see the culprit. The lead horseman's smirking, familiar face grew horrified as he focused on the bleeding figure before him. The crowd gasped and cried out as they rushed to Ana's side. The horseman lifted his chin before taking off in a gallop, pursuing the black-cloaked creatures, who were, in turn, following Silvine.

Silvine's return to reality jarred her. The bear was gone. In its place, the familiar face from the vision sat cross-legged, an arm's reach away, intently studying her face. *Taran and the bear are one being,* she realized. He was no mere Fae. He could shift forms. Even worse, he had been there that terrible day, sitting atop a horse, while her world crumbled.

Bav tucked her wings in. Her head was cocked. *Do you see now?*

Silvine covered her face with her hands. "What have I done? What does all of this mean?"

"There are forces that have been at war over you, long before you became aware of it," Taran answered gently.

"You," she whispered, fixing an icy stare in his direction.

His expression grew flat. "Yes, me, Regina."

"I—I need to go. Where can I go?" Silvine stood up, dusting off her leathers. "How can I ever make this right?"

You fight the usurper, Bav answered.

Pushing aside all thoughts of fighting anyone ever again, Silvine studied the courtyard. Phos and the other men were attending to a few wounded Fae. Silvine probed the area with her powers, detecting that no one had been gravely injured.

Breathing shakily, she praised the Skies above and The Creator that she hadn't become a murderer. She didn't bother to thank the Earth Below. That seemed a bit self-aggrandizing, and she clearly didn't deserve praise for the destruction she'd unleashed.

What kind of queen, however confused and irate, entered her castle for the first time ready to shed blood? Bile rose up in her stomach, heavy and acidic.

In a moment, her impulsive rage had ruined the few good days she'd had. She still hadn't understood her powers or her purpose fully, but she was beginning to embrace what her role in the Fae world could have been. Now, they would never look at her the same way again.

No one would forgive her. She didn't know as much about Fae custom as she should have, even after all those months, but she assumed this was an offense that could be punishable by death.

She surveyed the damage around her. Her skin went clammy as her heart continued to beat wildly. She wanted to flee, but her feet had become leaden. As she bent down to begin healing those she'd injured, the heaps of foliage disappeared from the courtyard, vanishing through the fabric of The Realm into one of Taran's infinite elsewheres. The injured Fae slowly rose to their feet, looking past her.

Taran stood in the gate of the courtyard, his figure straight and regal. He'd taken it all away. He'd washed away the evidence of her injustice, her fit of rage.

"The Heart sees the Earth for what it truly is," one of the injured Fae called, falling to her knees.

The others joined her, including Phos and their men. "The Earth loves its own."

Unsure of what to do, the depth of her shame changing the song of her blood, Silvine dropped to her knees, hanging her head. Could they crown Taran instead? He was The Enduring One, after all. He was the one they admired and respected. He had proven himself, time and time again, to be a natural leader, willing to serve alongside all he called. He knew these people intimately, understood their inner workings and customs.

Calloused hands reached for hers, gently pulling her up. "The Modrona bows for no one," he said.

Hanging her head, Silvine began to mutter something pitiful and apologetic. Taran's hands tipped her chin up to look at him. "*No one.*" His expression hardened.

A chorus of voices called, "Hail The Euron, The Enduring One. Hail The Modrona—power will blind the world in her light." Bodies flooded back into the courtyard, joining the other voices.

Taran turned Silvine so she could face her people. She forced herself to study them, holding her breath in anticipation of the fear, resentment, and anger she would have to accept. Instead, her magic sensed nothing but admiration and understanding.

Silvine started to sob. Wiping away her tears, Taran took her into his arms. Even though she resented everything about him and his lack of transparency, she needed to be held. She clung to him until the sobs subsided, the courtyard slowly emptying of all but a few strag-glers. When she settled down, she yanked herself out of Taran's embrace.

A tall Fae woman with silver hair and eyes the same otherworldly hue as Taran's approached, wiping at crusted blood on her temple.

Silvine swallowed. "I hurt you. I cannot apologize enough. I do not know how to make amends."

The silver-haired Fae patted Silvine's hand. "It would take a great deal more than some branches from my queen to truly hurt me. We were just waiting for the storm to subside." She frowned. "How-ever, there is much that could be said about The Enduring One's lack of communication. I told him that if he didn't tell you more, you'd be confused. You thought we were kidnappers, arsonists, and murderers, I'm sure. You will need to prove that you can be less impulsive, but we all knew the circumstances wouldn't earn us your favor until you knew the truth."

"But—but I caused so much damage. I was reckless, and I could sense everyone's fear." Silvine tried to lower her head, but Taran lifted it up again.

"They were afraid because, while they're not unfamiliar with the Earth's Wrath, they hadn't ever seen it do battle against the Earth itself," he said. "It was best to ride out the storm, so to speak." Thunder rumbled in the distance as if to illustrate his point. A few of the Fae in the courtyard glanced around.

Silvine's eyes widened. "The wind... you were the wind I felt, pushing against my powers."

Taran's only reply was a smirk.

The silver-haired woman continued, "We are impressed with your powers, certainly, and we have seen a few of The Euron's tantrums before. Through experience, we have learned to wait for them to pass. He was angry and reckless in his formative years. We just weren't accustomed to him using his powers to save us, nor were we prepared for the might of the two of you together." The woman gazed at Taran fondly.

"I use my powers for good every day, Mother," Taran argued.

"Mother?" Silvine blurted.It should have been obvious, but she'd been too preoccupied with the aftermath of her rampage.

"I see you've told her a great deal about yourself, too," Taran's mother noted dryly. "She probably assumed you were orphaned and raised by a wolf in the wild. He was, in fact, raised here by his father and me."

"I had assumed he'd crawled out of a hole and into existence," Silvine said.

This earned her a hearty chuckle from Taran's mother, who Silvine found herself instantly liking. "That's a fair assumption, given his behavior. By the way, you may call me Ethna. Allow me to show you to your tower, My Queen," she continued. "It was your mother's before yours, and I'd imagine you could use rest after... this. I can only imagine what The Euron has put you through."

"I have only done what is necessary to fulfill my duty, Mother, and show her what her true purpose is," Taran said.

Ethna shot him another look, which he countered with a shrug. "He shan't be joining us."

CHAPTER 43

FORGET-ME-NOT

Silvine

Moments later, Silvine was in her mother's tower, running her fingers along the coarse, woolen tapestries that lined the walls. The woven hangings reminded her of the paintings at home in Ainmean. All manner of mythical creatures, Fae, and lush greenery had been sewn into idyllic forest images.

"When did she live here?" Silvine asked.

Ethna pointed toward a blonde-haired figure on a tapestry. "Pulchra lived here for over a thousand years."

Silvine gaped. She stumbled over her words, finding no way to articulate her thoughts. The villagers had spoken of Morair's young second wife from a tiny, nameless village in the north. The younger spouse in that marriage, however, hadn't actually been Pulchra.

Ethna walked toward the four-poster bed beside them. Each post was made of a living aspen tree. The four met to form a leafy, green canopy overhead. The ceiling above had been glamoured to look like the night sky, complete with thin clouds and a crescent moon. The room smelled of jasmine and moss. Glowing emerald lichen formed a perfectly round rug underfoot.

Waiting patiently at the edge of the bed, Ethna asked, "Breathtaking, isn't it?"

Silvine could only manage an awestruck nod as she took a seat beside her. This room, through what she did not doubt was an abundance of magic, felt like the grandest place in The Realm. It did not have the stuffy pretense of Lord Morair's estate nor the cold grandeur of Court.

"I imagine you don't know much about Pulchra," Ethna said. "Would you like me to tell you about her?"

Desperate for a distraction and searching for answers long withheld, Silvine answered, "Yes, as much as you can."

"Your mother became The Modrona after the usurper slaughtered her mother in his greed. That single moment introduced rot, decay, and Death in a way The Realm had never been designed to experience. The Euron, coming into his own position at the same time due to the same misdeeds, had lost his seat as well."

"And The Euron is The Great Silver Bear, isn't he?" Silvine asked. She knew the truth before she heard the answer.

"According to the humans in Ainmean." Taran's mother scoffed. "No Fae has ever thought of The Euron as just a *bear*. The Euron holds the balance of The Court of Earth Below with The Modrona. She serves as the embodiment of the Earth itself—the love, beauty, hope, and cultivation of new and old Life. The Euron is Earth's protector, the Wrath of nature, the need for transformation, the moments that call for change and transition. Their powers complement one another, keeping everything in order.

"When The Euron found himself without a seat, The Modrona invited both courts to unify as one. Pulchra invited us all with open arms. We all staged a battle, feigning a loss that destroyed Dùn Falaich and its newly crowned queen. Now, to all who have greed in their heart and do not seek to see the truth, Dùn Falaich appears as a ruin."

"It—it looked like a ruin at first to me," Silvine said.

"Then you opened your eyes to truth. You are meant to be here.

You are Pulchra's heir," Ethna reassured her. "We have been biding our time. Bav advised us to wait for the prophesied moment. Key players had to be born, come into their powers, and see for themselves. Eventually, The Euron, my partner, lost his life at the hands of the usurper. He was in Asturia, trying to glean secrets. We never have been able to bring him north to lay him to rest. I am told where he lies is... beautiful.

"After The Euron's death, my son stepped into his role. Without Pulchra, he would have stumbled far more than he did. She had this gentleness and patience that drew everyone to her. She showed him what it meant to lead. He learned to endure from her."

Silvine struggled to put the pieces together. She tried not to begrudge Taran's time with her mother that she'd never gotten to have. Her lessons in leadership came from a petty, manipulative man.

Finally, she asked, "Why would she marry my father? What appeal did *he* have, when she had all of this?"

"It had been foretold long ago. She knew her greatest gift to The Realm, her greatest contribution, would be you."

Grief tore fresh wounds into Silvine's soul. Pulchra had entered into a marriage to her father because it meant Silvine would be born. She brought her into the world, knowing it would mean her end. Tears welling in her eyes, Silvine pressed for more. "Why not her? Why me? I am not patient or gentle or enduring."

Taran's mother studied her.

She has her son's knack for observing the emotions of others and continuing on without acknowledging them, Silvine thought.

Taran's mother continued, "The prophecy reads:
'When the blood of the hunter unites with the blood of cultivator,
Power will blind the world in its light.
All will seek her,
But only when he wins her,
Will victory occur.
As life leaves the one,
Who loved her first,

Will she shake The Realm from The Curse.'

Pulchra was not the prophesied Modrona. *You* are the blood of Owain the Hunter—the traitor—joined to the blood of the cultivator —The Modrona. You are the one who can right the wrongs and restore balance."

Understanding struck Silvine. Guval's motives for marrying her became much clearer. "Does Guval know the prophecy?"

Ethna's chin quivered, her expression distant. "The usurper knows those lines, probably recites them to himself when he goes to sleep each day and again when he rises. That is why he wants to mingle his blood with yours."

Silvine wished her mind worked like others. Her father would have picked apart each sentence of the prophecy, coming up with an answer or plot for each one. Ana would have viewed it as a challenge to defy. Silvine could only fixate on one alarming detail at a time: the fact that her mother willingly entered into a union with the descendant of a betrayer to bring her into existence.

The pressure not to squander her mother's sacrifice made her numb. It felt as though she was being pulled by her own desire to tuck tail and run while pushed by duty to the woman who sacrificed everything in hopes Silvine would one day save The Realm. Taran's mother patted her hand reassuringly and left her to sob in peace.

Following a good cry, Silvine pulled the tattered pieces of herself together. The time to feel would come later. The time to act, to take what she'd observed from her father and her betrothed and create something better, had come. Her mother said in her vision that Silvine could do what must be done. She couldn't let her down.

Taran appeared in her tower as she finished the final touches of her outfit. She'd found an array of flowing linen dresses hung along a vine in one corner. Opting for a white one with forget-me-nots embroidered on the hem and sleeves, she slipped into it.

"The true Regina," Taran said, leaning against the tapestry Silvine had run her fingers along hours before.

Heat rose from her chest. This man knew her mother. This man had the gift of time with Pulchra, a gift she would never receive. He'd known her purpose all along, known the prophecy that set into place so many terrible events and deaths, all in the hopes she would be the savior of their world.

Silvine harumphed as she ignored him.

"That was a cute noise," he commented.

"Can you glean intelligence on the meaning of it?" Her voice dripped with sarcasm as she tightened her boots. She pretended her laces were the most fascinating things in the room.

"Oh, I am *well aware* of the message you're trying to convey. I'm simply choosing to ignore it. Anger is a secondary emotion anyway."

Silvine rolled her eyes. "That sounds like mage-speak. Anger is my primary emotion and my sole companion these days."

Taran clutched at his heart. "Must you always hurt me with your delusions and sharp tongue? I am certain I've been your only true companion for a long while."

Rather than acknowledging any of his words, Silvine strode past and began the descent down the winding, spiral, stone staircase.

Halfway down, there was a flash of silver and a strong arm linked with Silvine's. "I can't have my Regina making her appearance unattended, can I?" he asked.

He led her to the dining hall, where will-o-the-wisps lit the area with an otherworldly glow. They bobbed and danced, hovering over them all.

Silvine, standing at the head of a long, low wooden table, addressed the multitude of Fae sitting around it on various pillows, tapestries, blankets, giant mushrooms, and mossy stones. Dùn Falaich's every detail exemplified Earth, forest comfort, and Faerie culture.

"I know many of you knew my mother," she began. Goblets clinked and murmurs of acknowledgment followed. "As you probably noticed this morning, I am not her."

Silence followed. All eyes were on her.

"I grew up a human, in a world where we were told the forest was dangerous. Although there *are* dangers in the forest, I know now that not all is as it seems. My home was cold. I never knew my mother, and her death made my father even more hard-hearted than before. After watching my village burn and fighting to survive in the forest, I was taken to Court. My father promised my hand to Guval, who many of you call usurper, Donadas. I did not know my own power until it was too late."

She cast a glance at Taran. His typical mirth was gone, his expression unreadable.

Her hands shook, but her voice remained steady. "I have seen and battled creatures of Death, creatures born of The Great Betrayal that frayed the fabric of our realm. I see my duty as your queen, as The Modrona. Together, we can restore the balance."

Phos rose to her feet, and several followed her lead, placing their hands over their hearts.

"I must go back. I must learn Guval's secrets and overthrow him from within. I will need you all to stand guard. I will need you to support me as I learn how to rule and how to use these powers. I will not be perfect, but I vow that I will never let my anger rule me again. So let it be promised from my heart. I look forward to the day I can be in Dùn Falaich with you, when the balance is restored."

Wings flapped behind her. *Well said, My Queen. You have chosen the correct path,* Bav croaked.

Silvine raised her wooden goblet, waiting for the crowd to join her. "Do you trust me enough to learn with me? I will never be Pulchra, but I will be the best Silvine I can be."

Those who had remained seated now stood. All of them raised their wooden goblets. Bav flew out of the open wooden doorway without another word.

"The Earth loves its own," the crowd said in unison.

Silvine lifted her chin. The ominous, bewildering phrase that had so startled her in Ainmean had become her battle cry, her motto.

"And the Heart sees the Earth for what it truly is," Taran cried, tapping his goblet alongside hers. The notes of all the magic around him, joyful and proud, did not drown out his melancholy melody. This time, though, she heard hopeful notes.

As the meal finished, Taran whisked away the table. Wild, erratic music began playing. Faerie wine flowed as the Fae danced. Taran pulled Silvine aside beneath a canopy of moss and flowers in the corner.

Silvine whispered, "I am angry with you. You lie. You keep secrets."

Taran flashed her a smile that didn't reach his eyes. "As I said before, anger is a secondary emotion. You want to be closer to me, more than anything. You're just frustrated out of a yearning for me."

"I—I cannot even—"

"You cannot even bear every moment we are apart. I may keep secrets, but every secret kept is for you." Taran took her hand and kissed it.

She yanked her hand away. "I am still engaged to the king of The Realm, usurper or not. I am not lusting after another man. I have some honor. I cannot even bear to think about *all of your deception.* But I have questions. Can you answer them truthfully?"

"I have never lied to you. I will answer every question I am able."

"Is Guval supposed to win me over to fulfill the prophecy?"

Taran crossed his arms. "I cannot answer that. Have you been won over?"

I think I am yours, her heart cried. Silvine shoved that thought firmly aside. "That remains to be seen. Does Cardoc have to die?"

"Was he not your first love?"

Silvine wondered how much Cardoc knew. His knowledge had to be significant. Memories of what he'd said in Ainmean and outside Court came flooding back.

She changed the subject quickly. She'd promised her people to no longer let anger rule her. For now, her alarming thoughts needed to be locked firmly away.

"When are we supposed to take on the felipentis and bananach?"

Taran threw his head back. "I may or may not have commanded

some false intelligence. It was the perfect excuse to have Donadas send us away to show you what you needed to see. Your eyes are almost fully opened to the truth now."

"That's not a lie?"

"I do not lie. If we want to play semantics, your betrothed lied to you about the dangers of felipentis and bananach up north. I did acquire the head of a felipentis to present for our return, however."

Glaring daggers, Silvine stalked off toward Phos, who was on the other side of the room. Phos threw her arms around her, leading her toward the dancing Fae. Taran did not leave his spot in the corner. Every time Silvine cast a glance in his direction that night, she found his eyes fixed upon her.

CHAPTER 44

THE RUSE

Silvine

After days of dancing and feasting, Taran surprised Silvine with her pack and the news they must return to Court. Their people gathered by the gate of Dùn Falaich to send them off.

"Must you leave so soon, Son?" Ethna asked, hugging Taran tightly.

He ran a hand through his hair. "You know the nature of my obligations, Mother. Phos and the others will hang back for a few days. Phos is much better company than I am, anyway."

Ethna smoothed stray hairs away from her son's face. "A mother still worries."

"Enduring One, remember?" Taran gestured toward himself.

This earned him a sharp look from his mother. Silvine stood by, watching awkwardly. The affection between the two of them was simple and tangible. She begrudged him for getting to know the warmth of his mother as well as her own. Later, she promised herself, she would bring it up. All of her rough edges and insecurities stemmed from a lack of mothering. What excuse did he have?

Suddenly, Ethna wrapped her arms around Silvine, pulling her into an embrace. "Be safe, and be brave, My Queen."

Her throat tightened. All she could manage to do was nod as Ethna stepped back.

Tightening the straps of her pack, she braced herself for their long journey. There would be much to do, much to observe, as she prepared to figure out how to fulfill the prophecy. The thought of a world where she could thrive without being under the thumb of a power-hungry man, filled her with hope.

Her one wish was that the prophecy did not mean she would have to be won over by the king. The knowledge of how the people of Luteche lived, coupled with the darkness of Court, made it impossible to truly give her heart to him. The Fae she'd encountered on this journey were nothing like the schemers of Court.

The threads of her destiny had woven into a tangled mess. She'd been promised to Guval based upon a lie, which by some Skies-blessed luck turned out to be true. Rather than relishing in the privilege of being the consort of The Realm, instead, Silvine fixated on the fact that everything about their match was wrong.

At Dùn Falaich, she was a queen in her own right. She could change the world so that those like Ana and Cardoc did not have to perish. She did not need a Blooding Ceremony. She did not need to risk her life to produce heirs. She only needed to fight and learn to lead.

True, the Fae of the forest were tricky and had their wiles. However, nothing Silvine had seen of the Earth she presided over showed the dark side of human rule or Guval's leadership. Though Fae morality did not make an even comparison with that of the humans, it did not come with the blinding malice of Guval's world, nor did it feed power structures that left many subservient, as was the case in Ainmean.

This world deserved a fight for its restoration.

"How's your delicate stomach today, Regina?" Taran winked.

"It's never been better."

He placed a hand on her shoulder, and before Silvine could protest, they were hurtling through the world. Unlike usual, there were whorls of light, blurs of Life, and buildings, which seemed to pass by them for a solid minute. Her stomach lurched. As she prepared to protest, she realized they'd landed on the plains outside of Guval's castle.

Taran clutched his knees. "Your face was priceless. Long-distance travel is a shock to the senses."

She narrowed her eyes. "You mean to tell me we traveled on foot for days when you could have taken us there with magic?"

"No. I can't shift six people that far. I am a little out of breath from transporting just you and I through The Realm, and I won't be able to shift for hours." He straightened his posture. "Besides, as I've said, there were things you needed to do and see on our journey."

"A little out of breath? I have a feeling Phos and company won't appreciate traveling back on foot," Silvine said.

He waved a hand dismissively. "I have things for her to do on the way. Have you forgotten? There is always a method to my madness. You had much to see and learn. The point was the experience, not the destination, Regina."

Taran retrieved the snarling head of a felipentis from a sack before sending their packs away with a flick of his wrist. They made their way to the drawbridge, up the steep hillside. Guards greeted Taran from the barbican before lifting the creaking steel gate.

With a sureness in his step, Taran led Silvine through parts of Guval's castle she'd never seen before until they arrived in the throne room.

Per usual, all manners of depravity were transpiring in the alcoves. Multiple Fae cozied up to one another in one area. Others were relieving themselves in the corners. The rest passed around crystal flagons and smoked earthy substances.

Silvine did her best to fix her gaze on the dais at the end of the room.

Guval lazed on his throne. He tapped his fingers absentmindedly.

For him, the acts of his court were an everyday occurrence. Silvine didn't think she would ever grow accustomed to public acts of indecency.

The arm of the throne was occupied by Minuet, whose legs—exposed by the deep slit of her violet gown—nearly brushed against Guval's.

When Silvine and Taran approached the dais, Taran tossed the felipentis head onto the amethyst rug in front of the king before bending a knee. Silvine stood beside him, studying Guval. He appeared entirely uninterested.

The music in the king's magic was its usual ill-timed dissonance. Minuet didn't shift her body at all, staying closely tucked beside him.

The king gestured at Taran to stand. "I see you vanquished our... enemies. I hear there may be an Unseelie rebellion to the north as well. Did you see anything?" Guval flexed his long, ring-adorned fingers. Minuet reached out as if to stroke them. He swatted her hand away.

"All is as it should be. I continue to work to detect the source of the surge in undead creatures," Taran said. "If there is an uprising brewing, it is too small to be notable. If that changes, I will notify you."

"Very well." Guval waved Taran away in dismissal. Taran strolled to the exit door behind the dais. Silvine knew this would lead him to the dungeons. Her heart stuttered as she wondered if Cardoc was whole again.

The din of Court's alcove-going Fae hummed behind her. She waited for Guval to say something.

Finally, he asked, "Have you eaten?"

"I have," she answered.

Minuet clasped her hands together. "You are just in time for all kinds of entertainment. Phelip's long-awaited ball is tomorrow night, and we are to have an execution in the morning."

Silvine's heart sank. She knew whose execution would happen in the morning.

Guval snapped his fingers. "Phelip."

His crimson-eyed brother appeared at his side.

"Go catch Lady Silvine up on your party and anything you would like her to know before the event. You know I don't care for those details."

Silvine's heart slowed; the music in her soul matched its funereal pace. Numb to everything, she let Phelip take her arm and whisk her away to The Mirror Room to practice his intricately choreographed dances. Now was the time to draw within herself. She would be ready when the time came to strike down the King of Donadais.

CHAPTER 45

AS LIFE LEAVES

Silvine

The rest of Silvine's first day back at Court went by in a blur of last-minute visits to the grumpy seamstress, tripping over her feet in The Mirror Room, reviewing dining etiquette, and pretending Phelip's plans were interesting. She cast her magic in every room, searching for unique powers and vulnerabilities.

While she glossed over the pages of Phelip's self-published, illustrated guide to Court etiquette, he interrupted her with a pointed clearing of his throat.

"Yes?" she asked.

"I can tell your excitement does not match mine. I smell boredom and desperation."

Silvine closed the book, narrowing her eyes at him. "How does it feel to smell the emotions of others?"

Phelip stifled a chuckle into an embroidered handkerchief. "Honestly, it usually feels just fine. Most of the leeches here at Court have the emotional depth of a fishpond. You, however, overtake my senses with the emotions you have. There are as many surprises in your feelings as there are in the great ocean. It is so... lively."

His comment bordered on praise. She'd never heard him speak so candidly about life at Court. She wondered what spurred this vulnerability from him. "I see," she said.

"No, you do not see, but you do *hear*. Everything you hear incites new feelings, new emotions, new depths of experiences that I cannot unlock myself. It is as though there is music in your very soul, your very blood. I remember the first battles I waged for Guval. I was so drained by them," Phelip said.

Silvine shrugged. "I'm far from drained."

Phelip produced two crystal wine glasses, pouring rich, dark liquid into each cup. "I admire your denial. I hardly feel anything most days. Dull your emotions, but don't ever give them up. They make you unique around here, a beacon of light in a sea of red Death. I am honestly... glad that you will soon be my sister."

Silvine gulped down the wine, eager to numb the intensity of her pain. "Spoken more like a mage than a courtier."

Phelip scoffed. "My wife wishes she had an ounce of the wisdom I do. She's still girlishly devoted to my brother's every flight of fancy. I have battle scars on my heart and body that refuse to allow me such naïveté."

Silvine swirled the last bit of wine around in its glass. The match between the mage and prince seemed to be a poor one. "Do you ever feel alone at Court?"

"Always. That's why I've carved out my own niche. When my brother isn't forcing me to go wage his wars, which have become more infrequent since Taran's arrival and then yours, I would rather spend my time creating something beautiful, something that the people can enjoy. Guval sees it as frivolity, but it's my only creative expression."

The warmth of the wine lightened Silvine's spirits a little. "Do you think I could have dinner brought to my room? I think I'd rather be alone. Could I go to the Court library afterward?"

Phelip rose, smoothing his tunic. "It's absurd that the future consort should have to ask permission for either, but I will grant it to you nonetheless. I'll have your attendant bring dinner. Do as you please afterward. You're more apt to be able to keep yourself safe than I am."

Silvine pondered Phelip's honesty. She related to him more than she'd thought she could. In marriage, Silvine and Ophelia had the gift of separation from one another. Phelip's marriage, however, bound him to a life under Guval's thumb. She wondered how comfortable the king's brother felt about the king's closeness with his wife—if centuries would dull the jealousy that sparked in her own chest.

After nibbling at a rich spread of five courses, she snuck away to the library. Books often revealed hidden information and long-forgotten secrets. She hoped she could uncover truth among the king's tomes.

Few courtiers appeared to bother reading, and there was no librarian at Court. Dust and cobwebs covered the expansive room, made more evident by the white marble walls, floors, and bookshelves. The violet windowpanes cast an eerie glow throughout the room. The smell of must hung heavy in the air.

Silvine's obsidian necklace, the true companion throughout her trials and tribulations, turned ice-cold. Her teeth chattered. The library at Court lacked all the warmth she felt in other archives. Even Lord Morair's personal library felt more inviting.

There appeared to be no organization of the books. Silvine began trying to read spines, all in The Old Language, to find books about avartaghs, prophecies, and the three Fae courts. She exhaled. Most of the books were about mining and its history, with several on accounting. There were also atlases of Galanthe and historical accounts of the provinces.

A few books on the opposite side of the room wiggled from the shelves. They whirred through the air, landing on the table in the center of the room. Misplaced dust particles coated the air, causing Silvine to cough and splutter.

Four titles had been magicked onto the table: *Secrets of The Realm, Guide to the Three Courts, The Magic of Rafflesia,* and *The Oracle and Her Sisters.* Silvine looked around for Taran. Sending books flying through space was something he would do. She could hear his signature melancholy song fading in the distance. He did not make himself known, however. She scooped the books into her arms and retreated to her room, welcoming the opportunity to lose herself in research rather than think about Cardoc's fate.

Early the next morning, she found herself in the throne room. The walls were lined with Fae, most of whom sported crimson eyes and were bedecked in finery.

Guval's voice echoed through the great expanse. "Court, today you are here to see justice served. The blood of a trespasser will be shed. He will learn what the powers of our Court truly mean. No weak human, no other Fae court, can ever compare to what we are capable of."

Silvine stood beside him, silent and frozen. She'd tried to convince her attendant to dress her in funeral black, but her request had been denied. Instead, she wore a purple silk gown and a velvet cloak. The two luxurious fabrics felt as heavy as her soul.

She scanned the crowd for Taran. She hadn't laid eyes on him since Guval dismissed him the previous day, after Taran laid the head of a felipentis at his feet. He'd given the king a reason to believe they'd accomplished the mission he'd sent them on without betraying their secrets.

The door behind the throne creaked open. Taran walked out, arm linked with a hooded figure wearing a silken black tunic with violet stitching. His cloak billowed behind him. His eyes were hard, but the rest of his expression was mirthful. For the briefest moment, he scanned Silvine's face, and she felt a twinge of apology in it.

She fidgeted with the obsidian beneath her neckline, rubbing her fingers around its silver cage. The crystal remained as cold as it'd been in the library the night before. *Danger*, she thought to herself. *We are all in danger here.*

You will be safe, Bav croaked in her mind.

Taran led his prisoner to the center of the room, above the opening in the floor where Silvine had slain the felipentis months before. With barely perceptible gentleness, he eased Cardoc onto his knees, removed the hood from his face, and unbound his hands from behind his back.

Silvine glided across the floor, a single stride behind Guval, as they approached Cardoc and Taran. She broke out in a cold sweat and forced herself to focus on the music within her soul.

Guval folded his arms. "You are charged with treason per viam transgressionem. What do you say for these charges, mortal?"

Treason by way of trespassing is a ridiculous reason to kill someone, Silvine thought. Not even Lord Morair would execute someone for such a minor offense.

The deafening roar of jeers, hollering, and cries for execution came from all sides of the room. Silvine hated Guval's bloodthirsty monsters.

Cardoc fixed his gaze on Silvine, unflinching. "I say, if those are the laws of the usurper, I have violated them. I am bound to higher laws than yours."

The king tensed beside Silvine, the dissonant notes of his magic ringing in her ears. "Such insolence. Are you prepared to die for your folly?"

"I would die a thousand deaths for my queen," Cardoc replied. His brown eyes softened. In another life, another place, maybe he would have been hers. "Silvine, do not forget my sacrifice. Do not forget my family. Most importantly, do not forget who you are at your core."

"Silence!" Guval's shout quieted the crowd of eager courtiers. "This is not a province court. You are not entitled to final words."

Silvine thought of their stolen kisses, their loving words, and the way she'd felt running with him in a field of wildflowers. She knelt in front of him and mouthed "I love you." The corners of his lips curved upward, and he gave a slight nod, his only acknowledgment and declaration of affection. She may no longer have been in love with him, but a part of Cardoc would always live in her heart.

A puzzled look crossed Guval's face. "My consort need not kneel beside a traitor. Rise, Lady Silvine. I know your tender half-human heart feels compassion, but it's misplaced." His patronizing tone made her sick, but she complied.

Hold yourself together, Bav said.

Guval lifted his palms.

Taran interrupted, "Erm, King, if I may—"

The king pressed his lips together before asking, "Yes, Dando?"

"The prisoner has the right to choose his means of execution."

Silvine's belly fluttered. She eyed Taran, waiting for an elaborate plan to unfold.

Guval groaned. "I am aware." He turned to Cardoc. "Do you not prefer a painless death from your king?"

"I would prefer to die by blade, with some of my dignity intact," Cardoc answered.

Guval exhaled sharply. Cardoc's request seemed to please the bloodthirsty crowd, however. When the king slaughtered the guards, it looked both quick and miserable. For his courtiers, a blade provided far more entertainment.

Silvine's hopeful flutters faded, replaced by knots. She held her breath, forcing her eyes to stay open, although her every instinct screamed at her to look away.

The sound of a sword unsheathing twanged in the air. Taran revealed the sword at his side and steadied himself to swing his blade. Cardoc held steady on his knees. He did not falter or break eye contact with Silvine.

Her knees threatened to buckle, but she urged her body to hold itself together. The cold sting of betrayal from Taran hurt as much as Cardoc's impending death. She couldn't fathom why Taran, who had crowned her queen in the forest and fought alongside her in every trial, would slay Cardoc.

The blade soared through the air. There was a sickening squelch and crunch as it made contact with Cardoc's neck. His decapitated head fell to the floor, body crumpling beside it. The metallic smell of blood filled Silvine's senses as it pooled and ran like a river across the floor, staining her shoes and the edge of her gown in sickly crimson. Her breaths came in ragged gasps.

Bav whispered to her mind, *This is for the best.*

Silvine dug deep for her magic and shoved the raven out of her mind. She didn't think she could forgive Taran for killing Cardoc. She'd overlooked his deception and his scheming, but this level of betrayal could not be forgotten.

The throne room rang out with cheers.

The power within Silvine, always a comforting hum, grew louder and louder, begging to be let out. She tamped down on it, trying to conceal her emotions. Guval bent to dip his fingers in Cardoc's blood then raised his hand in the air.

"May Court dominate and direct The Realm for eternity," he called.

"Hail King Guval of Court! Hail King Guval of The Realm! Death overcomes all," his people answered.

Taran bent beside Cardoc's dismembered body. His cloak lay on the floor in the puddle of blood. He collected the body and head, placing the pieces of Silvine's first love onto his mantle. In a voice so low only Silvine could hear, he sang:

"May the sun shine upon you,

May the darkness turn its back from you,

May the rainfall be gentle to you,

May The Creator smile upon you

As you look upon His face and enter into His arms."

Bav's voice appeared in her mind, harmonizing with Taran in the funeral song. Tears streamed down Silvine's face.

Where are you? she asked.

Watching as always, Modrona.

Her mind went quiet as Bav severed their connection.

Realization hit like a punch to the gut. All of her Ainmeanian friends were dead. Her sister had never been an ally, and her father had sold her out for more power.

Silvine lifted her head at Guval, whose eyes had grown wild as he chatted with Minuet and Phelip. Minuet's frenzied expression matched his. Phelip raised an eyebrow in Silvine's direction, no doubt smelling her grief and despair. She left the throne room without a word.

As she roamed the empty halls on the way to her bed chamber feeling numb, she remembered the prophecy as Taran's mother had told it.

"When the blood of the hunter unites with the blood of cultivator,
Power will blind the world in its light.
All will seek her,
But only when he wins her,
Will victory occur.
As life leaves the one,
Who loved her first,
Will she shake The Realm from The Curse."

If the prophecy served as a guide to the future, it seemed the key events were set. Life had left the one who loved her first.

CHAPTER 46

BLOODSTAINS AND BALLGOWNS

Silvine

Silvine's nameless attendant slipped her into a blood-red, split-sleeved dress for the ball that evening. She tightened a red leather bodice outside of the dress so firmly that Silvine had no idea how she'd breathe. Finishing the look, the attendant placed a swipe of kohl around her eyes, a heavy dusting of blush on her cheeks, and red paint on her lips.

The color scheme made Silvine's stomach lurch, a cruel reminder of what had happened that morning. She'd taken three baths in an attempt to scrub away the stain of Cardoc's death from her soul. Nothing brought relief.

Phelip had apparently given the seamstress very specific instructions on the color of her gown. The theme of the ball was "brimming with excitement for The Blooding Ceremony." The only person who could be considered *brimming with excitement* was Guval and perhaps his mage.

"You are stunning, Lady," her attendant commented.

All Silvine could muster was a nod.

Phelip entered her room, adorned in head-to-toe ruby and white.

His sharp cheekbones were painted as red as hers. "Come! You are the guest of honor. First, we feast." Phelip waved his hands in the air. He'd clearly indulged in a few goblets of wine.

She tried to muster enthusiasm. It didn't come. Feeling flat, she offered him her arm. Phelip murmured constant reminders about the appropriate way to walk as they entered the dining hall. Normal Fae grace and agility would not suffice for this special occasion. Steps had to be measured, toes pointed, as they glided down empty hallways.

The dining hall's magical discordance overwhelmed Silvine's senses as she strode through the marble archway. So many notes, so few of them producing beautiful sounds. She fought the childish urge to clamp her hands over her ears, knowing it would be futile anyway. The magic in her blood, not her ears, felt each dissonant note.

Four tables lined the perimeter of the room, an array of hors d'oeuvres and wines laid out on them. In the center, more Fae than she'd ever seen mingled. Some paused to plant kisses on the mouths of others. Some swayed to the eerie music playing in the corner of the room. Some wore hideous masks. Others slathered their faces in layers of intricate paint and makeup. The only thing all the Fae in attendance seemed to agree on was the color of the evening: bright red. Bile burned Silvine's throat.

A crimson-eyed usher announced, "Introducing Lady Silvine—promised to King Guval—and Prince Phelip—Master of Festivities and General of War."

Minuet wove through the crowd, pointing a bony finger in Silvine's direction. "My Lady, you look simply marvelous. Red is your color." She turned to Phelip, who bowed his head in acknowledgment before departing.

"I thought purple was the color of Court?" Silvine asked.

Minuet flipped her hair over her shoulder. Her skin-tight dress left little to the imagination. "It is the official Court color. Red is much better, though, don't you think? It reminds me of so many wonderful things. Like blood. Blood represents Life. And Life is so *delicious.*"

Silvine could not suppress her shudder. "I need air. Excuse me."

Weaving her way through the crowd, she sped toward a purple stained-glass door that led to a balcony. The people of Court seemed content to stay indoors. The sepulchral marble ceilings, however, felt more like a tomb than a home to Silvine. She knew a few moments' solitude with the evening air would help her collect herself.

A woman in a shimmering dress leaned over the balcony's railing, studying the twinkling stars above.

So much for solitude, Silvine thought. Few at Court bothered to interact with her. Perhaps she would still be able to settle her nerves in peace.

"Silvine," the woman called. Her voice was familiar. Ophelia.

Silvine flinched. She knew she'd see her sister frequently, as her husband presided over Guval's capital city. She just hadn't thought she'd have to face her right then.

Ophelia approached, her vermilion skirts trailing behind her. Torches lit the perimeter of the balcony, revealing a face more powdered and painted than even Silvine's. "You look as though you've seen a ghost."

"I've seen more than you can imagine."

Ophelia lowered her voice and drew her face closer. "I believe that. Do you believe *it*?" None of her usual disdain laced her voice.

Silvine sucked in a breath. "Do I believe what?"

Her sister gestured behind them. "This. Do you believe in all of this?" The stained glass obscured the inside of the dining hall but concealed none of the noise. A few screams rang out. Others cheered. Metal clanged against metal, the sound of hungry Fae scraping their plates.

"I—I don't know what to say."

"Then you don't believe in it. I don't either. Something is *wrong* here. Something is wrong with my husband."

"What do you mean?" Silvine grimaced. She longed to tell someone about the burdens that weighed her down, but her sister had never been a confidante.

"I mean that I have true sight now. I know you do, too. The duc and I... we... shared a bath once. Nothing has been the same since then. I thought the bath would be romantic... This is a *sinister* world. The duc is a monster. Your king is a monster. Nothing here is as it seems."

Ophelia clutched Silvine's hand. Silvine bit her lip, trying to find the right words. The tales said one way to gain true sight was to bathe in the bath waters of an Old One. *The duc must be one of Guval's Fae*, she thought. Words failed her.

Her sister continued, "Stay out here with me. They're having their quarterly feast, and I can't stand to watch. You shouldn't, either. They're truly depraved. They round up anyone who is on the streets in Luteche and bring them here. If they survive the feast, they become servants to the king or the duc."

"You know?" Silvine whispered.

The screams from inside the dining hall grew louder. Ophelia tightened her grip. Silvine glanced at the glass door, but her sister grabbed her head, making her face the night sky.

"You cannot marry him. You cannot be 'brimming with excitement about The Blooding Ceremony.'"

Silvine balled her fists. "I am not excited, nor do I plan to marry him." Instead, she was planning to overthrow him.

"Can you fight it? Can you fight *him*?"

Silvine sucked in a breath, staring at the stars that mirrored her necklace. "I think I can."

"There was always something different about your mother. I never knew what it was, but she was one of them. You're one of them. You're not *them*"—she motioned toward the dining hall— "but you are Fae."

"I am."

Ophelia eased her hold on her sister's hand. "I was never a good sister to you. I didn't know how to be one. Our mothers died. Father always pitted us against each other. I did some truly despicable things. I didn't know what the world was really like."

Silvine nodded. Acknowledgement was more important in this moment than responding.

"A band of Fae give aid to the peasants in Luteche at night," Ophelia continued. "The way peasants live there would make Father have a conniption, as cold and useless as he is. I slipped away and found them once. I've been helping ever since. The man who leads them is good. He's not like my husband or the king. He's everything a leader should be."

Silvine would have agreed a few days ago. Now, she wasn't sure if anyone in this Skies-forsaken realm could be considered good. Taran hadn't hesitated for a moment while executing Cardoc. In the vision Bav had shared, it appeared Cardoc knew and trusted Taran. Why would he have taken his life?

"*That man* killed Cardoc," Silvine blurted.

"Good. He tried to give you over to Earth-knows-who," Ophelia said. "I never thought he was good enough for you. Now he can never endanger you again."

"I don't think it's that simple. I don't think *anything* is that simple," Silvine said. Cardoc had given his life for her in a round-about way.

The stained-glass door swung open. Both sisters started. Guval stood, bathed in light, swaying slightly. He wore a crimson jacket. His lips were unusually red.

"I wondered where you ran off to. You missed the last feast of its kind I ever hope to host." He strode toward them and slipped his arm around Silvine's waist. Ophelia studied him coldly.

The smell of blood on his breath made Silvine's stomach roll. The constant reminders of the bloody morning had her in a state of constant nausea, but this was the final straw. She coughed to avoid getting closer. He pulled a handkerchief from his pocket and dabbed at his lips. The white cloth returned to his pocket with blood stains all over it.

Taran had called him an avartagh. The word, according to *Magic of Rafflesia*, meant dwarf. Dwarf, however, did not fully convey what

Guval and his people were. *Secrets of The Realm* said that, corrupted by greed for the power of Life, The Avartagh of Galanthe had been condemned to an eternal, half-dead existence. The only thing that prevented his slow descent into madness and living decay was drinking the Life force of others.

A part of her had been in disbelief until this moment. The horrible truth was laid before her eyes. Guval drank *blood*. She knew, in her heart, that The Blooding Ceremony would involve his blood mingling with hers. It would bind her to him forever.

She had read about blood ties during her late-night reading marathon. Blood ties, a dark magic form mastered by mages, were a means of joining powers or attaching them to the one who initiated the bond. Life and Death were opposites. They should have remained in their respective domains, never mingling.

An awkward silence hung in the air. Ophelia sniffed, her fists clenched at her sides. Silvine, meanwhile, was attempting to conceal her abhorrence with silence.

Guval furthered the conversation, appearing oblivious to the hatred radiating from one sister and the disgust from the other. "You are both so quiet this evening. Duchesse de Luteche, I must say your gown is a masterpiece. You, my Silvine, look utterly *delectable*. May I escort you both to The Room of Mirrors? Phelip will be so displeased if we are late."

"Yes, we would like that," Silvine said, cautiously glancing at Ophelia.

He led the sisters through the stained-glass door, one of them on each arm, and through the dining hall. Bodies lay strewn across the marble floor. Red-eyed servants scrubbed the blood that had splattered everywhere. Guval did not look at the carnage once, but Silvine could not tear her eyes away. One particular body caught her eye, and time seemed to slow.

"I'll no' forget the graciousness o' the Seelie court."

The drunken man in Luteche, who had been so pleased to

receive their help, now lay dead. Taran, the supposed good leader, was nowhere to be found. Silvine felt utterly alone.

The Mirror Room, normally lavish with its gilded mirrors and amethyst inlay, had been decorated to new heights of opulence. Red roses covered the entire expanse of ceiling, their fragrance warring for dominance with mixture of perfumes from the courtiers.

A great clap echoed in the room. Guval steered Silvine and her sister toward the walls. Servants circulated, distributing crystal goblets of red wine.

Phelip burst into the room, a group of dancers behind him, a golden crown atop his head. Each of his dancers wore grimacing, red masks—except for a male in a blonde wig. They danced across the floor with ethereal grace as the band played soft, sweet music. Silvine struggled to swallow, the Faerie wine catching in her throat.

The dancer with a blonde wig spun closer and closer to Phelip. The music grew faster and faster, Silvine's heart pumping along to the rhythm. Phelip danced on the tips of his toes until the blonde dancer twirled his way into his arms.

No, no, no, Silvine screamed internally. Something was dreadfully wrong about this dance.

Twirling his long fingers, Phelip withdrew a gold-handled dagger from his tights. He dipped the postiche-wearing dancer low to the floor, seductively sliding the blade across his neck. As slick, scarlet droplets fell to the floor, Phelip lapped at the blood coming from his partner's throat. The backup dancers glided around the floor, twirling long, golden sashes, depicting a bright flash of light and power. As they twirled the sashes, their grimacing masks turned to ash, revealing expressions of ecstasy.

This was Phelip's choreographed story of The Blooding Ceremony, Silvine realized. She began to hyperventilate.

Phelip portrayed his brother. The dancer in the wig was intended to be Silvine. This performance foreshadowed her future. Everything in her body urged her to run.

With a blood-stained kiss to his partner's lips, Phelip helped him to his feet. Dancer Silvine pulled green scarves from his sleeves, tossing them at members of the crowd, who clapped and cheered. The dancers bowed to thunderous applause, the lights flickered, and the dancers vanished.

Silvine swore she heard her sister mutter "sick bastards" under her breath. Knowing that acknowledging this would've caught Guval's attention—he seemed in rapture with the performance—Silvine focused her attention on steadying her breath. She grew woozy, her corset preventing her from drawing a deep, cleansing breath.

Guval gave slow claps long after the others had ceased. "Well done, Phelip. The height of creativity, a portrayal of what is to come and the hope to be found in my lady, my future consort. Now, we dance the courante."

The band struck up strings, flutes, and oboes, beginning to play a song of hope and longing. Couples found their way to the dance floor. The Duc de Luteche joined his wife. The two exchanged bows before he guided her away.

Familiar, black-cloaked figures slithered around the room, running their fingers along the arms and faces of unwitting dancers. Only Silvine seemed to notice their presence. These murderers were Guval's creatures—more harbingers of Death in a court gluttonous for it.

The king turned expectantly toward Silvine. Her heart pounded and black spots clouded her vision. He reached for her hand, but she clutched it to her side.

"I—I can't. Don't touch me."

Guval's mouth flung open, and he reached for her hand once more. Lifting the skirts of her dress, she fled.

A few couples had wandered into the halls, embracing in the shadows. They hardly spared her a glance as she ran. The corset slowed her down. Summoning a vine, she fashioned it into a dagger, slicing her leather cage in two. Her corset fell to the marble floor with a clatter.

She did not look back as she sprinted over the drawbridge, left down for guests to come and go. Her lungs drew in the cool night air, steadying her mind. She kept her eyes forward as she ran through the plain, where plants had started to blossom. Visions of endless bloodshed, from Cardoc to Ana to the drunken man, filled her head.

She spotted a lone bananach, watching from across the valley floor. She reached into the depths of her power, finding comfort in the familiar melody of her magic. Not in the mood to be trifled with, she shot a beam of light at the creature, and it crumbled to ash. She ran until she reached the purple mountains, her only thoughts centered on the need to escape it all.

CHAPTER 47

REPROCESSING

Silvine

The beating of wings overhead interrupted Silvine's racing thoughts. She sparked her power in her palms before looking up, bracing to face another enemy. A familiar raven descended and landed on her shoulder.

You must deal with your trauma, Bav croaked in her mind.

How can I when there are constant reminders? I am useless to save anyone I love or anyone that matters to the people I care about.

Switching to speaking aloud, Bav said, "That's your core belief. It's wrong."

Visions of death played in Silvine's mind on repeat. She clenched her fists. "How is it not true? I am powerful and useless all at once. I didn't save Cardoc. I didn't save Ana. Phos lost the love of her life. I could have stepped in at every turn."

"Cardoc knew his purpose. Someone had to love you enough to lay their life down for you. Fate is cruel that way." Bav shifted her weight from one foot to the other. "Demetrius was not the first to die due to the undead creatures. You cannot blame yourself for these things."

Silvine let out a sob. "What is the point of having power if I can't do anything meaningful with it?"

Bav cackled. "You slew a bananach without a second thought. Thanks to you, no one leaving Donadas's ball will become its prey tonight. I will repeat myself. You must deal with your trauma."

Silvine ran her fingers through her hair, smoothing her sweat-drenched locks. "How am I supposed to do that? I try to hold it in, and it festers. I let it out, and I look deranged."

"You are The Modrona. You aren't deranged. You simply aren't processing your negative experiences."

Silvine rolled her eyes. She had no interest in semantics at the moment. Rather than maintaining a cool demeanor, she'd lost it and fled from Court. "I mean that I behave as though I am mentally unwell."

"That's a much better term. *Are* you mentally unwell?"

Silvine couldn't find a rebuttal. Silence filled the air between them.

Do you trust me? Bav asked.

Yes, Silvine said.

We are going to try an ancient healing technique. It will be intense, but I will draw energy from the skies to power you through. You need to let yourself feel those feelings, or the wound will fester like an incurable poison. If you want to be the ruler you promised you would be at Dùn Falaich, you must confront your feelings so they do not control you.

Silvine shivered. *Is your method safe?*

Yes, Modrona. Macha invented this technique millennia ago. Many have benefited from it. It will not take the pain away, but it will allow you to function.

Bav's galaxy eyes turned white, illuminating the mountainside.

Close your eyes. Tap your knees, left then right. Do not stop.

Despite her nerves, Silvine did as she was told. She quickly fell into a rhythm. The taps felt soothing as she readied herself for the unknown. Trusting anyone felt difficult, but she knew Bav had served her Modrona ancestresses faithfully for eons. The raven entered her mind, projecting scenes from Silvine's life.

A little girl with blonde hair and pointed ears lay on the floor of Lord Morair's kitchen: Silvine. Tears streamed down her face. Tension hung thickly in the air. A dark-haired woman had dragged her into the room by her ears. Heating a knife over the flames of the stovetop, she began to hack away at the little girl's ears.

Silvine screamed, begged, pleaded, and fought. It was no use. The woman, a lady from Asturia her father had been courting, continued to carve away the pointed tips of her ears. Silvine finally lost consciousness.

"I will rid The Realm of this abnormality. No more of this wicked forest creature nonsense."

After what felt like an eternity, Master Fluellen flew into the kitchen, scooping Silvine into his arms. He summoned his men to carry the Asturian lady away. Lord Morair followed, emitting guttural sobs.

Silvine relived the burning pain she had felt as a little girl. Nausea rolled through her gut, and her breathing grew ragged.

Realization struck her. Her father, seeking another wife, brought a woman into their lives who had harmed her. Her Fae ears, the one indication she was different, were the reason she'd been attacked. Her father's avoidance of the topic made sense for the first time; he'd felt guilty.

Stop tapping and open your eyes, Bav encouraged. Her gentle tone surprised Silvine. *What did you notice?*

I was useless to stop it, she answered.Tears streamed down her face and she began to shake.

Were you useless? You fought and others came to your aid, Bav insisted. *Now, resume tapping.*

They returned to an image of the village square in Ainmean—the scene of Ana's death. Silvine's chest tightened. Ana had died because Silvine hadn't spoken up. She did not confront the black-cloaked creatures. They slithered through the crowd, just as menacing as they'd been moments before in The Mirror Room. Silvine did not say a word to spare Ana.

Ana put her hand over her heart, a gesture of love and goodbye Silvine did not understand until it was too late. Her mind struggled to comprehend what was happening around her as she fled, her heart's desire to turn back conflicting with Ana's command to run.

She hated herself for what had happened. Ana's blood pooled on the cobblestone street, and the crowd gathered around her body.

Silvine continued to cry as she replayed Ana's death in her mind. Her chest was tight, as though a heavy weight pressed her down.

I am useless and worthless, she thought. She stopped tapping and opened her eyes once again. Bav's white gaze pierced through her.

You fought and others came to your aid. Others have always come to your aid. Now, resume. This time, I want you to focus on the fact that you are powerful, and others come to your aid.

In the next vision, Silvine was in Guval's throne room. The hood had just slipped from Cardoc's head. He stared up at Silvine with a look of adoration on his beautiful face despite his impending death sentence.

His thoughts echoed in her head as if he'd spoken them aloud, "I must endure so she can create a better future for us all. I will lay down my life so she can live hers fully."

Silvine froze, struggling to draw breaths or articulate words. Her body did not move, did not cry out, did not save him.

The exchange continued as it had that morning.

"The prisoner has the right to choose his means of execution," Taran said.

"I am aware. Do you not prefer a painless death from your king?" Guval asked.

Voice steady and assured, Cardoc replied, "I would prefer to die by blade, with some of my dignity intact."

In his mind, he thought, "I am glad to die by the hand of a friend. That is the greatest mercy I could ask for in this life. Creator guide me and send me into your arms."

Bav explained, Cardoc made a noble choice for you. Once he had trespassed at Court, he knew he would be killed. He cared that much for you.

The raven's words did not fill the void in Silvine's heart or ease

354

her grief. Her body was overtaken by sobs, her limbs growing heavy. She almost stopped tapping, but Bav brushed a wing along her forearm. A surge of energy flowed through her veins.

I am powerful. Others always come to my aid.

Good. Repeat it.

I am powerful. Others always come to my aid.

Let us picture your mother's dagger, the one with wings, Bav instructed.

The silver dagger, with its winged handles, gleamed in Silvine's mind.

Take all the feelings, all the negativity, all the past experiences that hurt you, and put them into that dagger. You are powerful, and others always come to your aid. Open your eyes.

As Silvine obeyed, Bav's eyes returned to their strange galaxy hue. Silvine's necklace warmed her chest, and she realized the night air had chilled her skin. As Bav brushed both arms with her wings, sending another surge of energy and warmth, Silvine realized her sobbing had stopped and her muscles had relaxed.

A calloused hand touched her shoulder. She knew it was Taran before she laid eyes on him. The hatred that had burned for him all day dissipated. Before her stood the man who fought for her, who gave Cardoc mercy in death, who always came when she needed him.

"We have to get you back. Donadas is pretending you took a 'toilette' break, but he is going to get frantic soon. We do not want to see what he will do. We need to maintain the status quo, at least for tonight. Can you do that?" His voice was soft.

Embracing the calm she'd found, Silvine answered, "Yes, take me now. I have to deal with with Guval." She was not alone in the battle against him, but she knew she needed to lead the way.

"There's that power."

He shifted her through The Realm. They arrived outside the doors to The Mirror Room where the king waited, pacing. The dissonant notes of the magic in his blood crescendoed. His emerald eyes scrutinized them as they approached.

"My Silvine, where did you go? I was about to send my men to search for you." His tone was harsh. Taran bowed to the king before shuffling into The Mirror Room.

Silvine lifted her chin. "I needed time, so I took it."

A glare crossed his face for a moment. "You have missed an hour of dancing. Phelip is offended."

Silvine snorted. "No concern for my well-being? You made me watch you condemn someone from my village to death this morning. Blood stained my shoes and dress. Then, you brought me to an event soaked in blood, in more ways than one. You slaughtered innocents tonight. Your main concern is that I've missed an hour of dancing?" Silvine held up a finger. "You may have one dance, and then I will require time away from you."

She sought to sow seeds of doubt in the king's mind. Watching his reactions would give her an advantage in the fight against him. She would remain calm; he would spin out, or so she hoped.

"I didn't think of it that way," he said, twirling a ring on his finger. She'd never seen him fidget. "Do not think this is who I am. This is why we are having The Blooding Ceremony in four days. I will become my true self when you are bound to me."

Four days was far too soon. Silvine clenched her jaw. "One dance, Your Majesty. I won't be treated like this *ever* again, so I hope you will have a sudden change of character."

She marched inside without another word.

Ophelia studied her sister carefully as she entered. The crimson-eyed duc spun her around the dance floor. She exchanged a brief look with her sister, seemingly trying to reassure her that she could manage. Suppressing a shudder, Silvine allowed Guval to place his Death-marred hands on her waist. As they danced, she planned her next steps.

356

CHAPTER 48

SEEDS OF REBELLION

Silvine

After that singular dance, Silvine retired to her bedchambers. The exertion she'd experienced left her groggy.

The next day, Guval sent a servant to ask her to join him for breakfast beside the underground river. She said she would have her meal in bed.

Minuet was sent next to deliver a message from the king. She brought a red rose with a black stem and sharp thorns, placing it on the dining table in the center of the room. The sun shone through the floor to ceiling windows, emitting a warmth wholly at odds with the cold mage in her bedchamber.

"My Majesty—" Minuet began. Silvine rolled her eyes. "He sends this rare rose. It grows in his underground gardens. It is the only remaining bush from a far-off land. He says it is as rare and beautiful as you."

"And as deadly," Silvine muttered under her breath, noting the funereal hum emanating from the thorns.

Minuet pursed her lips. "You seem ungrateful."

Silvine waved her hand away. *The Magic of Rafflesia* lay open in her lap, turned to a page about poisonous plants. She studied the rose. "You must be confused, Minuet. I don't care how I seem. Tell Guval I am resting. I have done enough for The Realm in recent weeks."

The king's mage glided across the floor until she stood an arm's length from Silvine. "I will order you to be sent to my study. I smell some kind of vapors that have enchanted you. Did you eat or drink from strange Fae on your journey?"

The Silvine from a day before would have felt panicked at the threat. The Silvine of today remembered that she was powerful and chose to keep reading the book that rested on her knees. She flipped the pages slowly, careful to keep the cover of the book concealed.

Eventually, the mage stomped off.

Lord Tylon arrived minutes later with three hooded guards in tow. The only thing Silvine could see of the guards were their pale claws. These were Guval's creatures of Death, his assassins. Silvine tensed. These creatures did not belong in her space.

She sprang from her bed, summoning vines to her side, palms aglow. "How dare you bring those creatures to my room. Further, how dare you come into the bedchamber of the king's betrothed." Her vines wrapped around his legs.

He held out a hand. "I come in service of Lady Minuet. She believes you have been enchanted. Seeing you attack a member of His Majesty's court leads me to agree with her."

The hooded guards slithered closer, and Silvine sucked in a breath. The song in her heart crescendoed until she could not hear Tylon's protests and chiding, although his face had turned red from shouting. She blasted them with beams of power. Their bodies slammed into the marble wall, going limp as they crumpled to the floor.

Screeching, staccato notes beat out from Tylon's blood. He bent down, pricking his fingers on the thistles of the vines as he grabbed them. His touch withered the plants, which blackened and died. Silvine shot out a beam of power at him. Stumbling backward, he collected himself and continued toward her.

Death powers exist in more court members than just Guval, she realized. Mentally filing that detail for later, she braced herself for the fight to come.

Tylon stalked closer, kicking aside the legs of one of Guval's creatures. "I will drink your blood before that king of yours can try. He's been putting it off for too long. I've waited long enough. It is time for my resurrection."

Silvine glowered. She would not let him anywhere near her blood. "Take one more step, and the guards will have to haul your carcass from my chambers."

Seeming undeterred, he moved closer. She shot him in the chest with another blast of her power. This time, she hit him hard enough to send him crashing into the wall. He slumped on the floor, unconscious.

Stepping past the four bodies, The Modrona marched into the hallway.

The solitude of the corridors that led to the throne room gave her time to collect her thoughts. Guval wanted to dine with her. Instead, she would serve him her fury.

She trod into the unusually quiet throne room. Minuet and Guval were the only two there. They were locked in a passionate embrace at the foot of the dais, kissing in a frenzy.

Of course, she had been right about their relationship. Her jealousy hadn't been misplaced. Her bitter laugh echoed through the room. "This is what you expect me to marry into?"

Guval shoved Minuet off him. They smoothed their clothing and faced her, wide-eyed.

"Oh, have I interrupted something?" she crooned.

"Interrupted what?" Guval asked, adjusting his coronet.

She approached the dais, fists balled at her sides. "Have I interrupted my betrothed shoving his tongue down his *brother's wife's* throat."

Minuet tried to pat her arm, but Silvine twisted away before she could touch her. "Lady Silvine, I think your eyes are deceiving you. I really would like to take you to my study and test you. My Highness, I warned you that letting her wander Galanthe before The Blooding would leave her vulnerable to this sort of thing. We know Pulchra had a weak constitution as well."

Heat flared in Silvine's chest. "My eyes see perfectly fine. Does Phelip know about this?"

Guval's voice shook. "Minuet and I have been friends for longer than you can imagine. She and I predate any attachments to my brother. They have an *arrangement* that suits each of their tastes quite well. This... dalliance... will end as soon as you are mine."

Silvine shook her head. "I am wholly uninterested in playing the polite wife who looks the other way. And Mage, keep my mother's name out of your harlot mouth."

To illustrate her point, she shot a beam of power at the throne. The mage gasped, and the king ducked. The throne fell backwards, clattering onto the floor below.

Silvine could no longer endure thinking of Guval as the king of The Realm. Even though he had bestowed the title upon himself, she would thereafter only consider him the usurper. She would shatter his throne, literally and figuratively.

Guval reached out for her, and she stepped back.

"My Lady, I need you," he said. "You need me. I will not let you slip from my grasp. You are not well. I sent you to fight too early. I see that now. Once we are blooded and wed, none of this will continue. Not Minuet and I, not Death, not this shadow existence. Can we please take you to my mage's study?"

Her jaw clenched until it ached. She lifted her palms in warning. Their white glow cast shadows on the faces of the usurper and his mistress. Minuet paled and fell to the floor, coughing and spluttering. Silvine's eyes widened.

"Did your power do this?" Guval asked.

Silvine shook her head.

"Poison," his mistress rasped. "I have been poisoned."

The usurper waved his hand, black tendrils emanating from his fingertips. Purple-clad guards ran in response to the summons of his power. "Take her to her room and find my brother. We need an antidote."

Minuet let out delicate gasps as the guards carried her away.

Guval turned his attention back to Silvine, gritting his teeth. "We need to talk."

Silvine crossed her arms. "We do. Shall we start with your pale creatures and Lord Tylon coming to my room at Minuet's behest? I think we should."

Rubbing his temples, Guval took a seat on the first step of the dais. He patted the space next to him. Silvine opted to sit two arms' lengths away from him.

"The pale things are... undead creatures," Guval explained. "We call them true avartaghs. They are useful for some purposes, and they only do my bidding."

"Avartaghs like you?"

"Yes," he admitted.

"You've been trying to deceive me. Those true avartaghs were there that day in Ainmean. They slaughtered my best friend when she took a stand to save my life. You need my blood bound to yours to restore your court to life, don't you?"

Bav rasped into her mind, *You can't restore Life, Modrona. You can't create it. You can only cultivate it. You are the sower of seeds, not the creator of them.*

I suspected as much, Silvine replied. *How do you know what I'm doing?*

I see, and I serve, Bav said before severing their connection.

Guval put his face in his hands. "I sent them because they can move undetected. I thought it would be the safest way to get you to me without your father. Morair had agreed to the betrothal the day before. Unseelie rebels, however, caused the fire and the rest of the chaos. My creatures made a poor call, and they have paid for it. Everything has been done in the name of winning your love."

Silvine looked him up and down, wrinkling her nose. "There's a long and valid list of reasons why I question your love. And no, I haven't been enchanted. If I hear mention of an enchantment one more time, I am going to destroy more than just your throne."

Guval lifted his palms. "Jealousy has sent you into a fit of passion. I love the vibrance of your feelings. You feel everything so intensely. I have not... felt... in a millennium."

She would not be baited into feeling empathy for him. "Back to the subject of Lord Tylon and the true avartaghs that tried to kidnap me in my chamber. Lord Tylon threatened to drink my blood. He and those *things* are currently unconscious."

He clenched his fists. "Lord Tylon was in your bedchamber? He threatened you?"

Silvine rolled her eyes. "I mentioned that already."

"I was distracted. I did not send Lord Tylon."

Silvine raised a brow. "You didn't? He said he was taking me to your mage's study to test for any enchantments."

Guval sighed. "Minuet means well. Sometimes, she acts without my permission, but always with my best interests in mind."

Silvine raised her palm toward him, hinting that his time to speak was done. "I am a queen. I am not interested in playing games with your mistress. She doesn't have *my* best interests in mind."

"You *will be* a queen *consort*. You are not one yet. But I will deal with Lord Tylon. We are all so excited about your powers that I am sure he was overzealous. He can be tiresome."

If only you realized that I know the full truth, she thought. *I am already a queen.*

She glowered at him. "I am not sure I wish to be your queen consort. The reasons to not marry you increase by the minute."

Black tendrils wafted toward the ceiling as Guval raised his voice. "You will marry me. You will want to." His magic had no effect on her, but she softened her face to let him think it had.

With a gentler tone, the king asked, "Do you want to go back to your room? I will ensure it remains safe."

"Yes, Guval," she said, keeping her tone even.

When they reached her chamber, all signs of altercation had been removed. Guval summoned a guard, using his dark tendrils of magic, and checked the room for danger. Once it was determined that the room was safe, he said, "I must check on my sister-in-law's welfare. Not because I am in love with her, but because she matters to my brother."

A single whorl of black magic drifted through the keyhole as the sound of his footsteps grew distant. Silvine checked the door, finding it locked from the outside. Guval must have felt threatened enough to lock her in. A part of her was satisfied that she'd finally won his attention—another worried that she'd taken it too far. He still had the upper hand.

The usurper pretended to be apologetic and sincere, only to lock her in her chamber to control her. The poisoning of Minuet had been Silvine's saving grace. She had no doubt Guval would have resorted to further extremes if he hadn't been concerned about his mage.

She rushed to the windows, trying to open them. They'd been enchanted shut as well. Her hands began to shake, but she reminded herself, *I am powerful, and others always come to my aid.*

CHAPTER 49

WHAT IF I ESCAPE

"Trapped?" a familiar voice asked.

Silvine spun from the windows to find Taran studying the garnet-colored rose on her table. "Regina, did you touch that?"

"I have no interest in touching that. It's a poisonous antique rose from Rafflesia. It's toxic to Fae and dwarves," she said.

"Good, because *someone* used the milk from its thorns to poison the usurper's beloved mage. I am glad to know you didn't trifle with the poison." He gestured to the books on her nightstand. "I take it you've been doing a bit of reading?"

She sighed. "I don't want to have literary discussions right now. I want to know what to do."

Taran leaned against her table. "You need to leave. The Blooding Ceremony is coming soon. Thanks to your emboldened behavior, Donadas is paranoid. He is ready to guard you like a dragon hoarding its treasure. We can't risk your safety." He flicked his wrist at the rose, shifting it away.

Silvine studied her outfit. Her dress would not do for an escape. Taran, perhaps noticing her hesitation, turned his back, giving her a

moment of modesty. He magicked a change of clothes onto her. A tunic, pants, and his cloak replaced the dress, which lay in a heap on the floor. He twirled back to face her.

Glancing at the window, Silvine felt a lump form in her throat. "Are you coming?" she asked. The thought of facing the forest without him felt unbearable. Taran, for all his wrongs, had been the reason she'd found her power. He was the reason she knew she was a queen, not simply a consort-to-be. He'd crowned her himself and opened her eyes to truth.

His face fell. "I can't come with you."

Silvine swallowed. "You can't, or you won't?"

"I can't. I am... sending you off... to battle against... Donadas." He seemed to struggle with each word. "I ... cannot... join you. I need you... to win." By the time he'd finished his sentence, he was gasping. Blood trickled from his nostrils. He hastily wiped it away.

Silvine lifted her hand to touch him but let it drop at her side. "You're bleeding," she said.

"It's... no matter... Regina. You have... to fight."

She frowned. "I don't understand. Are you planning to betray me?"

He drew close and ran his fingers along her jawline. His warm, calloused hands were so reassuring—so at odds with the fear his words were stirring in her soul. "I would never betray you. I need you... to win this battle... so I can have... your firstborn child. Remember? Our bargain... is very important... to me."

She wanted to know what had him so distressed, but she knew he kept his secrets locked away. She opted to continue prying about their deal. "I still don't understand why you wanted that bargain. What if I never have a child after this? I can't imagine there is a Fae in the world who wouldn't be intimidated by marrying The Modrona, especially if he knew my firstborn child was going to become *yours*."

"I have... very good... intuition. The opportunity... will come along... for me to collect... what I am owed." He winked and then wiped his nose again. "Enough talk. You need... to go. Phos and Bav... are waiting... in the cave... that leads to Luteche."

"Can you shift me there?" she asked, wondering how much his powers could do in his weakened state.

He shook his head. "Not until you break the enchantment in this room."

Her heart began to race. "How can I do that? I wasn't aware I had spell-breaking powers."

"Must I help you with everything?" he teased. "What will you give me for my aid this time?"

She punched him in the chest. "I will give you a realm that doesn't have a cheating, lying usurper for its ruler."

He rubbed the spot where she'd struck him. "Calm down. I don't need anything from you. You are the cultivator of Life. He is the wielder of Death. Flood the room with Life, and the spell will be broken."

Of course. It's that simple, she thought. Tuning into the rhythm of her heart, she amplified her power as she reached out, sensing the dissonant notes of Guval's magic. Her white light overcame the dark traces of his magic that reached from the door and wrapped all the way around the windows. White sparks flew from her fingertips, and she felt the enchantment break.

Taran's eyes sparkled, despite his wheezing breaths. "There's... that power. You're so... quick to... doubt yourself." He snapped his fingers, and she found herself shifting through space.

Without Taran there to steady her, she landed flat on her bottom. The collision with the cave's firm surface knocked the air from her lungs. Green light bobbed toward her, and Phos and an old woman appeared at her side.

"Modrona, it is time," the crone croaked.

Silvine shivered. She knew that crone.

"I met you at the market, and you gave me this." She pulled her necklace from its resting place. It glowed in response, its colors the same as the crone's eyes. The same as Bav's.

"Yes, I am Bav," the crone said, seeming to sense Silvine's realization. "This is my other form. I told you that I have always been there. I see, and I serve." An undeniably creepy expression spread across her worn face, revealing a total of four blackened teeth.

Phos shook her head. "I much prefer your raven form."

Bav ignored the comment. "Your army waits for you. We must lay siege tonight. It is time to undo the plague that has haunted this land for a millennium."

"What about Taran?" Silvine asked. The thought of leaving him behind, gasping for air and bleeding, made her stomach clench.

"You must free him as well."

Her eyes widened. "From what?"

Bav coughed. "Skies above, I hate talking the way you all love to do. He is bound to Donadas. The Euron bound himself to the usurper to be able to keep an eye on Court and ensure events went as expected. Not everything has gone well, but then again, Macha is not here to read the stars for us."

He was dangerously close to breaking his bargain when he came to me, Silvine realized. That was why he had been so unwell. Taran was actively dying while sending her to fight. She began to wonder if her own deal with him had anything to do with the usurper's struggles when he kissed her.

A heavy feeling made her heart slow. "Does Guval know Taran is The Euron?"

"Heavens, no!" Bav scoffed. "He thinks he's a common Earth Fae with powers of intelligence-gathering. You can save him. You need to battle until Life dominates Death, and then you must free him. It is the only way to restore the balance."

Phos rubbed Silvine's shoulder. "You can do this. He believes in you more than anything. I believe in you. We are here to aid and ensure victory. Besides, Dùn Falaich is so boring without your sharp wit."

A few Fae Silvine recognized from her coronation and Dùn Falaich approached, adorned in green and silver tunics. They rode on horseback with will-o-the-wisps lighting their path. Two women held the reins to two additional horses with shiny, gray coats.

One led the horse to Silvine. "Modrona." She dipped her chin. "This is The Euron's best steed. He will not fail you."

Phos mounted a horse, taking the lead. Silvine put her foot in the stirrup and lifted herself onto another. She didn't have Ophelia's passion for equestrianism, but she'd always been a proficient rider.

Following her glowing friend, she rode until they reached the mouth of the cave. Its opening revealed the purple mountains overlooking Court. The plain below twinkled with yellow lights; her flowers were overtaking the once-lifeless grounds.

One of the men in their company put his lips to a silver horn, blaring a single note. In response, a multitude of Fae and creatures of all kinds appeared. Trolls, dryads, naiads, and all manner of creatures that would have given Nene a heart attack began a rapid descent down the mountainside.

The cavalry trotted down the slope as well, but Phos hung back, gesturing for Silvine to do the same.

"I know nothing of battle strategy," Silvine said.

"*We* know plenty. All we must do is catch him by surprise and weaken his undead army. Then, you step in with your powers and do the rest. But for now, we will watch," Phos said.

Silvine wanted to share Phos's confidence, but she knew this war had been waged for a thousand years. Guval had been victorious every time. What if she couldn't fulfill the prophecy? After all, it could have been wrong. Macha no longer lived. The stars could have changed.

The magic of hundreds of Fae resounded in a symphony as bolts of power, gusts of wind, and waves of water were hurled along the plain. Silvine watched in awe as they crossed the valley, drawing nearer to Guval's castle.

"Shouldn't we do something? Doesn't a queen fight alongside her people?" she asked.

"You've been fighting for us. We can't risk you getting hurt. The timing must be perfect."

An alarm sounded in the distance. The royal guards had been alerted. Silvine hoped Taran would not have to participate in the battle. Her heart couldn't bear the thought of losing him when so much had been left unsaid.

The silver horn blared another eight-count note. The army, *Silvine's* army, continued charging forward. The drawbridge of the castle lowered, and a sea of black and purple soldiers descended upon her people. The human part of Silvine wondered at the keenness of her Fae sight, her ability to see details from afar. Metal clanged with metal as warriors grunted and cried out.

Slowly, the yellow lights winked out one by one, replaced by great clouds of dust. Silvine could sense music dying out sporadically. Her chest tightened, matching her roiling stomach. Her people were dying on the battlefield.

"I can't do this," she blurted.

Phos cocked her head. "We can't call off the battle. There's too much at stake."

"That's not what I meant. I can't keep watching. I *need* to be down there. But I won't ride Taran's horse into battle. I want him to have it... when he goes home to Dùn Falaich." A vision of The Modrona who came before perishing on the mountainside flashed in her mind. If she didn't make it out, she wanted to leave him something.

A touch of pride colored Phos's voice. "I would be honored to fight alongside my queen, but you must be careful."

They tied the horses up and made their way toward the battle in a sprint. Just one night ago, Silvine had been a broken woman running to the mountains to get away from Guval. Now, she was running toward the fate that awaited her at his castle.

CHAPTER 50

THE QUEEN AND HER WRATH

Silvine

No description of battle could accurately describe the experience of being in the midst of the worst outcomes possible. No words could do justice to the horrors. The culmination of the metallic tang of blood, the screams of the mortally wounded, and the bellows of warriors who fought to live another day was indescribable. Those who went to war rarely came back whole. Even when they survived, pieces of them died along with those who never returned.

The only true victor in battle was Death.

During this particular battle, the queen of The Realm resolved that the fighting would end quickly. She would cut down the enemies in her path and make her way to Guval. She would claw her way to him, only taking down those who came for her first.

In the midst of chaos, walking along that forsaken plain toward her enemy, Silvine reached deep within her soul for her heart's song. She repeated the mantra Bav had given her, searching for peace to steady her thudding heart and racing thoughts.

Her magic flowed through her veins, lulled her into a state of calm with the song of her foremothers. This was not the first time a

Modrona had come here to wage war. However, Silvine was determined it would be the last.

Bav hovered far overhead, croaking and chortling. Every time she circled, the soldiers beneath her fell. She wielded her powers, the powers of the Skies above, scattering the enemies below.

On the other side of the battle, Silvine was spurred on by the knowledge that Taran remained in Guval's clutches, bound to him. Taran—the man who gave himself in service to the usurper when she was born in hopes that someday she would end Guval's reign of terror and save The Realm. It did not matter if he did not love her the way she loved him. And Skies above, she *did* love him. She hadn't realized it until she'd fought her way through the battle to save him. It did not matter if he had killed her first love. All that mattered was that he had chosen to fight for her, long before she'd even known of the storm that was brewing.

Thunder rolled behind Court, and lightning flashed. Silvine listened for Taran's signature melancholy notes, which reached her in faint pulses, and she knew he was fighting the pull of his bargain as much as he could.

Calling to the Life nearby, her beckoning reaching out for miles, she fired arrows of thorns and launched spears forged from poisonous oleander. Guval's army seemed to have been warned not to harm her. They gave her a wide berth—a treatment her people did not receive.

They danced around her, seemingly preparing to lunge for her and take her back to their king without causing her bodily harm. She felt no remorse as she struck them down. A few of the bolder men fired arrows tipped with a numbing agent at her.

She refused to succumb. She would fight this every step of the way. She shot out beams of power, obliterating each arrow into dust.

Phos's glow led her onward. The glowing woman swung a blade in each hand, striking down every soldier who stepped toward Silvine. Blackish blood splattered both of their faces, ran down their hair, and coated their hands.

A lone guard approached Silvine and lunged for her hand,

reaching for her mother's wing-handled dagger. Phos whirled her twin blades in the air, decapitating him with a single swipe.

They fought on, amidst the dust and blood, cutting a path toward the castles with bodies lying in their wake.

A cloud of dust grew as a group of Guval's men rode toward Silvine on horseback. Her infantry retreated, bows drawn. A purple-cloaked figure rode ahead of the rest of them. Beneath the starlit sky and Phos' green glow, the purple looked more like decay than grandeur.

"Lady Silvine!" Phelip shouted from atop a white stallion. "I implore you: stop this!"

She turned to face him, her voice low and deadly. "You have had a thousand years to stop this. You know who Guval is. You drink the blood of innocents to feed *this*. Your brother killed the Fae of this realm to fuel his power. You want me to stop it? I am doing *just that*."

Before he could utter a response, she shot twin bolts of white-hot power from her palms. It struck the ground where the horses stood, and in an instant, the horses were spooked enough to fall back. Phelip gave orders to his men to retreat.

Silvine hollered at him, "Let the king come talk to me himself, Phelip, and stop using others to do the dirty work for him!"

"Very well," he called back. His red eyes shone in the light. The way he hunched his shoulders, normally so erect, exuded defeat.

The fighting came to a standstill after all of Guval's army retreated to the castle. An eerie silence blanketed the plain. The only sound emanating around them came from the waves crashing against the red rock cliffs behind the castle.

Beside Silvine, Phos wiped blood away from her face. Silvine raised a brow.

"It's not mine," Phos whispered. "You do incredible work, My Queen."

Moments later, three figures made their way toward them. Silvine recognized the auburn-haired figure in the middle as the usurper, flanked by Taran and Phelip. He must have been angered enough to step foot onto the battlefield. Ever the coward, he did not fight alongside his men. Loud, angry notes emanated from his magic. *Good*, she thought. She wanted him riled up.

Wings flapped beside her. Bracing for Bav's arrival, she thrust out her arm expectantly. Instead of Bav, a figure with jet black hair landed beside her. Luc Ollam.

He bowed. "I am at your service. Always."

She tilted her chin in acknowledgment. Surprising even herself, she no longer harbored a grudge against him. She'd been safer in his cave than she'd ever been at Court. He'd cared for Cardoc in his final days. Despite the way she'd once raged at him, he chose to be at her side. *The Heart sees the Earth for what it truly is.*

The rest of them, the true Fae of Galanthe, gathered behind her. Bodies from both sides were strewn across the plain.

The air hung thick with anticipation. This act of defiance would define the future of The Realm.

Guval's figure became clearer as he approached. His hair shone garishly under the glow of the moon, his jaw tight. He dragged Taran behind him, who thrashed and kicked the entire way. Phelip strode beside his brother, gaze fixed on the mountains in the distance, avoiding eye contact.

Bracing herself, Silvine called upon the full force of her power.

Luc murmured, "Your body, Modrona. You are aglow."

Indeed, Silvine's entire body radiated with visible power. The glow of her palms had spread until her entire body outshone even Phos.

The three figures halted ten paces from Silvine, Phos, and Luc.

With a sickening thud, Guval hurled Taran to the ground. Sterling eyes, filled with defiance, flashed up at Silvine. Lightning struck the ground a dozen paces away, shaking the earth.

Silvine knew that every recalcitrant act Taran made, fighting against the bargain he'd struck to do Guval's bidding, wore him ragged. The circles under his eyes revealed his exhaustion, and blood spilled from his nose.

Guval shook his head. "Modrona, I am disappointed in your actions. But it is nothing that cannot be forgiven or fixed."

"The Creator is disappointed in your actions, the way you ravage The Realm!" she roared.

The usurper's nostrils flared. He reached for Taran, lifting him by his neck.

Silvine balled her fists. Guval was mistaken if he thought he could harm Taran without her interference. She shot a bolt of power at his feet. A sickening hiss radiated from his boots.

"That hurt," the usurper said. "How badly will it hurt, I wonder, if I kill my General of Intelligence? You seem most disturbed by Death. All these Fae have died for you, and you dare attack your future husband?"

She jutted out her chin. "I will only marry an honorable man."

Guval tightened his grip on Taran's throat. "Be that as it may, your father promised you to me. I will start killing off as many as I must to get you to surrender. This will hurt us both, but you leave me no choice. Phelip, hand me the antique rose venom."

Taran began to choke. Silvine's heart raced, and she took a step forward, but her friend shook his head.

Phelip produced a vial of thick, white liquid.

Before she could stop herself, she screamed, "Let him go!"

Guval shot her a sinister smile, throwing Taran to the earth with the force of ten men, knocking him unconscious. Silvine held in another shriek, opting to reach out for Taran's magic. Although it was faint, his sorrowful song assured her he was still alive.

The usurper lifted the vial. "Funny, this poison. It hasn't been used in more years than you can imagine. Minuet fights for her life even after an antidote was given. Would you like to know how it works?"

Reading *The Magic of Rafflesia* had given Silvine a solid understanding of how the venom worked. Its victims lay conscious, paralyzed, while their bodies slowly decayed from the inside out.

Gruesome was hardly a strong enough word to describe death by antique rose.

She pointed a finger at him. "You will take no more lives."

"Then you will come with me. Or I will destroy every one of these traitors, starting with Taran Dando. He behaved most inappropriately this evening." Guval uncorked the vial and leaned toward Taran's unconscious body.

Without Taran, there was no Realm for her.

But only when he *wins her,*

Will victory occur.

The "he" wasn't the usurper. It was Taran who had won her heart. To be victorious, she needed more than the power of nature; she needed its Wrath. She would heal him, and they would take on the usurper together.

Cupping her hands around her mouth, she shouted, "Retreat!"

"Modrona, no," Luc argued.

Foolish, foolish child, Bav chastened.

"I'll take that mouthy winged one out next," Guval threatened.

"Retreat!" Silvine repeated.

Tears streamed down Phos's face, but their queen had given a command. Wings beat, footsteps thundered, and water flowed as her army followed her orders. Although Silvine could sense notes of disappointment in the magic of her people, she needed the usurper to believe he'd defeated her. Though they had the means to succeed, the Seelie were missing something vital.

Guval relaxed his posture. "I knew you would come to see reason."

Phelip made a small noise in his throat. Both monarchs shot him a look. He resumed studying the mountains intently.

Determined to see her plan through, Silvine steadied her voice. "I will come with you, but I have one condition. Well, two."

The usurper cocked his head. "Name them. We will see if I choose to honor them."

"Bind yourself to my terms, or I stay here. I'll let him die." She hoped he would not catch her bluff. Time was of the essence as she planned her next steps.

"I am willing to entertain this, but I'm getting impatient. Make haste."

Silvine lifted a finger. "Number one: you will not harm Taran any further. Number two: I will destroy that vial before I take another step."

Guval waved his hand dismissively. "I will not harm Taran any further in this battle, and I will allow you to destroy the vial as long as it does not harm me or my men. You will come with me, and you will not harm more of my men. So let it be promised from my heart."

"I will destroy the vial in a way that does not harm you or your men. I will come with you, and I will not harm any more of your men in this battle. So let it be promised from my heart."

Magic buzzed between the two of them as their bargain was set.

The usurper tossed the vial between their feet. Silvine shot out a vine, which coiled itself around the container until it shattered. The poison spilled across the dust, shooting up and morphing into a rose bush. The roses bloomed, but unlike their parent plant, these flowers were yellow.

"Impressive," Phelip murmured. His brother glowered at him.

Silvine rushed to Taran's side. She could feel his heart pumping wildly, his melancholy notes playing all wrong. She placed her hands on his chest, playing her own song against his. The beating of his heart slowed until it was in rhythm with hers. His eyes fluttered open.

"Why would you do this?" he rasped.

Because I need you, she thought. *You are the other part of the prophecy.*

She helped him to his feet before dropping her voice to a whisper. "For the first time, I'm the one with a plan. Trust me."

Guval cleared his throat. "It is time to go, Lady Silvine."

Lifting her still-glowing palms, a gesture to remind all of Court of her power, she began walking toward the castle.

In her mind, she said, *Bav, I need a favor.*

I see, and I serve, even when you're foolish. What are you thinking?

Silvine scanned the plains, taking in the death and destruction the battle had caused. Her stomach lurched at the sight. *Can you keep taking out the guards? I promised I wouldn't, but I said nothing about you. It'll look as though they succumbed to wounds from the battle.*

It would be my pleasure, Bav croaked.

As Silvine trudged back to Court, flanked on either side by the usurper and his brother, the bodies of Guval's men started to stir. She jumped when one sat up suddenly, an axe still lodged in his head. Perhaps trying to stall her before she could get any ideas, the usurper cloaked her in his dark magic. She pushed her light outward to shake it off. Like oil and water in a glass jar, his Death magic hovered above her Life magic.

Bav explained, *Only you and I can end them for good. Life and the power of the Skies above are the only things that can truly do away with The Avartagh. Once the usurper is nestled back in his precious castle, I will finish what we started.*

Taking comfort in the thought that she was not truly alone, Silvine allowed Guval to escort her back to his castle. She needed The Euron by her side.

CHAPTER 51

A PRIMER ON COURTLY MANNERS

Silvine's plans shattered the minute they entered the courtyard. Wielding their bargain, Guval ordered Taran to retreat to the strategy room. The usurper's cocoon of dark magic retreated from around Silvine. She exhaled, releasing the tension the fight had built within her body.

Before she could realize what was happening, Guval wrapped tendrils of his magic around her wrists. They drained her powers, the sound of her music growing quiet and soft. Reaching for the song of her soul, she tried in vain to force her shackles off. Her pulse throbbed in her ears. She stared at Guval, wide-eyed.

"I am patient, but even I have my limits for what I will endure," he said.

Of course you do. You're not The Enduring One, she thought.

"Phelip and I will take you to your temporary accommodations," he said. "I cannot trust you until The Blooding Ceremony is complete. I have no doubt you will be more compliant afterward, and then, you will regain freedoms."

378

She hated herself for ever thinking Guval choosing her was an honor. This was not a man she could ever grow to love.

With Guval's cold hand on her back while Phelip led the way, Silvine followed through passageways and down flights of stairs until they reached the underground river. She called to her magic out of instinct. It sputtered, hopelessly dim.

Phelip veered to the left and placed his hand on the stone wall. One by one, each stone moved, revealing a tiny cell. It contained a straw bed, a woolen blanket, and a latrine bucket.

The usurper shoved her inside. "We will fetch you when it is time for The Ceremony. Until then, make good choices." He gestured at a stack of books in the corner opposite the bed. "You can pass the time reading about expectations for Court behavior."

Without warning, he released her magical bindings. Red, angry burns marked her wrists, and she hissed in pain.

Her voice shaky, she asked, "What are you doing?"

The usurper held a finger to his lips. "Quiet. I have had enough of your words. This is a lesson you will only have to learn once."

Frozen, she watched as he stepped out of the cell and placed his hand on the wall. Her breaths came in quick, shallow spurts. Stone by stone, the wall sealed itself, closing her in.

When the final stone was set, her power surged. The music was loud and frantic. Lifting her trembling hands, she placed her palms on the wall the same way Guval and Phelip had. Nothing happened. She wove a soothing song to the stones, calling for them to open. The wall did not move. She studied each stone, looking for gaps, trying to stave off claustrophobia. Being encased in the cell felt like dying.

She slumped down on the mattress and grabbed the first book from the pile. The title was: *A Primer on Courtly Manners* by Lord Phelip. It had been written in his handwriting, neat and elegant. Jaw clenched, she began tearing pages from the spine.

Even if Phelip would never know she'd done it, it felt like the only blow she could strike. Dozens of her people had been slain on the battlefield. Taran was bound to Guval and out of her reach. She focused on steadying her breathing, repeating Bav's mantra.

I am powerful, and others always come to my aid. Succumbing to her exhaustion, she finally fell asleep.

In her sleep, a recurrent nightmare played out over and over. The face of her tormentor alternated, bouncing between her Asturian assailant, Guval, and her father. Throughout the night, she fought to wake up, but every time, she fell back into the dream.

She finally awoke when something sharp jabbed at her hand.

"What?" she groaned.

Bav's obsidian eyes bored into her soul. *I brought food. If he starves you, you won't be at your full strength to fight. We have a day before The Ceremony is to happen.*

How did you get in here?

I see, and I serve, Bav answered. *The Court of the Skies Above is woefully underestimated. We avoid the Earth Below these days, with the treacherous political climate. Make no mistake; I am formidable, and I will not be restrained.*

Silvine rubbed the sleep from her eyes. *Good to know. Were you successful?*

Yes. I wiped out a third of his men. Their courtiers are racking their brains, trying to figure out what has happened. There are few things that can kill them, except for the usurper himself. She cackled. *Even better, no one can wake the mage.*

Silvine exhaled slowly. Weakening Guval's forces gave her a much-needed advantage, but the threat of The Ceremony still loomed over her. *How do I stop him from blooding me?*

You simply need to remember how powerful you are. I cannot tell you how it will go, but he will struggle without that trollop by his side. You have the wisdom of all the Modronas before you. Use it.

She needed Wrath *and* wisdom. *And Taran?*

Oh, child, Bav croaked. *Focus on the first problem. The usurper needs him and thinks their bargain is unbreakable. Rely on your wits, not your emotions.*

Still, Silvine needed to know how to free Taran. *But—*

No buts. Eat and prepare.

With that, she vanished.

Silvine gratefully devoured the food the raven had delivered. At the bottom of the sack containing her meal, she found a yellow flower.

Using the flower to form vines and branches, she began to craft weapons. She wielded a dirk, sharpening its long blade, and stabbed it through *Fine Ladies of Court.* Transforming the dirk into a crossbow, she fired a thorny bolt into *Conduct of a Consort,* splitting the book in half. Satisfied with her weapons, she shot a beam of light from her hand, disintegrating the remaining books.

She remained in her prison for the rest of the day, preparing her mind and body to resist at all costs. The sound of stones sliding away interrupted her meditation.

Guval held out his hand through the opening in the wall. "Come. I have sent your attendant to my room to prepare. Have you learned anything?"

Silvine forced tears to well up. "I did. I was so full of pride that I tried to rebel. I am not even sure how I came to fight with those Fae."

He squeezed her hand. "You are young. Passions run high in adolescence. The Blooding will humble you. Let's have no more troubles."

She bowed her head and lowered her eyes. "Yes, let's have no more troubles." She built her power up within her, a steadily rising well that warmed her chest.

As they walked, Guval shared his plans for The Ceremony. Phelip had been tasked with coordinating the event. The Blooding would be intimate, with only the most important courtiers in attendance.

"You will do your toilette in my chamber. For safety," he said.

An expansive, gold-trimmed bed with purple linens occupied the majority of his room. The furnishings were hewn in gold. Floor-to-ceiling windows overlooked the raging sea below.

Musky incense burned throughout the room. "Minuet says it cleanses our magic," Guval explained as he took a seat in a velvet chair.

I'm sure she does. She's a fraud, Silvine thought.

Her attendant waited beside a golden vanity. A purple bishop sleeve gown hung from the handle of the adjacent golden wardrobe. The Court insignia had been embroidered on it with gold thread. Silvine cast a questioning look at Guval.

"I think it's best I stay and watch, given how little trust we have between the two of us," he said.

She made herself beg. "Let me keep my modesty."

This seemed to please Guval, who lifted his chin. "Once we are wed, there will be no modesty between us, but I admire your virtue. I will look away. I brought reports to read." He lifted a stack of papers to prove his point.

The bathing chamber was, mercifully, behind a screen. She required two baths and intense scrubbing to wash away the blood and gore from the battle. Her skin wrinkled after her lengthy time in the water.

Her attendant brought rose oil and a fluffy towel as the water drained.

Silvine waved away the oil. "Please, I hate the smell." She'd never trust a rose again.

"Yes, Lady. I have some tallow."

Silvine accepted it gratefully and slipped into a lacy shift. No doubt, it was intended for Guval's enjoyment later. A wave of nausea hit her. She hoped things would not come to that.

The dress felt heavy and stiff. It had been starched to allow for little movement. Once her attendant had slipped it over her head, Guval gestured in approval. Silvine cringed inwardly.

After two hours of coiffing, her attendant patted her shoulders. "You are ready as you'll ever be, Lady." Something cold and metal slipped down the bodice of Silvine's dress. She felt the familiar shape of carved silver against her skin.

Guval rose and extended his arm to her.

She lifted a finger. "One moment. I need to use the facilities."

"Of course. You've sat for so long. I've no idea how ladies have such patience for their toilettes." He was obviously trying to placate her. She'd seen his darkness, though, and she would not forget it.

Giving him a little wave, she slipped behind the screen. Her mother's dagger had gone missing in the heat of battle. Now, it had been returned to her, nestled in her humble cleavage.

She lifted the rigid fabric of her clothing, transferring the dagger to the garter that held up her stockings. No matter the risk, she vowed to fight. She was The Modrona. She was powerful, and others would always come to her aid.

CHAPTER 52

BARING TEETH

Silvine

The usurper hauled her down corridors and into The Mirror Room. The first face she laid eyes on was Phelip's. He tilted his head and studied her intently. She fought to control her emotions, knowing he could smell them.

The room had no furnishings, save for a single gilded chair. Fae lined the walls, many of them holding incense sticks. The smell had never bothered her before, but it made her nauseous now. She wanted to snort at the thought of this gathering as "intimate." Lord Tylon, arm slung around his wife, who held their changeling child, shot her a heated glare. She offered him her most beatific smile in return.

She scanned the room until her eyes landed on the only person she cared about: Taran. He held her gaze, sneaking a wink. As she took in the sight of him, she let out a breath. He appeared entirely whole. Not a bruise or cut marred him.

Guval led her to the chair and motioned for her to be seated. Her music thrummed in response, vibrant and strong. Tendrils of black

power drifted from his fingertips to her wrists. She set her jaw and held onto her magic, wrapping her forearms in white light before the dark power could touch them. By all appearances, though, she was bound to the chair.

The usurper addressed the court. "We are gathered here for the restoration of Life. With my consort, we will grow more powerful than we have ever been. We will no longer thirst for that which is vile. We will no longer have blood feasts. We will be fully alive again."

Various cheers and shouts of praise circulated the room. Many of the normally sinister faces of the courtiers appeared almost pleasant, aside from their unnerving red eyes.

Guval continued, "The power of Death and that of Life will mingle, undoing The Curse, which has plagued us for one thousand years." His face hardened. "My Silvine, I cannot wait for this moment."

A buzz in her palm made her twist her wrist slightly. The tiniest of yellow flowers appeared, reminding her of who she was. She returned Guval's stare. "Nor can I."

A clap of thunder startled everyone in the room. Various shrieks and shouts rang out from Guval's courtiers. Heavy fog flooded the space, making it impossible to see anything. Silvine seized the opportunity, springing from the gilded chair. She turned her tiny flower into two sharp thorns. Using her magic to guide her to her target, she pierced the thorns through Guval's hands with a sickening squelch. He roared in response.

Taking a step backward, she used her powers to summon vines. One after another, she sent them slithering across the floor, wrapping around each magic signature of dissonant notes. The metallic tang of ozone drifted to her nostrils as lightning struck near Guval's feet, illuminating the room for a moment.

Pandemonium ensued. The babe began to shriek as courtiers thrashed, screeched, and cried out. Silvine used more of her magic, twisting the vines tighter around the members of Court until she was sure they were held in place.

The familiar scent of white birch and petrichor washed away the ozone and incense as calloused hands reached for Silvine in the fog. "My Regina," Taran whispered. "You've done so well."

Hands clasped tightly together, they made their way out of the room, dodging bodies and thorns.

In the torchlit hallway, she studied his face and frowned. "You're bleeding."

"It's... nothing," he gasped.

"I have to unbind you from him. Defying the usurper is killing you."

"I love... hearing you... call him that. But... you need... to leave." He pushed her weakly forward.

She crossed her arms. "I am never going to leave you in this Earth-forsaken castle again. This was a mere skirmish. I need to deal with the usurper once and for all."

Footsteps thundered behind them.

Silvine turned, only to see Guval glaring at her. "Deal with me? Let's try a more intimate setting, shall we? Taran Dando, you can watch. It only seems fitting."

Phelip snuck a glance from behind his brother, eyes darting from person to person.

Silvine reached for Taran's hand, gripping it tightly. "Where would you like to go?"

Guval gestured behind him. "Back to my chamber."

She narrowed her eyes. "Lead the way, usurper."

Smoke drifted from Guval's fingertips. "I am your king, your *true* king. I have proven stronger than anyone else. I'm the only one to ever rule over this entire damned continent."

"We can discuss semantics later," she replied, keeping her tone even. "The whole reason there's a curse is because of you. It sounds like The Realm was much better before."

As Taran and Silvine followed the brothers through the maze of torchlit corridors that led to the king's wing of the castle, Taran's wheezing lessened. Silvine thanked The Creator for his steadying vital signs. If he could stay stable, she would end this, but she would not leave him behind.

CHAPTER 53

POWER WILL BLIND

Silvine

A handful of courtiers loitered in Guval's chamber, gossiping about the failed Blooding Ceremony as Silvine, Taran, Phelip, and Guval entered.

"Clear the room," Guval commanded, his tone icy. He yanked Taran toward him, breaking the hold Silvine had kept on him. "Now, no more of these disruptions. I will be drinking from your Life source. You will drink from mine. And then Phelip will lead us in the marriage bargain."

After the last courtier fled the room, Phelip closed the door. He stared, eyes wide.

In that moment, as the sounds of bodies shuffling down the hallway echoed on the bare marble floors, there was nothing Silvine could focus on but Taran. In turn, he kept his gaze trained on her.

"Say it," she breathed.

The truth had been engraved in her heart long before she'd ever realized it. He'd kept her secrets, but the time had come to reveal one of them.

One side of Taran's mouth raised as he rasped, "She doesn't... love you. Nor can she ever... truly be yours."

Guval wrapped his hands around Taran's throat. Those beautiful emerald eyes that had once mesmerized Silvine were gone. They'd turned an angry shade of crimson. She shuddered.

Taran continued, "I know... she doesn't... love you... because... she loves me. The Earth... loves its own... and the Heart... sees the Earth ... for what it truly is." Those once-bewildering words had become the very axioms of Silvine's soul.

Guval's face reddened. The cracks in his veneer of regal beauty revealed his real nature. He lifted his free hand toward Taran's skull.

"Don't you dare," Silvine hissed. Although her hands were shaking and her heart pounded wildly in her chest, she forced herself to channel the queen within.

"My death... will be hers... as well. We have ... an unfulfilled bargain. It would... forever be... unable to... be met," Taran wheezed.

Guval froze. His gaze flitted back and forth between the two.

"It's true," Silvine said.

"Minuet detected no bargains," he argued, unable to conceal the uncertainty in his voice.

Silvine threw her shoulders back as she strode toward Guval and Taran. It was as though instinct and the lived experiences of all the Modronas before her were guiding her.

Phelip lunged, grabbing Silvine's arm. The unwelcome interruption made her blood boil. She listened to the music within her, and suddenly, a glowing bear cub sprang up at her feet. Her skin tingled as she realized she'd summoned a living being, not merely flora, to her side.

It growled at Phelip, who gasped. The bear cub opened its jaws. Phelip's fear, a high-pitched note emanating from his veins, made Silvine's head throb. The usurper's brother leapt backwards until he slammed against the gilded wallpaper of his brother's bedchamber.

"Leave, Phelip," Silvine ordered. He did not deserve the Wrath she would unleash. He was merely serving his brother even when he saw his wrongs, and she did not fault him for his loyalty to family.

She glared at him as she and her bear cub strode toward her betrothed and... and her true love. Phelip, clinging to the wall with each step, slunk out of the room.

It was just the three of them left in Guval's bedchamber.

Silvine fixed her eyes on the usurper. "Your mage cannot detect that which transcends what you have corrupted. Our bargain is of a magic purer than anything you know. It is the magic of love and light and creation."

Guval seethed. "Even if this bargain that you both claim will kill you if I do not honor it is real, you cannot have Taran Dando. He was bound to me two decades ago. It was sealed with his blood. It seems Taran will die either way. He'll die if he defies me, and he'll die if he breaks his agreement with you."

Drawing her dagger, Silvine drew nearer. The bear cub's mouth opened, revealing its sharp teeth.

Silvine asked, "There is no way the connection to you can be undone?"

The usurper began cursing under his breath as she and the cub approached. The bear focused its gaze upon Guval, eyeing him with hunger. Guval loosened his grip on Taran's throat.

Taran jerked his head toward her. "Silvine," he croaked.

It was the first time he'd ever said her name. It sounded like the sweetest note she'd ever heard. The melancholy song, the one Silvine knew so well, was not echoing through his veins anymore. She let out a small gasp. This was his song intertwined with hers, making something new. Something beautiful.

"Silvine. Silvine," Taran whispered, "say my name. Say it to the whole world, to the blood and—"

Guval's grip tightened once more. The bear cub emitted a low growl in warning.

Guval scoffed. "She can say Taran Dando as many times as she'd like. It'll make no difference. You sold your true name long ago. It's meaningless."

It was then that Silvine understood what she'd failed to realize before. *Taran Dando* had made a deal in blood with Guval. Foolishly, he'd bound his body to the usurper and then bound himself to her. A hopeless contradiction in which no one could live or die and abide by the bonds that held them all. But *Taran Dando* couldn't speak at all. Taran Dando could bind his body, his blood, but never his soul. In fact, *Taran* didn't have a soul.

Outside of Court, Silvine had never heard that name. Phos never called him by it. The Fae of the northern parts of The Realm greeted him as "The Enduring One." In the forest, she'd met him by another name. His true name.

He'd given her the key from the very beginning—the power to change everything. After all, his true name was the one tied to his soul.

"I know your name, and I will greet you."

His starlight eyes shone with recognition. A part of her knew that she had always been meant for this very moment. This had been the answer she'd been searching for. This was how it would end.

"I release you from your bargain to the King of Donadais. Tuum nomen est Cian The Enduring One, Cian The Enduring One, Cian The Enduring One."

The music that held together the very fabric of The Realm came to a crescendo so loud Silvine was certain she'd go deaf. She closed her eyes, bracing for the impact. Hot blood seeped out of her ears, the cost of using her power to such an extent.

Undeterred, she lifted her hands up. She was the conductor of the power holding the world together. As though orchestrating a symphony for the universe, she summoned every pulse of Life—every thread—to her. A white beam shot forth from her chest, leaving her gasping as it struck Cian in his. Her galaxy obsidian necklace lifted from her neck. It levitated in the air, catching her magic and amplifying it. Warmth sent tingles from her toes up to her scalp.

Her illumination flashed through the room, bathing the white marble in its brilliance. Light poured from her, out through the windows, igniting the moonless night in a glow that was brighter than any starlit sky.

Cries echoed through the castle.

The brightness continued to pulse out of her, with her obsidian vibrating as it pushed her power further and further, washing everything in its glow. The impact of Silvine's magic at its full force rattled the floors. The shaking earth knocked Cian from Guval's clutches and flung him into the wall. His body clattered to the floor. He grunted at the impact, his head colliding with stone as he closed his eyes.

A fleeting thought popped into Silvine's head; she wondered if repeated head injuries were as harmful to Fae as they were to humans. The song in Cian's blood reassured her that his heart was still beating, so she forced herself to focus on the task at hand. She would do what had to be done.

Before Guval could move, the bear cub sank its claws into his legs, holding him in place. The walls began to shake. A crack sprang beneath Silvine's feet through the center of the room, shaking the floor until it reached Cian. She expected the crack to swallow them both. Instead, it made a glowing, white path, connecting the two of them.

She stretched her arms out, feeling the magnetic pull drawing her toward The Enduring One. Nature and its Wrath. She focused her energy on closing the gap between them.

A sickening crunch interrupted her. The white path that led to her began to wobble as her attention shifted. Guval had snapped the neck of the bear cub and began gliding toward the crevice in the marble floor. A lump formed in her throat at the sight of her short-lived companion's body.

"You may be The Modrona, but you will not escape me like your predecessor once did. You will not die. We will have The Blooding Ceremony tonight. You are *mine*." He reached for her wrist.

The woman Silvine had once been would have cowered and backed down. Today, she searched within herself for traces of the scared human she had once been, but all she found was power. She pitied Guval for the existence he lived, but she would not give in.

With her purpose reignited, she strode down the path of light to Cian's slumped figure. Amping up her music, she pushed on despite the trickle of blood escaping from her ears. She would give every drop of herself to claim Cian.

The usurper attempted to touch her, but the light that wrapped around her and Cian seemed to burn his flesh with every touch. Her power formed a protective barrier around them. The usurper gasped and howled, gasped and howled, but to no avail.

Silvine knelt beside Cian, placing her palm on his hunched back. Reframing every memory she had of him into a love story, she channeled her Life force into him. Her touch sent a jolt through his body. An unseen force pulled him upward—like a puppet on invisible strings—until he stood. His eyes remained closed. She reached out to touch his face, capturing every inch of it in her memory.

A chorus, low and quiet, began to murmur, "If she can see truth with her own eyes and rid The Realm of its lies, Modrona and Euron will end Death's game. If she can see truth with her own eyes and rid The Realm of its lies, Modrona and Euron will end Death's game." The voices of all the Modronas, the Eurons, and the Seelie Fae who had lost their lives to the King of Donadais repeated the prophecy.

The smell of Guval's singed flesh as he continued his attempts to breach her shield, the sounds of all the music and a chorus of unseen voices, and the pounding of Cian's heart were too much to take. Silvine closed her eyes, breathing through the whirlwind of light and music around her, centering her attention on the man she loved.

If Cian didn't wake soon, she didn't know what she'd do. She could only use this much power for so long. Glancing down at her violet dress, she realized it was darkened with splotches of her blood. If she continued, she would risk burning out and losing her life in the process.

Gentle, calloused hands cupped her face. "The Earth loves its own," Cian whispered as he kissed her forehead. The sounds and smells disappeared. In the stillness, it was just Cian and Silvine.

The world had changed when she opened her eyes. The average-looking Fae had vanished. In his place was the most beautiful creature Silvine had ever seen. His hair was the same silver as his eyes, framing his strong jawline and high cheekbones. Everything about him radiated power. Even his brows shimmered silver, a lighter color than the swirling gray orbs of his eyes, and his skin was tawny. He still smelled of white birch and fresh rain, and his irreverent smirk remained. His glamoured form had been shed along with the bargain. This was the real Cian. He was *pure magic*.

Guval's good looks, which Silvine had once been brought to tears at the very sight of, seemed to be a mockery of the beauty of the male who she beheld now. Cian had transformed, and Silvine knew this was who he truly was.

He pulled her to her feet, one hand still resting on her face. He towered above her, tall and muscular. "You set me free," he breathed.

A sharp pang rose up in her, knocking the breath out of her as she realized the weight of what she'd done. By saying Cian's true name, she freed him.

Power will blind the world in its light.
All will seek her,
But only when he *wins her,*
Will victory occur.

For a moment, she wondered if she'd freed an even greater monster than the one she had already been facing. Cian had won her over, to the very depths of her soul. The prophecy had no mention of whether he'd stick around.

She tore her gaze away from the silvery heat of his gaze. Was this all just a ploy in his quest to overthrow Guval, the actual Unseelie king?

Cian seemed to sense her insecurity, in that infuriating way that he always did, and he wrapped an arm around her waist. "And I will bind myself to you in a thousand other ways from now until eternity. Silvine, I will never be free of you."

His other hand tangled itself up in her hair as he pulled her in for a kiss.

Nothing had ever felt more *right*.

She grabbed his hips, pulling him closer to her. She kissed him greedily. With urgency, her mouth explored his. She could feel every song of his existence—from melancholy chords to the sweetest symphonies—all at once. This was the strongest magic she'd ever felt. She wanted it to play for the rest of her existence, the kind of background music a bard would play as they recounted the feats of a great hero.

Guval's screech, muffled by their shield, interrupted their momentary bliss. They pulled apart.

"Silvine," Cian whispered. "You are the most glorious Modrona to ever walk The Realm, and I want to continue. But right now, we're going to have to fight our way out of Court. I cannot wait to put this undead monster in his place. Are you ready?"

"Yes," she said.

He continued, "We'll fight this together. Once you let this shield down, I will disarm him. I want you to send your senses out and see who you can find in the castle. Will you do that?"

"I will," she vowed. "Brace yourself. I have no idea what coming out of this shield is going to feel like."

As she cast her magic along the light still radiating throughout The Realm, she detected notes of joy, undeniably Phos, and the indescribable music she knew to be Bav. She blew out a breath when she found no more of their people in the castle.

We have it handled, Bav croaked in her mind.

"Now!" Cian coached, assuming a fighting stance in front of her.

Silvine's hands shook as she released the shield. The light dimmed, and her necklace dropped back down her bodice.

Guval sneered. "I knew you would not outlast me." Turning to Cian, he gloated, "I know her true name. Her father told me. Silvine

Belle Morair, I command you to complete The Blooding Ceremony."

She tensed, awaiting the sensation of a new form of captivity, but nothing happened.

"That's her human name," Cian said. "Pulchra would have never trusted Morair with her *real* name. Is that all you have? True name magic? I wish you'd make this more interesting."

Inky tendrils of power poured from Guval's fingertips. His eyes glowed, and his face contorted.

Cian applauded. "Now we're talking."

Guval sent a beam of Death magic toward him, but Cian shifted through space.

He tapped Guval on the shoulder. "Try harder."

The usurper tried to put his hands on his General of Intelligence's temple, but Cian vanished again.

The Euron clucked from Guval's bed, where he'd stretched out lazily, "Is that the best you can do? I thought 'she was yours, and you needed her.' This doesn't feel like a fair fight at all."

Something snapped in Guval's face at that final remark. He turned toward Silvine, seemingly ready to send his dark powers her way. She put up her shield again, shaking as she did so, her powers stuttering.

Cian shifted a few footsteps away from Guval. He snapped his fingers, sending a bolt of lightning through the usurper's chest. Gaping, the usurper studied the hole that went through him. The gilded wallpaper behind him began to melt, dripping into a puddle on the marble floor.

Remembering what Bav had said, Silvine took the opportunity to send one last desperate beam of power at the man who'd tried to force her hand. It struck him on the other side of his chest, leaving two holes where his heart and lungs should have been.

With a gasp, he collapsed to the floor. His skin shriveled and blackened as though he'd been burned. His russet hair turned white. With an open mouth and holes in his chest, he stirred no more.

396

Silvine tossed her charoite ring to the floor, finally free of him. It rolled and landed near his lifeless body.

Boots stomped down the hallway.

Guval's remaining men are coming, Silvine thought. Their marching steps reverberated as loudly as the discordant notes of their magic.

Cian took her hand, shifting them both to The Mirror Room where Phos was fighting a handful of lingering courtiers.

"It is done," Cian said. He sent a gust of wind toward Phos's opponents, launching their bodies through the mirrors. Glass shattered everywhere. Their corpses shriveled and blackened, just as the usurper's had.

"It's their real nature finally revealed," Cian explained as Silvine stared. He turned to Phos, "We need to get out of here. The Curse is broken, but they will swarm if we don't move quickly. I only gave the mage enough poison to keep her down until tomorrow. She's bound to put up a fight."

"What about the changeling?" Phos asked quietly.

Cian rubbed his face. "We don't have him?"

Phos shook her head. "Tylon and his wife are nowhere to be found."

Silvine raised a brow, asking, "Why do we want the changeling child?"

Her love looked at her with tenderness. "I promise I will shield you from all future pain. I will tear apart anyone in The Realm who ever causes you a moment's discomfort and envelop you in more love than you can imagine, but I can't spare you the pain of the past." He reached for her hand. "The child is Cardoc's. His wife died in childbirth."

Silvine bit her lip, fighting the tears that burned in her eyes. "I'm growing exhausted, but I can try to find Tylon. His magic sounds screechier than the rest of the courtiers' does."

Reaching out through the castle, she found staccato beats and dissonant notes. Phelip had returned to his room, likely tending to his comatose wife.

She continued to search until she heard the faint screeching.

"They're in the dungeon."

Cian shifted the three of them to the main room of the dungeon, beside his torture table. A shriek came from beneath it.

"I found you," Cian crooned, waving a finger and shifting two figures out from under the table. Lord Tylon glowered as his wife sobbed. The baby in her arms began to cry.

"Hand over the babe, and we'll let you live," Cian said.

Tylon sneered at Silvine. "Guval had no idea what he was getting into with you. I should have dealt with you myself. My wife and I could be back at our estates, away from this mess with our powers restored."

Silvine cast a vine out. It wound around Tylon's legs, his torso, and his neck, slowly tightening. He began to gurgle and choke.

"*He* promised to let you live. *I* made no such claim," she said.

Tylon collapsed to the floor, hate darkening his expression even in death.

Silvine held her arms out to Tylon's sobbing wife, who handed over the baby without a word. "Wise woman," she remarked.

The Modrona had held few children in her life, but this one felt special. Warm brown eyes looked up at her, and the child stopped crying instantly. The baby cooed. Her chest swelled as she admired its round cheeks and tiny hands.

"Come on," Cian said, "we'll leave through the dungeon exit. I'm as spent as you are, Silvine."

Clutching Cardoc's baby to her chest, the young Modrona ran after her friend and true love.

CHAPTER 54

AN UNEXPECTED HELLO

Silvine

Once they reached the dungeon's corridor, Cian said, "We'll use the cave system to travel into the mountains. It has an enchantment on it similar to Dùn Falaich's. None of The Avartagh's court will be able to pursue us there."

The cave's entrance happened to be in Cian's room, the place he had kept Cardoc safe. Phos held her arms out to take the baby from Silvine. "I'll take good care of him, I promise. I haven't exerted myself like the two of you have. Let me run ahead, and I'll gather troops and horses. Shall we meet in the forest?"

Cian nodded, and Phos sprinted forward. Her footsteps and her green glow faded in moments. Will-o-the-wisps lit up in her absence, leading Silvine and Cian toward their future.

She released the tension she'd been storing for as long as she could remember. Here she was, with the one who truly loved her, and she wasn't going to waste a moment.

"You love me?" she asked.

He entwined his hand into hers, lifting them to his lips and

kissing each of her fingers. "I do. I've loved you from the moment I laid eyes on you, when you first spouted your venom at me. I'd been trying to fill the emptiness inside me for centuries, longing for something I couldn't name. Little did I know, it was a half-human woman with a tongue like a sword who would free me from a bargain I'd made for her." Cian pulled her face close to his, planting a dozen kisses on her lips. Everything about his touch felt right.

She breathed in his white birch scent and pulled him closer. "I love you. I didn't know it until you couldn't come with me, but I've loved you for longer than I've realized."

"Some of us aren't as quick-witted as others. Don't feel inadequate, Regina," he teased. "I knew you couldn't resist me."

"I've resisted you for a year." She rolled her eyes. "There's one thing I still don't understand. The bargain for my firstborn child makes no sense."

"You haven't figured it out yet?"

"No. How are you going to take my firstborn child if I—we—"

"I said 'I will *have* your firstborn child.' I didn't say I was going to *steal* it or even that you had to *give* it to me. The first lesson in bargains: you must be very specific. Language is a tricky, tricky thing."

"You meant we will have my firstborn child *together*, didn't you?" It was so obvious when he put it that way, when she knew he'd loved her from the beginning.

"We will. And the second born. And the third. And as many unruly Fae children as your heart desires. I always knew you'd be mine."

She studied the way their fingers entwined, her small hand a perfect fit in his. "Is that why—with Guval—?"

Cian laughed again, music to her ears. "Yes. The bargain wouldn't let him touch you. If you'd tried any further, you would have passed out, and he would have gotten a bloody nose. Killed the mood, didn't it?"

Silvine sighed. "I think it's time to stop making risky bargains. You'd known me for only a few weeks before you bound yourself to having children with me."

"Nothing is too great a risk when it comes to you. You're the one thing in this realm I'm always sure of. Now that you freed me from my blood bargain, I can show you even more truth. Look at our wrists."

He held his out for her to inspect. A glowing, yellow flower had been etched into it. She held her wrist out and sucked in a breath. A glowing, yellow flower that matched his own shone on hers.

"You do intend to marry me, right? Then, in the distant future, have a firstborn child?" she asked. The only Fae marriage she knew much about was Phelip and Minuet's. She wasn't certain marriage was even a common practice among the Fae.

He ruffled her hair. "I told you I knew of a man who wouldn't be intimidated by your power—someone who would marry you. You're looking at him. I am the honorable man you will marry, whenever you feel the time is right."

Her heart swelled. She took his hand in hers again, leading him out of the cave.

He paused at a turn to the right, revealing a little room that opened into the red cliffs and the raging sea below. A few blankets, dusty books, and trunks littered the small stone room.

"I need to collect something." His eyes were alight with mischief. He reached for a single piece of worn parchment concealed beneath a stone.

Hand-in-hand, they trod through the cave system. Together, they would face whatever the future held.

The cave's mouth brought them to the peak of the mountains beyond Court. The sun had just risen, bathing the world beyond in its glow.

"Look down at the plain," Cian said.

She gasped. A river ran in the middle of the plain, which had begun to look more like a verdant valley. Wildflowers bloomed. Closer to the castle, a vineyard had sprung up with grapes in a rich array of colors. The castle shimmered in shades of salmon, huckleberry, jade, and serpentine.

"This is what *Life* is supposed to look like," he breathed. "I will forever be in awe of you. You did this." He planted a kiss on her forehead.

Silvine paused to take in the mountains. The sparse forest, the place where she'd first recognized the wonders of The Realm, had grown thick with trees and foliage. Life teemed around them.

They walked along the trail. The further they went, the less sunlight trickled in beneath the lush canopy of leaves. Cian assured her that Phos and their company awaited with horses in the distance, ready to take them home.

She yearned to go to Dùn Falaich, to become the queen she'd been born to be. Even more than Dùn Falaich, though, she knew she'd found her home in Cian.

A rustling in the trees disrupted her musings. She tensed instinctively. Though she'd never seen any of Guval's men in these mountains, she assumed they would be desperate after the events of the night before.

A dark-haired figure emerged from the trees, pausing in the trail a few yards ahead of them, hands confidently placed on their hips. Bav was perched on their shoulder.

Silvine strained her eyes and her magic simultaneously, trying to detect whether the figure was friend or enemy. Unlike the magic of The Avartagh and his court, this being's magic sang a beautiful song of hope and redemption.

Do not flee, and do not fret, Bav encouraged.

As they drew nearer, Silvine could not shake the unmistakable familiarity of the person on the trail. The joy of Phos's music reverberated from behind the figure, her glow casting light on a defiant facial expression and small stature.

Silvine could not believe what she was seeing. She wondered if exhaustion was clouding her vision. It was as though a ghost stood before her.

A warm expression illuminated her best friend's face. "Well done, Silvine. My sisters and I have waited for this moment for a thousand years," Ana said. "You won the battle. Now, you must win the war. Onward to Dùn Falaich."

AFTERWORD

As a little girl, I was intrigued by stories of those who came before us. I voraciously consumed stories of Troy, countless cultures' myths, fairy tales, and fables. I have always loved getting lost in other worlds.

While recovering from a severe concussion, I read *Outlander,* and it changed my view on what fiction could be. I am forever indebted to Diana Gabaldon for opening my eyes to the way romance, history, language, science fiction, and fantasy can intertwine to create a breathtaking book that transcends the confines of genre. *The Fabric of the Realm* is admittedly nothing like *Outlander.* However, I did a great deal of research in crafting this novel. In this book, I hope you have seen glimpses of the many influences that culminated to create Silvine's story.

I drew inspiration from *The Mabinogion* (primarily the story of Pwyll, Rhiannon, and Gwawl), the Latin language, Gàidhlig, French royal history, Celtic stories of the fairies, W.B. Yeats, Genesis, Ecclesiastes, and vampire lore. We stand upon the shoulders of giants, as they say. My humble work is a response to centuries and millennia of those who came before with great ideas and great stories. In Silvine, there are countless bits of myself: the good, the bad, and the ugly. For readers who have experienced trauma and loss, I hope you see glimpses of yourself as well and find the courage to stitch back together the fabrics of your own realms.

Thank you to everyone who has supported this journey. It's taken me years to get here. To my mother, I love you always. Thank you for modeling selfless sacrifice for others. To my children, I love you endlessly, and I do it all for you. To my sisters, I love you, and I promise neither of you inspired Ophelia. Thank you to Traci, my mother on Earth, for always believing in me. I owe my best friend, Sami, endless thanks for always being willing to discuss plot, excerpts, titles, and province names. Thank you to Tiera for being one of my earliest and most enthusiastic supporters. I am beyond grateful for my husband's support. Even though he is "not a reader," he listened endlessly as I read bits and pieces aloud and debated elements of the story.

Thank you to Jenn and Jenny for reviewing my EMDR scene. Thank you to Angela for providing feedback on fight scenes and breaking wrists. Thank you to Christi for your unwavering support and expertise in crystals, gems, and scent craft. Thank you to my critique partners for slogging through the nitty-gritty details in my roughest of drafts, and my editor, Serena, for the work you put in to make this story a book worth sharing. Thank you to my PA, Katey, for your hard work and "getting" the story from day one. Thank you to Nova B. Eames and all the incredible people *at Your Bookish Bestie* for the early support. It takes a village to raise a child, and it takes a village to bring a book to life.

If you'd like to stay connected, you can find me on TikTok (my favorite and most active app by far), Instagram, and Facebook. Readers are always welcome to join me in my Facebook group, Ryazakhov's Realms!

THE FABRIC OF THE REALM
FAMILY TREES

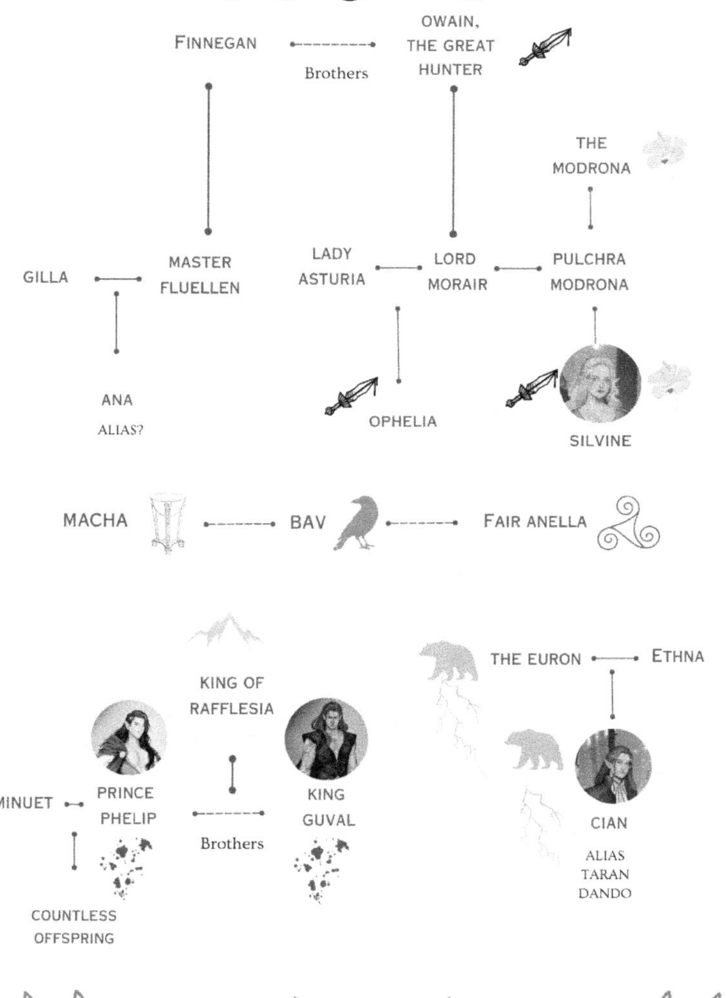

ABOUT THE AUTHOR

S.B. Ryazakhov lives in a remote place in the mountains, voraciously reading books, going on adventures in all four seasons, and studying history. Her educational background is in English literature and the Great Books tradition. She's a huge fan of medieval history and ancient languages. This is her debut novel, although she has written many shorter pieces shared in several other publications.

https://sbryazakhov.com
https://www.facebook.com/groups/1244750543391540
https://www.tiktok.com/@sbreadsfantasy
https://instagram.com/sbreadsfantasy
https://substack.com/@sbwritesfantasy